TROPHY GIRL

Marlis Manley

MARLIS MANLEY

Oct. 1, 2021

To Lynsey —
Enjoy the ride!

♡

Black Rose Writing | Texas

ISBN: 978-1-68433-773-6
PUBLISHED BY BLACK ROSE WRITING
www.blackrosewriting.com

Printed in the United States of America
Suggested Retail Price (SRP) $20.95

Trophy Girl is printed in Plantagenet Cherokee

*As a planet-friendly publisher, Black Rose Writing does its best to eliminate unnecessary waste to reduce paper usage and energy costs, while never compromising the reading experience. As a result, the final word count vs. page count may not meet common expectations.

TROPHY
GIRL

CHAPTER 1

Locking the door of the ladies' room on the side of the Phillips 66 Station, fourteen-year-old Sandy Turner sat on the toilet-seat lid, the front of her circle skirt with its poodle applique spreading out horizontally, buoyed by three pink crinolines. On her lap she held the morning edition of the *Enid Daily Eagle* for Friday, July 5, 1957, which she opened to the sports page. When the article she'd hoped would be there even had a photo with it, she whispered, "Bingo."

The picture was one the papers ran often, a close-up three-quarter shot with his racing helmet on. The angle of its bill against the dark background echoed the outline of his high cheekbones and strong jaw line. His eyes were so light they photographed like pale rings around the pupils, and there were fine sprays of laugh lines in the outer corners. In all the pictures she'd secretly pored over the past months, he was smiling like that, the relaxed grin of a born winner.

FAVOR FRANK HAGGARD IN HOT-ROD RACES
Drivers to Shoot at New Record

High-point leader Frankie Haggard has been tagged as the man to beat when the hot-rods resume action at Enid Raceway tonight, the 9-race card to be followed by a fireworks display.

Haggard shattered the track mark at Enid last week along with three other speedsters—Jerry Oakley, former record holder Buddy Lutkie, and Pee Wee Jones.

Haggard's team is confident that he can come through with the A-feature win tomorrow night after romping to the feature win on the Jayhawk oval in Newton, Kansas, last night, and will be on the Enid track tonight with his sights set high.

She opened a small, red-leather suitcase she had once stored her dolls' clothes in and removed a scrapbook labeled "1949" and a pair of cuticle scissors. Spreading the newspaper across her lap, she cut out what would be the newest addition to the yellow-paged album she'd discovered at the bottom of her late mother's hope chest. She tucked it into the last of four albums her mother had kept—secretly, as far as Sandy knew—until she died, when Sandy was five. The man she'd called Daddy had passed two years before that, and she had few memories of him. But she still missed her mother's voice calling her name and the way her hair would brush Sandy's face when she bent over her for goodnight kisses.

Over the years, Sandy had puzzled over scraps of whispered conversations between her aunts and Grandmother Parson that quickly died out when she drew near, no matter how quiet she was. And while Aunt Maggie had become like a mother to her, when Sandy lay in bed at night listening to the cicadas or walked home from school in the silence of a light snowfall, she felt the melancholy tug of something missing. And there it was all the time—right there in the scrapbooks.

The clock over the door to the gas station had said 11:30. Sandy figured it would be at least lunchtime before her Aunt Maggie back in Kiowa, Kansas, would get home from the meeting at the high school where she taught and wonder why Sandy hadn't returned from the sleepover yet. Her aunt would probably make some calls, or maybe check the bedroom right away, and find the note Sandy had propped up on the threadbare belly of Bobby, her first and still most favorite teddy bear. The note assured Aunt Maggie Sandy was not hurt or kidnapped, only going away for a little while, there was something she had to do. It also said she would be all right and call collect when she got a chance. Still, her aunt would probably take it hard. That part bothered Sandy. But not enough to keep her from hitching early-morning rides the 60-some miles down to Enid, Oklahoma.

Sandy would have to ask someone how to get to the racetrack, but first she had to find a safe place to stash her suitcase. Maybe a locker at the bus depot. She was punchy from staying awake all night plotting her getaway and was too excited to be hungry, but she knew she should eat something.

2

She took the key attached to a piece of wood with "Ladie's" written on it back to the office, thinking how she and her English-teacher aunt would have a laugh about that when Sandy got back home. She was about to ask the boy on duty for directions when she noticed a sign down the street that said Bus Depot. She turned to leave and saw a poster next to the door announcing, "Enid Speedway, 302 E. Oxford Avenue, Friday Night – Gate opens at 5:00 – Races begin at 7:00." Just as if it was put there for her to find. That could be significant, she told herself. Maybe some things really are meant to be.

She'd made up her mind she and Frank Haggard would first set eyes on each other at a racetrack, with the big lights beaming down around the dirt oval. There would be strings of red, white, and blue plastic flags crackling at the top of the stadium in the race-night excitement that always makes even the air crazy-jittery. He would win his heat race and the trophy dash. He could come in second in the semi-final—she didn't want to be greedy. But he would sail past the black-and-white checkered flag ahead of the others to take the A-Feature.

Afterward, they would open the gate, and all the fans would rush down onto the track and scramble through the pits. She would go up to him and hold out a program for him to autograph. And when he asked who to make it out to, she'd look smack dab into his eyes saying her mother's maiden name, pronouncing very clearly—Ruth Parson.

And then she'd know for sure.

CHAPTER 2

"I blame that Elvis Presley fella," said the principal of the Kiowa, Kansas, high school, slapping his palm flat against the Formica lunch table to drive home his point. Gathered under the uncompromising lights of the high school cafeteria, several of the attendees at the Friday morning ad hoc meeting called out their agreement.

"Last night," he went on, "some scoundrels took down street signs while the concert in the gazebo was goin' on. Found 'em this morning by the trash dumpster behind the police station."

"I read where it's worse where that Presley fella is giving live concerts," said the high school's vice-principal. "The fans form these blue-suede-shoe clubs. What kind of self-respecting man wears blue suede shoes?"

"You can thank Mr. Ed Sullivan for bringing that hip-wagger right into decent people's homes," said the school secretary, whose three sons had been hellions well before the new rock and roll sensation had hit the scene.

"Watched the show, did you?" the principal said, kidding his secretary, but on the square.

"Well, if you can't trust Ed Sullivan, I don't know who you can trust," she said. "Isn't that right, Maggie? You told me you watched that show deliberately, to see what all the fuss was about."

"Everybody and his dog watched that show," Maggie Parson replied. "But aren't we getting a little off topic here?" Maggie, who had been teaching English there for 14 years, had been fanning herself with the agenda and trying to keep her own counsel. With her mother still in rehab from a mild stroke and her niece Sandy no doubt still asleep after being up all night at a slumber party, Maggie was looking forward to having a little quiet time to herself as soon as the meeting adjourned, the sooner the better. She planned to give herself a facial and finish the paperback Shell Scott murder mystery she was reading—her only vice.

"I heard there's one of them blue shoes clubs starting up right here in Kiowa," the principal said. "Everything about this Presley fella seems to fly in the face of one convention or another. The television and popular magazines all show these hysterical wide-eyed girls with their mouths hanging open as Elvis shakes his hips and makes that snarly face. Used to be it was just the boys we had to look out for, but I swear, some of these girls are gettin' pretty crazy."

On that score, Maggie tended to agree. Even the so-called goody-two-shoes girls were getting restless and moony, swooning over more sensual idols than the usual teen heartthrobs. Seeing the writing on the wall, young boys were greasing their hair into pompadours and letting their jeans slide lower on their hips. And judging from what she passed on the street, some undid their second and sometimes third shirt buttons as they turned the corner between home and the local hangouts.

"Well," the vice-principal said, "I've got a lawn to mow and a date with some fish. I move we get back to the business of deciding whether we're gonna adopt stricter standards about decorum in the school and at school-sponsored functions."

"What about a dress code?" said the owner of Kresge's Five and Dime, who had no children of his own but lots of ideas about how to raise and educate them. "I swear, if I see one more cocky kid walk into my place his dungarees hanging by his hip bones . . . ."

Maggie sighed audibly and traced the pattern of little overlapping boomerangs in the table top with her index finger. She'd heard it all before. As far as she knew, there had been some outhouse tipping on Halloween. And the Witt twins had fed Harley Simms' prize hog, Gracie, a bucket of rotten hard-boiled eggs before sneaking it into the principal's basement while he was at Easter service. And of course, last night's escapade with the street signs. But aside from holiday crime waves, Kiowa was relatively clear of any juvenile criminal element.

In fact, Maggie thought this was another tempest in a teapot, and looked up with relief when she heard, "I move that we form a study group on how to enforce the dress code and respective punishments for violations."

"I second that motion," Maggie spoke up, to get people moving toward closure.

"All in favor" was followed by a unanimous show of hands.

"Well, that's that," the secretary said. "I'll take names of volunteers. Let's make it snappy." Squinting at her new easy-to-read Timex wristwatch, she announced to the room at large, "It's nearly 11:00, and I've got some hamburger patties that aren't gonna' thaw themselves."

· · · · ·

Maggie breathed a sigh of relief to be out of the stifling cafeteria, happy to be heading for home and her new Philco window air conditioner. It was just as well no one had brought up her trip to Wichita a year ago May with Sandy, her then 13-year-old niece, and Sandy's best friend Ralph to see the overnight rock-and-roll sensation bump and grind in the flesh. She had been appalled at the incessant screaming of the young girls, but having worked with them all her adult life, she wasn't particularly surprised by it. The music, on the other hand, she'd found very satisfying. Her Methodist, hymn-singing mother called the music Maggie liked too jivey and felt it was a decided flaw in her otherwise rational eldest daughter's character.

But if her love for a more stimulating strain of music and the desire to travel and perhaps discover a less predictable life were weaknesses as a person, as a caretaker Maggie was sensible and vigilant. Sandy had come to live with her after her sister Ruth's death ten years earlier, and raising a child as an unmarried, working woman had its moments—some good, some challenging. But no one could say she hadn't given it her whole-hearted effort. In fact, she took pride in the fact that she'd had no serious problems with Sandy. Maggie attributed it to her steadiness coupled with a profession that kept her abreast of the developmental stages of young females. She took her job as foster parent seriously. And the truth was she couldn't have loved Sandy more if she were her own.

Cutting over to Maple, she crossed in front of the Eldridges', where a gaggle of girls were sleeping off their Fourth-of-July slumber party.

Mildred stepped out onto the porch with a broom and waved at Maggie, saying, "What a nutty bunch of girls we're raising. No offense meant, and actually, your niece was one of the quieter girls last night. But it's like a cyclone hit this place."

"I don't doubt it," Maggie said. "I'm glad to hear Sandy is behaving herself. Make sure she stays to help clean up."

"She left before anyone else was up. Probably wanted to get home and get some sleep. You wanna come up and sit for a bit? I've got lemonade in the fridge."

"Thanks, another time. I just got finished with the meeting over at the school. When are they going to agree to air condition that place?"

"When pigs fly, or someone strikes oil on the property," Mildred said.

"Well right now, I'll have to settle for a cold shower."

Mildred laughed. "I'd be happy to turn on the sprinkler for you."

"Tempting," Maggie said, and waved as she headed for home. She felt it safe to say that the young girls in her town were not falling prey to the influences of either Elvis Presley or marauding locals with contraband street signs—this particular morning anyway.

She crossed the intersection to her house catty corner, a scofflaw in the steamy summer day, and felt a familiar tremor of longing for something more in her own life—something more stimulating on the horizon than another year of sentence diagramming and parent-teacher conferences. She looked up the street at the rows of tidy front yards and porches with their swings and planters. Whatever it was that might satisfy her longing wasn't likely to come racing down the street in Kiowa, and with Sandy to raise and her mother's health ailing, it was unlikely, now, that she'd ever go in search of it.

CHAPTER 3

"Sandy," Maggie called out. "Sandy, Honey, I'm home." When there was no answer, she tiptoed back to her niece's bedroom, expecting to find her sleeping off the effects of the slumber party, but the bed was still made. She looked for some sign that Sandy had been there, but the room looked exactly as it had the night before—bed made and piled with the usual stuffed animals, pink ice-cream-parlor chair parked at an angle in front of the ruffle-skirted vanity table, 1956 Kansas State Fair baseball cap hanging slaunchways on one bed post, a blue-and-white seersucker robe draped over another.

Maggie walked through the rest of the house calling her niece's name on her way to the back door to see if she'd fallen asleep sunbathing in the yard. Back in the kitchen, she dialed the Eldridge house.

"Yes, I'm sure she's not here," Mildred said. "She must have left pretty early. Before the girls came up for blueberry pancakes, anyway."

"Thanks, Mildred. It's just odd she's not here."

"Well, she'll be close by, probably be showing up anytime now. Did you check with Ralph?"

"Tried to. There was no answer," Maggie said.

"Maybe she's meeting him for lunch."

"Quite likely. Thanks, Mildred."

Maggie wasn't used to worrying about Sandy, and told herself it was too soon to get upset. But she was definitely uneasy, and there was also a substrata of anger forming that didn't bode well for a cheerful reunion regardless of how good Sandy's excuse might be for not calling to say where she'd gone off to.

Maggie wrote a note telling Sandy that she was going to pick up Grandma's laundry and to go ahead and fix herself a sandwich. She propped it against the fruit bowl in the center of the kitchen table and looked around the room once more for any evidence a groggy 14-year-old had been there.

•　　•　　•　　•　　•

"You're late," Olivia Parson complained. The nurse was wrapping a blood-pressure cuff around her impatient patient's upper arm. "Where's my granddaughter?"

"Is it late?" Maggie looked at her watch. "Sandy went to a slumber party last night. I told you about it. Which means they don't get any sleep until the next day, you know," Maggie improvised. "Have you seen the doctor today? Did he say how you're coming along?"

"Slow. Old-woman slow."

"He didn't say *that*, Mother."

"S'true anyhow. I thought I'd be back in my own home by now."

"Soon," Maggie reassured her. She walked the five steps between the bed and door, touching things as if to tidy the room. "We just have to be patient."

"*We* aren't sitting in this chair like a lump. I am. And it takes an act of congress to get me into a standing position. 'Nose over toes, nose over toes.' You'd think I'm in kindergarten again."

The nurse finished up, saying, "There we go, Mrs. Parson. All done."

"Thanks, Susie, you're a doll," Olivia said, giving her a genuine smile and patting her arm.

Maggie walked over and adjusted the sweater draped around her mother's shoulders.

"Quit fussing and sit down where I can see you."

Maggie sat in the visitor's chair, her purse in her lap, and smiled. "You look well. I just came by to pick up your laundry and to see if you needed anything. You need anything?"

"I need you to tell me what's on your mind. You're as jumpy as a frog near a pot of boilin' water."

"Don't be silly. I had the summer school board meeting this morning. It was tedious as usual. Anyway, I've just got a lot of work to get done back at the house, is all. Gonna put fresh sheets on your bed, get your room spiffed up for your homecoming."

Olivia reached out her right hand and grabbed Maggie's arm. "I'm a strong woman. No need to pussy-foot about. What has that doctor told you?"

Maggie was relieved to learn that her mother thought she was nervous because she was hiding bad news from the doctor. Because the stroke had been a mild one, the reports had been good for a full recovery. "Nothing you don't already know. Says you're making good progress. I promise. Irma will be up tomorrow. She'll bring back your laundry. And some of those butterscotch lifesavers you like. Okay? And I'll see you the day after."

Maggie leaned over and kissed her mother on the cheek, then stood up and grabbed the pillowcase of laundry the nurses had collected. As soon as she was out of the building, she hurried to the corner where she set the bag of laundry on the sidewalk and stepped into the wood-and-glass phone booth. She closed the accordion door to cut out the street traffic and called her sister Irma to learn whether anyone had heard from Sandy. As she dialed, she mentally went over the names she'd written down for Irma to call trying to think of who she might have missed.

Irma had said it might just be teenage forgetfulness, and that Sandy'd most likely come dragging in at dinner time with a sunburn and a story to tell. Fact was, Sandy sometimes took so much on herself that Maggie worried about her niece still feeling like the orphan, the outsider who had to constantly prove that she was worth having around. But Sandy was certainly making up for it now. If she had actually forgotten to tell Maggie of some plans, some outing with a friend, or...Maggie was running out of things to suppose, except for the unsupposable.

"She hasn't called here," Irma told her. "Lloyd's been out driving through town looking for her. He's back now, though. No luck. How's Mother?"

"Doing better, but she guessed something was up. I swear she's got a built-in bull-hockey detector."

"What did you tell her?"

"Nothing. That I needed to get back to take care of some things, which is true. Did Lloyd check the movie house and drugstore?"

"Yes. Nothing. No one's seen her. We did manage to track down Ralph."

Finally, Maggie thought. If Sandy wasn't with him, at least he'd be the person most likely to know what her niece was up to. "What did he have to say?"

"Nothin'. Lloyd went over and talked with him in person. Wanted to see if Ralph might be holding something back."

"Is he?"

"I don't know. He and Sandy have always been thick as thieves. Lloyd couldn't get anything out of him, but he felt Ralph was telling the truth, that he didn't know where Sandy has gotten herself off to."

Maggie was not given to spells of nerves, but the mishmash of anger and anxiety was taking a toll. She slumped down onto the wooden seat and leaned her forehead against the black metal base of the phone. If Ralph truly had no idea what Sandy was up to, that meant she really could be missing, and maybe in trouble. Maggie looked at her watch and then stared at the dial on the phone, wondering what other number they could call.

"You still there," Irma asked.

"Yes, I'm here. Look, you stay by the phone until I get there. I'm going to swing through town again."

"Where else can you look?"

Maggie fought against making a sharp reply. She wasn't mad at Irma, she was mad at the question, because she didn't know where to go, just that she had to keep searching. Her mother wasn't the only one with detection abilities, and Maggie couldn't shake the feeling that something was off.

CHAPTER 4

After circling back around to the finish line of the Friday-night Trophy Dash in Enid, Oklahoma, Frank Haggard pulled himself up through the cut-out top of red-and-white number 65, his Parker Special jalopy—an old '32 Ford coupé with a Chrysler V-8 engine, modified for high speed.

He waved to the cheering fans and jumped down to receive his prize. Wrapping his arm around the waist of a bottle-blonde girl in a yellow spaghetti-strap dress that fit like a casing around a spark plug, he accepted the silver trophy she was there to present. He flashed his signature smile at the photographers and then up at the fans, raising the trophy overhead as the cheering and whistles rolled across the track and into the infield. But he was mainly thinking that he was one trophy dash closer to holding on to the season's high points and a little over a week away from the first-ever Grand National Championship for Jalopies. He'd put his job selling insurance mostly on hold that summer, competing with other drivers who also tried to make it to every race on the circuit. They traveled throughout Kansas, Oklahoma, Nebraska, and beyond, competing several times a week. Sometimes he'd finish one race, load the car and gear onto the trailer behind his mechanic-partner Buddy Baehr's Chinook truck camper, and drive most of the night to make it to a race the next day.

The voice over the PA system encouraged fans to give "a big round of applause for Enid's own Miss Peggy Trilling, who's making us proud as a student up at Patricia Stevens Modeling School in Wichita, Kansas." Young boys sitting along the front row of the stands were whooping and yelling, "Kiss her, Frankie," and "What are ya waitin' for," more flashbulbs popping as Frank leaned down and planted a quick kiss on the girl's bright pink mouth. She wobbled on her three-inch heels as he escorted her back across the slick, rutted track and steadied her up the concrete steps that took her through the center gate and safely to the spectators' side of the chain link fence.

"Good luck, Frankie" she called to him, her fingers laced through the steel diamond openings, and then she turned back toward the crowd, her raised hands swooping in an energetic flutter of waves as if to capture the whistles and cheers.

Frank climbed back into the jalopy and pulled it into his pit area. By the time he'd climbed out of the car again and set the trophy on the trailer, his smile was replaced by a tight set to his jaw and the recently acquired furrows in his brow.

Buddy lifted the hood and leaned into the Chrysler V-8 engine to check it out before Frank's next race. He asked, "How are the Firestones working out?"

"Okay for now, but if the track gets much slicker we may want to switch them out for the A-feature." Haggard wiped the dust from his face with his handkerchief. "So, Bear," he asked, without looking over at the ace mechanic, "we copacetic?" It was a ritual they followed most race days. It meant not was the engine running outlaw—Buddy was too good to have to resort to outright cheating—but was there anything borderline on the car that track officials might question if the car got challenged and torn down at the end of the races, before any payout.

"All good," Buddy answered without straightening up. Any mechanic worth his salt had tricks to make a car run hotter, some flagrantly against the rules even for modifieds—easily discovered if challenged—and some the kinds of sophisticated adjustments made by men who love the intricacies of engines the way some men dedicate themselves to wooing women. Buddy found that engines responded more reliably.

Frank stretched his arms above his head, then bent over from the waist, grunting as his fingertips touched the tops of his boots. Straightening up, he swung his arms and twisted at the waist to loosen up and work off some of his nervous energy. He didn't usually tense up again after he'd worked out the bugs during the first few laps of his heat race, but over the past few weeks the tension had ratcheted up along with the stakes.

He'd first started hanging around the tracks when he got home after the war, and now in his 12th year of racing—8 out of the last 10 spent racking up annual high points on the Midwest circuit—Frank was the clear front runner. But several challengers were making bold moves to overtake him—younger men, mostly, although Henry Bowles, who had nearly as many years on the dirt ovals as Frank, had recently gotten into a rebuilt Buick that had an impressive history and promising future.

Buddy wiped his hands on a red grease rag and retrieved a bottle of Coca Cola from a green Coleman cooler, popping off the cap with the built-in opener. "You watchin' L. Ray on the inside like I told you?" Buddy asked, squinting out over the pits to where the cars were circling for the start of B-Feature.

"I'm watching," Frank answered, squinting in the same direction. "He hasn't got it tonight, not the way his car's handling."

"Looked like he might could of made it past you on the second-to-the last lap of the heat if he'd stood on it comin' out of turn three about two seconds longer."

Frank blew his nose to clear out the track dust. Buddy was right. The kid was hungry and a little reckless. With more experience, he might be able to crank his engine up another notch, shave two or even three seconds off his time. Frank was watching him like a hawk.

"Henry's got the pole. That ought to cinch it," Frank said, changing the subject to the race that was just starting up.

They watched as the green flag dropped. Henry Bowles out of Tulsa driving cherry-red 05 shot into the lead. By the backstretch, Bowles had put two car lengths between him and the fight for second place. He stood to time into the field for the national the way he'd been running, and he had nine years of experience under his belt.

Frank stepped up onto the tongue of the trailer for a better view and watched the action with a keen eye and a knot in his chest. The growing tension as the day of the first-ever Grand National for Jalopies approached had become as much a part of the racing scene as the steady pitch of the engines as they whined and growled down the straightaway or the smell of hot rubber being laid over the track that grew slicker and potentially faster with each lap. The National was

14

expected to usher in a new era for dirt-track racing—larger, hotter fields, greater recognition, bigger gates resulting in bigger purses. The man who took the checkered flag on the first grand national victory lap was likely to ride the crest of a new wave of popularity and prosperity.

All that had allowed Frank to distinguish himself in 34 years of an otherwise lackluster life—besides his service to his country—was his natural skill behind the wheel and his love of the race. His home was filled with trophies of all sizes and shapes, attesting to who he was and what he'd done with his life. But this year it would all come down to a single July afternoon and 100 laps.

Single and making a modest living selling insurance to people who agreed to meet with him in the first place because of his racing reputation, he couldn't see how he could live with that kind of falling off. It was too soon. But then, whenever the time came, it would be too soon.

Buddy tossed his empty Coke bottle into a steel drum that served as a trash can and yelled, "Awright!" as Billy Mahler edged up on Henry Bowles on the inside at the white flag and the two cars flew nose-to-nose into the back stretch. "We got us a race!"

The two lead cars held even in turn three, Mahler hugging the groove, as close to 05 as he could run without scraping paint or dipping down into the loose dirt on the inside of the track.

The fans were on their feet screaming as the lead cars shot toward the checkered flag and across the finish line, Billy's nose half a flag wave in the lead. Frank jumped down from the trailer knowing he'd just witnessed the kind of superior driving that could eventually get the driver of a B-feature car a better ride.

He climbed into his car and dropped down into the seat. After he pulled his goggles into place and fastened the chinstrap of his helmet, he spit a fine spray onto the palms of his hands, rubbed them together, and took the gloves that Buddy handed him, ready for the final race of the night, the A-feature.

They looked at one another for the flick of a second, then Buddy tapped him on the helmet. Frank flexed his hands to stretch the gloves and rolled his head once to loosen his neck and back, then pressed the starter. He listened for a moment, taking stock, before winding carefully through the pits to the edge of the track. Driving up the front-stretch, he lined up next to Harvey Little, who'd drawn the pole position. The popular new rookie, L. Ray Chenoweth, was behind Little, with Jerry Oakley behind Frank. It would be a rugged start unless one of them could get the jump while the other three were battling for second and third. Frank adjusted his helmet and eased ahead, leading the pack as they jostled and realigned themselves into formation. Rounding turn four, he kept an eye on the green flag Dewey was holding close to his body while he concentrated on the brightly colored river of metal and horsepower growling up the straightaway toward the starting line, watching to see how the cars were lining up. Frank knew from experience that, if the formation looked tight enough for a fair start, Dewey would lift the flag a fraction between his waist and his chest—a tell that gave the observant driver with lightning reflexes a one- or two-second advantage in slamming the pedal to the metal.

The lineup held, and a second before the flag began to rise, Frank slammed down the throttle and laid on hard through turn one, coming out of turn two half a car length ahead of Little. He floored it on the back stretch and stayed on it hard enough into turn three to grab the groove coming around four and slingshot down past the grandstand. He backed off just enough to hold the groove through turns one and two, fighting to keep the rear end from drifting wide and letting Little get under him.

The car was handling the way he liked it, super responsive but not loose enough to get squirrelly on him with every knock and bobble. On turn four he caught a quick look back at the scramble for second place between Little and Oakley, took advantage to open his lead to two car lengths, and cake-walked to the checkered flag.

It wasn't until he pulled into the pits that he found out that Chenoweth had spun out on the far turn in lap four and disappeared down the back side of the embankment, causing a brief but intense flurry of excitement in the stands.

Frank stood next to Buddy and watched as Chenoweth's car bobbed up over the embankment and pulled into the pits.

Haggard said, "That was unlucky. His car damaged, you think?

"Couldn't tell you," said Buddy. "He came on in on his own power. And screw luck. You just keep your eye on the prize."

That was exactly with Frank intended to do. He was already thinking about tomorrow's race in Winfield, and beyond that the Grand National.

•   •   •   •   •

In Kiowa, Maggie had gone through Sandy's room, closet, and drawers, but she knew pretty much what would be missing since her niece always packed for slumber parties as if she were going on a road trip. And earlier questioning of the others at the slumber party had turned up no leads. The official police position was that Sandy was probably just mad about something or on a lark, and would show up by dinner time, but she hadn't. There was nothing to do but wait—and hope for a call.

It was well past the dinner hour when Maggie sat down on the edge of Sandy's bed and looked around once more. Her weight displaced the menagerie of stuffed animals, including Sandy's favorite, a well-worn stuffed polar bear that tumbled onto the floor. She wondered at what age girls left those things behind to grow stiff and stale in the back of a closet or boxed up in a basement. Was Sandy already there, Maggie not noticing the latest surge toward maturity? She reached down for the bear and caught a glimpse of a pink note card half hidden by the bed-skirt. The message in it was written in Sandy's loopy cursive— "Dear Aunt Maggie, I'm all right, so don't get upset or worried or call the police or anything. There's something I need to do, even though other people might not understand. Don't worry. I'll call you soon to let you know I'm all right. Love, Sandy."

Maggie read the note a second time, more slowly, to see what she might have missed. Surely there had to be an indication of where Sandy had gone, when she'd be home. She said she'd call, but from where? And why mention the police? Maggie jumped up like someone in a hurry, but with no idea of where to go as she looked around the room to figure out what in the world her niece was up to.

CHAPTER 5

The knocking on the motel room door was so unexpected that Frank turned over and slipped off the edge of the bed, taking some of the covers with him. Standing up, he started to wrap the thin chenille spread around his waist, but Tina was trying to draw the covers up over her, so that they engaged in a brief tug-of-war through the second volley of knuckles against the door.

"Hold your horses!" Frank called out, finally managing to separate the spread from the sheet and wrap it around his waist. "Who is it?" he said, and turned to Tina, who had turned on the lamp on the bedside table. "You expecting company?"

"Right," she said, rolling her eyes. "I invited my family to stop by. Get your autograph."

"Police. Open up."

"Holy shit!" He eyed her suspiciously. "Just how old are you?"

"Nineteen. Want to see my driver's license?"

"Hunh. You seem older."

"Well, you *are* older."

He opened the door part way—a man's fist following it into the room in an aborted knock.

"Officer?" He smiled at the blue uniform as he read the name badge, "McDonough. What can I do for you?"

"Good evening, Sir. Are you Frankie Haggard?" The policeman looked him over. "Yeah, it's you. Didn't recognize you at first without your, um... helmet." He laughed at his own joke.

"Mind comin' to the point?" Frank asked. "We're lettin' out all the cold air."

McDonough adopted a serious tone, but his face sported a lopsided grin and his eyes clearly were enjoying what he was seeing. Frank had seen that look before, on fans who felt like they knew him but got awkward when it came to actually talking to one of their heroes. "I've got a young lady who says you were supposed to pick her up at the bus depot this evening before the races. Found her asleep on a bench. I guess there was some misunderstanding about the time."

"Whoa! There's some misunderstanding, all right. I don't know anything about a woman at a bus stop. You've got the wrong man." He started to push the door closed.

"Not so fast there." McDonough pushed the door open again. "She says she's your daughter and you were supposed to meet her, but I guess you sorta lost track of time," he said, glancing over at Tina.

"My what?" He stepped back, his foot caught in the spread. "You've definitely made a mistake."

"She wanted to wait there," McDonough went on, as if Frank hadn't spoken, "but I figured you'd be staying over this way. I recognized your rig." He pointed in the direction of the camper and trailer—loaded down with Frank's race car and enough tires to start a small business. "I go to the races regular myself."

"You're kidding me, right? Someone put you up to this." Frank scrutinized the policeman's face. "Buddy talk you into doin' this?"

"Buddy Baehr? No, sir, this is no joke."

"Now hold on." Frank's confusion was giving way to irritation. "Someone's trying to pull a fast one on both of us."

The officer reached around behind him and pulled Sandy into the doorway. "You're sure, now, that this here's your daddy?"

"Yes, sir. That's him," she answered softly. Tina, leaning to one side to peer around Frank, looked at Sandy and muttered, "Great balls of fire!"

Frank held up a hand—palm out—and laughed uncomfortably.

"I guarantee you this is some kind of joke or prank or somethin'. I don't have a kid. Look," he turned to Sandy, who was staring at him open-mouthed, fingering the slight dip in her chin—not unlike the one in his. "I don't know what you're up to, young lady, but I suggest that you tell this nice officer here where you live and let him take you on home."

"It's not a joke." Sandy's voice, thin and reedy at first, grew steadier with resolve. "My mother was Ruth Parson. I mean Ruth Haggard, of course, like you." Frank's mouth dropped open as he sucked in a sharp breath. If this was a hoax, it was a cruel one.

"'Cept they made her change it back, after you left, I guess. Then it was Turner after she married my other father, on account of me, I figure, but he was pretty old."

"Wait . . . wait just a minute," Frank said, needing time to get his head around not only what she was saying but the unwelcome visions she was conjuring up of painful events fifteen years ago he'd struggled hard to keep buried.

"He died when I was little, then she died." She watched as Frank's jaw, which had been slowly descending as if he were going to interrupt her, snapped shut, so she pushed on as if racing through a script. "That was ten years ago. When I'm eighteen I can have it officially changed to Haggard." The final string of words had been forced out with a steady push of her diaphragm. She took a breath and let it out. "Hi."

Frank automatically shook her outstretched hand, the charms on her bracelet tinkling daintily above the drone of the air conditioner that had failed to prevent the temperature of the room from warming considerably.

Officer McDonough motioned for Frank to follow him to the parking lot, well away from where Sandy stood by the open door looking back and forth from them to Tina. He placed one foot on the bumper of Frank's new buckskin-and-white '55 Mercury and bit down on a toothpick. "So what's really goin' on here?"

Frank gazed out across the lot and patted his chest in a nervous reflex, feeling for a pack of cigarettes. "You wouldn't happen to have a smoke on you?"

McDonough pulled out a red-and-white pack of Winstons and tapped the top against his index finger to coax a cigarette out. Frank took it and put it between his lips, then ran his hand down his hip, getting it caught in the folds of the bed spread.

"Shit! Gotta light?"

McDonough lit Frank's cigarette, then one for himself.

"So, Frankie. Is she your kid?"

"How the hell would I know?"

"You ever married to her mother, like she says?"

Frank took a pull on the cigarette and exhaled hard. In less than five minutes, fifteen years had peeled away so that it was like thinking about something that happened yesterday. The weight of it nearly crushed his lungs. Back then, Ruth was just about all he could talk about, bending the ears of the other soldiers, who were mostly as lonely as he was, though few as angry. But that was when he'd still believed in reason and justice, was willing to serve his country while he waited for Ruth to come of legal age when they could marry again, without her parents sticking their noses into it. He'd stopped talking before he stopped believing. And now she was dead.

"Uncle Sam knocked on my door. I had no idea where the Army would send me, so we eloped. April 16, 1942." Smoke-tinged saliva pooling on his tongue, he cleared his throat and spit onto the strip of grass separating the walk from the parking lot.

"A week later, her old man came after us, and took her back home. They had me officially annulled." He had dragged out the last two words, exaggerating each syllable.

"A week," McDonough said. "Wow. What are the odds? Anyway, you'd think a girl would mention something like that."

"Yeah. You'd think."

"So she never said anything?"

"I got shipped overseas." He exhaled some smoke, which drifted back into his eyes, causing them to water. "My letters went unanswered." He looked at McDonough. "And no one in all these years has ever said anything to me about a baby."

McDonough looked up at the green and yellow neon wagon wheel that appeared to be turning in place above the motel office. "Long odds, all right. But not impossible. Since you're not exactly dressed for company, why don't I take the girl across the road and get her a Coke or something while you get respectable? Then you can come on over and we can get this thing straightened out."

Frank pursed his lips, exhaled through his nose, and nodded. He had to turn sideways to get past Sandy, who was still standing in the doorway, her eyes fixed on the girl in the bed, who was staring back at her. When McDonough clamped his hand over Sandy's shoulder, she flinched.

"Let's you and me go get something cold to drink while your . . . while he gets dressed. Come on, now. We'll get this worked out." He tipped his cap to the girl in the bed. "Sorry, Miss . . . ."

"Tina," Frank said, making the abbreviated introduction.

"Miss Tina, for warmin' things up in here a mite. Evenin'."

Tina waited until the door was closed to ask, "What in the Sam Hill was that all about?"

Pulling on his pants, he said, "You know just as much as I do."

"What are you gonna do?"

"I'm going to go over to the truck stop, sit down with that policeman and a little girl who is saying that she and I are related, and make sure that the police do their job. By which I mean they find out where she's from and send her back there." He was a little winded from talking fast and hopping first on one foot and then the other while he pulled on his boots.

"Want me to go with you?"

"Hell no. This is enough of a circus already."

"Well, t'hell with you!" She tossed off the sheet and hopped out of bed, snatching up her things.

"Here! Come on, stop that!" He pulled the wad of clothes from her and held it behind him. "What do you think you're doin'?"

She tried to reach around him to grab them back. "I'm thinkin' I'll just go where I'll be better appreciated. You ain't the only hot rod on the track."

Frank tossed her things onto the bed and then pinned her arms to her sides with his, bending his knees so that he could look into her face. "Trust me, I appreciate you. Just calm down. This whole thing is crazy. I don't want you mixed up in it."

She stopped struggling and scrutinized him, her head cocked to one side. "Who do you really think she is?"

"Some moony kid who goes to the races. Probably a runaway. Or maybe just a local kid out on a dare." He wondered if it could really be as simple as that, but doubted it. "It's nothin' for you to worry about." He kissed her on her forehead. "I won't be long."

"All right. But be careful." She pulled on one of his chambray shirts and wrapped it around her like a robe.

"What the hell is that supposed to mean?" He stuffed his wallet into his back pocket and grabbed a pack of cigarettes from the suitcase.

"I dunno. Just used to sayin' it, I guess."

"Well, it's not like I'm goin' to the Indy 500." He made an attempt at a smile as he left, but his long strides betrayed his urgency.

Tina leaned against the doorframe, the lights from the neon wagon wheel sign casting different hues across her face as she watched Frank lope toward the highway. "Just the same," she called out. "And she's not all that little, either, in case you haven't noticed!"

CHAPTER 6

The truck stop was still packed at 10:00 p.m., typical after a race. The closer Frank got to the entrance, the slower he walked, but his pulse was racing. His head had filled with names and faces from the past. At first, early scenes of Ruth had come back—her face partially lit from a streetlight as he kissed her gently before taking her hand and leading her up the steps to meet with the Justice of the Peace in Alma, Oklahoma. That night, for the first time in his life, he'd felt absolute bliss, lying with his arms around her, his face buried in her hair, drunk on the scent and wonder of her. Caught up as he was in a dream come true, he could not then have foreseen the swift and unending wrath destined to swoop down upon him, even when Ruth's phone call to her mother the next day ended in tears.

Four days after they'd said their vows, he ran out of Lucky Strike cigarettes and was down to his last book of matches, which called for a quick trip into town. He kissed Ruth goodbye where she was sitting in a lawn chair next to the cabin, writing a letter. She needed some of her things and was asking her older sister Margaret if it was safe to come home for them or if their father was still angry.

On the way back, Frank stopped by a do-it-yourself car wash, then picked up some Chinese take-out as a surprise for dinner. When he returned at dusk, the chair was empty and the lights in the cabin were off. He called out from the empty front room in case Ruth was in the bathroom, but there was no answer. He started to step back outside to search the grounds but stopped short. Ruth's things were gone.

There was only her small gold-cross necklace lying on the nightstand. He picked it up, then closed his fist around it. At the door he looked around and sank down on the threshold. Setting the sack of food next to him on the porch, he cradled his head against his fists. The aroma of fried rice filled the air, and a nervous, sick feeling lodged in his stomach. His mind was churning as he imagined the scene. At first, he'd held out hope she'd just stepped out for a moment, maybe gone to the office for more towels or something. But then he thought her father must have come for her, forced her to go back with him. She would never have left on her own. He tried to think of what to do next to make things right again. To get her back.

He'd jumped when the phone in the cabin had rung and lifted the receiver saying, "Ruth, where are you?" But it had been one of her sisters, whispering a warning to stay away for the time being.

He returned to Kiowa immediately, demanding to see his wife, but had been told she wasn't there. He phoned the house for two days with nothing for his efforts but the sound of the receiver being replaced in the cradle. On the third day, there was a pause, and he could hear voices in the background before her father's voice shot through the wire. The choice laid out for him was painfully clear—he could sign annulment papers or go to jail.

Ruth had given in first. One week after they'd said "I do," he stood off to himself at one end of the Parsons' dining room table as Ruth, flanked by the parents and two sisters, leaned over and signed her name at the bottom of the document, having to be reminded in the heat of the moment to add the newly acquired Haggard. She'd looked up at Frank, her face glistening with tears, and mouthed I'm sorry. Her father set the document in front of Frank, who looked over at Ruth, waiting for some sign, for her to change her mind. When she looked away, he signed his name over hers, and before he'd added the date to make his one-week marriage a thing of the past she'd run sobbing from the room. The first door to slam was to her bedroom. The second was the front door as he stormed through it, followed by the screech of rubber against asphalt as he raced away from the Parsons, away from Kiowa all together. He drove in circles, until his outrage finally wore down along with the tread on his tires.

When he'd gotten it through his head that he would not be allowed to phone her and his first letters went unanswered, he rode a wave of bitterness into the army recruiting station and wound up at boot camp two days early. He'd finally be getting the fight he'd been spoiling for.

25

Now, Frank hesitated at the entrance of the truck stop, trying to get his head around what had to be a practical joke or at least a case of mistaken identity. Maybe someone was trying to mess with him, throw him off before the big race next weekend. *Well just let 'em try,* he thought, as he pulled the door open and headed for the booth in the back where McDonough sat with the girl who claimed to be his long-lost daughter.

CHAPTER 7

Sandy glanced up and saw that Frank's mood hadn't improved on the walk over. She thought if she could get him to talk about her mother, that would change. When he swung into the booth next to the officer, all three started to talk, their words scrambling together over the table. McDonough cleared his throat as a preface to a second attempt. "She says that you were supposed to get a letter."

She nodded eagerly, loose curls bobbing against her shoulders. It was the best lie she could come up with on short notice. "From Aunt Maggie," she said. "I guess maybe you didn't get it?"

"She'd be one of Ruth's sisters," he said.

"She's the oldest. Aunt lrma is the baby."

"Yeah. Well, it's been a lot of years since I saw any of them, and we weren't exactly on the best of terms." He realized that he was taking inventory, not of the obvious features—most pretty girls resemble one another—but of how her left ear stood out a little farther than the right one did, and the way her little fingers curved inward. He remembered Ruth's hands clinging to the edge of the swimming dock at Crystal Lake where he'd been lying on his stomach, watching her paddle around. She'd said she was practically a freak because her pinkies curved so much. She'd crossed them over her ring fingers as if to prove her point, then laughed at him, reaching down and scooping a cold stream of lake water over his sun-warmed back.

Frank leaned back and crossed his arms over his chest. "So why would Maggie suddenly think to write me a letter?"

"To tell you I was coming?" She smiled at him ruefully and shook her head in disbelief, the way adults do to children who give the appearance of being dense. "To visit. Just for a little while?"

Frank looked at her hard, and she could meet his eyes for only a moment before looking over to McDonough and then back down at her Coke. She could feel a trickle of sweat between her shoulder blades and her nose itched. She thought of Pinocchio, and gave it a tentative rub with the tip of her index finger. This wasn't how it was supposed to go. She was making it up as she went, hoping to delay being sent back right away, before she got to know him and find out exactly why her mother had kept all those newspaper clippings in all those albums right up until she got sick and died.

"Just like that?" His voice grew louder with his frustration over not being able to catch her in the lie. "Out of the clear blue, she decided to write me that some kid I never heard of before is coming to visit? To a motel—in Enid, Oklahoma?"

"I thought … well, we thought you would know. That my mother told you about me."

The people sitting nearby had stopped talking and were looking over at the threesome in the booth. She widened her eyes hoping to appear sincere and said, "Anyway, it was sort of an emergency." His eyes were squinty with suspicion, and she began to chew on her lower lip, trying to think up an emergency that he would believe.

Frank rubbed his hand over his face. "How did your Aunt Maggie find me, anyway? We've been on the road more than off it this whole season."

"Sports pages. They always give the racing results and list the big ones coming up."

"That's just great. And what if we decided to go someplace else this weekend? Or stayed home?"

"You wouldn't of. You need to make up points for two weeks ago when you blew an engine in the heat race."

He was surprised that she had actually been following him so closely, and his expression registered it before he got his game face back on. "Think you're pretty smart, don't you? And what if we'd had problems last week? What if we'd . . . well, just what if! Listen, something's fishy about all this." He looked at McDonough. "Wouldn't you say?"

McDonough shrugged and offered, "What about calling this aunt? She'd want to know the girl got here all right, anyway."

Sandy sat up straight, her hands gripping the edge of the table. "I did that already. Right when I got off the bus, just like she said to. And she's not home now, anyway. She's at rehab with Grandma Parson, getting her wash. Grandma Parson had a stroke, so I've been going back and forth between Aunt Irma's and Aunt Maggie's. But Uncle Lloyd has been real sick, too, with prostrate trouble, and they're all real busy." She frowned, took a sharp breath, and gave her head an earnest little shake. "That's why I needed to come see you for a little while. Get out of everybody's way. Just a few days."

Frank shook his own head in disbelief and looked over at McDonough.

"Prostrate trouble? You know that for a fact, do you," McDonough asked, trying to suppress a smile.

"I overheard them talking about it. And he lays on the couch a lot."

"I'll bet he does," McDonough, said, chuckling openly at Frank.

"Aunt Maggie said I'm not to be any trouble or anything, and it'll just be for a little while. Because it's an emergency. She'll send me bus fare whenever I need it."

"And you don't have bus fare home right now?" Frank asked.

She solemnly shook her head, her fingers curling tightly around her purse where seventeen dollars and 79 cents—the former contents of her piggy bank—resided.

Frank rolled his head around and let out a sigh, then motioned the waitress over and ordered a bottle of Coors for himself. While she refilled McDonough's coffee, Frank decided to take a different approach. "Listen, I'm sorry about your family's troubles and all, but this is no place for a young girl. You understand?"

She pinched her lips together and shook her head no.

"Well, you would if you had the sense to think about it!"

Her voice rose to meet his. "I have thought about it. A lot!"

"Good for you! It comes as pretty sudden news to me! How old are you, anyway?"

"Fourteen and a half."

Frank shook his head. "Lord, just a baby. Tall for your age, aren't you? What in the world do you think you're doin' runnin' around by yourself?"

"I'm not hardly a *baby*. Myra Gale Brown just married Jerry Lee Lewis, and she's only 13."

Frank looked at McDonough who grinned and shrugged, as if to say she's got you there.

"That is the worst argument I've ever heard. And she's his cousin. There's an example for you."

"My best friend Ralph is 14 and already has a driver's license."

"He does not," Frank said.

"He does too. He works on their farm, so he's got a special one. And he lets me drive sometimes when he has to go get the cows in for milking."

"You live on a farm?"

"No. I live with my Aunt Maggie and Grandma Parson. I told you."

They stared at one another for a moment before Frank tipped up his beer and drank half of it down. McDonough suggested it might be better if he let them talk things over in private, but Frank said for him to stay right there. While the two men were debating whether McDonough should get up or stay put, Sandy scrambled out of the booth.

"Where you think you're goin'?" Frank called after her.

McDonough motioned for Frank to get up and let him out and called to her, "Hey, wait up. Where you goin'? You can't go wandering around at night."

They caught up with her at the door, where she turned and faced them, her cheeks streaked with watery streams of black mascara. "Just you never mind!"

The two men looked at each other and back at her. "Never mind? Just like that? Never mind?" Frank practically yelled, then brought his voice down to a raspy whisper. "You come bouncin' in here, with a police escort, and tell some crazy story about being Ruth's and my kid—of which I have heard absolutely nothing in all these dozen years—"

"Fourteen and a half!"

"And your Aunt whatever—"

"Maggie!"

"Whatever! Sends you off to a strange man in a strange town—because her husband has medical problems—and it's summer vacation! Holy shit!" He threw up his hands in exasperation and appealed to McDonough. "You hearing this load of—"

"Let's be watchin' our language," McDonough cautioned, but there was no heat in it.

"Aunt Irma's husband!" Her voice, too, had become a raspy pseudo whisper. "Aunt Maggie isn't married. Just forget it! Forget I was ever here!" She pushed through the door, the two men following close behind. Frank shook an unheeded finger as he trailed her into the parking lot. "Listen here, kid—"

She whirled around so fast that the thick sweep of her skirt and petticoats caught against his shins, and yelled, "I'm not a kid! I'm almost 15. Almost as old as my mother when you married her. And anyway, I'm leaving! That's what you want." She started sobbing, and her words tatted out on tiny explosions of air. "I've done all right without any fathers. I don't care if I never see you again. I hope you lose tomorrow night! I hope that your car breaks down pulling out of the pits, and you drop your transmission, and . . . your car just . . . ." With all of her fantasizing and plotting about how it would be when they finally met, it had not occurred to her that she might be angry with him. She lurched toward the patrol car and leaned against it, her face buried in slender arms that didn't come close to containing her hot, angry sobs.

"McDonough!" Frank looked around for the officer, who was leaning against a light pole in front of the cafe. "Do something."

McDonough walked over to him shaking his head. "You two sure fight like family."

Frank gave him a warning look.

"All right," McDonough offered. "Here's the way it is. If she's not your relation, then technically she's a runaway. That makes her a ward of the court, until we find out more about the situation. Shouldn't be too hard to check things out, locate this Aunt Maggie and see what's what."

Frank glanced over at the girl, who was quieter now, but her shoulders were still shaking. He asked, "What'll you do with her?"

"We don't throw them into the holding tank, if that's what you're wondering. There are people who take charge of kids who for one reason or another can't be in their own homes. The city pays them to sort of oversee things until the court rules. Unless the kid's a hard case, has a history of running off and like that."

Frank called over to her, "You hear that? Do you see the kind of trouble you've created for yourself here?" He lowered his voice to McDonough, "The way I figure it, she's not telling the whole truth. It just doesn't add up. On the other hand, she is Ruth's kid . . . ."

"And yours?"

Frank glanced over at her, shaking his head. "Regardless ... I wouldn't want anything bad to happen to her."

Sandy turned around to lean back against the car and wiped her face with the back of her arm. McDonough had taken a toothpick out of his shirt pocket and was chewing on it, working it from one side of his mouth to the other while Frank lit a cigarette. "Well," McDonough took the pick out of his mouth and used it like a tiny pointer, emphasizing his words as he spoke, "she's traveled here from somewhere to meet up with the man she seems to think is her father. Of course, so far, I don't imagine she's too thrilled with what she's seen."

Frank shifted his weight from one foot to the other. "You know, what I've got a mother lode of right now is aggravation. I don't need you trowelin' it on."

"I'd say you've got that right."

"And what would you say I do about it?"

"Find out who she is for sure."

"And how might I be able to do that?"

"Get the aunt's number and call her."

Frank thought about that briefly. "What if she's part of this?" His head was aching from trying to calculate all the possible angles.

"People who depart from the truth eventually trip themselves up. Talk to the girl. Talk to the aunt."

Frank took a hard drag on the cigarette, then flipped the butt out into the parking lot. "Look, kid—what's your name, again?"

Her answer was muffled, and he had to ask her to repeat it.

"Sandy," she said. She had calmed down considerably, but still sucked in erratic gasps of air, her bottom lip quivering against her front teeth.

"Well look. Sandy, nobody wants to upset you or make you cry, so calm down now. Lt. McDonough here says that they might have to put you some place until all this is straightened out. Now, I don't think that's such a good idea. What I mean is, I think maybe we'd best go call your aunt and get this worked out. What about that, McDonough? You agree with that, don't ya?"

"Okay by me. I've got her stuff in the car. I can drive you back over to the motel."

Frank looked at Sandy. "Well, what do you say?"

She chewed on her bottom lip and looked over at the neon wagon wheel spinning in front of the motel. "I guess."

"Okay." Frank pulled out a handkerchief, clean but still permanently discolored from oily track dirt and car grease. "McDonough, you got something she can use here?"

McDonough leaned into the car and pulled out some tissues from a box on the dash, handing them over the car to Frank, who passed them to Sandy.

"Blow your nose," Frank told her, "and wipe that crud off your eyes. You look like a raccoon." He opened the door, packing the fortress of petticoats in after her before closing it. He hadn't meant it to sound as harsh as it came out, but he couldn't seem to get control of the situation. Crazy as it sounded, the girl who was yo-yoing back and forth between bravado and hysterics could be his child. In the hot, still night, Frank felt a rush of air, as if another driver was breathing down his neck coming out of turn four.

CHAPTER 8

Back at the motel, McDonough waited on the sidewalk with Sandy and her suitcase while Frank went to the office to see about getting a second room. His agitation was obvious as he strode back to where he had left them. "You're not gonna believe this. All the rooms are full. They don't even have a roll-away left."

McDonough took Frank's arm and led him up the sidewalk a little ways. "Just a word of caution, here. In the event that the girl really isn't any relation of yours . . . I mean just suppose that she's mistaken, even—well, you see the problem."

"Terrific! You picked a great time to bring this up."

"I just thought you'd best be prepared for any possibility. Isn't there someone in your crew who can put you up?"

"I'll work on it. In the meantime, I not only have to tell Tina that Sandy is staying tonight, I have to break it to her that they're going to be bunkmates. Unless you'd like to break that news bulletin too."

"Thanks, I'll pass. I wouldn't mind staying around to watch while you tell her, though," McDonough said, laughing to himself as he followed Frank back over to where Sandy was waiting, McDonough nodding genially at her, saying to get a good night's sleep, that everything looks better in the morning.

Frank and Sandy watched until the black and white police cruiser had-pulled onto the highway, then looked at each other. Sandy thought they ought to be saying things, maybe about her mother—the scrapbooks, or the way she died. After a moment, Frank said they'd better go on in.

"Is that girl still in there?"

"You two are going to be bunkmates tonight."

"Where will you sleep?"

"Fine time for you to think about that."

By now, the room had cooled down again, and Tina, who was wearing shortie pajamas and a bathing suit cover-up, was sitting in a chair with one leg tucked under her, the other one swinging back and forth throwing off nervous energy. She took one look at the two of them and blew a long, hard stream of smoke at the ceiling. The bed had been pulled together and the clothes were back in the suitcases. "You're sure there aren't any other rooms?" Sandy asked him.

"I'm sure." He swung Sandy's suitcase onto the built-in counter that served as a TV stand and desk. "Tina James, this is Sandy Parson."

"Turner," Sandy corrected him.

"Haggard." Tina corrected them both.

Frank flinched. "Looks like you two have everything you need for now."

"More than a body could hope for." Tina's sarcasm was lost on Sandy, who was holding her suitcase and yawning, as though she were watching them from a great distance.

Frank headed for the door. "Don't stay up all night talking girl talk."

"You mean this isn't a slumber party?"

"Not for some of us. I'll see you in the morning."

Sandy disappeared into the bathroom, and Tina followed Frank to the door. "Where will you be?"

"In the car, until Buddy shows up."

She looked at the Mercury. "It's probably better than you deserve."

"Thanks. I appreciate your concern."

"All right. So I'm not being a very good sport. But this wasn't exactly what I had in mind when I agreed to spend my vacation on the circuit with you."

"This wasn't in my plans, either. Look, we'll get it straightened out. Okay?" He touched the smooth skin of her cheek and realized that she didn't look much older than the girl in the bathroom. The thought was like a poke in his solar plexus, and he struggled to push it away.

Tina locked her fingers through the hair at the back of his head and pulled him down so that she could kiss him. "I guess I can take a smudge-eyed teenage girl for one night. It is just for tonight, isn't it?"

"Absolutely. This is just to keep her from havin' to spend the night with strangers."

"Is that right? You know, she and I don't exactly go way back."

"Get some sleep."

She watched him climb into the back of the Mercury and pull his boots off. Disappearing for a few minutes, she returned with a blanket.

"Are you crazy? It's gotta be eighty degrees out here."

"It's to use for a pillow, you dope." She leaned in the window and kissed him, and he pulled her in farther until she squealed and squirmed back out of the window. She ran the three yards back to the room, pausing to wave before she shut the door.

The bathroom door was still closed, and she could hear Sandy brushing her teeth. Tina lit another cigarette and sat in a chair with a magazine open across her lap. At least ten more minutes passed before Sandy reappeared, huge rollers all over her head, except for her bangs, which were still damp and clung to her forehead. With the makeup washed off and the stiff petticoats standing in a corner, she looked younger and smaller. The two of them stared at one another through the strips of smoke that hung in the air like the flat yellow shelf of clouds that carry embryos of tornadoes.

Tina cleared her throat and snubbed out her cigarette. "Why don't you take the side by the window? I might read for a little while."

Sandy walked to the other side, where she slipped under the covers and hugged the edge of the bed.

"If it gets too cool for you, we can turn the fan down."

Sandy's voice, muffled by the pillow and drowsiness, seemed to come from far away. "Doesn't matter." She drew her knees close to her chest, taking up as little space in the double bed as possible. She hadn't counted on falling asleep at the depot, and she certainly hadn't counted on the girl on the other side of the bed. She couldn't be much older than Sandy, who had noticed that, figure-wise, Tina had already filled out substantially. In fact, she was probably done.

With fatigue washing through her, it was hard to keep her thoughts straight, but she needed to reconsider her strategy. Nothing was going the way she had planned. Except that she was really there. And so was he. She tried to recall everything she and Frank had said to each other, but what she kept zeroing in on was the way he'd gotten her the Kleenex, and told her to wipe her eyes in a disgruntled, fatherly way. That could be significant.

CHAPTER 9

Late in the warm summer night, sitting on the back-porch swing, Maggie told Irma, "I can't help it. I'm furiously worried—if that's even a legitimate emotional state." With her left leg tucked under her and her arms wrapped tightly around her ribcage, Maggie stared out at nothing in particular. The huge owl Sandy had named Sir that lived in the cottonwood at the far back of their property took off and landed several times, as if the tension throughout the house radiated into the yard and stirred up the night air. She leaned her head back and listened hard. She wanted to be like Superman on TV who could pick up conversations from all over, maybe even Sandy's voice, giving her a clue of what was happening and why. Between the squeak of the swing and the hooting of Sir, she could hear Lloyd on the phone in the kitchen, his voice as big as the rest of him. There was the clinking of cup on saucer, the scraping of a chair on linoleum, dogs barking intermittently, no doubt agitated by the popping firecrackers being set off by some kids unwilling to accept that Independence Day was over.

"You remember when Ruth had come home from the hospital with Sandy and stayed at the house for the first week?" Irma asked. "Dad had grumbled about the lost sleep. We three took turns heating bottles and sitting up into the wee hours?"

"How could I forget?" To Maggie, the sounds that had come from the crib were wondrous, the quick bursts announcing feeding time and the petulant whimpering that receded when the tiny mouth finally caught hold of the nipple and focused all the strength in that small body on long pulls of the formula they took turns giving her. Sandy would ball up her tiny fists and hold them close to her face, like a miniature prizefighter.

"Then the next week, Fred Turner moved Ruth and the baby back to his apartment, and you and Joe got engaged."

Maggie nodded in time with the swing's back and forth. "Seems a hundred years ago." Maggie had accepted Joe Hersch's wartime proposal and a promise ring. She vowed to herself that she would get pregnant as soon as they were married, regardless of the town gossips who would undoubtedly be counting the months with glee and relishing the speed with which the Parsons girls got pregnant, nodding knowingly to one another.

But the gossips were denied that pleasure by a draft notice and soon after by a fragment from a German grenade. It was not even a very large fragment. It had stayed lodged in the front of Joe's head for three days, until he was finally delivered to a hospital where they could remove it safely. Then they sent him stateside, saying that he would be fine, but he wasn't. Or maybe he was, but he was never the same. He came to see Maggie a few times, even had supper with her family, but he was nervous and often smelled of whiskey, and the subject of marriage never came up again. The last time she'd talked to his mother, while trying to run down former classmates for their ten-year high school reunion, she learned that he had married, finally, a woman he worked with at the Montgomery Ward store in Raleigh, North Carolina, someone who hadn't known the Joe who went off to war and never really came back.

Lloyd called to them through the screen door, asking if they wanted any more coffee or iced tea. She didn't, but asked for coffee anyway. She was afraid she might fall asleep and not hear if Sandy called in the night, so she opted for jittery wakefulness and a series of imagined disasters that grew darker with the night.

CHAPTER 10

It took the sun hitting him full in the face to finally rouse Frank from what had been a cramped night of semi-wakefulness. And yet, he had managed to dream. The noise of gunfire slipped back into the undifferentiated web of memories in his subconscious. The curiosity was that it hadn't seemed to be a military setting, but more like a black-and-white movie—home movie—of his old neighborhood. His old border collie had been in the dream, rubbing against his legs.

Dreams about the Army always left a bad taste in his mouth, but even before he'd fallen asleep, his head had been full of uneasy memories. He hadn't thought of Ruth for a long time, couldn't recall what his last thoughts of her had been. Curiosity, maybe. Or a brief, nostalgic flash of her as the girl he'd courted, out in the open somewhere, beside the river in fair weather.

At first, after her father had taken her back home, Frank had fed his grief by imagining how her stricken, tearful face must have looked through the car window. But he never actually saw her like that. He'd gone to the drugstore to buy cigarettes, and when he returned, she was gone. Gradually, when it became clear that he wouldn't be allowed to see her and she wasn't going to run back to him on her own, he signed up for duty. When he'd returned to Kiowa on leave to bury his father, he'd heard that Ruth had married soon after he'd gone, and that had ended it—except for a residual bitterness that rose up from time to time like bile, usually after particularly bad periods of thankless jobs or burnt-out love affairs. Then he would spend whole Sunday afternoons or those shapeless hours in the middle of the night mulling over what might or might not have been faithful renditions of those heady months he'd given over to loving the slim girl called Ruth—

Ruth with the widest, most beautiful smile in the county, and hair as thick and silky as mink fur.

He scratched the stubble on his face and looked at his watch, swearing aloud when he saw that it was only six-fifteen. It wasn't the early hour that troubled him. Dirt-track racers were used to early-morning and even late-night drives from one track to another a hundred miles or more away. Right now, it was the early-morning heat that bothered him. He remembered that it had finally felt cooler one of the times he'd awakened, but it was already warming up again. Easing up to look around, he spotted the pickup camper at the back of the parking lot, and decided it was wiser to wake up Buddy than to have to tackle the two girls asleep in the room. Anyway, he needed time to sort out his thoughts in the clear light of day.

He started to sit up, had difficulty negotiating, and discovered that his ankles were bound together with red grease rags. "Damn it, Buddy," he swore, loosening the knots and working up a sweat in the process. He opened the trunk and took a bottle of beer from the melted ice. He took a swig as he headed for the camper, opening the door carefully so as not to make any noise, and climbing in. It was fairly dark, but he could make out Buddy's outline in the bunk over the cab. Stepping up on the bench in the eating nook, he steadied himself with his left hand, clamped the thumb on his right hand over the top of the bottle, and shook it vigorously before releasing the spray in the general direction of Buddy's choking-on-a-chicken-bone snore. The shrill, female shout that accompanied Buddy's curses left Frank as startled as the two who sat up yelling at him.

The woman, one of the Enid regulars Frank had seen around the track, wiped the side of her face with the edge of the sheet and said, "Awright, Buddy. Who's the joker with the sick sense of humor?" Frank decided to let Buddy explain it to her since he was the one who started it all with the rags stunt.

"Sorry, Ma'am," Frank said, by way of apology, any sincerity getting lost in his laughter. "I didn't know the Bear had company." He quickly walked to the back and stepped into the narrow cubbyhole that served as a toilet, sink, and shower. He washed leisurely, in spite of the hammering on the door and a few choice curses. Once the water was off, he yelled at Buddy to get him some of the clothes he kept in the top of the closet. Getting no response, he wrapped his shirt around him and opened the door, saying good morning to the woman who was already dressed in Capri pants and a sleeveless blouse. She was wearing sling pumps, and he noticed the nice turn of her ankles and calves, and that the line was slightly spoiled by the broadening thighs and buttocks. Her hair had come unpinned in several places and sprang up awkwardly, giving her a surprised look which was enhanced by the fact that most of her eyebrow pencil had rubbed off. She ignored his greeting and busied herself making coffee while he found his clothes and got dressed behind the open door to the bathroom. Buddy came in from the outside, wearing only his jeans, which he was still closing up.

"Darn it, Frank, whatcha tryin' to do? First you nearly give me a heart attack, and then you try to bust my bladder."

"I thought you were alone."

"What the hell difference does that make?"

Frank reached into the pile of clothes he'd stuffed into the closet and threw the red grease rags onto the table.

"Aw hell," Buddy said. "It was just a little joke. Insult to injury, like they say. What were you doin' sleepin' in the car, anyway? That scrap of a girlfriend too much for you to handle?" Buddy leaned over, kissing the woman on the neck, and sniffed the coffee. "Got any of that for me?"

She handed him the steaming mug and said, "You'll have to see hot shot there if you want another chaser."

The men laughed, but Frank saw that she still wasn't amused.

"I really am sorry about that. I had no intention of inconveniencing anyone but the Bear, here." She shrugged, as if to dismiss him. "No, really. Here," he pulled out a five-dollar bill, "Use this to get your hair done." She looked at him sharply but there was no heat in it as he gingerly tucked the folded bill into the side pocket of her Capri pants. "It's the least I can do. It'll make us both feel better. Truce?"

She bit the side of her mouth, but smiled anyway. "Truce."

Belatedly, Buddy said, "This here's Louise Jurgis. This is Frankie. Frank Haggard."

Louise reached for Frank's extended hand. "Of course, I recognized you. Not right off. Must have been the beer in my eyes. But when you came out of the bathroom."

"Well, I'm pleased to meet any friend of the Bear's."

"Likewise." She patted her hair. "If you boys will let me at the powder room, I'll try to dilute this beer rinse. The truck stop will be the only place open this early, if you're hungry."

"I'd better see if Tina is up."

"Want some protection?" Buddy chuckled.

"It's not what you think. Believe me, I wish it was."

"Are you trying to say something? Cause if you are, you ain't gettin' it done."

"Later. Meet you for breakfast. Try to get the big booth."

Frank's slap on the bathroom door was met by a yelp. "Sorry! Just wanted to say it was nice meetin' you. And don't hurry. There's no rush."

"Not much point in taking my time," she called through the door. "You used up all the hot water."

Frank grimaced at Buddy. "I don't think she's a fan."

"You blame her?"

Frank gulped down some of the coffee Louise had poured and opened the back door. "What time you planning on taking off for Winfield?"

"Around noon. Time trials are at 5:00. I'll drain the gas tank after I install the new starter at Wilbur's garage and she'll be ready to go."

"Did G.D. say he'd actually pay for the new starter?"

"I think he and Coralee are still at the Grand Canyon. But he's the owner, he'll pay. If not, we'll take it out of the winnings."

"Bold talk."

"Will you let me take care of my end of things? You're gettin' to be an old lady." Buddy grabbed Frank by his shoulder, spun him around, and propelled him through the door and down the camper's retractable step.

Frank thought the problem with the starter was almost a welcome diversion from the real setback that was sleeping next to Tina. But he headed back over to the motel room to take the bull by the horns and set things right. The last thing he needed with the biggest race of his life coming up was this kind of distraction.

CHAPTER 11

Frank walked over to where Tina lay curled on her side and grinned in spite of himself. He jiggled her shoulder and watched as she slowly opened her eyes and lay there for a moment staring at Sandy, whose nose was only a few inches from her own. The girl's mouth was slightly open, and some of the large, pink curlers had slipped loose.

Tina turned her head to look at him.

"Snug as two bugs in a rug," he said softly, grinning at her.

"What time is it?" Tina whispered back, closing her eyes again.

"Half past seven. How'd you two get along last night?"

She yawned. "Swell. Tons of giggles."

"Really?" he asked.

She shot him a look that said otherwise and propped herself up on her elbows. "What about you?" she whispered, "What time did Buddy show up?"

"I slept in the car. Any way the Bear had company." He sat down on the corner of the nightstand.

Tina slipped out from under the covers and stood up, pulling the blanket back up next to Sandy, who rolled over onto her back and threw one arm up over her eyes. They walked across the room, Tina stretching her arms above her head, the pajama top covered with violets inching up to the top of her thighs. She saw Frank raise his eyebrows in an admiring look, and brought one hand down in a caress along his cheek. "Poor baby. You must be all kinked up. Why don't you take the first shower, and I'll give you a rubdown?"

He gestured at the sleeping girl. "I think that might be just a little awkward. Anyway, I showered in the camper."

"I thought you said Buddy had a girl in there . . . Never mind. I can't use my brain until I've had some coffee." She tipped her head in Sandy's direction. "What have you decided to do about this little matter?"

"Feed her, buy her a bus ticket, and send her home."

"Just like that?"

"I thought you couldn't wait to get rid of her."

"Well, I don't exactly see us as one big happy family. But I think you ought to talk to her. And you never did answer me. Is she your kid or not?"

He took the pack of cigarettes out of his shirt pocket and glanced over at Sandy, then put it back. He really didn't relish conjuring up his past right there, in a motel room, stuck between Tina's natural curiosity and the remaining evidence of Ruth's existence. "She has her hair and eyes. And her hands."

"That's not what I asked."

"She's the right age." He gave Sandy a long looking over. "On the other hand, maybe she is that Turner fellow's, and made this other up when he died. Found out about her mom and me. Formed some kind of psychological attachment." Saying it out loud, Frank suddenly realized that while that would be the easy way out for him, he was no longer sure if he wanted that to be the final verdict either. "Hell, you know more about the way a little girl's mind works than I do."

"I had to start thinkin' like a big girl a long time ago. What I do think is that if I were in your place, I'd wanna know for sure, one way or the other. But that's your business. S'got nothin' to do with me. Should we wake her up? She showered last night."

"Not yet. Let her sleep a little longer. I told Buddy and Louise we'd meet them for breakfast across the street. I'm going on over there."

"Louise?"

"Buddy's new friend."

Tina went into the bathroom. "What happened to Delores?"

"Dunno. Different track? Different state?"

As she closed the door she said, "I thought they were having a good time."

"Me too. Changed her mind, I guess. You know how unpredictable women are."

46

She opened the door a sliver and said, "I heard that." There was the sound of running water and shower rings scraping along the rod.

"How long you gonna be?" he asked.

"What?"

"How long . . . never mind. I gotta go talk to the Bear."

"So, git."

Stopping at the door, Frank watched Sandy long enough to reassure himself she was still asleep before he quietly closed the door behind him, relieved at not having to face her again just yet. It would be easier once he'd laid down a nicotine and caffeine base.

After the door closed, Sandy took her arm down and stared up at the ceiling, tears pooling in her eyes until she blinked hard and they spilled down her temples and onto the pillow. She slipped out of bed and took shorts and a sleeveless blouse out of her suitcase, then started yanking the curlers out of her hair. If only they could have met at the track the way she'd planned. She sat down on the bed and wiped her eyes with the collar of her pajamas. She thought about leaving without saying anything, but she heard the shower shut off, and she needed to use the bathroom. She wiped her eyes again and sniffed hard to clear her nose. She wasn't going to let her maybe-father's girlfriend see her being a crybaby.

CHAPTER 12

The truck stop was packed, and several men turned to watch Tina walk in with Sandy in tow. They wound through the tables toward the large corner booth in the back where Frank was sitting with Buddy and Louise. The two men stood up as the girls slipped in on Frank's side, Sandy followed by Tina, who seemed to Frank a shade reserved. He leaned over, his mouth close to her ear, and asked, "Anything wrong?" Her tight smile in response wasn't reassuring. She turned and said in a low voice, "She wasn't sure she wanted to come over here. I'm pretty sure she's been crying."

Frank nodded, then said, "Louise, this is Tina. And here's Sandy."

Buddy looked at Frank and then back at the girl, clearly puzzled.

"Hi, there," Louise said. "Nice to meet ya both."

Buddy gave Frank a questioning look and then reached his hand across the table to Sandy. "Howdy. I'm Buddy."

She shook his hand, saying "How do you do," and then looked down at her lap. In a ruffled pink blouse and pink and blue plaid shorts and with her face still soft from sleep, she looked more like a story-book doll than the obstinate teenager who was causing Frank more grief than he'd known for some time. As she sat there primly between the two couples, her hands folded in her lap, he wondered what had happened to the stubbornness and fire of the night before. He turned to Tina, who raised her eyebrows and shrugged. Leaning closer, she whispered, "Maybe she's not a morning person."

"We've already ordered," Frank told the girls. "Buddy's got to pick up a part we need for tonight. You two know what you want?"

"Would it be too much trouble to get a menu?" Tina asked with a hint of irritation at being rushed along.

Frank waved to the waitress, who was too loaded down with dishes to respond right away.

"So," Buddy asked, "everyone sleep all right?"

When no one answered, Sandy looked over at him and said, "Fine, thank you."

"That's good," Buddy said. "Nothing like a good night's sleep to clear out the cobwebs."

Sandy looked back down at her hands, and Frank saw that her upper lashes had mascara on them again, forming perfect fans over her rouged cheeks. He fought off the inclination to tell her to lay off the makeup, that she was too young to paint up like that. But hell, she'd be gone soon, and the Parsons' problem again.

Frank said, "Glad someone did."

Buddy suppressed a grin, said, "Gonna be a scorcher today."

Frank stiffened when he felt the toe of Buddy's boot graze his shin. He looked over at him, frowning. "Right. Yeah. A real hot one."

"Paper says 90 or better," Buddy continued. When he didn't get a response, he picked up the Enid Gazette from the bench and held it out. "Anyone else interested in seeing what the world's up to?"

Tina stretched her arm across the table and took it. "Thanks." She noticed Frank frowning at her, and said, "Sorry, but there are very few things I'm good at in the morning, and small talk isn't one of them." She popped the paper open in front of her and Buddy gave up trying to jump start a conversation. He went back to making sketches on a paper napkin.

Louise nodded. "I know just what she means. I, personally, am no good whatsoever until I've had my second cup of coffee." She turned her attention to Sandy. "I'll bet you're real hungry, aren't you? You kids can just eat and eat, and it never shows." She nudged Buddy. "Can't you two he-men get someone over here to take their order?"

Frank lifted himself out of the booth, jostling the table, and went to retrieve two menus from the counter. He dropped one down between Tina's arms—which jerked together in reflex, causing the paper to collapse—and held the other out to Sandy, who didn't notice it at first. She was watching intently while Louise peered into an inch-long mirror and applied lipstick with a brush, then blotted her lips on a paper napkin and placed it on the table, the tidy print of her mouth a bright red circle that gaped up at them. Noticing Sandy's interest, she smiled and held out the gold tube for her to examine. "It's called Candied Apple."

Frank thrust the menu between the lipstick and Sandy's outstretched hand. "Better order. It's gettin' late."

She took the menu from him in silence, her eyes meeting his for only a moment, but the accusation in them was enough to make him feel a mixture of anger and guilt, the emotions circling like boxers readying themselves for the first blow. He ran his thumb across the top of his belt buckle, a metal replica of his race car that a fan in Wichita, Kansas, had given him the first year he'd been high-point man. It was a nervous habit he'd acquired. It reminded him who he was.

He watched Sandy read down both sides of the menu, a slight frown on her face. Regardless of where she came from, she didn't belong here. He needed to stop pussy-footing around and settle the matter of the stray child once and for all, so he could get back to the business of preparing for that evening's race in Winfield, and beyond that, the Grand National.

The waitress came with the three orders and waited impatiently for the other two to make up their minds. Frank's resolve had relieved his tension some, and he figured he'd wait until after everyone had eaten breakfast to tell Sandy what was what and that she was going to be on a bus home in a matter of hours. That was best all around, though she might not see it right off and cause a fuss.

Tina put down her menu. "Two eggs over medium, toast, dry, hash browns, and coffee with cream."

Sandy studied the menu a moment longer, then said, "I'll have orange juice and an order of sausage, please."

"That's too much grease on an empty stomach," Frank told her. "Get some eggs and toast with it."

"I don't want eggs."

"What'll it be," the waitress asked, shifting from one foot to the other.

"Get toast and hash browns with it, then," Frank said.

"I'm not very hungry."

Frank was still scowling at Sandy as the waitress repeated the original orders and marched off.

"I was a picky eater myself," Louise said, smiling at Sandy and reaching across to pat her arm. "Drink your juice first, and you'll be fine. Here, take this piece of toast. I'd never finish all this if I ate until noon. Go on now."

Sandy accepted the toast reluctantly, and periodically took mincing bites that grated on Frank so much that he began to grind his own food relentlessly as if to compensate for her lack of effort.

Louise managed to engage Tina in small talk about the heat and the density of dust that sweeps up during the races when they don't water down the tracks enough. The two women agreed that they would like racing a lot better if there was less dust and noise.

As if suddenly energized from the food, Sandy spoke up, saying that she loved the noise, and that when the cars were coming around the fourth turn at the beginning of a race she could feel the racing engines "in here," she tapped her sternum lightly, "and the sensation changes when they shift gears or speed up and slow down. If you concentrate, you can hear the different engines and gears—like in an orchestra." Her face had grown more angular, more mature looking with motion and intensity, and she had the men's full attention.

"You go to a lot of races?" Buddy asked.

"My uncle used to take all of us kids over to Alva, and sometimes even down to Oklahoma City. His dream was to invest in one of the new modifieds himself, so he could really be involved. He even used to go into the pits and help out sometimes."

"Doesn't he go anymore?" Buddy asked.

"Not for a while. Not since Alva, I think." She glanced at Frank and shrugged, then looked at her toast thoughtfully remembering one of last night's spur-of-the-moment lies. "He's been kinda sickly lately."

Buddy leaned forward. "Alva's not a bad track, considering the size of the place."

"You all came in second in the heat there, lost the trophy dash to that creep Hays who bumps into everyone, and came in fifth in the feature. The car wasn't handling right. I think it was because of Hays. You should have challenged and had him torn down after the race."

She shook her head at the memory and took a big bite of toast. "You let him off too easy."

Buddy tapped the tabletop with his fist. "I'd say you're right, kid, but we didn't have the twenty-five dollars to put up at the time."

She looked surprised. "But you win a lot. More than most others."

"We win some," said Buddy, "but this kinda racing ain't for people who are lookin' to get rich."

She looked at him thoughtfully and chewed her toast intently. "I see." She turned to Frank. "Then how do you make a living?"

"I," he paused and shot Buddy a look, "sell insurance."

Louise stopped eating, her forkful of hash browns halfway to her mouth.

Sandy thought a moment longer, and asked, "Life?"

"And accident."

Louise burst out laughing and clamped her napkin over her mouth."Sorry, but that does take the cake. Get many customers?"

Tina was smiling too. "He's pretty good. That's how we met. He said he wanted to sell me some car insurance."

Louise, who was still chuckling, asked, "Did he?"

"Not hardly. I was driving my boyfriend's car. Sold *him* a policy," she said.

Louise laughed so hard that she snorted each time she inhaled, which made even Frank laugh out loud. She was the last to finally calm down, opening her mouth wide for a gulp of air. "That's a good one! I hope I can keep all this food down."

Buddy patted Frank on the shoulder and said, "That's pretty good all right. How much commission you make off the poor son-of-a big . . . dog . . . catcher?"

Frank looked at Tina and grinned sheepishly.

She used her index finger and thumb to make a circle. "Nothin'. Chauncey got real upset when he found out I was going out with Frank, and while he was chasing us down the road on our way out of town, he ran into a mailbox. Broke his leg and messed up the car somethin' awful. He put in a claim, and Frank hasn't seen a nickel from that deal." She nudged him with her elbow. "Isn't that right?"

He said, "Not exactly," but his response was lost in their laughter, so he just shook his head in resignation.

Sandy stopped laughing first, and after the others had quieted down, she asked, "What about the big race coming up? The one in Oklahoma City? I mean, if it's for the first championship of the whole country, the whole world, almost, for dirt-track cars, won't they have to pay you a lot?"

Frank's voice carried a trace of irritation. "Only if we win, which we won't, if the world's jolliest mechanic here doesn't get the car runnin' right."

Buddy chuckled and lifted his brows at Frank. "Looks like you've got a genuine, bona fide fan here." He stood up and pulled out his billfold.

"I guess I'd best be gettin' over to the garage. You comin', Speedball?"

He took out some bills and handed them to Frank to cover his and Louise's breakfasts.

"I've gotta check the bus schedules," Frank said. "She'll be heading back to Kiowa. I'll catch up with you."

Buddy said, "You do that." He looked over at Sandy. "Seems a shame, though, a big fan like this missin' the Winfield race tonight. Buses roll on Sundays, don't they?" He cleared his throat in the silence. "Whatever. Louise, you goin' back to the camper or what?"

"Seein' as I gotta five-dollar bill burnin' a hole in my pocket," she looked over and winked at Frank, "I thought I'd go on over and get my hair done at that place over by the hardware store, if they can work me in. I'll catch up with you all at the track."

Frank saw that Sandy's plate still held most of the sausage patty, the congealing grease smeared across the porcelain from where she had toyed with the food. "I guess we better get goin'," He said. "You ready, Tina?"

"I think I'll go on back to the motel and read some. Maybe take a nap. I didn't sleep so good."

"Suit yourself. Sandy, you go on over with her and get your bag packed up."

Louise had applied more lipstick and was watching Sandy over the top of the mirror. "I think I'll have another refill of coffee since it's included before I get beautified. It was real nice meetin' you, Sandy. I hope we'll see you again, real soon."

The two girls walked out ahead of Frank, who stood in line to pay the bill as he watched them through the window, Tina's red short-shorts and Sandy's pink-and-blue-plaid Bermuda shorts swaying in unison as they walked across the road.

At the counter, the hostess took the money and asked if everything was okay. "I'm workin' on it," Frank answered as he pocketed the change and started after the girls.

CHAPTER 13

Holding the phone in the motel office, Sandy turned her back to Frank and Tina as she pretended to place a call to her aunt's house. She was pretty sure that her friend Mary's family had just left for the Oregon Coast in their new RV, so she dialed her number, and sure enough—Sandy held the receiver out for Frank to hear the unanswered ringing.

Sandy hung up and said, "I guess we can try later,"

"I guess we will," Frank said. "From the bus depot."

Tina looked from Sandy to Frank, then said, "I'll wait here until you get back."

Frank and Sandy drove to the T.G.& Y. to get a bottle of Maalox and a jar of Clary's waterless cleaner for Frank and to let Sandy buy snacks and magazines for the bus ride home.

Frank glanced at his watch while waiting for her to work back up the jewelry aisle toward the checkout counter. "Quit dawdling," he called out to her, then excused himself and stepped back to let what looked to be a mother and daughter step up to pay for a Lilt Home Permanent and two substantial bras that he determined could have been for either one of them.

He pretended not to notice the daughter's nudge that sent her mother's wallet tumbling down onto the counter, the change making a dull clatter as it sprayed across the white cotton cups. The girl whispered something to her mother, both of them glancing up at him and smiling self-consciously—the girl a little less so—while the salesclerk dug out the coins and finished bagging their order.

Sandy—holding the latest issue of *Modern TEEN Magazine*, featuring Tab Hunter on the cover, and two rolls of fruit-flavored Life Savers—watched as both women glanced back over their shoulders one last time to smile at Frank, the younger one's grin flashing a little more boldly as her mother pushed through the door ahead of her.

"Who's that?" Sandy said.

Frank let it go, concentrating on paying the cashier. "Separate sacks, okay, darlin'?" he asked with a smile as he separated out Sandy's items for the bus trip.

"Do you know those two women?" Sandy asked him. "They sure acted like they knew you," she said, squinting up at him.

"Nope," he shook his head and handed a sack to Sandy. They had looked familiar, but he couldn't have said whether it might have been the mother or the daughter he could have run into sometime. That was a detail that wouldn't have mattered before Sandy came bounding into his life. He had to get her on a bus home and his life back on an even keel. He saw that Sandy was still eyeing him suspiciously.

"Look," he said, "sometimes people feel like they know you if they've read about you in the newspapers."

"It looked like more than that," Sandy said. "It looked like that young one thought she knew you real well."

He gave her a little shove toward the door. "Well, maybe she's read a whole lot of newspapers."

He crossed the street to the bus depot with long strides that she had to hurry to keep up with. The hollow raps of his boot heels resounded against the tile floor as he led Sandy to the ticket window. "Gimme a one-way for the next bus to Kiowa, Kansas."

The agent pulled out a carbon ticket book and said, "That'll be eight dollars and twenty-five cents." As Frank was counting out the money, the agent said, "She pulls out at 7:45 p.m. You should be in here and ready to load by 7:30."

"Hold on," Frank said. "Don't you have anything earlier?"

"The 8:45. You just missed her."

Frank took off his baseball cap and slapped it across his thigh. "Dammit! You sure there's nothing else?"

"Yep. You still want a ticket?"

"Gotta get to Winfield. I suppose they have a connection from there."

"Yep. Be farther away, though. Cost ya more."

Frank just shook his head, muttering under his breath, then asked where there was a phone.

"Booth's back by the restrooms."

Frank started for it at a clip. "What's the number?" His voice resonated through the empty waiting room.

Sandy followed reluctantly. "She won't be home."

"Well, we're gonna give it a try anyway." He dialed zero. "Just a second, Operator." He cupped his hand over the mouthpiece. "Come on."

Shrugging in resignation, she crossed her fingers behind her back and gave him Mary's number, hoping they really were on vacation and hadn't been out for breakfast when she called earlier. While he repeated the number to the long-distance operator, Sandy stared at the black box, blinking with each metallic ping as he dropped nickels and dimes into their slots.

Frank tapped a coin against the wooden shelf under the phone as it rang four, five, six times, and then slammed the receiver down. "Not home. Which hospital you say they got the old lady in?"

"It's a rehabilitation center."

Frank turned to face Sandy as the coins clattered into the metal return cup. "I'm losing my patience. What's the place called?"

Sandy started to say the name, then thought better and asked, "What time is it?"

His arm automatically lifted and turned so that the face of his watch was in clear view. "Now what. You gotta take a pill?"

She studied the watch thoughtfully. "They'll be working with Grandma Parson in the pool this time of the morning. To rebuild her muscles, you know. I don't think there's a phone in there."

He stared into the space just above her head for so long that she shivered. His uncertainty gave his face a soft, open look that almost made Sandy want to confide in him. If she explained about the scrapbooks, her feeling that there had always been something missing in the story of her mother's life, and hers, maybe he would open up, tell her about his time with her mom. Maybe he would see that he just had to be her father.

"I don't suppose you can wait around here all day," he said, sounding exasperated. "But don't think you're getting away with anything," he shook his finger at her. "Your aunt answers next time or not, you're going to be on a bus home before today's over, and that'll be an end to this little game you're playing. You understand?"

She just looked at him, the urge to come clean caught up in the constriction in her throat.

"All right," he said, as if it were settled. "Tina'll probably have to take you to the bus station in Winfield. She's not gonna like it much."

That'll make two of us, thought Sandy as she trailed after him to the car.

CHAPTER 14

When they got to Winfield, Kansas, the first stop was the bus depot to buy a one-way ticket to Kiowa, leaving at 7:35 pm. Tina said to drop her off at The Mane Event downtown so she could get a manicure. Sandy opted to go on to the garage, where she helped Buddy roll number 65 into a workspace. She tried to peer around and between the men to see what they were doing, but Frank kept warning her to get back and be careful. After several minutes of being ignored, she went through the door to the tiny office. The desk was cluttered with papers and small metal parts that left oil stains. There was a calendar on the wall with a picture of a woman at the top that looked to be naked under her sheer black nightgown, but it was hard to see exactly.

Sandy opened the front door, causing a buzzer to go off from inside the garage. Squinting, she shielded her eyes with her hand and studied the red, white, and blue fireworks stand across the street with a big hand lettered "SALE" sign propped up on the counter. Two small children gripping the edge of the counter and standing on their tiptoes were pointing out displays on the back wall to their mother. Sandy crossed the street and moved into the shade of the bright green-and-white-striped awning.

"How's it goin'," the boy behind the counter asked.

"Fine," she said, glancing over at him. His hair was orangey red, and he was covered with freckles. She turned her attention to the displays of do-it-yourself explosives.

"Gonna shoot off some fireworks?" he asked. "Got some Jim-dandy bottle rockets here. Guaranteed to go off first time you light 'em. Half Price."

"Just looking." She studied the strings of firecrackers, and the colorful cardboard cones that looked innocent as ice cream.

"You're new around here, aren't you?" he asked.

She looked over at him, letting her fingers trail softly over packets of Black Cat Lady Fingers. "What makes you say that?"

"Haven't seen you around before."

"You the mayor, or something?" she said. "You supposed to know everyone who sets foot in Winfield, Kansas?"

He grinned at her in a way that made her feel both self-conscious and fairly pleased with herself. "Heck, I'm a lot better than the mayor. They're not ever around long enough to know what's goin' on. Anyway, I'm not from here. I go with the races."

"What does that mean, go with?"

"It means that I don't live anywhere in particular during racing season. I just follow the circuit. Work the major tracks. I'm just watching this stand for a guy to pick up a couple extra bucks."

"Don't your parents object?"

"Heck no." He stopped to wait on the woman who had gathered up 10 strings of Black Cats, 6 bottle rockets, and 10 boxes of sparklers. Sandy watched him make change and say something that made him and the lady both laugh. He was nice-looking except for his ginger hair, which sprang into loose curls on top of his head where it was longest. When he'd finished with the sale, he ducked under the corner of the counter and stood in front of the stand, studying the intertwined loops of red, white, and blue crepe paper that had come loose at one end and were flapping in the wind. He stretched up over the counter and pulled out the tacks, then reattached the decorations.

He eyed her briefly before he ducked back into the booth. "Aren't you a little dressed up to be hanging around a garage?"

She looked over her shoulder to see what he would have seen as she walked over.

"I saw you pull up. You know Frank Haggard?"

"Well enough."

"Enough to hang around garages with him?"

"What's it to you?"

"Nothin'. Nothin's nothin' to me. You're a little young, though, even for Frankie."

60

She lifted the hair off her neck and tossed her head. "A lot you know. It just so happens he's my father."

He laughed and said, "You wish!"

"I don't have to wish, because it's true. So I guess you don't know everything after all." She pivoted neatly, in spite of the gravel, and walked briskly back to the curb. As she paused to let some cars pass, she heard the boy call out, "Hey, don't go away mad. See you at the track. Miss Haggard."

She put an exaggerated bounce into her walk as she headed for the garage. Once inside, she stayed in the office, periodically checking the action at the fireworks stand across the road. Who cared what anyone else believed? Anyway, she might have a bus ticket in her purse, but today she was going to the races with Frank Haggard.

CHAPTER 15

An hour and a half before the first race at seven o'clock, Tina and Sandy dropped Frank at the entrance to the Cowley Fairgrounds race cars and drivers' gate and drove back around to the parking lot near the ticket gate, where he had passes waiting for them.

"I'm gonna hang out down here for a bit," Tina said. "I'll be doin' enough sittin' when the races start."

"I think I'll head on up into the stands," Sandy said. "I want to get a look at the track."

She hopped up the nearly empty benches to the top and walked from one end of the grandstand to the other, burning up nervous energy. She was really here, and her maybe-father was down there in the pits talking with his mechanic and some other men who had joined them. The oval infield was a crayon box patchwork of cars and trucks and campers and trailers. There were folding chairs and coolers set up next to the cars and a concrete bunker-like building near the front straightaway with Restroom painted in black on the side.

She turned around to lean over the top railing and watch people filing through the ticket gate, people who had to pay to get in because their fathers weren't famous race-car drivers. She spotted Tina down at the stand where they sold stadium seats with backs on them, her butter-yellow crop top and white shorts gleaming in the noonday sun until she disappeared from view, heading for the center opening between the two sets of bleachers. Sandy leaned back against the top railing and looked out over the track again, her heart racing as she took a mental snapshot so that she would have this day forever.

Even that high up, the air was rich with the smell of oil and dust, and the sun bouncing off the race cars made them shimmer. Sandy made a game of judging the colors and shapes of each car as it pulled onto the track to warm up, rating those high that had clean, sleek lines and clear primary colors.

She muttered "zilch" to herself as a clumsy looking pink and gray Ford lumbered over the ridge of rough dirt at the inside of turn four and started down the straightaway. She thought that Frank's car looked the way a race car should, lean and fast, the white and silver 65 distinct on the dark red body. She gave a little bounce as she saw Frank climb into his car and head for the apron and crossed her fingers on both hands.

Bounding down the steps two at a time, she descended to where Tina had set up two stadium seats and plunked down beside the spare cushion.

Tina lowered her *True Romance* magazine to her lap and flicked her cigarette ash beneath the bleacher. "That's for you," she said, indicating the seat. "How's the view up there?"

Sandy moved over. "Thanks. It's windy. He's up next."

Tina squinted out at the pit area.

"Over there." Sandy pointed to where red-and-white 65 was idling at the edge of the track near turn four.

"So he is."

They looked at one another, then back at the car. Tina asked Sandy if she was hungry, and got a head shake in response.

"The best time so far is 22.50," said Sandy. "He can beat that easy."

"You really like the races, do you?" Tina asked.

Sandy shrugged. "Sure. My Uncle Lloyd sometimes takes us kids. Don't you?"

"I like them okay. Mostly, I like Frank."

Sandy frowned slightly but kept her face toward the track.

"What I mean is that he's really a nice man. You know? Fun to be with. I didn't go to the races that much before I met him."

"It's okay," Sandy told her.

"Beg pardon?"

"It's okay. You don't have to explain anything to me. I mean, well, it's none of my business if you're my father's paramour."

Tina looked at her and barked out a laugh. "His what?"

"There he goes," Sandy yelled over the growl of the engine. They watched as Frank took his warm-up lap, slowing in turn four and signaling the flagman that he would take another lap before timing.

He revved the engine several times, pausing for what seemed to Sandy an agonizingly long time before pulling back out and heading for turn one. On the back-stretch, he let it all out, flying into turn three and coming out of turn four like a rock from a slingshot. He crossed the starting line dead center and geared into the first turns as smoothly as if the car was a magnet on a strip of steel. Sandy leaned into turn three with him and held her breath as he blasted down the straightaway and into his second timed lap, not shutting down until he was back around and well past the flag stand.

She waited anxiously for the announcer's voice to lift over the engine noises and static with the results, squinting against the cloud of dust blanketing the stands.

"There you have it, ladies and gentlemen, our fastest time so far today—20.05! Let's give a big hand to Frankie Haggard as he pulls into the pits, let these guys know how much we appreciate the time and skill that goes into putting on a first-class event like the one coming up this evening. And there goes L. Ray Chenoweth, a freshman driver, not new to the racetracks, but this is only his second year of being on the business end—behind the steering wheel. Looks like he's set to go!"

Sandy watched the new driver turn in a time of 21.90, and commented to Tina that he was running good. She felt Tina's eyes on her and finally looked over.

"Look, Sandy. I guess you've had some problems. You're not alone in that, but never mind. What I want to say is that you were right about my relationship with Frankie being nobody else's business." She waited for some response from Sandy, who wrinkled her nose as if it itched.

"Personally, between my stepbrother and his gossipy wife and some of those nosy old biddies back home who claim to be friends of the family 'cause almost everybody livin' there was born there—well, I'm pretty well burnt out on self-righteous busybodies. If we—you and I—can get along, well and good. If not, let's just agree to let one another alone. Okay?" She dropped her cigarette and ground it out beneath her strappy white wedge sandal.

Sandy had been staring at Tina with her mouth open, struck by her bluntness. Most adults she knew didn't talk straight out like that. But then Tina was just barely an adult at that. Sandy nodded at her and said, "Okay."

"Okay what?"

"We can try getting along." As if to seal the deal, she offered Tina a piece of Juicy Fruit gum.

"Thanks," Tina told her, and said, "Maybe later. Right now, I'm more interested in a barbeque beef sandwich and an ice-cold Coke. You game?"

"I could go for that." Sandy picked up her purse and led the way, descending the bleacher steps two at a time.

The girls walked around behind the stands with their sandwiches and drinks, only Tina noticing the appreciative glances that followed them. They stopped in front of a souvenir stand that had pennants with the name of the track and the outline of a race car, printed T-shirts, and hundreds of 8x10 glossies of drivers and their cars.

"Darn!" Tina looked down at the blob of barbeque sauce that had slid out of the bun and onto her blouse. She tossed the remainder of the sandwich into a trash can and asked to see one of the T-shirts in a size small.

Sandy was studying a print of Frank and Buddy standing on either side of a young girl in a tight skirt and high-heels who held a trophy in the crook of her arm when something hard pressed against her right shoulder blade.

"'Scuse me. Rather, 'scuse my tray. Hi there."

It was the redhead from the fireworks stand, although a white cap that had "Cowley Fairgrounds, Winfield, Kansas" stitched on it covered much of his hair. He had a tray of sweating cups of Coke and 7-Ups hanging from a wide strap around his neck.

"Gonna buy a souvenir photo of your dad?"

Ignoring him, she moved around a little to the side of the souvenir stand to wait for Tina who was holding up a T-shirt with crossed checkered flags on the front and checking the label.

"I already said I was sorry about that crack I made this morning," he said. "What do you want? Blood? A free Coke?"

"No thanks. I have both," she answered, holding up her cup with a "so there" smile.

"Are you really Frankie's kid? I mean, I never figured he had any. But why not? Right?"

She took the last bite of her sandwich and chewed self-consciously.

"Okay, I get it. Racing royalty doesn't fraternize with the hired help. I won't bother you anymore, Your Highness."

"Wait." She followed him back toward the opening between the stands. "I'm not mad. Or stuck-up or anything. But I don't know you, and what you said at the fireworks stand was—"

"I know. I'm sorry. I'm humbly sorry. Will that take care of it?" He stuck out his right hand. "Madam, I'm Adam."

His formality made her smile a little, and she shook his hand. "My name's Sandy."

"That was a palindrome. What I said. The letters go the same way forward and backwards. My name really is Adam, too. People call me Ad 'cause I'm always sellin' something. That's how I make a living. So where're you from?"

"Kiowa, Kansas."

"There's no track there."

"I know that," she said.

He was grinning at her again. "Well . . . I'd better get these into the stands 'fore they get lukewarm. Where you sittin'?"

"About halfway up on the middle aisle over there."

"I'll look for you after the A-feature, when they'll start up the fireworks. We don't work the stands while that's goin' on."

Sandy said sure, and looked over to see if Tina had heard her agree to be around after the race, but she was getting change from the man behind the counter.

"Come here," she said, pulling Sandy under the stands where she used her as a shield so she could change into the T-shirt. Sandy couldn't help noticing that the cups of Tina's bra were made of lace and covered her only about halfway up. Sandy's own bra was a sturdy cotton number with bands sewn into an X across her chest, designed to separate and lift according to the ads. Her size As were already pretty separated and there wasn't all that much to lift, but she could see that, for making the most of what you had, a lacy low-cut bra was a better bet. They went to find a water fountain and wash out the stain before climbing back up into the stands, the damp blouse flapping like a yellow caution flag on the bench between them.

CHAPTER 16

By six o'clock, the stands were three-quarters full, and people were still streaming up the aisles and squeezing between kneecaps and backbones to claim the good seats in the center of the stands. Tina said that some of them were probably folks who came out every Fourth of July weekend to see the fireworks display. After she said it, she realized that Sandy wouldn't be around to enjoy the display, and changed the subject by offering to buy her some peanuts from a vendor passing by.

"Not supposed to eat peanuts at the track," Sandy told her. "It's a superstition."

Tina shrugged and bought two boxes of popcorn and passed one to Sandy. "Why not? Peanuts, I mean."

"Well," Sandy said, "my Uncle Lloyd told me a guy flipped his racer and was killed, and afterwards, they found peanut shells in his car."

"That really happen?"

"Dunno. But none of the guys eat peanuts at the track." She looked at her Minnie Mouse watch. "Cars are warmin' up."

Spectators cheered as their favorite drivers pulled onto the track as soon as the water truck pulled off, conversations getting louder as drivers tested gears and revved engines while packing down the dirt that was now tacky. Frank was currently first in overall points for the region, and Sandy was surprised at how proud it made her to hear the thunderous clapping and shouting when the announcer said his name.

Because the heat races were short, the first two, for the slower cars, passed quickly. Tina kept looking at her watch. She opened her purse to make sure that the keys to the Mercury were in it, then closed it and placed it on her lap. Sandy was clutching her own purse, with the bus ticket, waiting to make her move. She looked at her watch and saw it was almost 7:00. She stood up abruptly, then bent down to whisper to Tina, "I have to go to the bathroom."

"Hold on, I'll go with you," Tina said.

"Have to go bad," Sandy said and flew down the steps. Tina called out that she would meet her in the car, but Sandy kept going, giving no indication whether she'd heard or not.

By the time Tina got her things together and located herself so she could see both the admission gate and the Ladies restroom—a rustic shed at the south end of the stands—Sandy was nowhere in sight. The announcer called out the line-up for Frank's heat race, and Tina ran back up to the front of the stands to see what his position was, looking over her shoulder every few moments to see if Sandy was back from the bathroom yet. She waited until all the cars had cleared the first two turns, and ran back to the gate.

According to her watch, they had only twenty minutes to get Sandy to the bus. She paused to have her hand stamped at the entrance and ran to the car, which was empty. She lit a cigarette and paced in front of the car, trying to hear the announcer and scanning the grounds for Sandy's pink shirt. Perhaps she'd forgotten where they'd left the car. Running back inside, Tina headed for the Ladies room. She waited until the two women and a little girl using the stalls came out to be sure Sandy wasn't there before hurrying back out. She wasn't certain at which point she'd become suspicious, but the possibility of the girl's running off seemed more and more of a certainty, and Tina grew more frustrated by the minute.

She looked from side to side as she retraced her steps to the car— which was as empty as when she'd last left it—and strode angrily back to the grandstand, just in time to hear that Frank had placed second. She continued to scan the area for Sandy as she headed back up the aisle to their seats. It was too late to make it to the bus depot in time. Frank would be furious, but it wasn't her fault. The girl wasn't her responsibility in the first place. Tina hadn't signed up to be a babysitter. She'd had enough of that with her four younger siblings to last a lifetime. As the six fastest cars from the three heat races lined up on the track for the trophy dash, she couldn't tell which one she was more put out with, Frank or the kid.

CHAPTER 17

Sandy scampered under the grandstand until she got to the far north end, then went around to the front and climbed to the top, where she sat by herself on the top row. That put her well away from Tina and gave her a head-on view of the third and fourth turns with no one in the way of the rest of the track. She had to stifle the impulse to jump up when she saw Frank's red 65 pull up to the front row and line up on the outside of maroon 12, the car that had won Frank's heat race. With only six cars competing and only three laps to complete, she felt sure that his chances of winning the trophy dash were good.

As the cars passed by, she felt the vibrations of the engines in her chest, and the noise filled her head so that for a moment she couldn't hear the yelling all around her. She lost sight of the numbers in the scramble along the backstretch, but by the end of lap one Frank was in second place, hugging the pole and trying to nose up on the inside of number 12. As they opened up on the front stretch and closed up again in the far turn, her whole body tensed. Squinting hard, she willed red 65 ahead, the front tires aligning with the back tires of number 12. She felt light-headed as she watched the cars, locked into position as they passed under the white flag, and realized she'd been holding her breath. Both cars bobbled going into turn one, their backends doing a quick little shimmy, but in unison so that they didn't collide. Then the lead car seemed to be inching away, coming out of the second turn with a half-car advantage as they moved as one down the back stretch and torqued into turn three.

Suddenly, the front end of the lead car slipped just a of couple inches to the right, up over the groove, giving Frank a slim opening. He stayed low and steady, his left front tire lifting off the track once, twice, then settling back down coming out of turn four. Inching ahead as they roared down the straightaway, 65's nose shot past the checkered flag no more than a foot ahead of number 12's. Sandy was screaming as one with the general roar coming from the stands and bouncing up and down in her seat. Any worries about her immediate future were swept away with the track dust blowing through the stands.

During intermission, she waved a vendor over and bought a hotdog, eating it while she tried to follow the activity in the pits. She pulled the bus ticket from her purse and read the number and departure time. There were no two ways about it. Frank was going to be really upset when he found out she didn't go home. Tina too, probably, but it was really none of her business. Sandy might be able to get the ticket reimbursed, which would give her enough to hide out a little longer. Ad might know of a place she could stay until Frank calmed down. But then maybe he would just think good riddance and not even bother to look for her anyway. Tears stung her eyes, though with her brow furrowed and her eyes all squinty and lips pinched together, she looked more angry than sad. Maybe she was. Processing her own array of feelings was as hard as guessing at Frank's.

Stuffing the ticket back into her purse, she wiped her index fingers under her eyes, sniffed, and looked out at the pits. She saw his white racing uniform moving through the cluster of men near the flagman's stand. She stood up to get a better look, and saw that it was Frank heading across the track. She sat down, her pulse racing as she watched him come through the gate that led to the grandstand and head up the center aisle. He shook the outstretched hands and waved and smiled at fans who called out greetings and good luck. When he reached where Tina was sitting, she scooted over to the stadium seat she'd gotten for Sandy while he dropped down next to her. They looked excited, and Tina's hands were moving a lot. Then they both looked out over the crowds on either side of them.

Dropping down between the benches to conceal herself, Sandy waited until she saw Frank loping back down toward the track, no longer acknowledging the calls and raised hands of the fans. Then she duck-walked to the end of the row and stayed hunched over as she descended the steps. Halfway down, she sat next to a heavyset man wearing overalls and a baseball cap. Her view of the track wasn't all that good, but then neither was anyone's view of her.

She watched the B-Feature half-heartedly, the dread of facing Frank filling her like an electric buzzing. By the time the B was over, she was feeling a little sick and sorry she'd eaten the hot dog. The announcer used the time between the two feature races to give the points the drivers had accumulated so far for the season.

"And in first place for overall point standings so far this year," his voice boomed and crackled through the speakers mounted along the poles in front of the stands, "no surprise for those of you who come to the races regularly, in first spot we have Frankie Haggard!"

Once the cars were lined up for the A-feature, they took a parade lap. "All right, folks," the announcer shouted above the blasts of the engines, "this is what you came for. Let's get on your feet, put your hands together, raise your voices, and let these racers know that you appreciate the fine show they're putting on for us tonight!"

People whistled and cheered as the cars snaked past the grandstand. Not satisfied, the announcer called to the flagman to have the pilots take one more parade lap. "Now let's really hear it for your favorite drivers as they come by," he shouted, working the crowd into a frenzy.

By the time Ad set his cold drink tray down on the bench in front and moved in next to Sandy, her palms were sore from all the clapping. He handed her a Coke and got one for himself. She shouted thanks and turned back to the lineup. Frank had pole position. If he could get a jump on the rest of the field, that would save a lot of wear and tear on the car as well as her nerves.

Ad said, "Frankie could make a real pile tonight, since they're paying lap money for leading the race. He's in a good position to get out ahead for most of the thirty laps."

"He's going to lead all the way," she said.

Ad grinned at her and said, "Woman's intuition?"

She grinned back at him and bumped her shoulder against his as they watched the cars pour around the north end and accelerate toward the starting line where the flagman signaled them to take one more lap. She took a deep breath, set the Coke down by her feet, and crossed the fingers on both hands.

The cars at the back moved into tighter positions, and as the first cars rounded turn four, all but the last row held together as the cars tore down the straightaway for the green flag. They bunched up gearing through the first two turns. Frank used his advantage on the pole to pull away quickly. By the end of the back stretch, he had nearly a half-car length lead.

Adam had to put his mouth close to her ear to be heard. "The car's runnin' good!"

She nodded, keeping her eyes glued to Frank's car and her fingers tightly crossed. She wasn't taking any chances. "They worked on it today," she yelled. By the second lap, Oakley in number 12 was running a close second and being challenged by car number 19, a bright orange job she remembered from the heat races.

"Ad," she shouted to be heard, "who's in the orange car?"

"L. Ray Chenoweth. He's a rookie, compared to most of the guys he's runnin' against, but he's a comer!"

"How old is he?"

"Almost twenty-two. The L stands for Littlebuck. He's part Indian."

Sandy counted "five" out loud, keeping track of the laps. The muscles in her stomach and along the backs of her calves had begun to tighten. She reached down for the Coke she'd left near her feet, and drank some of it, feeling self-conscious about her crossed fingers, but fearing an instant conversion from good luck to bad if she uncrossed them in the middle of the race.

By lap eleven, Frank had pulled wide to pass some of the slower cars at the back when a maroon car he'd just gotten by began to cross up, its nose turning toward the infield. The orange car with the part-Indian driver dodged low to slip under. Sandy saw sparks shoot up where the orange front fender clipped the maroon car's hood before jerking toward the infield, the men standing at that end scattering like billiard balls. When Sandy looked back at the maroon car, it was flipping sideways down the straightaway right behind Frank. Pieces of metal were showering the other cars and track and a tire shot into the air as the car slammed into the concrete barrier just beyond the front of the stands.

"Can you see anything," Sandy asked Ad, who was a head taller than her. "Is the driver getting out?"

Adam's reply was swallowed up in the drone of the crowd. She shook her head to show she didn't understand, and he leaned down. "I don't see any movement." The ambulance siren had started almost immediately, but the panel van seemed to Sandy to be barely inching along the track to where men were working to free the driver from the battered car.

Adam grabbed Sandy's arm to steady her as she climbed up onto the bench to get a better look. She was glad not to be alone in the eerily quiet stadium. It was impossible to see through the crowd of men around the car, but the movements of the group indicated that the driver was being taken to the ambulance. Sandy thought that she heard the heavy back doors close. She'd lost sight of Frank.

"Do you think he'll be all right?"

Ad shrugged. "Hard to tell, but that was a bad one. The flips were low but fast."

They watched in silence as the track officials set fire to the oil and gasoline that had spilled out of the overturned car to clear it off the track, yellow-blue flames leaping up and dying just as suddenly. The flagman was consulting a clipboard and pointing to where the cars should be as they pulled into position again. Frank was still in the lead, but Sandy saw he would have to fight his way free of the pack again, and her insides felt queasy. She crossed her fingers even tighter.

The drivers got the green on the first lap of the restart, and Frank slipped ahead easily, orange 19 close behind, but not close enough to challenge. A few laps later, two more cars spun out in front of the stands, but pulled far enough up on the bank to be out of the way. Adam pointed at them and yelled, "The track might still be slick there from the wreck."

The rest of the race dragged on interminably for Sandy, who jumped every time someone sitting around them screeched or jumped up to get a better view. By the end, Sandy was so drained that she almost forgot to cheer as Frank crossed the finish line in first place, the new driver with the Indian name close behind him.

Adam got up and strapped on his drink tray. "I'm gonna try to get rid of some of these before the fireworks start. Save me a place."

She nodded that she would, placing her clutch bag on the bench next to her. Ad grinned at her and said, "You can uncross your fingers now. It's all over."

She thought to herself, that's what you think, then settled in to watch the trophy girl riding on the top of the red leather backseat of a white convertible with a sign on the side door that read "Balzer Cadillac." Sandy noticed the girl had on a tiara, but the announcer didn't say what she was queen of.

"Let's have a round of applause for our A Feature trophy girl Miss Minnie Wright," said the announcer. "A recent graduate of Winfield High School."

Sandy watched as Frank, Buddy, and a short, heavy-set man the announcer introduced as the car's owner, G.D. Parker, walked over to stand in front of 65. The announcer yelled, "Let's have another round of applause for the winner of tonight's feature event, high-point holder, long-time champion of the oval circuits . . . Frankie Haggard!"

As they posed for the pictures, the announcer said, "She's a little old for you Frankie." Sandy didn't appreciate his comment, or the laughter that accompanied it, but Frank just wagged his finger at the press box and grinned, then waved at the crowd and escorted the young lady back to the car. Sandy noted he didn't give her the traditional winner's kiss.

As soon as the Cadillac lumbered up over the embankment, the lights around the track and along the top of the stands began to go out, one by one, until the work lights still being used by the drivers and their mechanics made the infield look as if it was filled with fireflies. Big booming ear poppers went off, announcing the start of the fireworks show.

The crowd oohed in unison as the streaks and sparks of colored gun powder whistled and popped overhead, then erupted like blown dandelions that drifted toward the upturned faces before disintegrating into thin streams of smoke. Leaning her head back as far as she could, Sandy bumped against Adam, who had slipped in next to her. He pointed across the infield, to where some ground works were being lit along the back fence. First a gold and silver pinwheel spun around, next to it a flag that burned red, white, and blue from the top down. Another red pinwheel lit up on the other side of the burning out flag, and finally, right behind those, a pulsating fountain of red shot at least twenty feet into the air turning to blue, then white, and finishing out in brilliant shafts of gold.

Even before the last ashes had fallen, the sky lit up once again and seemed to be raining glitter down over them. It was magical, Sandy thought, as upturned faces glowed the colors of the fireworks as huge sprays filled the night sky. The whole night had been magical to Sandy. She felt as if she'd been waiting for a night like that her whole life. That's what she would need to make Frank understand once the fireworks were over. But first, she would need to make him believe she'd lost track of Tina and forgotten where the car was parked. Maybe winning all but one of his races would have Frank in such a good mood that he would be open to understanding how important it was that she could be there to share all this with him, just the way her mother would have, if whatever it was hadn't gone wrong all those years ago.

• • • • •

By the time Sandy pushed through the small gate in front of the stands and was within shouting distance of red 65, Tina was already in the pits, talking heatedly with Frank.

"That was some A-Feature," called out Sandy, with a little wave. Frank strode over and grabbed her upper arm, asking, "Where in the hell have you been? Tina said you just disappeared?"

She couldn't tell from his expression whether he was angry or worried.

"I don't know," Sandy started, then said, "I mean, I couldn't find her, and then I got confused about where the car was parked." There was a tremor in her voice that was real, all the more so because her explanation wasn't.

"You're lying. You thought that if you got away from Tina, you'd miss the bus and get to stay here and then everything would be . . . what? What is it you think is gonna happen here?"

Sandy was pulling to get free, but he held on. "I just wanted to . . . a little more time. To get to know each other." Her chin started to quiver for real, and she said, "And there were fireworks."

"What say we all calm down here," said Buddy, who had loaded the car onto the trailer. He nodded at fans milling around. "Maybe you wanna take it to the camper? Have a little privacy?"

Frank let go of her arm, which she began to rub. "Well, here I am," he said, throwing out his arms. "This is it. Now you can go back to where you came from and die happy."

Sandy looked at him for a moment, her mouth dropping open, and said, "Like my mother?"

Frank stared back at her, the only indication that she'd hit a nerve the working of his Adam's apple as he swallowed hard. He turned to Tina and said, "You two take the car back to the motel."

Tina started to protest that he couldn't order her around, but she decided her irritation with them both didn't match his anger by half. She touched Sandy lightly on her shoulder and said, "Come on. Let's get out of this dust."

Frank watched as they crossed the track between trucks hauling trailers, making their way back up to the grandstand and parking lot. He flinched as Buddy slammed a toolbox closed, but wasn't going to get into it with him as well. He wrapped his two trophies in a towel and climbed into the passenger seat of the camper truck, weighing his options for getting through one more night with this teenage girl who had gotten so far under his skin. He couldn't tell if the churning in his head was caused by her obvious lies or because of the truth that might lie just beneath them. Buddy stowed the rest of the gear without saying anything, which for Buddy said a lot.

CHAPTER 18

Saturday night, sitting at Sandy's vanity table, Maggie counted as the phone rang two and a half times before it was picked up. She'd placed the note from Sandy next to an ashtray filled with tiny white Avon lipstick samples, assorted hair bands, a travel manicure set with the cuticle scissors missing, and a local theater ticket stub from the previous weekend with red hearts doodled all over it. She sat perfectly still until she heard the receiver hit the cradle and Irma call out, "Just Sandy's friend Melanie, wanting to know if we've heard anything yet."

It would be two more days before the police department would reclassify Sandy from a runaway to possibly missing. Until then, they were on their own. Maggie turned her attention back to the vanity table where even the note held no clues to where her niece had run off to. She felt her sister's skirt brush against her back as Irma stood looking over her shoulder.

"What's that?" Irma asked, indicating the ticket stub Maggie was holding.

"It's from last weekend."

"Those girls sure have been good about calling," Irma said.

"Yeah, well, they're not about to miss out on any chance to engage in a drama."

"Now Maggie, they seem sincere to me."

"Oh, they surely are that. Sincerely interested in other people's business. As long as they're dealing with local gossip instead of historical information." Maggie had long ago reserved the right to harbor accurate and pointed assessments of the children who passed through her classroom, a right earned through years of devotion to her job as their teacher, guidance counselor, sponsor when one was needed, and often mother-confessor. Sometimes she felt that they held more shares of her life than she did. But right now, there was only one girl she cared about, and she could be scared or hungry or even hurt, and unable to call home.

Maggie handed the ticket stub to Irma and said, "Do you remember what movie they went to last weekend?"

"Some romantic thing with Tab Hunter and Natalie Wood. Called *The Girl He Left Behind?* Tab's a goof-off who gets drafted. I don't know the plot."

Maggie looked up at her sister, and said, "Maybe you do." She went to the walk-in closet and moved a comforter and extra pillow from the hope chest to the bed. Irma followed her back to the closet and said, "What are you looking for in there?"

"The remnants of our sister's too-short life. And maybe a clue."

Maggie dropped to her knees and unlatched the chest, the sharp aromas from the cedar lining filling the small space. Irma sat down next to Maggie, watching as she carefully lifted out Ruth's blue-linen nurse's aide apron and stiff white cap and placed them on the floor beside her. Next she retrieved high-heeled satin pumps dyed pale blue and placed them on Irma's lap. Slipping sideways to pull her legs out from under her, Irma kicked off her right shoe and put on the blue slipper. "From my prom," she said. "And then something borrowed and blue for Ruth's second wedding. What else you got there?"

Maggie reached deep into the chest and pulled out a scrapbook labeled simply "1948."

"Oh, wow," Irma said softly. "The secret scrapbooks." She peered at the pages Maggie was turning over, gently tucking loose bits of newspaper and photos back against the spine. "I used to get goose bumps helping you smuggle extra newspapers over to Ruth. You think Fred ever knew she was clipping out all those articles about that boy she ran off an' married? Frank?"

"Haggard." Maggie said the name matter-of-factly as she handed the scrapbook to Irma and pulled out three more. She opened the one marked "1947." The first page held a loose newspaper article from September with a large picture of Frank leaning with one hand against the hood of a race car and the other arm raised in a wave toward the camera. He'd looked like a movie star back then, and had been just as sure of himself. She said the name a second time, with more emphasis, "Frank Haggard." She quickly turned the pages, scanning the articles and close-up glossies of race car drivers standing just to the side of the numbers on their cars, some holding trophies with local beauty queens by their sides. Some of the photos showed upended cars frozen in mid-air, perpetually on their way toward a collision.

"Irma, did you ever see Sandy looking at these?"

"No. I'd forgotten all about them. Why?"

"What do you think she would make of all this?"

The sisters exchanged a look and read snatches of the articles aloud. Irma had unfolded a long double-column article and held it up for Maggie to see. "He really was a handsome man. Do you think Ruth ever saw him again? In later years, I mean?"

"I don't know. I think she would have told us." Maggie closed up the book.

"Not to me she wouldn't of. You two were always closer," Irma said. "She thought of me as the bratty kid and never confided anything worthwhile."

"You *were* the bratty kid."

Irma elbowed Maggie in the side before helping her return the contents to the chest.

"Come on," Maggie said, "I need some air. I have to think." She led the way to the backyard, where she stopped and looked up at the stars. Irma linked her arm through Maggie's as they strolled along the narrow walk that ran along the flower garden, cut across the center of the yard and stretched back along the vegetable patch.

Maggie took Irma's presence for granted much as she had when they had been children, Maggie always leading the others to this place or that as she went on her way, hardly noticing their smaller hands in hers. She realized now that, regardless of her youthful nonchalance, none of the children she'd ever tended had gotten hurt or lost. Until now.

She thought about Mildred saying Sandy had left the slumber party before the others were up, and some of the girls said that she'd been quieter than usual—hadn't cracked jokes or even danced around, which would have been the more typical behavior for Sandy. A born actress, Maggie called her. Once when Maggie was in bed with influenza, Sandy had mimicked her teachers and the principal at assembly earlier that day trying to adjust the microphone until Maggie was laughing in spite of her fever and nausea. And Sandy could be equally melancholy, with the normal teenage girl's penchant for high drama.

Maggie stopped so suddenly that Irma was two steps beyond her before she jerked to a halt. Maggie took off running across the lawn and up the steps, Irma right behind her. Back in the closet, Maggie dropped down onto her knees and pulled the scrapbooks out, spreading them across the floor. "What's the last one Ruth would have kept?" They lined up the years—1946, 1947, and 1948.

"Ruth died in the fall of '49," Irma said. "Do you remember if she kept one for that year?"

"She did." Maggie stood up squeezing her sister's first scrapbook to her chest.

"You think Sandy knows about these?" Irma asked. Maybe that's what she meant, about having something she needed to do. Good lord."

"I don't know," Maggie said, "But I'm going to find out."

"What are we going to do?"

"Your husband is going to get ahold of some of those people he knows connected with the races and see what he can find about Frank Haggard. Someone will know how to find him."

"What about his parents?" Irma asked.

"I read his father died in a tractor accident a few years ago. His mother went off to be with her sister. I don't remember where to. I don't know if she ever returned to Kiowa."

They both jumped up and rushed to the kitchen, where Lloyd was drinking a glass of iced tea and reading the evening paper. "Lloyd," Irma yelled, "where are the racing results? Maggie has a hunch."

Maggie ran up behind him to look over his shoulder, asking, "Where are they? Anything about the races." Her heart was pounding and her upper arms were indented from where she'd been hugging the album to her chest.

"What in the Sam Hill are you two yammering about?"

"Cars, you dope," Irma said. "Race cars. The kind that Haggard boy started driving when he got back from the war."

"Good grief. You don't suppose—"

"Look and see if there's anything in the paper about the local races."

Lloyd snapped the pages open and turned to the sports pages. "There it is," he said. "Haggard won the trophy dash and A-feature at Enid last night."

"How can we find out where he might be tonight?" Maggie asked, reading over his shoulder to see what other news there might be.

"Well," Lloyd said, "He won't want to run too far out on the circuit with the Grand National a little over a week away. Go get me the atlas."

The three of them pored over the maps of Oklahoma and Kansas as Lloyd circled towns with racetracks. "He lives in Hutch, and I imagine he'll want to get back there soon to get ready for next weekend down in Oklahoma City. That's the big one. First Grand National ever. I'm plannin' to go."

Irma squinted at him and asked, "How do you know all this? You haven't been to a race in months."

"I read the papers. I highly recommend it."

"Smart aleck," she said. "I guess we could wait until Monday and track him down in Hutch."

"No," Maggie said. "This is only Saturday, and what if we're wrong? What if she's not with him?"

Irma said, "Honey, we're all worried sick, but we can't just drive all over hell and back without some idea of where she might be."

Lloyd looked up from the map and said, "Tomorrow afternoon, I call all the tracks within a 200-mile radius of Hutch. I can ask them if anyone on Haggard's team has picked up pit passes, and if not to call me collect as soon as one of 'em shows up. Maybe we'll get lucky. As soon as we locate him, I can hightail it over there."

"That's real good, Lloyd," Irma said, putting an arm around Maggie's shoulders. "Don't you be thinking this is your fault, Sister, 'cause it's not. And Lloyd will track her down tomorrow and everything can get back to normal around here."

Maggie nodded, but without conviction. She thought about the scrapbooks and what they might have held for a young girl who'd lost her step-father before she could remember him and then her mother at only five. Perhaps Maggie should have told Sandy about her real father, but Ruth hadn't chosen to. Or maybe she just hadn't gotten around to it before it was too late. And what if Maggie had told Sandy and then somehow had to deal with the Haggards after all that bad business between the families? She might have lost her, and she couldn't imagine life without Sandy.

CHAPTER 19

SPEEDSTER DOES TRIPLE ROLL,
RACER CRITICALLY HURT

Jerry Oakley, 29, of 835 South Dobbs, Stillwater, Oklahoma, was taken to Memorial Hospital Saturday night after the car he was driving overturned at the Winfield Fairgrounds track.

Oakley is said to have suffered a fractured back, shoulder and leg, as well as received lacerations to the face.

The accident happened during the A- Feature, which was won by veteran Frank Haggard. An official of the track said that freshman L. Ray Chenoweth attempted to avoid Oakley's racer as it crossed up coming out of turn four, but the two machines collided, causing Oakley's rear-end to lift and the racer to flip three times sideways in front of the grandstand.

Frank's tirade after the races at Winfield the night before had kept replaying in Sandy's head, keeping her awake well after midnight. His anger seemed all mixed up with worry about the driver whose car had flipped, so she'd given up trying to explain herself. Opting to start the morning's drive with Buddy in his truck camper, she sat in the eating nook with her head resting on her arms for the first hour, wondering what Frank and Tina might be saying about her in the car just ahead.

They stopped for breakfast in Medicine Lodge just as the sun crested the horizon. Next stop would be Kiowa. As much as Frank chaffed at returning to the town, it looked to be the one sure way to get the girl back where she belonged.

Breakfast was a solemn affair with little conversation. They were all groggy from the late night and early start, and Frank's frustration with the Sandy problem was taking a toll on the group.

"What if she can't locate her aunt?" Tina said, dipping her toast into the runny yolk of an egg, which made Sandy queasy.

Frank stared out over the table as if considering it. "Won't get any help from her, you can be darned sure," he said, indicating Sandy with a tip of his head without looking at her. "Can drop her off at the police station."

Buddy glanced over at Sandy, then took another bite of his chicken-fried steak and looked out at the parking lot, chewing thoughtfully.

Sandy had been toying with the raisin bran Frank had ordered for her when she'd insisted she wasn't hungry. She used her spoon to separate the raisins into a pile on one side of the bowl and the bran flakes into a soggy clump on the other, her stomach churning while she waited for his decision. She was starting to not care where they went; she just wanted him to lighten up. It seemed unfair that he could be so mad at someone just for wanting to get to know him. He was a whole lot nicer to the fans who asked for an autograph or to have a picture taken with him and the race car.

Sandy excused herself to go to the restroom, where she splashed cold water on her face and neck, but she couldn't shake the sick feeling in her stomach. As soon as she sat back down at the table, Frank motioned for her to finish her cereal, and she made an unconvincing effort at spooning through the mushy bran, now soppy with milk that hadn't been all that cold even when she'd opened the carton.

"Quit playing with your food and eat it. We don't have all day."

"Frank," Tina started to intervene, but he cut her off.

"She already wasted eight dollars on a bus ticket. Darned if she's gonna waste the price of her breakfast."

When he continued to glare at her, she forced down a mouthful of the soggy bran, then another, and one more. She started to get up for another trip to the ladies' room, but Frank said not until she finished her cereal so they could get the heck on the road. She was good for one more bite, then quickly lowered the spoon, cast an alarmed look around the table, and projectile vomited. The thick, creamy mixture spread across the slick Formica, slowed by dishes and silverware and heading for the black napkin dispenser in the middle of the table that Tina snatched up at the last second.

"What in the hell do you think you're doing?" Frank yelled, jumping up and pulling his chair back from the advancing stream of bran and milk and stomach acid.

Sandy yelped back, "I think I'm throwing up. What do *you* think I'm doing?"

Tina pulled out napkins and dropped them strategically over the mess while Buddy walked around the table to put his hand on Sandy's forehead.

"He wouldn't let me go to the bathroom," she told Buddy, though it was meant for them all to hear.

"You all right now?" Buddy asked.

She gulped some air and said, "I think so," her eyes watering.

"Come on," Tina said, as Buddy scooted out Sandy's chair with her still in it. "Let's get you to the ladies' room."

Tina dampened some paper towels, saying "You're gonna be all right. Just need to cool down and let your stomach settle." Sandy cupped her hands under the faucet and rinsed out her mouth. Thanking Tina for the towels, she blotted her face, and then, turning her back to Tina, she eased her shirt up to run the towel under her arms and over her ribcage and then reached around to her back. Tina glanced over and froze, her lipstick halfway to her mouth. There was a long slice of a scar running diagonally from Sandy's left shoulder blade nearly to her waist. It was hard to tell how deep it had been, but it spiked out wider in a few places, as if it hadn't closed up quite right.

Sandy pulled down her shirt and turned around, then lifted her hair and ran a second damp towel over the back of her neck. "Thanks again," she said.

"You feelin' any better?" Tina asked, staring at bruises on the undersides of Sandy's arms. She didn't think Frank's grabbing her the night before could have made them, and he'd only held her by one arm. There was also a pale bluish bruise the shape of an amoeba along the outside of Sandy's right thigh.

"I guess."

"'You bruise easily, huh?"

Sandy looked down at her leg to see what Tina was looking at. "I dunno. Maybe."

"How'd you get those scars on your back?"

Sandy turned away slightly and said, "It was an accident."

"That must have really hurt."

Sandy dropped her hair back down and shrugged. "Yeah. I don't really like to talk about it."

Tina turned back to the mirror to finish applying her lipstick and said, "My dad forced me eat split-pea soup, once. We were visiting his sister, and he knew I didn't like it, but wanted me to be polite."

"What did you do?"

"Same thing. Kid's revenge. It's the only way they ever get even."

Sandy smiled sheepishly. "I really didn't mean to."

"Neither did I. That's what makes it so perfect."

They laughed at that, and Tina handed Sandy her lipstick. "Try this color. It's called Persian Melon." Sandy dabbed the lipstick onto her lips and then rubbed it in with her middle finger, the way she'd watched Tina do it.

"That's right," said Tina. "Makes it look real soft and natural."

"Thanks," said Sandy. She was starting to feel better, but reluctantly followed Tina back out into the July heat and Frank's angry silence, dreading the scene when they got to Kiowa.

Outside, Tina asked Sandy to go see if Buddy was ready to go. Then she pulled Frank around to the front of the car where they couldn't be overheard, and told him what she'd seen in the bathroom.

"What makes you so sure those scars weren't caused by an accident like she said?"

"Experience. And if I'm right, and we just drop her off without being sure about . . . . We could be placing her in a bad situation. Think you can ask her about it?"

"If she wouldn't tell you, she sure as hell won't confide in me."

"So what do we do?"

Frank leaned both arms against the hood of the Mercury and let his chin drop to his chest. "Shit. I don't have time for this right now. Let's go."

"First I'm gonna see if they have any Pepto Bismol in there," Tina said, "and get some cold water."

Frank looked over to where Sandy was leaning against the camper, fighting back tears as Buddy spoke with her.

"He just needs a little time," Buddy said, "and he'll calm down."

She shrugged. "Then will he stop hating me?"

"He doesn't hate you. He's more confused right now than anything. He's run up against something he can't out-think, out-talk, or out-drive. A man doesn't like to lose that much control."

He looked out over the stretch of highway. "Ya know, you two are gonna have to actually talk to one another eventually." He looked down at her. "And you're gonna need to be straight with him. That's the only way this is gonna work. You understand me?"

She held his gaze long enough for some of her own anger to die out and then nodded, relieved that, even though Buddy knew she'd been bending the truth some, he seemed to be on her side. They turned to watch Tina coming toward them carrying a paper cup.

"Here," she said to Sandy, handing her the stomach medicine and water. "Take a swig of this, and keep the water to sip on."

Frank walked over and said for the girls to get into the car. "I'm thinking the motion in the camper might have upset her stomach. Might be better for her to ride in the car for a while." He exchanged a look with Tina, who led Sandy back to the Mercury.

"We might have a situation," Frank said to Buddy. "Can't take her to Kiowa just yet."

Buddy frowned, but just said, "Liberal then?"

Frank nodded.

Buddy stepped up into the cab and said, "Let's roll."

· · · · ·

The warm air siphoning in through the windows whipped Sandy's hair into her eyes and mouth, so she laid her head down on the seat and closed her eyes. She wondered how far they were from Kiowa and whether she should just ask to be dropped off at a gas station and call her aunt Maggie to come get her.

It was a good 40 miles farther down the road before Sandy awoke, surprised to discover she'd dozed off. She could tell because she remembered listening to "Your Cheatin' Heart" on the radio, waiting for her favorite part— *When tears come down, like falling rain, you'll come around, and call my name,* but she never heard it, and the next thing she heard was ... *and the wayward wind is a restless wind....*

Her mouth was dry and her nose felt as if it was stuffed with cotton. She sat up and saw that the cup of water was still upright on the floorboard. It was warm, but wet, and she finished it all before turning around to see if Buddy was still behind them in the camper. He gave her a smile and raised his index finger up off the steering wheel the way people living in the country greeted each other on the dirt roads. She gave him a little wave and turned back around just in time to catch the start of a row of Burma Shave signs. Leaning her head out of the window to get a better look, she read out loud, "The safest rule," and paused until the car got up to the second sign, where she continued reading, "No ifs or buts ...."

By then Tina, who was looking out of her window too, read the last three signs in unison with Sandy: "Just drive ... like everyone else ... is nuts." There was a slight pause before they came to the last sign and said in unison, "Burma Shave."

After a few more miles had slipped past with the only sounds the rhythm of the tires on blacktop and the wind shushing in through the open windows, Tina stretched her arms up and said, "I drank too much coffee."

When Frank didn't respond, she said, "You hear me?"

"We're making good time."

"I said I need to use the ladies' room."

"Want me to pull over?"

Tina looked back at him with an expression of disbelief, and said, "No, I don't want you to pull over. What do you think, I'm five years old?"

"Where are we?" Sandy asked, looking for familiar landmarks around Kiowa.

Right after a sign that said Coldwater, Frank pulled into a gas station with trees around it for shade and plenty of room for Buddy to pull the camper off the road.

"Come on," Tina told Sandy, heading toward the building. "We're goin' on over to Liberal so Buddy can get right to work on the car."

Sandy stumbled and caught herself, then followed Tina around to the door on the side of the station. Confused and a little apprehensive, she realized she would need to call her aunt soon, and wondered if things were getting out of hand.

CHAPTER 20

THERE IS A NEW WAR CRY
AT LIBERAL SPEEDWAY:
"Beat Frankie Haggard"

Frank Haggard manages to win features on other tracks without trouble. Last night he won the feature at Winfield Fairgrounds.

Last year, he scored enough championship points on tracks in Kansas to win the championship of the state.

But the Jinx is on the Sunflower flyer here at Fairgrounds Speedway, where he has failed to pilot his G.D. Parker special to one feature victory in the last four attempts although he has consistently placed high.

Fans for Saturday night's card will see whether Haggard can be stopped once again. Odds are the would-be Jinx Killer will cop yet another big win in his growing string of victories on the way to the first-ever Grand National Championship one week from tonight at Taft Stadium in Oklahoma City.

Sitting in the shade of the camper parked at a roadside campground just inside Liberal city limits, Tina fanned herself with the *Liberal Monitor*—reaching over periodically to move the air over Frank where he half-reclined in a lawn chair next to her.

His voice sounded husky because he was keeping it low. "Do you know what you're sayin'? If you're right, it's a matter for the police, or some agency who takes care of things like that."

"I hate to disillusion you, but most folks don't want to get into the middle of what they consider family matters, not even the cops. I should know." She turned her face away from him, took a long drag on her cigarette, and blew out hard. "Everybody on our block knew that my old man knocked us around. They still slapped him on the back, like he was a good old boy, and drank his beer on the stoop, sending us inside for refills as fast as our red-welted legs could carry us." She sighed deeply and raised her knees to let what little breeze there was cool the backs of her legs. Frank reached over and ran his palm along her arm. "I'm sorry."

"Water under the bridge."

He waited for her to say something more, his thoughts skipping back and forth between the image of a small Tina being hit by her father and the long, welt-like scar on Sandy's back that Tina had described to him. "Do you think you ought to ask her about it again?"

"She didn't trust me enough this morning to confide in me."

Sandy, who had started out of the camper to join them, was frozen with the screen door ajar to keep it from slapping closed and drawing their attention. She had been trying to overhear what they were planning to do with her.

"Then you really think she ran away because they abused her, and she came lookin' for me?" He paused. "Why?" he asked, trying to sort out his relationship with her, which had gotten a lot more complicated with this news of her possible mistreatment.

"As far as I can see, you're in way over your head here," Tina told him. "I heard what that cop in Enid said. If she's not who she says she is, you could be charged with kidnapping. Maybe even if she is. But if you send her back to Kiowa and she is being knocked around, she may just run off again, or worse, and we'd be responsible for not doing anything about it."

"Damn. This just keeps getting better and better." Frank ran his thumb across the top edge of his belt buckle, flinching as Tina slapped at a fly that had landed on her arm.

92

Easing the screen door closed and sitting on the bench behind the driver's seat, Sandy tried to recall exactly what she and Tina had said to each other about the scar and bruises. It was clear from the tone of the conversation she'd just overheard that they thought she had been beaten and that it was a regular thing. She thought the bruises must have come from bouncing around in the back of the pickup she'd hitched a ride in to Enid. The whole notion was so far-fetched that she couldn't decide whether it was truly terrible or the best thing that could have happened. At least they weren't still talking about dumping her onto a bus. On the other hand, she felt like a traitor letting them think anything that bad about her Aunt Maggie, who had always been there for her, even before Sandy's mother had died. She resolved to phone her aunt as soon as she could sneak away to a pay phone where the others couldn't see her, and let her know everything was all right.

Tina stepped up into the camper to get some ice and smiled at Sandy. "You look like you're thinkin' hard."

"Sort of," Sandy said. "Thanks for the sandwich."

"There's more if you want. You were smart to stay inside," Tina told her. "The flies are biting. I guess the heat is getting to them, too." She opened the refrigerator and called out to Frank, "There's not enough beer in here for tonight, and we could use some more ice and soda for the cooler. Why don't you run me in to town so we can stock up the cooler before we pick up Buddy and head to the track?"

Turning to Sandy, she said, "There's a grocery store just a ways up the road. Want to ride along?"

Sandy thought about it. She'd done enough hard time that day riding in the backseat with Frank not talking except when Tina asked him a direct question. "No thanks. I'll wait here."

"It'll be cooler drivin' than sittin'," Tina said.

"That's all right. If I stay, then you won't have to close up the camper."

"Suit yourself. There's a strawberry pop left."

Sandy watched the car pull onto the highway, then retrieved Tina's *True Romance* magazine from the straw bag next to the passenger seat in the front, dragging out an open pack of cigarettes that fell onto the floorboard. She bent down and picked it up, staring at the cigarettes that were sticking out. Kool menthols with filter tips. She held them under her nose and sniffed the mixture of menthol and tobacco. She glanced out of the windows, then clamped her lips over one and drew it out. She worked the matches out from under the cellophane. Striking one, she held it to the end of the cigarette, sucking steadily until she got it burning, then shook out the match and tossed it out of the door.

Putting the cigarettes and matches back, she sucked smoke into her mouth—her cheeks ballooning slightly as she held it there before spewing it all out. She and Ralph had practiced a few times behind his house, and he was good enough to blow rings that she caught with her fingers. She watched herself in the small mirror next to the sink, experimenting with the way she held her fingers and placed the cigarette between her lips, which pouted out to receive it.

She went outside, where she stretched out in the chaise lounge facing the entrance to the park, the magazine propped against her knees. She didn't dare get too comfortable, but might as well make the most of whatever reprieve they were giving her for now.

"Crushed in His Arms," she read the article title aloud. "Can love with the wrong man ever go right?" She dove into the story using speed-reading skills she learned her freshman year, halting periodically to swat flies with the magazine.

By the time the Mercury drove back into the park and Tina climbed into the camper to put the beer and pop in the fridge, Sandy had carefully tucked the magazine away and laid cards out across the small table in a game of solitaire. She could hear Frank's voice mixing in with someone else's just outside the door and looked up to see Tina opening three beers.

"Who's here?"

"One of the drivers. We ran into him in town. He's from around here. You want a soda?"

"Thanks," she said, then turned to the door to look outside just as the screen door swung open and found herself face to face with a man with black curly hair and pale eyes. The phrase "dream boat" came to mind.

"Can I give you a hand," he asked, smiling at Sandy and looking past her to where Tina was getting their drinks. "Howdy," he said, looking at Sandy again.

"This is L. Ray Chenoweth. He drives number 19. This here's Sandy, Frank's daughter."

"Well, this is a pleasure," he said, holding out his hand. She took it, her own hand pretty much going along for the ride as he pumped it with enthusiasm. "You must be real proud of your dad."

He let go of Sandy's hand to take the two bottles of beer Tina was holding out to him.

Tina handed a bottle of strawberry Nehi to Sandy and whispered, "That's the driver that got tied up with Jerry Oakley just before the accident. He's feeling pretty bad about things right now. Not that it was his fault." Tina rolled the cold bottle against her cheeks and then held it against her sternum briefly before grabbing a portable radio.

Sandy followed Tina out of the camper, the girls taking the chaise lounges. Instead of straddling it and flopping backwards as she normally did, Sandy rolled in from the side and swung her legs up together. When she tipped her head back to drink, she sneaked looks at L. Ray, who was in a lawn chair next to Frank. He looked bigger, but L. Ray sat taller. They were going over the details of the accident, and from what he and Frank were saying, it sounded as if a driver named Hays had been as much to blame as anyone or anything else, slamming L. Ray from behind and pushing him into Oakley.

"Up in Platte, Nebraska," Frank said, "Hays forced me plumb off the track."

"Why don't the officials ban him," Sandy asked.

"Because he hasn't broken any written laws," Frank answered her. "He's just a squirrely driver."

"But if he runs people off the track, and causes accidents?"

"Well, I guess those things are sorta like occupational risks," L. Ray chimed in. "And part of why fans keep coming back week after week. Why do you figure promoters give roll-over trophies?"

Sandy thought about that.

"You like the races, do you?" L. Ray's deep voice slipped over her smooth as silk.

"I've been going to them with my uncle since I was . . . pretty young." Her voice lifted as she warmed to the subject. "I have scrapbooks that go back to 1946."

"'46!" L. Ray's laughter shot out on a rush of air and she felt her neck and face grow even warmer. "Boy, you aren't kiddin' when you say you started young. I was only seven myself back then. They give ya them little plastic scissors with the round tips?"

They all laughed at the soft tease, and then Frank leaned forward and asked, "Scrapbooks?"

"They were my mother's."

L. Ray nodded and everyone was silent for a moment. Then Frank, who was studying her face, asked, "How many?"

"For 1946 to 1949, except for part of '47 and the end of '49. I came down with pneumonia in '47 and was delirious for a time." She wanted Frank to ask her about that, but he was silent. Instead, it was L. Ray who asked, "What happened in '49?"

"She died."

They were all quiet for a beat, and then L. Ray said he was sorry to hear that, that she must have died a very young woman. Sandy waited for the sensation that came whenever she said it out loud, the odd, precise hole she imagined that burned through her chest, like when the hot tip of a cigarette is held to a sheet of paper, consuming just so much and no more. Her pulse thumped in her neck, and she wanted to know what Frank was feeling, if anything, wanted to see some evidence of loss on his face, but he'd turned away. Then L. Ray turned the talk to that night's race in Liberal, and her chance to press Frank to a response evaporated as talk of drivers and cars and mechanical terms she wasn't familiar with filled the air.

CHAPTER 21

Just as they were packing up the chairs and getting ready to head to the track, a silver Cadillac pulled up next to them. Sandy watched as Buddy got out of the passenger side and a short, stocky man wearing a light-blue-and-white striped seersucker suit and a straw hat got out of the driver's side. He had a cigar sticking out of the side of his mouth and was wiping his face with a handkerchief.

"G.D.," Frank said, glancing over at Buddy, "when did you get to Liberal?"

A ring of sweat glistened just below G.D.'s hat brim, and his cheeks and nose were road maps of broken blood vessels. "Ain't got there yet. Saw the rig while I was drivin' by. And if you'd check in now and again," he said to Frank, "you wouldn't have to ask. More important, I'd know what in the hell—'scuse my French, ladies," he touched the brim of his hat with his index finger—"I'd know what in the hell is going on with that little toy car you're so fond of that's already cost me twice as much to keep running this year as it did last and isn't running near as good." There were tiny bubbles in the corners of his mouth, and Sandy nodded to Tina to indicate that Frank was running his thumb across the top of his belt buckle in that habit he had when he was tense.

"G.D., meet Tina, and this here's Sandy. My . . . daughter."

Sandy managed to nod at Parker, but a chill was shimmying between her shoulder blades, and she had a lump in her throat. Tina and Buddy looked from Frank to Sandy and then back to Frank while the word daughter seemed to hang in the air.

G.D. slapped a hammy palm against his thigh and said, "No kiddin'? You got a kid? We'll I'll be a monkey's uncle." He turned to Buddy and said, "I don't suppose this other one's yours," then winked at Tina and laughed loudly at his own joke.

Frank said, "Girls, this here's Mr. Parker," then cleared his throat of the frog that had formed there. He'd decided almost without realizing it that if Sandy was Ruth's from that far back, then she was probably his. But the timing of his declaration of fatherhood had surprised him as much as anyone. He wondered uneasily if maybe he'd sensed it might deflect Parker, get him to ease up on his nagging, which was getting to Frank more than usual this close to the Grand National.

Buddy was saying, "G.D's the owner of the car, in case you haven't figured that out yet."

"I never took you for the family type, Frank," G.D. said. "Where you been keepin' her?"

"I stay with my aunt, a lot," Sandy spoke up. "I can be here with my," she hesitated for a split second, which was caught by everyone except Parker, "father because it's summer vacation. And of course, the big race is coming up."

G.D. nodded, squinting as he scrutinized her. "I do believe I see a family resemblance, now I study on it."

"I don't know what you're griping about," Frank said. "We won last night."

"I know that," G.D. said. "We got newspapers in Wichita. And I know what your time was, and what the others were running laps in, and the car should of been faster than that as hot as the track was runnin'. What tires you have on?"

"We dressed out for dry/slick, and we guessed right."

"The big Firestones?"

"Yeah, the big Firestones."

"They should of worked all right. I thought Buddy had the engine primed. You let up, or what?"

Frank hesitated a beat before he responded, his voice low and careful. "I don't let up."

"Your time was two seconds off what you ran there last month. I'm beginning to wonder if you're losing your edge."

"Track conditions were different last month. And the only thing I'm losin' is patience with your repeated accusations that I'm not runnin' all out."

"Let's stop by the cafe on Highway 54 so I can get cooled off," Parker said." I have an idea about seeing if we're getting all out of her we can."

Buddy and Frank exchanged a look while the girls put the last of the lunch items into the camper, Sandy giggling briefly as Tina leaned over and whispered, "Guess we know what G.D. stands for."

· · · · ·

At the café, Sandy kept thinking about Frank's referring to her as his daughter, right there in front of everybody. Surely he wouldn't just pack her onto a bus now and send her back home before the biggest race of their lives. She thought about calling her Aunt Maggie, but as she sat there drawing hearts in the condensation on her glass of Coke, she realized that there had been a significant shift. She'd been busy scheming ways to avoid getting sent home, and now she wasn't sure how or when she would get back there.

It was Buddy who got around to asking Parker what his idea was about getting more out of number 65, but he didn't expect much. He'd decided some time ago that Parker was too heavy to race and too arrogant to know how much he didn't know about engines. But he'd bought his way into the life with a decent car and put up enough money to allow Buddy to turn it into a competitive racing machine.

Parker got a grin on his face, finished his iced tea, and wiped his mouth with a paper napkin that he waded up and tossed onto the table. "I got the idea while some Jehovah's Witnesses were leaning on my doorbell. Wouldn't let up. Saw my car in the drive, I guess. Figured I was needin' saving."

Buddy just frowned and said, "Yeah, they're persistent buggers. What's that got to do with racin'?"

"What makes a doorbell go off," Parker asked, without expecting an answer. "Someone leaning on it. And as long as he leans on it, it keeps clanging or buzzing—I've got those chimes, myself—and so you know the son of a mother-dog is still there. 'Scuse my French, ladies."

"Yeah, so?" Buddy asked.

"So I figured how we can tell how she's runnin' when ol' Frank has got the pedal to the metal." He looked at Frank and then Buddy to make sure he had their undivided attention, and said, "We mount a red light on her. Locate the button right under the accelerator." He leaned back in his chair and hooked his thumbs under his navy-blue suspenders. Sandy had been studying him and didn't like the smug way he was smiling and the way he talked about Frank as if he wasn't sitting right there at the same table. She turned to look at Frank, who had been leaning his chair back on two legs, his arms crossed over his chest. Anyone could see from his stony expression that he wasn't taking well to Parker's idea. Frank let the chair snap back upright and leaned his arms on the table, looking G.D. in the eye. "I don't need a red light to tell me when I've got her wide open."

Parker leaned as far forward as his stomach would allow and said, "Maybe not, Sport, but I do." He reached out and slapped Buddy on the back. "You can hook it up easy, get one of them cherry lights they have on the tops of cop cars."

Buddy shifted uncomfortably glancing over at Frank. "I don't think that's such a good idea, G.D."

"Well, I do, and it's my nickel you boys are riding to the Grand National, and I don't intend to leave there an also-ran. I want the hottest car with the hardest driving son of a bitch in the country behind the wheel."

Sandy noticed he didn't ask them to excuse his French that time, and there was a thin line of white foam in the corners of his mouth. He wasn't smiling anymore, either.

Buddy said, "I don't know. Whadda you think, Frank?" not really wanting to hear the answer. "Maybe we could try it out for a couple of laps. Check the time, like the man says."

Frank, who had seemed to be looking at a spot on the table, raised his eyes first to Buddy, who cringed when he saw the anger in Frank's face, and then to Parker, who returned the look like a man who knows he's holding the winning cards.

"It ain't up to Frank," Parker said, turning a hard look to Buddy. "You boys want to accompany 65 to Oklahoma City, we're gonna run this little test Wednesday night at 81 Speedway in Wichita, soon's they open up for the Wally Lutke Memorial race. That'll be our best chance to check her out."

Frank stood up abruptly, sticking his hands in his back pockets as he shifted his weight from one leg to another like a racehorse eager to get out of the chute. "One time. You hear me? That's all. Just to get you off my back." He took out his wallet and dropped a twenty-dollar bill on the table. "Let's go get a motel room for the girls before it gets any later and head out to the track."

"Well, I best be gettin' out there as well," Parker said, bracing his hands against the table as he raised himself up out of his chair. Sandy noticed that, without the smile cutting across the lower half of his face, his jowls were more prominent, giving him the appearance of a bulldog.

"You get that light hooked up, Buddy, and then we'll see what's what."

Tina waited until Parker had gone out the door before asking Buddy, "How angry do you think Frank is right now?"

Buddy just shook his head. "I'd steer clear for a while if I were you. I'm afraid it's gonna get a lot hotter before things cool off between those two."

Though Sandy wasn't clear on what harm could come from the red light, she wished that Parker had stayed away. But at least the focus had shifted away from her. Everyone was thinking about G.D. and the red light.

CHAPTER 22

The field behind the grandstand at Liberal's Carnival Speedway was a grid of small tents and rides being set up. Left to her own devices while Tina went into town to buy more ice, Sandy wandered over to check out the booths and rides. She stopped in front of a mechanical fortune teller's glass cage being set up. The soothsayer's head was lying on its side on the counter. A carnival worker in grease-stained jeans and a faded T-shirt with a cigarette pack rolled up in one sleeve was setting it up, and Sandy watched with fascination as metal rods sticking up from the opening of the neck torqued and quivered. The recording that came out sounded like a woman speaking with an exaggerated accent, and said to no one in particular, "The clouds of dreams are dust from the eyelids of those who have gone before. They are watching over and protecting those whose hearts make them worthy of . . . worthy of . . . worthy of . . . . "

The worker made an adjustment at the back, and the voice stopped and started over, completing the sentence this time, with "worthy of the star's messages." When the movement stopped, the worker picked up the head and lowered it over the mechanism. It came to rest in a tilted position, the eyes slanting down and a little to the left, as if studying the over-sized deck of cards fanned out on the inside of the glass front, forming a red arc of miniature dragons. When he backed out of the side flap, Sandy saw that his hips were weighed down with a semi-circle of tools stuck through loops on a canvas belt. He saw Sandy watching and smiled at her. "Hey," he called out in greeting.

"Hey," she answered.

"You wanna get your fortune told?"

"Maybe later," she said.

"Madame Yolanda knows many things." He grinned at her. "Come on over. You can help me test her out. See if she's working right."

"I don't think so," she said.

"Be doin' me a big favor. Everbody else is busy, and I gotta get the old girl up and runnin'. Just take a minute. Put your hand on the counter in front of her and see what she says while I duck inside and check out her movin' parts." He held up a token that looked like a gold coin from a treasure chest.

She looked at the gaudily decorated red and gold booth with the glass front and little window to stick a hand through. "If it won't take too long."

"Spend a minute now to learn about your whole future." He stepped back a little, still smiling.

Sandy looked around to see if anyone was watching, telling herself there was no harm in it, but there was also a sense of adventure that she might have read as a warning if she'd been home in Kiowa instead of out practically on her own on the racing circuit. She reached through the opening and said, "Here?" fitting her fingers into the black outline of a hand.

He pulled up the canvas skirt behind Madame Yolanda and told her, "Turn it over, so she can see your palm."

"Sandy rolled her eyes and said, "Right. Like that makes all the difference."

He squeezed in behind the mannequin, and said, "Put the token into the slot and punch the button for your sign."

"Uh, shouldn't Madame Yolanda know my sign?" Sandy teased.

He laughed and said, "Wise guy, huh?" Sandy flipped her hand over and listened as the coin rolled through the mechanical works, then pushed the button that said Pisces. It lit up and made a tinny chiming noise. That was followed by a slight grinding noise, and then the yellow banner lit up above Madame Yolonda's head flashing the words "Your fortune" in red. Suddenly, the gypsy's head dipped forward as if nodding, and then turned from side to side, pausing a moment over the spot where Sandy's hand was. After another slight grinding sound, the head popped upright, the mouth opening and partially closing: "Your planet is Neptune, your sign is two fish swimming in opposite directions, signifying inner tensions. Pisces yearns for new sensations and travel to remote and exotic places. You are intensely loyal and faithful. Be careful that you place your trust in those worthy of it. Your birthstone is aquamarine. Your ideal partner will be a Gemini or a Scorpio."

Sandy listened as the gears stopped turning in Madame Yolanda, whose head rocked to one side and froze there so she was staring at the fan of cards again.

Sandy called out, "Okay, that's a little freaky." She stepped back and bumped into the worker who was standing behind her with his hands resting against the glass booth on either side of her.

He grinned. "So is that true? You like excitement and travel?"

"Sure," she answered, "who doesn't? I have to go now."

"What's the hurry? Nothing else going on right now."

"I have to get back to the track. They're waiting for me."

"Yeah? You got a boyfriend over there?"

Sandy gave his chest a shove, but he didn't budge. Then she lowered her head to dip under his arm, but he let it drop to prevent her from leaving. "Listen," she said, "I'm telling you to let me go."

"Or what?" he said, leaning in closer.

"My dad is Frank Haggard. He's a champion driver, and he's expecting me right now."

His voice turned from suggestive to something more menacing as he mimicked her with, "My daddy's a champion driver. Wow. Ain't I special? Yeah, I know who he is."

She looked around to see if there was anyone close enough to call out to, but they were alone. "Just let me go."

"First you're all smiles and come on, and now you're too good for me?"

Sandy pushed hard against his chest, saying, "Move, you creep!"

"Sure," he said. As soon as you've paid for your fortune, Princess."

"Fine." As Sandy reached into her pocket for some change, he grabbed the back of her head and pressed his mouth over hers. She could feel his jabbing whiskers, and he forced his tongue between her lips. She kept her mouth pinched as tightly as she could as she pushed against him, her hand catching on the head of the mallet hanging on

104

his utility belt. She grabbed the top and yanked it down hard, driving the thick handle up into his crotch. He backed off so fast that the hot breeze that blew across her wet mouth caught her like a slap.

He doubled over, squeaking out, "Jeez Louise!" She ran back to the main entrance of the racetrack, holding her hand up at the window to show her stamp, and came to a halt at the concession stand just inside.

Leaning over the counter, she gasped for air and wiped the back of her hand across her mouth several times. Just as she straightened up, she felt a hand on her shoulder, and let out a yelp. It took a second before the red hair registered.

Adam looked as startled as she did. "Hey there. You all right?"

She nodded, the back of her hand still pressed against her mouth.

"Did I scare ya?"

"Yeah." She let her hand drop.

"Hello." He smiled tentatively. "You don't seem very happy."

"I'm not." She turned to face him and worked up a smile. "But I'm really glad to see you. Really." She looked back over at the carnival grounds.

"Thanks," he said, his smile widening. "I was thinking the same thing myself. About you, I mean. Been here long?"

"Too long."

"Yeah, well, I guess it can get kinda boring, just sitting around waiting while the guys work on the cars."

"I wouldn't say boring, exactly." She looked over at the fairgrounds again. There were cars pulling in along the drive that separated the racetrack from the field behind it.

Adam followed her gaze. "You staying for the carnival? If so, maybe we can meet up there after."

"I don't know about that."

"About going or meeting up?"

"I don't know if we'll be staying around or not."

"Well, I have to help get the concessions set up. You know where you'll be sitting yet?"

"Not really. I have to wait for Tina to get back. She drove back into town for ice."

"That's okay. I'll find you. Stay close to the middle, about halfway up to the press box."

"That's where we sat at Enid, on the right. Left if you're facing the press box."

"Gotcha. Want a Coke or something? My treat."

"No thanks." She watched him lope over to a truck with "Weissman's Franks" painted on it, where some other boys were already unloading boxes of hotdogs packed in dry ice.

"You want somethin'?" the woman inside the concession stand asked.

Sandy stepped back from the counter and said, "No thank you. Wait. Are the snow-cones ready?"

"Machine's goin'."

"Then may I please have a plain one?"

"What flavor?"

"Plain. Just the plain ice."

"You don't want no syrup on it?"

"Just plain, please."

"Suit yourself. Costs the same."

Sandy climbed the bleachers slowly, blotting her mouth on the shaved ice and running her tongue over it. When she got to the top, she leaned against the railing and watched the activity below. The carnival was nearly set up, bright flags and lights strung from tent to tent, and the merry-go-round doing a test spin in the middle of the compound. Thready strains of circus music radiated out from it and wafted up to the stands.

Her fright, having long since abated, was replaced with a gnawing disgust and angry internal dialogues in which she revealed the creep for what he was, publicly. Her sentencing him to an indeterminable incarceration with the gypsy dummy gone berserk occupied her time so compellingly that she was content to suck the ice and remain in the sun and wind at the top of the stands while the parking lot filled up.

She debated whether to tell Tina what had happened, but when it came down to it, she felt a little queasy about her part in it. She didn't want to hear them tell her that she should have known better than to talk to strangers when she was alone. And anyway, she'd taken care of herself pretty good. She smiled, recalling how he'd doubled up helplessly as she escaped—something to tell Ralph about when she got back home again. She frowned at the thought, her tongue circling the shaved ice, wondering exactly when that might be, and what Aunt Maggie was thinking right now, whether she was angry or mostly just sad about what Sandy had done.

CHAPTER 23

It was nearly six-thirty before Tina came looking for Sandy in the stands carrying orange stadium seats. She was trailed up the steps by two women. The first looked matronly in a navy-and-white sailor blouse and red pleated skirt, and the second was Louise, Buddy's friend. Sandy stood up and waved at them, then bounded down the steps to meet them halfway from the bottom, where they set up their seats starting at the aisle. Sandy took the stadium seat Tina held out to her and set it on the bench in front of the three women, where it would be easier to hear them.

The watering truck had already finished wetting down the track, and a dozen race cars were running slow laps to pack it down for time trials and to check out their engines. Tina told Sandy, "This is Mrs. Jones, Pee Wee Jones' wife." Then she pointed to black and white car number 12x passing in front of the stands. Sandy nodded and turned around to say hello.

"You can call me Gladys," the woman told her.

"It's real easy to remember," Louise said, "looking over at Gladys, who actually blushed and laughed behind one hand.

"Oh dear," Gladys said, "I guess she's old enough," Her cheeks were rosy and her eyes full of mirth. "Just think 'Happy Bottom.'" She giggled again.

Louise and Tina were grinning as they looked to see if Sandy got the joke, and then Tina leaned closer and said, "Happy Bottom . . . Glad Ass?"

Sandy's grin got a lot wider and she said, "Happy to meet you," but mostly she was happy to be considered one of the gang. She took the Baby Ruth that Tina held out to her and secured it under the edge of her seat cushion for later, feeling very much like an old hand, as if she had been coming to the races to watch her father do his thing for years.

For the first three heat races, Sandy didn't pay much attention since she didn't recognize any of the drivers' names, but she joined the other fans in cheering and clapping as the checkered flag flapped and the cars shot over the finish line. By the start of Frank's heat race, she'd swallowed enough dust blown up from the track to be thirsty.

She looked around for Ad or one of the other boys who sold concessions in the stands, but there was no one close enough to signal to, and no time to go to one of the stands below before Frank's first race of the night.

She pulled out the Baby Ruth, which was partly melted. She worked the paper loose but kept it partially intact while she took bites and licked chocolate from the wrapper as she went. By the time she'd eaten and licked what she could without getting the chocolate all over her hands and face, she let the wrapper drop under the bleachers and crossed her fingers just as the cars in the fourth heat sped into their first lap and another of the endless waves of track dust blanketed the stands. Behind her, Louise was screaming all-out as Frank circled the track in tight formation with three other cars, including Pee Wee Jones in 12x, who was a little behind and to the outside of the other three.

Sandy cried out along with the other three women as the cars jostled against one another going into turn three. Pee Wee rode high on the bank and then dove straight down behind the others and gunned up into the opening made when the two cars battling for first drifted wide. Frank shot to the left behind Pee Wee and followed him through, pulling his front tires up only inches from Pee Wee's rear-end. As they flew around for lap two, they held position through turn one, and then Frank eased forward on the outside half a car length. They held their positions for another lap, the three women behind Sandy straining forward, and Tina's fists resting on Sandy's shoulders. Their cheers were swallowed by the roar of the cars' engines as they sped up along the straight-a-ways.

The drivers in third and fourth positions were also locked into a tight race, and still close enough to challenge Frank and Pee Wee.

Sandy's shoulders sagged when Frank backed-off and trailed Pee Wee, his own rear-end dangerously close to the racers battling just behind him. By the eighth lap, Frank and Pee Wee were ready to pass the cars at the tail-end of the pack, and before the flagman could give the "move over" signal telling the slower cars to move to the outside, Frank shot around the outside of the car in last place with the throttle all the way out. Pee Wee moved with him, but a second behind so that Frank dipped down into turn one and caught the groove, firing on all cylinders down the backstretch and rocketing out of turn four on the outside. Pee Wee ducked in right behind him as they lapped the remaining stragglers.

Sandy had been glancing back at the rest of the cars to check on L. Ray, who had started near the back. She had counted him seven back by lap five, but by the eighth lap he had passed two cars for fifth place and was challenging the cars just ahead of him. As Frank took the white flag, Sandy held her breath, her head turning slightly from Frank's race with Pee Wee to L. Ray's struggle to pass the cars fighting for third position and finish in the money. On the backstretch, Pee Wee went low and pulled his nose even with Frank's rear tires, which could give him the shot he was looking for coming out of turn four if he held position. Suddenly, the fourth car—number 99—wobbled in front of L. Ray and skidded into a slow clockwise spin. He steered hard to the left to straighten up and was clipped by L. Ray as he slipped by and pulled up under the third-place car and passed it as well.

White 99 completed a full revolution and stopped against the wall a quarter of the track short of the finish line while Frank and then Pee Wee roared across it, with L. Ray close behind.

The fans were on their feet, yelling and applauding, and trying to see the condition of 99. Some men gathered around the car, making it hard to see the driver until he was up and over the side. Another man jumped into the race car and two others pushed it into the pits behind the driver, who was gesturing angrily.

"All right!" Louise yelled, applauding with her hands high in the air. "Way to go! Boy, is Hays gonna be hot at L. Ray."

At the mention of L. Ray's name, Sandy twisted around in her seat.

"The guy who spun out was Hays?" Sandy asked. She'd heard about his reputation as a reckless racer and a hothead.

"He got shot right out of the saddle. L. Ray just popped around him like a flea on a hot griddle for third place! There's gonna be some sparks in the pits tonight!"

CHAPTER 24

During the B Feature, Sandy borrowed a program from Louise and pored over the pictures. She read about the upcoming Grand National the following Sunday in Oklahoma City and studied the picture of L. Ray standing by his car, his left arm resting along the cut-out top. The cameraman had taken it so far back that the face was no bigger than her little finger and the features hard to make out. Ad was closer to her age, and fun and flirty in a juvenile sort of way, but Sandy had replayed that afternoon at the campsite with L. Ray at least a dozen times.

Before she knew it, cars were lining up for the A-Feature, the announcer inviting everyone "to stand up and stretch." The crowd obliged as the last-minute adjustments and driver-mechanic conferences took place in preparation for the big event of the night. Frank was outside in row two, with Pee Wee in front of him and L. Ray only two rows back. She winced when she recognized the car just in front of L. Ray as Hays', and tightened her crossed fingers.

"All right, fans and fanatics," the announcer's voice boomed, "this is your chance to let these drivers know how much you appreciate the great show they're puttin' on for us tonight here on Carnival Night. Let's give 'em a big round of applause as they take a parade lap and get ready for the feature event of the night."

His volume ratcheted up along with the revving engines as they crept along the backstretch. "And don't forget to visit the Wynn Brothers' Carnival and Road Show set up just the other side of the stands." He was nearly screaming to make himself heard. "Visit the booths and ride the rides and get your own thrills and chills. Even win a prize for your Honey. All right folks, here they come!"

The building roar of the engines as the cars accelerated out of turn four was like a physical pressure in Sandy's chest. When they all cleared turns one and two, the announcer shouted, "We've got us a race!" The lead cars were on their second lap before the fans had settled back into their seats. Sandy pressed the ring finger of her left hand hard against her thigh to mark lap two and strained forward as Frank rode high on the bank coming out of turn two, trying to pass Hays and Peewee on the outside as they fought for first position. L. Ray and yellow-and-red number 33, a car whose driver she wasn't familiar with, were in a tight race right behind. Frank lost ground as Pee Wee opened a slight lead on Hays in turn three, so he slipped back down to the pole and paced himself, waiting for a chance while Hays dogged Pee Wee in 12x down the front stretch.

The muscles in Sandy's stomach and calves tensed as Frank got sandwiched between the two pairs of cars. Red 65 seemed to be running all right, but she couldn't tell if it had enough power for him to move up. She pressed the little finger of her right hand against her leg, marking lap five, and made a mental note that the race was one fourth over. He was still in fourth position—which at least for the A feature was in the money, but probably too low in regional points to be significant. Her mental figuring had cut into her concentration, and she sucked in a quick breath when she realized that L. Ray and 33 were right on Frank's tail, their cars so evenly aligned that they seemed to be welded together, L. Ray on the outside and hanging on 33 like a side car on a cycle.

As they slipped up the embankment, it looked to Sandy as if L. Ray was going to be forced up into the goofballs along the top edge of the track and lose control. She held her breath as L. Ray held his ground, the two cars circling in tandem going for lap seven.

L. Ray began to edge ahead, but with nowhere to take it since Frank was holding tight on the outside next to Hays. Sandy pressed her fists against her thighs as she willed Frank to pull ahead, his front end even with Hays' steering wheel, then his front tires, and finally by turn four inching past his radiator. Suddenly, a shower of sparks sprayed up between the cars and red 65 jerked to the right and began a double spin that carried it backend first into the retaining wall in front of the grandstand.

The screams of the crowd were so shrill that Sandy couldn't tell if any noise was coming out of Tina's open mouth. They steadied each other as they balanced on their cushioned seats to see if Frank was all right.

"Get down and get your purse," Tina said. Sandy followed her down the steps and stood as close to the gate as the gathering crowd would allow.

"Can you see anything?" Sandy asked Tina, who was all of two inches taller. Tina shook her head, and tapped on the shoulder of a man standing right in front of them. "Can you see Frank Haggard?" she asked.

He looked through the crowd and called out "Not from here. Too many fatheads in the way."

"Can I get up on your shoulders for a minute?" Tina asked the man standing next to her.

He looked surprised, then turned to look at the woman standing next to him, whose own expression showed she clearly didn't like the idea. Tina hugged Sandy to her side and said, "This here is Frankie Haggard's daughter. We need to see if he's all right."

The woman was still frowning, but the man shrugged and said, "I guess so." He turned his back to Tina and bent down. She threw her right leg over his shoulder and then got the left one up with Sandy's help. From her elevated position, she could see the emergency crew working with Frank and yelled down to Sandy, "Frankie's all right. They're pushing the car back to the pits, but he's walking on his own." The people standing behind them cheered and whooped at the good news. Tina tapped the man on the head and said, "Thanks. You can let me down now."

When Sandy finally located Hays' car, it was stopped along the infield with its front end balanced on one of the half-buried tires that edged the inside of the turns. Hays gestured angrily as he yelled something to the swarm of men around him. Over the P.A. system, the announcer made repeated requests for the fans to take their seats, but the final laps of the A-Feature were completed before a standing audience. Their shrieks and applause as the announcer called out the numbers of the cars as they crossed the finish line sounded all the more emphatic to Sandy. Pee Wee had finished in first place, 33 came in second, and L. Ray's number 19 placed in the money in third. She cheered along with everyone else, but her throat felt tight, the way it gets just before you start crying. All she wanted now was for the trophies to be handed out quickly so they would let people cross the track and she could get into the pits and see if her dad was really all right and how banged up the car was.

CHAPTER 25

Sandy and Tina were in the first wave of spectators to squeeze through the narrow gate and down the uneven steps onto the track. They hurried to Frank's pit area and found the car ready to be loaded onto the trailer.

"Are you all right?" Tina asked, hugging Frank around the waist while Sandy inspected the bandaged cut on his left hand.

"Does it hurt much?" Sandy asked, her face tight with concern. He pulled her to his chest for a quick hug, the familiar smells of motor oil and dust somehow reassuring to her.

Louise, who'd been close behind them, said, "Gee, Frankie, that was a shame. Someday somebody's gonna set Hays straight. Is the car hurt bad?"

"The U-joint is banged up," said a voice from behind them, "and the drive shaft will have to be replaced, and that's just for starters."

Sandy thought she saw a shadow pass over Frank's face. She turned around and saw the car owner, Parker.

Buddy called over from where he was working on loading the trailer, "Could of been worse."

Parker stood with one chunky leg on a tool chest, his thigh supporting his protruding belly, an unlit cigar in the corner of his mouth. "Sure, it could of been worse. Coulda been banged into scrap metal. Point is, the car was runnin' great a quarter of an hour ago, and now it ain't runnin' at all."

Sandy said, "It was running good until it got hit from behind." which earned her an annoyed glance from Parker. He waved her off and said, "I agree, that's how it looked, but there was nothing wrong with the car at the start of the race." He chewed on the cigar, working it to the other side of his mouth. "Buddy! You be sure to have that red dome light set up for Wichita Wednesday night. Hear me?"

Frank and Buddy exchanged looks, and Frank walked over to the trailer to load tires. Sandy glared at Parker, who ignored her while he held forth with fans and other pit crew members making the rounds.

She joined Frank at the trailer to see if she could help. She was staring at the grease and dust that had settled into the creases on either side of his nose and the clean rings around his eyes where the goggles had protected them when he noticed her.

"Come here. Hold this for me," he said. He handed her the end of the chain he'd put through the tires and hopped down off the trailer. He showed her how to work it tight and loop it to a brace and put the padlock on. She saw he was favoring his bandaged left hand and asked, "You sure you're all right?"

"I'm sure. I just got scraped up a little." He flexed his hand as if to prove it was no big deal. "Tough luck tonight, is all. It happens."

She looked down and her voice had a catch in it when she said, "But what if you'd been hurt bad?" Her chest felt as if a bubble had expanded there, and she thought she might cry, but she didn't understand, because the worst was over with.

Frank squeezed her shoulder with his good hand. "But I wasn't, was I?"

She looked up and shook her head.

"Listen, kid. Don't spend time on the what-ifs. It's a waste of worry." He picked up his helmet from the back of the trailer and looked at it. It was dirty and scuffed on the left and there was an older, deeper gash along the right side. When Tina had asked why he didn't replace it with a shiny new one, he just shook his head and said, "It suits me." Tina had said that was nuts, but Sandy thought she understood—that all the marks and scratches were sort of trophies, too.

He slipped the helmet over her head, and said, "Take care of this for me, okay?" It was heavy and slipped sideways on her. She pushed it level while he took out the car keys and handed them to her. "Goes in the trunk."

Glancing around them, she was aware of the admiring and perhaps envious looks she was getting from the fans who had come to get a glimpse of Frank or even to call out a self-conscious "Hey, Frankie, how's it goin'," before they stepped closer to take a good look at the car or ask Buddy about its condition.

Frank stuck his thumb under her chin and raised her face so he could see her expression, the helmet remaining horizontal on her head. "Don't take it so hard, Junior. Think of all the fun you'll have helping Buddy get 65 back in shape."

Her mouth pulled to one side in a crooked smile as she eased from the urge to cry to an attempt to show she was game. "Oklahoma?" she asked.

"Yep. It'll give us a chance to get her squared away."

Her smile broadened. "Now you look like a raccoon," she told him, "only like in reverse."

"Is that right?" He pulled out a handkerchief and wiped his face. "Family trait."

He knocked on the top of the helmet. "Why don't you go put that in the trunk for me?"

She started for the Mercury but stopped when she heard shouting. She looked around to see where the yelling was coming from, and saw that a sizable crowd had gathered near where L. Ray's racer was parked.

Frank was looking over at them, too. He said, "Tina, you keep Sandy over here," and walked over to the growing circle of shouting and jostling men.

"Frankie. Frank!" Tina yelled. "Stay out of it!"

Buddy went after him, and Parker waddled after Buddy.

The three girls looked at one another, and Louise said, "It's gotta be that fool Hays." The three of them took off after the men, stopping just short of the outer ring of onlookers. Sandy could see glimpses of L. Ray's head and shoulders and heard what she thought must be Hays yelling, "You stupid punk! You shouldn't be allowed on the same track with real drivers."

She climbed up onto the fender of a nearby truck to get a better look. She watched as a short, stocky man with a thick neck and large arms ranted and gestured angrily at L. Ray, who was standing on the other side of his race car, giving Hays a menacing grin. Then all at once, L. Ray darted around the front of his car and tried to break through the circle of men who were trying to subdue Hays. The crowd lunged back and forth, the men closest to L. Ray blocking him with outstretched arms until he turned and walked back, his right arm raised as he gave L. Ray the finger. Suddenly he leapt up on top of his car, his legs spread wide over the cut-out roof. Then he swung his arms up over his head and dove out over the sea of heads, his hands catching on Hays' shoulders, L. Ray's momentum dragging Hays and a half dozen men to the ground with him.

They scrambled to their feet, some trying to keep the two men apart and others yelling, "Let 'em go!"

Sandy saw that Buddy was shouting at Hays and L. Ray to cool down.

Hays shouted back at him, "Stay out of it, Baehr. You can go to hell, and take that son-of-a-bitch you work for with you!"

Sandy wasn't sure whether he meant Parker or Frank, but her skin began to crawl. Louise was standing behind Parker and yelled, "Buddy, get your ass out of there before you get hurt!"

Frank reached in to grab Buddy's shirt to pull him out of harm's way and said something to Hays, who took a swing at him. Frank ducked, but knocked into L. Ray.

From her elevated vantage point, Sandy saw that there was a slight swell in the crowd standing behind Hays, the bodies spreading apart like a balloon just starting to fill with air. In the opening, she could make-out Louise's blond bouffant with the filmy red scarf as she bent down and the blue-green glow of a cigarette lighter in her outstretched hand. Louise touched it to the cuff of Hays' pant leg where he stood with restraining arms across his chest, his own arms taking swings in L. Ray's direction. Her heart pounding, Sandy watched in fascination as the cuff blackened and then there was an orange puff as the fabric caught fire. Louise quickly ducked back to the outside of the circle and ran back over to stand next to Tina while the men closest to Hays, who'd watched Louise at work, waited until she was clear to yell at Hays that his pants were on fire. It took a moment for their words and the smell to register and him to look down to see the smoke curling upward from his burning cuff. He slapped at the smoking fabric while several volunteers poured their beers and soda pops over his leg and quickly put out the fire.

Louise and Tina were laughing so hard Sandy was afraid Hays would realize who'd done it but then everyone else was laughing too.

"Hicks!" Hays called out, spit flying from the corners of his mouth. He located L. Ray, who had been pulled back and was standing next to Frank with an unfriendly grin on his face, and warned, "You better watch yourself, Sonny. You're runnin' with the big dogs now." Hays stormed back over to his car, followed by his pit crew and a few enthusiastic "woofs" before the crowd dispersed.

Sandy jumped down and went over to stand with Frank. She had been trying all night to think of what she would say to L. Ray when she got close to him again, but after all that excitement nothing she could come up with seemed to fit. Finally, she pulled out a pack of Juicy Fruit gum and tapped him on the arm to offer him a piece. He did a double take at first, then bent down to peer beneath the bill of the helmet and knocked on the top of it. "Hey, Sandy. That you in there?"

Blushing, she grabbed it off her head. "I have to go put this in the car."

He took her by the arm. "Hold up, Hot Rod. Not so fast. How about that gum?"

She pushed the pack into his hand and darted off for the Mercury. After stowing the helmet, she slid into the front seat. She adjusted the rearview mirror so she could check her hair and lipstick. She combed furiously and dabbed at her face with a Kleenex and holding it up to the light to see how much dirt she was getting off, the way she'd see Louise do between races. Her face felt gritty, and her skin grew tender from the dry scrubbing. She applied more lipstick and was about to hurry back to where the camper and trailer were parked, but just then Tina leaned in the window and said, "Stay there. We're all gonna drive around and check out the carnival."

Sandy liked the sound of "all," but wasn't keen on running into the creep from the fortune teller's booth again.

Frank and Tina got in on either side, laughing and talking about Louise's crazy stunt to break up the fight. Sandy was picturing herself strolling through the carnival beside L. Ray, maybe even going on a ride with him, which was sweetened by the thought she might even point out the creep who tricked her, watch him turn tail and run off at the sight of a real man who wasn't afraid to stand up for a respectable female.

The car lurched over the top of the embankment and headed for the gate out to the parking lot. Sandy, rocking back and forth where she was sitting on the edge of the seat, said, "For a race car driver, you're sure poking along."

He and Tina looked at her and then grinned at each other. Tina said, "Well, somebody sure must like carnivals."

"Well, who doesn't," said Sandy, scooting back in the seat and trying to get control of her emotions as she scanned the traffic for L. Ray's rig.

CHAPTER 26

The carnival looked a lot more inviting with all the tents up and crowds moving through the fairway. The booths were packed with every kind of trinket and stuffed toy imaginable in all the colors of a 64-count crayon box. Rides were accompanied by galloping organ music in counterpoint to the raucous voices of barkers encouraging passersby to try out their skills and win valuable prizes.

Buddy and Louise had already met up with L. Ray and others of the racing crowd at the barbeque stand. Sandy was too keyed up at first to think about food, but by the time the men were washing down their pulled-pork sandwiches and curly fries with their beers, she had accepted half of Tina's sandwich and was accepting the fries L. Ray offered her, dipping them into the pool of ketchup on his paper plate. Her right arm and his left arm bumped twice in the tight quarters, but neither of them said excuse me.

"I'm tired," said Buddy. "I think I'll enjoy the action from here."

"No way, Jose," Louise said, getting up and throwing their plates and cups into a nearby trashcan. "Come on, Lover Boy. You can lean on me."

He shook his head and pushed himself up, then draped one arm over Louise's shoulders and said, "Well, come on, then. Let's see what kind of trouble you can get me into." Tina and Sandy strolled along behind them with Frank and L. Ray bringing up the rear. Frank saw Sandy crank her neck at a candied apple stand as they passed, and handed her a five-dollar bill. "Here," he said, "You need to have some walking around money."

"Thanks," she said. It was a strange and satisfying sensation, having walking-around money from her very own male parent, and she was eager to complete the transaction with a purchase. She hurried back to the small stand with one red and one brown apple painted on it, selected a gooey, caramel-covered apple, and ran to catch up with the others. Buddy was saying he wanted to go someplace and sit down for a spell.

"I know just the place," Louise said, and led them all to a self-photo booth. L. Ray walked up beside Sandy and tapped her on the arm. "You forgot this." He handed her the pack of Juicy Fruit gum. She took it, then looked up at his profile as they walked. His presence dwarfed and muted the scene around them into a backdrop to the main event of their being together. He turned to look at her. "You gonna eat all that?" he asked.

She held the bitten-into caramel apple out to him. "Help yourself."

"I usually do." He grinned at her, then took hold of her wrist as he pulled the apple up and took a bite out of it.

Sandy was so intent on watching his chewing and licking the caramel from his lips that she stepped on Tina's heel. She stopped to watch as Louise ducked into the booth and pulled Buddy in after her, the black curtain flapping as they positioned themselves. Tina pulled the curtain open to reveal Louise with her arms around Buddy's neck and her head leaning close to his, and said, "You two comfy in there?"

"Like two bugs in a rug," Louise said.

"So put the damn quarters in," Buddy growled.

Tina dropped the curtain back into place, and called out, "Don't do anything we wouldn't do," hooking her arm through Frank's. "That doesn't leave much, does it!" She laughed lightly until he jerked his arm and told her to cut it out.

She looked at him as if he couldn't be serious, but the scowl on his face convinced her otherwise. Glancing over at Sandy and L. Ray, she said, "I was just kidding."

Frank said, "I don't like that kind of kidding."

She released his arm and said, "Well, excuse me, if you can't take a joke." More quietly, she asked, "Are you still sore from the wreck?"

Frank looked away and said, "Just drop it."

That brought a look of controlled anger to Tina's face that Sandy had seen twice before, once when Parker had been complaining about Frank's driving, and once at the garage where Frank had complained about Tina's wearing shorts and a halter top while joking around with the other guys there, fooling around as if she was a green kid. Her reply—that there was nothing wrong with the way she dressed and that she was a kid, just tougher and smarter than most—had put an end to the conversation but not the disagreement. Sandy had been fascinated by the red splotches that had blossomed on Tina's cheeks and the way her eyebrows had stayed slightly raised for what had seemed like a long time.

"Listen," Tina told him, "don't take it out on me just because Parker's being an ass. This damned Grand National is making everybody crazy, if you ask me."

"I didn't."

Buddy climbed out of the photo booth first, followed by Louise holding a thin strip of pictures. He looked over her shoulder and said, "Waste of two bits. Don't even look like us."

"Course they do," Louise said. "It'd been a lot better if you'd cooperated and smiled once. What a baby."

"You wouldn't stop squirmin' around trying for this pose and that."

Louise handed the pictures to Sandy, who said she liked the third one best. Louise, combing the hair at the nape of her neck back up with her fingers, took another look and said, "You think? I'm turned too much there. Makes my nose look a foot long."

"I think your nose looks fine," Sandy told her, "and Buddy's almost smiling in that one."

"You can keep 'em," Louise told her, "for a souvenir. I'm going to pour a couple more beers down him and try it again."

Buddy agreed that the beers were a good idea, but said he'd be darned if he'd cram himself into that torture chamber again. They spotted a place with a bottle of Coors on the sign and wooden picnic tables out in front and said they'd be over there.

L. Ray clamped his hand around the back of Sandy's neck and said, "Come on. Let's go find some action."

Sandy looked over at Frank and Tina, who seemed to have gotten past their spat, and the four of them headed into the arcade where the games of chance were lined up. Sandy and Tina stopped at the Bust

'Em booth and tossed darts at balloons that slipped this way and that as the darts skimmed past them. They each popped two out of six.

"Didn't even finish in the money," Sandy said, causing Frank and L. Ray to laugh.

Tina, who still seemed a little subdued, said, "I guess it's up to these big, strong men to win us some prizes."

"Yeah, let's let the men do it," Sandy said, copying Tina's tone so it was a playful challenge, but inside she was jumping up and down at the thought of leaving the carnival with a prize won for her by L. Ray.

"All right, Farm Boy, we've got our marching orders," Frank said, leading them over to the shooting range booth, where the object was to clear the red-dot eye out of a cardboard turkey.

"Right behind ya, Old Man," L. Ray said.

They put down two quarters each and lifted the rifles to their shoulders. Sandy saw that the guns had short plastic cords securing them to the counter. She grinned at Tina and glanced at the crowd that had gathered, race fans, some of them, coming to see the drivers up close. The guns popped loudly as they unloaded the pellets at the turkeys. She studied the cards at the back of the booth as the worker walked back to get them. He pulled them down and called out, "Close but no cigar." She watched as he hooked up two fresh cards and then headed back to the counter. Her stomach did a roll and she took a step back as the worker she'd fought off at the fortune teller's booth handed the cards to the shooters. He was looking from the cards to Sandy and back again, a slight smirk on his face.

"What are you talking about?" Frank asked him. L. Ray had taken out a little over half of the red dot, but Frank's looked as if it was all gone. Frank held the card up. "That eye is plumb out."

"Nope," the man said. "S'gotta be clean through." He was half-smiling, and when he looked over at Sandy again, she could see in his eyes that he was enjoying himself at her expense.

"Take another look," Frank said, still sounding reasonable but with an edge in his voice. "There's nothing but a hole there."

The carney took the card and studied it, then took his fingernails and plucked some of the fuzzy edge of the hole back into it and pointed. "I see some red there."

Frank looked the worker in the eye, then pulled out two more quarters and stepped up to a loaded gun. The crowd around them had grown considerably, but Sandy's attention was riveted on the worker, standing to the side with his eyes mostly cast down, a thin smile on his face. She started to ask if they could just go, but suddenly Frank unloaded the rifle, and there were cheers as the red disappeared from the new card. He laid down the gun, smiled at L. Ray, looked around at the crowd, and said, "If that's not clean through, I'll eat the damn thing."

The carney walked back up with the card, peering at the hole and testing the edge with his fingernails again. He held it up shaking his head and pointing to what might or might not have been a strand of pink fuzz.

"Bullshit!" L. Ray said. "What kinda gyp joint is this!"

There were shouts from people standing around as well, saying, "Give him his prize," and "This place is a rook, Frankie. Get your money back!"

Smiling, Frank leaned across the counter and took the card, studied it, then reached out with his left hand and clasped the carney by the back of his neck, pulling him forward so that their noses were inches apart. The worker tried to jerk away but Frank also had a handful of his shirt that twisted around in front of the man's chest as Frank held him there, still smiling with his lips. "Now listen, son, let's be reasonable. You know that both shots were right on target. You just let my girl pick out a prize, and we'll get on out of your hair."

The carney cut his eyes to Sandy and said, "Yeah, well I don't think we have anything special enough for that little prick tease, so you can just get the hell on outta here before there's trouble."

Frank's smile disintegrated into a scowl, and all at once he was shoving the cardboard turkey into the carney's mouth, saying, "You punk. Where do you get off saying something like that!"

The carney got his face turned sideways and spit out some the paper tinged with blood and screamed, "Rube!"

Frank shoved him backwards and let go, the carney sprawling on the ground. L. Ray called out, "Oh shit!" just before he cocked his right fist and drove it into the face of one of the other carnival workers who had rushed up to them ready to fight.

Frank yelled, "You girls get out of here now! Get to the car and lock the doors!"

Sandy could hear the word "Rube!" echoing all around them as other carnies took up the war cry and came tearing in from all directions, some of them carrying boards and swinging chains.

Sandy screamed, "Stop! Stop it!" but only got bounced around in the crush of the race crowd and carnival workers getting caught up in a free for all.

She turned toward the outer edge and pulled her way toward it with whatever scrap of cloth or body part she could grab, twisting through openings when men who were wrestling with each other staggered or tumbled to one side or one got knocked down. She was almost clear of the mob when she tripped over someone on the ground and reached out to keep herself from falling. She caught a glimpse of a fist, and suddenly her head exploded. She instinctively squeezed her eyes shut, little white sparks shimmering behind her eyelids. She was surprised to still be upright when she finally got her eyes open again, then realized that she was too socked in to fall down. She thought she heard Frank's voice say, "Come on!" and she felt a hand clasp her arm and pull her forward. She leapt over two men rolling around on the ground and sprinted for the car, Frank right behind her. Rocks shot past them and skimmed alongside, but none hit her.

Tina had the car doors open and engine running and was yelling at them to hurry up. Sandy climbed into the backseat, Frank telling her to stay down as he slid into the driver's seat and took off toward the street exit. Sandy peeked through the back window and saw two men still heaving rocks in their direction, one pinging off the car as Frank pulled out around the line of cars snaking out of the speedway and cut in at the street, horns honking behind them as they took off for the motel.

Sandy's eyes were watering, but she didn't think she was crying. She'd been too excited for that.

"Everyone okay?" Frank asked.

Tina said, "What in the Sam Hill was that all about?"

"Damned if I know," Frank said, checking his rearview mirror for anyone following them. "Crazy fool!" At one point, his eyes met Sandy's and he frowned, but then looked back at the road.

Two police cars with sirens on passed them going the other way, and Frank said, "We need to get out to the motel and lay low until this blows over."

"What in the hell got into that bunch," Tina said, looking behind them to see if they were being followed while Frank opened and closed his right hand to see if he'd damaged it.

Sandy leaned her aching head back against the seat and fingered her right cheek and jaw, which were tender and felt swollen. Now that they were safe, she began to shake. She wondered if she'd have a big bruise and what her aunt would say if she found out she'd been in a fight. Started it, actually, though it hadn't really been her fault. She kept telling herself that as they rode back to the motel in silence, parked the car around back, and went in without turning on the lights.

The words the carney had spit at Frank kept repeating in his head, causing the anger to resurge. "Either of you know that guy from before?" he asked, peeking through the curtain to see if they'd been followed.

"Are you kiddin'," Tina asked, sitting down on the bed. Then said, "Why?"

It was quiet except for the restless shifting of bodies in the darkened room.

"He said something that made it sound like he thought he knew one of you."

"Which one?" Tina asked.

"Doesn't matter. Damn, I wish Buddy would get his butt over here with the camper and tell me what happened after we got out of there. You two pack up so we'll be ready to pull out as soon as he gets here."

"I can't see where anything is," Tina said. "Why can't we turn on the lights?"

"Just wait. I want to make sure there's no one out there."

A moment later the glow of a red light slipped in around the drapes and was followed by a firm knock on the door that caused all of them to jump. "Open up. Police."

"Shit!" said Frank. "You two get over there and sit down. Keep quiet."
He flipped on the light and opened the door.

"Frank Haggard?" the policeman asked.

"Yes?"

"I need you to come with me to the station. There's some questions
we need to ask you."

"If it's about that ruckus over at the track, I did not start that. Those
carnies got way outta line."

"We just want to ask you some questions," he repeated, reaching
down and pulling Frank's right hand up, examining the knuckles.

Frank looked out at the squad car and saw another officer leaning
there, watching them.

"Look, I didn't start the trouble."

"Yes, sir, that's what some of the others involved said, but there's a
carnival worker who's had his eye popped out of the socket, and you
need to come in and answer some questions. Now."

"Can I drive my car?"

"You can ride with us, Sir."

Frank walked over and handed his keys to Tina, then put his hand
on Sandy's shoulder and gave her a look that made her stomach churn.
He asked quietly, "You got anything to tell me?" He studied her face,
the darkening eye and swollen cheek, and said, "Oh, wow."

She considered how much trouble she would be in if they found
out she'd gone onto the fairgrounds with the carnival worker and
whether they'd believe her that she hadn't meant to lead him on. She
turned her head to the side and back to the center to indicate she had
nothing to say.

"Tina," he said, "Get some ice on this for her. Please." If Buddy
shows up, tell him where I've gone and to park the rig around back of
the motel for tonight." He suspected there was something Sandy wasn't
telling him, but wasn't sure how it might matter. "Be sure to get some
ice on that and keep the door locked."

After the men left, Tina said, "Good grief, what happened to your
face, girl?" She got the ice bucket and headed for the door. "What was
Frank talking to you about?"

Sandy just shrugged and opened her suitcase on the bed, then went into the bathroom to gather up her shampoo and cosmetics. She called over her shoulder, "What if the carnival people find us before Frank and Buddy show up?"

"They won't," Tina assured her, but she scanned the lot before going to the ice machine, listening carefully for the sounds of tires in the gravel lot.

CHAPTER 27

When Frank returned to the motel a little after 11:00, the girls were groggy but still awake with worry. Tina sat across from him at the small round table and asked how bad it was. She and Sandy were relieved to know the police had discovered the carney's eye had been popped out by one of his own swinging a chain.

"So it's over then?" Sandy asked. "Nothing to worry about?"

Not from the cops. They hinted the judge might still ask for a hearing tomorrow, suggested I might want to pay a fine of fifty dollars on the spot and hightail it out of town by first light."

"Those crooks!" Tina said. "So there went the winnings, right?"

Frank made a sound between a grunt and a laugh. "And then some."

"Are we safe here now?" Sandy asked, the memory of rocks thumping the back of the Mercury still vivid in her mind at least.

"Yeah," Frank reassured her. "I'm thinking this town's done its worst. Best get some sleep and an early start home to Hutch."

Sandy crawled into bed and gingerly fingered the bruise on her jaw. She thought about what Frank said. They were going home, to his home, in Hutchinson. Nobody had said boo about Kiowa lately. She would need to check in with her Aunt Maggie soon. She was probably starting to get worried.

$\bullet \quad \bullet \quad \bullet \quad \bullet \quad \bullet$

A sound like a sticky valve woke Buddy just as he'd finally gotten to sleep over the cab of the truck. He called out, "Hey! Who the hell's trying to break in?"

Frank, who had just settled into a restless sleep himself, sat up and groped around in the dark until he found his pants. Half expecting more trouble from the carnival, he pushed the door open abruptly, banging it against the hand of the woman who was preparing to knock again.

The only light was coming from the motel and the pale wash of moonlight behind gauzy clouds. Frank pushed his hair back and squinted down at the woman, who was sucking on the scraped knuckle of her index finger.

"Frank? Frank Haggard?"

He squinted at her "Who's askin'?"

"I …. " She shifted her feet in a maneuver that carried her back a step without it seeming to be an actual retreat. "I know it's late, but I just found out from the police that you were staying here, and, well, I'm trying to find someone."

He flicked the edge of his nails across the bristles on his cheek with one hand and stepped down onto the step to get a better look. Her hair was darker, but the resemblance to her younger sister as well as to Sandy took the wind out of him.

She gazed at him steadily. "You don't remember me, do you?" When he didn't answer, she said, "It's been a long time."

Frank stepped down from the camper and let the door close behind him, its snap eliciting a curse from Buddy.

"I had quite a time finding you. You live pretty much a gypsy's existence, don't you?" The tone of her voice kept it from being a real question. In fact, to Frank, it sounded like a cold appraisal.

"Doesn't sound like you came by for an autograph."

The woman took in a deep breath and let it out in a rush. "My name is Maggie Parson. You were married to my sister. Briefly."

She waited, but when he didn't respond, she added, "About fifteen years ago." When he still didn't respond, she said, "You do remember that, right?" with just the slightest hint of sarcasm.

He hadn't answered because memories—welcome and unwelcome—were whirling through his head like dust devils. It might have been a trick of the dark or just his imagination, but he felt as if he would have recognized Maggie's voice blindfolded. But the last time she'd spoken to him had been when she had called the motel the night Ruth had been taken away. She'd spoken in a whisper, and at first he'd thought it was Ruth, hoped it was. Until she'd said, "Please don't come after my sister. It will be better for everyone if you just stay away." He'd heard a man's angry voice in the background, and then the dial tone of a broken connection.

Frank leaned back against the camper, his arms folded across his bare chest, which was rising and falling in shallow breaths. "Just what is it you want?"

She raised her chin and opened her mouth in preface to speaking, but hesitated, as if not certain how to proceed. She glanced over her shoulder to where a dark blue Pontiac was parked, and smoothed her skirt unnecessarily before turning back around. "I'm looking for someone. A girl." Again, she hesitated.

"Anyone I know?"

"I'm not sure," she said.

"Then it wouldn't be your sister we're talkin' about."

"My—no. No. You mean Ruth. I don't suppose you would have heard. She died some years ago."

He looked down at his feet for a moment, his face all shadows. "Some years ago, you say?"

"Ten." His response to hearing of Ruth's death didn't have the impact she'd expected. "Here's the situation," she said in a more congenial tone. "I'm looking for a young girl."

He thought he saw her hand flutter slightly as she drew it across her forehead and down one cheek. "Hot night," he said, looking her up and down. "A lot of girls come to the races. How young is she? What's she look like? And why do you suppose I'd of seen her?" He could see Maggie was growing more uncomfortable under his steady gaze.

"Because she likes the races very much, and you know how kids are. They think that, because someone drives faster than someone else, he's a sort of a hero, something special."

"A fan, huh?" Frank uncrossed his arms and pushed off the camper. "Well, now, Maggie, you're wrong about me knowing about kids. I never had any, so I'll just have to take your word for it. Your word's good, isn't it, Maggie?"

He could see she hadn't liked the tone of his question from the way her eyebrows went from a worried furrow to arches. The look of suspicion was certainly familiar, more like the mother than Ruth.

She crossed her arms over her chest and gave her head a little shake. "You haven't changed much."

He awarded her a grim smile for her directness. Rocking back on his heels, he tucked his hands into his back pockets and asked, "What did you expect?"

"I'm not sure, exactly. I guess I thought a person might be able to have a conversation with you by now that might prove useful. No, I take that back." She squinted slightly, her gaze taking in his face. "You have changed. You're less impetuous now, more cynical perhaps."

"I think you're just telling yourself a story you want to hear."

"Have you seen her? Is she here?"

"I don't know what you're talking about, but there's no girl here. Wanna take a look inside?"

Her hands dropped to her sides. "You wouldn't help me if you could, isn't that right?"

"I don't know why not, Maggie. You sure took care of me. Hanging up. Not letting Ruth take my calls. Intercepting my letters, no doubt."

She hesitated for a beat, then said, "I called you that night so you would understand and stop trying to make trouble. I thought you had a right to know that Ruth hadn't just disappeared or—"

"But she did!" He took a step toward her as if to drive the point home, then said more softly, "She did just . . . disappear." He took his hands from his pockets and held them tight to his sides. "I'm not clear on exactly what it is you want from me, but I can tell you what I feel I owe you."

"That won't be necessary." Her words were clipped. "All you've ever given my family is grief. You just about ruined Ruth's life. I should have known better than to try to talk to you as if you were a responsible human being with ordinary decency." She spun around and started back toward her car.

As she opened the car door and got in, he called out, "Now maybe you Parsons will get out of my life for good!" He stood there for a few moments, thinking that actually he was about to become entangled with that family in a whole new and undoubtedly hurtful way. He scooped up some rocks, rolling them in his hand, and then flung them one after the other into the cloud of dust that was settling back over the lot as Maggie Parson drove away.

Climbing into the camper, Frank hung in the doorway while he waited for Buddy to walk back to the lower bunk.

"Hear all that?"

"Yep."

"Want a smoke?"

"Might as well," Buddy said. "Wide awake now."

Frank handed a cigarette to Buddy and lit it, then leaned back against the counter and lit one for himself.

Buddy blew smoke toward the window. "Seemed hotter out there than it is in here."

Frank started to respond, but nothing that came to mind seemed to match the intensity of his feelings.

"Think she knows you've got the kid?"

"Maybe. She sure as hell wasn't gonna volunteer any information herself."

Buddy climbed back up onto the bed and laid back. "How do you think she found us?"

"Hell. Sandy didn't have any trouble. We're public property."

"So, what are you gonna do? About Sandy, I mean."

Frank threw his cigarette butt through the door and pulled it shut before settling onto the lower bed.

"Sandy's a prize, all right," Buddy said. "Not the kind you're used to. Worth fighting for, but you'd better be sure what you're doin'."

Frank lay perfectly still, working his way backwards through fifteen years of anger and sorrow, caught up once more in an enigma that held Ruth at the center.

CHAPTER 28

DIRT-TRACKERS, CARNIES FINISH IN DEAD HEAT

Tempers flared and a fight erupted after last night's racing card at Liberal Speedway. Several hot-rod pilots took exception to the way the Liberty Carnival was being run.

An exchange of words and blows ballooned into a free-for-all that left a carnival worker named William Cobb with an injured left eye and several others with cuts and bruises.

Local police held four workers and three drivers for questioning before releasing them a few hours later. No formal charges were filed.

On Monday morning, Tina and Frank talked quietly by themselves before heading across the road to a convenience store with a pay phone.

"Well the hell," Frank said into the receiver. "You're the one's supposed to know about things like this," Frank said into the receiver. Tina stood with her index finger tucked into his belt loop as she leaned in to try to hear the other end of the conversation.

"Just let me know as soon as you get in touch with him," Frank said. "You can't call me back. I'll be in Hutch later."

Tina stepped back as he turned around. "What's he say?"

"Nothin'." Frank walked over to the cooler and bought a six pack of Budweiser, and Tina tossed a pack of beer nuts onto the counter. They walked outside to a picnic table where Frank popped the cap off a bottle with a church key hanging from his key chain and drained a third of it before sitting down.

"Chester doesn't think he'll find anything out today," Frank said. "He has to talk to another attorney in Hutch who knows about custody laws and abuse cases, and that guy's in court all day."

"What'll you do in the meantime?"

"Keep her out of sight until I'm sure the barracuda's gone back to Kiowa."

Tina said, "I realize you're upset. So am I. But a beer breakfast?"

"What are you, my mother?" he said.

She tore the sack of beer nuts open with her teeth.

"Don't do that," he snapped at her.

"Don't take your bad mood out on me," she snapped back.

"You'll ruin your teeth."

"They're my teeth. What are you, my father?"

He gave her a hard look. "It that supposed to be funny?"

"Will you lighten up? Just . . . just stop being so crabby." She waited until he'd taken another swallow of beer and asked, "What's she look like, anyway?"

"I don't know."

"Bullshit."

"It was dark."

She turned the opening of the sack toward him. "Eat something." When he didn't take any, she shrugged and took the nuts back, popping them into her mouth one at a time and tapping her fingernails to the rhythm of the music coming from the jukebox. "How old would you say she is?"

"How the hell would I know?"

"She's your wife's sister. Didn't you talk about things like that when you were married?"

"We weren't married that long."

"When you were dating, then."

He looked at her. "Why you harpin' on this?"

She thought for a moment. "Why not? Seems to be the subject at hand."

Ignoring the question, Frank stood up and drained the last of his beer. "Let's go," he said, starting across the street as she scrambled after him.

·   ·   ·   ·   ·

Clouds created a cotton-candy sky and kept the sun from shining into their eyes as they headed toward Hutchinson, but Frank was still squinting as if the road ahead were a puzzle he was trying to piece together, and driving faster than Tina was comfortable with.

She was the first to see the series of Burma Shave signs looming in the distance and pointed them out to Sandy who sat forward, resting her chin on the top of the seat between Frank and her. The girls read together, their voices flat as the land stretched out in billowy waves of wheat on either side of them. "The Hero . . . was brave and strong . . . and willin'. . . she felt his chin . . . then wed the villain . . . Burma Shave."

Sandy sprawled back against her seat and recited the first three signs just under her breath, smiling to herself. It was just a silly ad, but still—it could be significant. She wanted to ask if L. Ray would be at the memorial race Wednesday in Wichita, but didn't want to get teased about it.

The second time Frank sped up to get around a car on the two-lane road , cutting it close as a car shot past them in the opposite direction, Tina looked over and said, "Will you slow down!"

Hot air was whipping through the car, stirring up the dirt and scraps of paper on the floor and twisting their hair around. Sandy who had been passing the time counting herds of cattle and watching for more Burma Shave signs, had enjoyed the sharp sway from side to side, but clearly Tina hadn't. Sandy listened to their silence for several miles, wishing one of them would say something. She finally spotted a series of signs extending the other side of a large hump in the road where railroad tracks crossed.

Right after the tracks, the road made a jog to the right, and there were four peeling white crosses stuck in the ground indicating four people had died there. Frank didn't slow for the rise or the curve, and the sudden drop just past the tracks made Sandy's stomach do a roll, and her head bounce off the window frame as she leaned half out the window and read under her breath, "Don't leave safety . . . To mere chance . . . That's why . . . Belts are . . . Sold with pants . . . Burma Shave."

She leaned back against the seat and closed her eyes, her mouth dry as cotton and her bladder starting to send out signals. Sandy felt the car swerve left and accelerate.

"Holy moly!"

The alarm in Tina's voice caused Sandy's eyes to pop open and she stared down her nose at the car coming at them as Frank sped up even more to pass a pickup truck rattling with milk cans. As soon as they swerved back across the white line, Sandy began counting, "one-thousand-one, one-thousand-two, one-thousand-three, one-thousand-four, one-thousand-five," until the car shot by them in the opposite direction. It hadn't been as close as it seemed, but Sandy could see that didn't matter to Tina, who was glaring at Frank.

He looked over at her casually, saying, "Never realized you were a religious woman." He had stressed the word *woman*, and Sandy quickly looked over to see if Tina had picked up on it. She had.

"There's a lot you don't know, apparently."

"Is that so?" he said.

"And at your age, I find it somewhat amazing and very disappointing."

Frank's jaw flexed, but no one said another word until they got to Greensburg, where Frank announced that they would make a rest stop.

For miles, billboards had been inviting them to stop and see the "World's Largest Hand-Dug Well." As Frank drove through town, Sandy cranked her neck to look back down the street where a big red arrow with a painting of a well on it was pointing. "Can we go look at it?"

No one responded, and Sandy wondered whether Frank and Tina could have completely missed the barrage of signs leading up to what was surely the biggest tourist attraction in western Kansas.

"Didn't you see the signs for the big well? The Largest Hand—"

"Yeah," Frank cut her off, and got yet another piercing glare from Tina. Sandy wondered if it was hard to stay mad that long, and felt some admiration for Tina being able to carry it off. He gave in to the silent pressure, saying, "I imagine they'll have bathrooms."

He swung the car around in a U-turn and drove back along the tree-lined residential street to where the well sat, a roof over it and a curio shop behind.

For a hole in the ground it was impressive. It looked like a person could park a car in it if he could get it down in there. Sandy read the marker aloud, "Built in 1887 at a cost of $45,000, the world's largest hand-dug well, at 109 feet deep and 32 feet in diameter." There were even black metal steps spiraling down to the bottom, which was bone dry, and where there looked to be a cat lying on its side.

Sandy watched for a moment in spite of the strong need to go into the shop and find the bathroom, but the cat didn't move. She picked up a small pebble and let it drop to the bottom. She couldn't tell if the cat's tail moved slightly or it was just wishful thinking.

The souvenir stand was a frame two-story house with the living and dining room converted into a store front. Sandy made her way toward the restrooms sign at the back wondering how the cat had managed to take such a tumble, and why no one had removed it. The more she thought about it, the more apparent it seemed to her that no cat would be stupid enough to take a leap into a well like that. Especially with steps going down.

Someone must have tossed it in—probably some stupid boys, trying to see if it would land on its feet. The idea of it made her feel a rush of indignation. How could such a thing go untended at what was probably a national monument, a place where dozens of little kids might see the cat and maybe have bad dreams or, worse yet, get bad ideas about the possible uses for cats?

By the time she was out of the bathroom, there was a family of five wandering from display to display, fingering the wooden signs with funny sayings burned into them and holding up Indian bead necklaces and leather pouches for one another to see. Frank was standing in the doorway, smoking a cigarette while Tina held up a t-shirt that said, "I dig the big well, Greensburg, Kansas."

140

Sandy stepped up to the counter with the cash register on it and said to the woman standing behind it, "Excuse me, did you know that there's a cat in your well?"

"Yep."

Sandy and the woman stood there looking at each other.

"It's just lying there," said Sandy.

"That's 'cause it's dead."

"Are you sure?"

"If it weren't, it'd climb back out."

"But what if it's only injured? Or sick? Aren't you going to do anything about it?"

"Nothin' *to* do."

"But . . . ." Sandy looked around the room, and saw the others looking at her and talking among themselves.

The clerk moved down the counter towards the woman shopper who was holding several small souvenirs and postcards in one hand and digging through her purse with the other. "You wanna go get it," the clerk said over her shoulder, "the well's open. Cost ya a dollar. Pays for the upkeep of the stairs."

Sandy looked over at Frank and said, "I'm going to go down and get it."

She could see by his expression that he didn't favor the idea. "Hold up. You're not going down there."

"It's only a dollar. I'll use my own money."

Tina had come over and stood halfway between them. "What do you need a dollar for?"

Frank said, "Forget it. Now let's get back on the road."

Ignoring Frank, Tina repeated her question to Sandy, who told her about wanting to go get the cat out of the well. Tina turned to Frank and said, "You hold up. If it's important to Sandy, you ought to let her do it."

The set of his jaw warned that he wasn't interested in Tina's opinion. "You mind your own business. Now get on out to the car, both of you." Frank stepped through the door, the screen slapping closed behind him.

His anger had been spiraling up all morning like the metal stairs inside the well, and it came from so many dark places, he didn't know where to direct it. And Parker's digs about his maybe not being up for the Grand National and Tina's harping about his driving kept the bile stirred up.

Sandy trailed Tina to the car where Frank was grinding out his cigarette with his shoe.

"Hey," said Tina, "who died and made you the king of the world?"

Frank gave her a hard look. "You can't rescue a dead animal, you idiot!"

Sandy, who had been standing by the car, said, "Let's just go."

"I'm the idiot? That's rich coming from you." The red splotches in Tina's cheeks were in full bloom.

Frank pointed his finger at her. "Listen to me. No one's going down into that well. That cat has probably been there for days. It for certain has maggots by now and is probably diseased to boot."

"Some big shot," said Tina, "afraid of a dead cat. Can't you see how upset she is?"

Sandy looked at them both and said, "Just stop it. I'm not that upset. Really, let's—"

"Why don't you try being a hero off the track for a change? She's your daughter, for Pete's sake."

"I don't need you to tell me that." He slapped both palms down against the trunk of the car and leaned there, shifting his weight from one leg to another. Then without looking at either of them, he walked around and yanked open the car door on the driver's side and said, "We're leaving. Now get into the car and try to keep your mouth from flapping for the next hundred miles."

Sandy quietly opened the back door on the passenger side and stood there looking at Tina, who was taking a long measure of Frank.

"You're more of a fool than I thought, Frank Haggard, talking like that in front of her. I don't know what's come over you, but I don't like it. Give me the keys."

"What for?"

"I need to get in the trunk."

He handed her the car keys and watched her in the side-view mirror as she walked back to the trunk and opened it, and when she slammed it down again, Sandy saw a suitcase sitting on the ground. Tina walked over to him and held out the keys, dropping them into his open hand and pausing, as if waiting for him to say something. "I used to think you really were some kind of hero," Tina said. "But you're not." When he didn't say anything, she said, "I'll tell you what you are. You're just some guy drivin' fast circles in the middle of nowhere, trying to prove he's not yesterday's news."

Frank and Sandy watched as she picked up her bag and walked back toward the souvenir store. Frank motioned for Sandy to get in while he started the car, turning it around and slowing to a creep as they pulled alongside Tina, but she wouldn't look over, instead cutting across to the door of the shop and disappearing inside.

Peeling out, Frank took off around the corner and down the street toward the highway.

"Stop," Sandy said, "You can't just leave her there!"

"I didn't leave her. She's the one who left."

"'Cause she's angry. You don't just go off and leave someone stranded."

Frank took a deep breath and slapped his hands against the steering wheel as he slowed and made a U-turn.

CHAPTER 29

As soon as Frank stopped the car back in the parking lot at the World's Largest Hand-dug Well, Sandy jumped out and ran inside to convince Tina to come with them. Frank stayed in the car and lit a cigarette, wondering how things had gotten so messed up. If he could just keep his cool until they got to Hutchinson, then they could sort things out.

Sandy appeared at the door and shook her head to indicate Tina wasn't there. He motioned for her to get back in the car. They looked up and down the cross streets as they headed back toward the highway, but there was no sign of her. Sandy, who had gotten into the back seat from habit, rode in silence, turning around to peer out the back window every few seconds as if Tina would suddenly materialize behind them, until they were several miles down the road. She thought of her Aunt Maggie and wished she'd called her from the well.

As they approached Pratt, there were signs for Highway 281, the turn-off for Kiowa. Sandy thought of getting Frank to stop so she could get out at the turn. She wouldn't have any trouble getting rides south. She decided that she would wait until they were almost into town and ask him to stop at a filling station. Then she could walk off the way Tina had, until he drove on without her too. Tears pooled in her eyes, and she knew that as soon as she blinked they would pour out, and he'd know something was up. If she ran off and he called the police, maybe she would get into trouble. Ralph would have to hide her in his shed until she could figure what to do. She stared ahead, forcing herself not to blink, and willing her eyes to dry.

"You okay back there?" Frank's question caught her off-guard, and she didn't answer.

"Sandy? Are you all right?" He turned around briefly to look at her. "You still worried about that cat?"

Her voice cracked when she answered "No," and she coughed to disguise a sob that slipped out.

"Oh shit," he murmured under his breath, then only slightly louder said, "Don't do that. Please don't . . . ."

Slowing down, he pulled over onto the shoulder, the car listing to the right and rocking slightly before he cut the engine. They sat there for a while as cars passed by in both directions. Then he got out and went around to the passenger side, where he stood looking out over the field. If he had any sense, he would take Sandy back to her aunt and admit that she and Tina were complications he needed like a hole in the head just days before the big race.

"Sandy? I'm sorry." He turned around and leaned down to look in at her. "Think you'll stop crying any time soon?"

Even as she was nodding her head yes, her lips, which had been pinched shut, parted and let out ragged little sobs. Everything seemed to have spun out of control.

He opened the door. "Come on. Let's get out for a minute and stretch. You've covered a lot of miles in three days."

She scooted forward to slip out past him and stood on the side of the road, staring out at the cows heading toward them just other side of the fence.

"You worried about Tina?" he asked.

She sniffed and cleared her throat. "Aren't you?"

"Yeah. But there wasn't much I could do. You saw that."

Sandy looked up at him, shading her eyes with her hand. He had his hands in his pockets and was looking toward the cows. "You didn't even try to make her come back."

Frank sighed heavily and nodded his head slightly to acknowledge the truth of what she'd said, then looked at her. "She knew I didn't want her to leave like that. But she had the right to walk."

She squinted at him. "Walk home?"

"Walk away."

Sandy thought about that for a minute. "Me too?"

He looked surprised. "I guess so. That's what you did last Friday morning, isn't it?"

She shrugged and walked down into the ditch and back up the other side to the fence, placing her hands carefully between the barbs along the wire and pulling on it to feel its tension while she thought about that.

Frank called after her, "That the only reason you were crying?" When she didn't answer or turn around, he sat down on the mowed shoulder and lit a cigarette. "If it's not, we can talk about it."

She called back, without turning her head, "Nothing to talk about."

"Maybe. Maybe not. All this has been kinda sudden for you too, you know."

Turning around, she frowned at him. "What do you mean?"

"Well, until four days ago, we hadn't even met. We still don't know each other very well. Is that fair to say?"

"I suppose so." She thought about sitting down, but her Bermuda shorts were no protection against the uncut buffalo grass laced with cockleburs along the fence line.

"Tina may be right in her assessment of me." Frank's head was down, and he seemed to be talking to himself. When he looked up, his gaze seemed to go right through her.

"You're not that old, and you're one of the best race car drivers who ever lived."

He smiled at her. "Well, I might be gettin' old for racing with this crowd. Lot of young punks itching to get past me. But true, I've won my share and then some." His voice was so low, Sandy could barely hear him. "Without that, there wouldn't be much to me."

Taking long strides, she crossed back over to the shoulder and sat down beside him.

He flicked ash off his cigarette. "The way I see it, we could use us a little time to get to know one another." He took a drag on his cigarette. "You agree, or do you have a better plan?"

She looked up, a faint smile beginning. "I guess that's an okay plan. Can we call Aunt Maggie soon so she won't worry?"

"Yeah. Once we get some things straightened out."

"What things?"

"Grown up things. We better get back on the road." He stood up and held out his hands for her to grab onto. "Buddy will be wondering what happened to us. We've got a lot to do in the next five days."

Sandy rode in the front seat, watching the passing scene with renewed interest. She felt excitement coursing through her as they sped eastward toward Hutchinson. They didn't talk much, but he let her pick the station they listened to on the radio, and they sang along with some of the songs, Frank trying a harmony part to "So Lonesome I Could Die" that caused Sandy to get the giggles.

When the song ended, she turned the radio down and asked, "Did you and my mother ever sing together?"

"I don't remember."

"She used to sing to me at night. I still remember that pretty well. And she sang in the kitchen." When Frank didn't say anything, she started humming "You Belong to Me," one of the songs she remembered her mother singing while working at the sink or breadboard. By the second chorus, Frank was humming along softly, and Sandy launched into an extra chorus to keep him going. With her dad all to herself, she didn't think of Tina again, or the turn-off to her Aunt Maggie's house, until she saw the sign for Hutchinson city limits.

CHAPTER 30

After they unloaded their things at Frank's two-bedroom house, he and Sandy went to the nearby garage where Buddy had 65 up on a rack. Sandy helped out by handing him tools and small parts, and eventually she was under the car herself, holding a wrench tight and directing the work light so Buddy could see around and under things.

Buddy loosened the wrench he was working with and handed it to Sandy to place on the workbench. "You're good help. You pay attention." He handed her a small cylinder that was covered with grease. "Think you can brush some solvent on there and clean it up for me?" He pointed to a glass jar with a brush in it.

"Sure."

"Don't splash any in your eyes."

She sighed audibly. "I'm not a child, you know."

"I pretty much figured."

She walked over and stood next to him. "Frank said I can phone my aunt this afternoon. He needs to do something first. You know, he doesn't seem to remember my mother at all. He hasn't even asked how she died." She dropped her head, and tears came together along her upper lip.

Buddy wiped his hands on a rag and put his arm around her shoulder. "Come on now. You're gettin' yourself all worked up for nothin'. You're still here, aren't you?"

She sniffed loudly, and nodded.

"And you're wrong about him not remembering your mom. When you get to know him better, you'll see how he carries the important things real deep inside." He handed her the rag. "Here, now, dry your eyes. You're gonna get salt on everything, and then you know what happens?"

"What?"

"We have to eat it."

She laughed at that, more a gust of relief, but she did start to feel better. She used his rag to dry her face, leaving greasy streaks on her cheeks.

Buddy patted her on the back. "That's better." He held out the bearing and brush and showed her how to work the solvent around, and said that after it was good and soaked she should wipe it clean with a rag. She cleaned and polished vigorously, then held it up and asked, "Is this clean enough?"

"Like new. You're gettin' to be a real little grease monkey. Get you a set of overalls, and you can really go to town."

She wrinkled her nose at the suggestion. "I think I prefer jeans, thanks just the same. But I would look pretty official in a racing jacket. Don't you think so?" She grinned at him and pointed at what looked like a high school letter jacket hanging on a peg.

"Think so, huh? Well, I think mine might be a little big for you, but you're free to try it out, as long as you can stand the heat."

Wiping her hands as hard as she could on the rag first, she took down the satiny blue jacket with white trim and held it up so she could see the back. Black and white thread spelled out "81 Speedway," with the Bardahl Oil Company trademark in a black and white circle just below it. On the front, it said "Buddy Baehr" and "Parker Special, High Points, 1956." She put one arm in, pulling several times to get the opening for her hand to stay up, and then put the other one in. Immediately, both arms of the jacket fell straight down again, so she worked her hands through again and rolled the sleeves until they were bulky enough to stay up. Then she picked up a baseball cap that was lying on a stack of tires and put it on, tucking her hair up into it. She struck a pose like a model and turned slowly in front of Buddy, who chuckled and gave her the "okay" sign. She sauntered around the garage, then walked by the office to look around. She thought that there might be a girly calendar of some interest, but there were just tacked up jokes and hand-scrawled notes. There was a cartoon taped to a closed door of a guy sitting on a toilet, reading a newspaper with the words "The job's not over till the paperwork is done."

Frank was still talking on the phone, so she wandered over to the large overhead doors that were open and looked around the lot and the field beyond. A lot of evening traffic was moving on the streets, and the gas station across the road was full. She squinted, trying to see what kind of gum-ball machines they had over there. The one at the garage had lots of peanutty stuff and mints but no gum or jawbreakers.

She walked to the curb, waiting for some cars to pass. She started across, and then jumped back at the sound of a horn as more cars swept by. Finally, she saw an opening coming and got ready to lope across. Suddenly she stepped back up onto the curb. Directly across from her, Maggie's blue Pontiac pulled away from the pumps and into the street. Sandy watched as Maggie reached for the sunglasses she always left tucked up in the sun visor. She felt her aunt's eyes flicker over her and shivered, as if eyelashes had brushed her cheek, like the butterfly kisses they used to exchange when she was little, but the car kept moving down the street, the license tag gradually growing fuzzier, until it was too far away to be made out if you hadn't already memorized the number.

"Here you are," Frank said from the office door of the garage. "Didn't recognize you at first." He walked up to her and took a good look. "Swell get-up. You an official member of the pit crew now?"

Sandy nodded. "I mean no. Buddy said I could try it on."

"That was nice of him. He loan you the grease, too?"

Sandy just looked at him blankly.

"Have you seen your face recently?"

Sandy shook her head.

"Are you all right," Frank asked her."

"I'm fine."

He smiled and said "Good," but kept glancing over at Sandy as they walked back in to the garage.

She went over to the peg to leave the coat and hat where she'd found them. She took out her compact and wiped at her face with some Kleenex, then held the tiny round mirror away from her, to get all of her face into it. She tried to imagine what Maggie had seen. She hadn't recognized her at all.

That her aunt was there in Hutch looking for her took Sandy's breath away. She began to feel for the first time since she'd made up her mind to learn if Frank Haggard was her natural father and at least see for herself what her mother had seen in him that perhaps things might be getting out of hand.

She looked in the mirror again, but what she was seeing were Maggie's eyes just before she put the sunglasses over them, her gaze open and sad, as if she were lost and just looking at everything at once, and nothing in particular.

Frank suggested they go out to the camper parked at the edge of the lot and fix sandwiches. "I'll bet you're hungry." Sandy just shrugged and followed him, wondering how to get word to her aunt that everything was fine, so she wouldn't keep driving around with that lost look in her eyes.

CHAPTER 31

The field on the far side of the garage was full of golden rod and witches' broom. There were also clusters of cockleburs that latched on to Sandy's bobby socks and blue canvas sneakers. She was cutting a swath parallel to the road, chewing disinterestedly on her tuna fish sandwich and fine-tuning her explanation to Maggie. She'd explain she had to try to make sense of the scrapbooks her mother saved, left like treasure maps in place of the words she never spoke to tell Sandy which parts of their lives were lies, and which parts true.

The safest thing to do would be to call Aunt Irma after lunch and ask her to get word to Maggie that Sandy was doing fine, and would call again later. She would say that she didn't know how long she would be gone, but that she would stay in touch and they were not to worry.

Sandy turned around and started back almost at a skip, her spirits lifted considerably now that she saw her way to clearing everything up. She figured she could run use the phone in the garage office and reverse the charges. As she hurried toward the camper, she saw a red light going around on the top of a car and a small crowd gathered near it. At first she thought it must be the red light Parker was harping about and wondered what it was doing out there. Unable to see through the bodies pressed together, she squatted down to peer through the legs and saw a police car parked next to the camper. Her instincts told her this couldn't be good.

She pivoted on her heels and stayed low hoping to slip away as the people nearest her glanced down and then turned toward her. That slight parting of their ranks drew a bead on Sandy's backside. A woman called out, "This here the girl y'all are askin' about?"

"Sandy?" Maggie's voice traveled right up Sandy's backbone and chimed in her head.

"Sandy!" Frank's voice reverberated, deeper and louder.

She looked over her shoulder and saw Frank and Maggie hurrying toward her. They each took an arm, more or less helping her upright, although it felt briefly as if her shoulders might pop out of their sockets.

They were asking questions, but she couldn't have answered if she'd wanted to because they were also peppering each other with accusations that tatted around her head like bullets from machine guns.

"Hold up there," the policeman told them. "Everybody just calm down." He looked at Sandy and asked if her name was Sandy Turner. She nodded, looking from one adult to another.

"All right, then," the policeman said. "Now that we've located her we can get this straightened out."

"That man," Maggie said, pointing to Frank, "deliberately lied to me about knowing where my niece was. She's a minor. I'm holding him personally responsible."

"For what?" Frank slashed back. "She found me so she could get away from you and your abuse. And I'm holding you personally responsible."

Their voices escalated as they exchanged accusations. Sandy muttered, "Oh, no, don't, that's not . . . ." but her soft mutterings were no match for the adults' raised voices.

"Quiet!" the policeman yelled.

Frank looked at Maggie and asked, "Who am I to her?" When she didn't answer, he repeated his question, "Who... am... I... to... her?"

"You happened," Maggie was breathing hard, and she enunciated her words as if giving very important information to a class, something they would be tested over later, "through a stroke of great misfortune, to have been married, ever so briefly, to my sister . . . a long time ago." The color had risen to her cheeks and her eyes flashed at him, but their pale blue color was giving way to a moist pink and her voice wavered toward the end.

"Say it!" Frank demanded

Her voice rose with exasperation, the sad, awful secret finally out in the open in the middle of nowhere, years too late to do her sister any good at all. "You are her father in name only."

"And whose fault is that?"

The policeman, who had kept his left arm across Frank's chest and his right hand around Maggie's arm turned Maggie toward the squad car. "You folks aren't settling anything like this. We're gonna have to go down to the station. You, Sandy, come over here. Come on."

Buddy, who'd stepped up and put his hands on Sandy's shoulders, called out, "Why do they have to go to the jailhouse?"

"Because we're not havin' a family brawl out here in front of God and everybody. The captain is going to have to hear all this. Maybe the judge. Now, unless you want to be arrested for obstructing an officer in the line of duty, I suggest you hand the girl over." The officer opened the front door of the squad car and steered Maggie toward it, but she turned before getting in to watch Sandy, who walked slowly to the rear door he had pulled open.

"I'm sorry," Sandy said softly, her voice catching. " I was going to call you."

"Then why didn't you," Maggie asked just as softly, reaching over, her fingertips just grazing Sandy's arm as the officer guided Maggie into the front seat.

Sandy thought her aunt looked younger than she'd ever noticed, and scared, not at all like a teacher, or the only person who could get Grandma Parson to pretend to cooperate when she didn't want to do something.

Sandy climbed into the backseat and Frank followed, tossing his keys to Buddy, and telling him to follow with the car.

No one in the patrol car spoke, and all the way to the station house Sandy tried to think of how to begin. She felt Frank's hand engulf hers for the first time, and she squeezed back, wondering if it would be the last time.

At the police station, the officer took them back past the front desk where a young policeman and an older man in plaid Bermuda shorts, a Polo shirt, and baseball cap were laughing and drinking coffee. He led them to the captain's office door, which was open. The officer went through the formality of knocking, but walked right in, motioning for the others to wait outside. They could see brown shoes and legs in a beige uniform with wide brown stripes running down the outsides resting on the corner of a desk and heard the squeak of a chair spring as the feet dropped to the floor. A policeman with a big head and a close-cropped crew cut leaned forward to peer at them and moved back out of range again.

Maggie put her hand under Sandy's chin and looked into her face. "What is this all about? Why did you do it?"

"I left you a note," she said, but saw that that clearly was not what Maggie had tracked her down to hear.

"Nothing about why you left or where you were going. Do you have any idea how worried sick I've been? We've all been?"

Sandy's cheeks blossomed crimson with a remorse that had been brewing from her first glimpse of her aunt that afternoon. "I'm sorry you were worried."

Maggie nodded solemnly. "I believe you. But why did you have to do this? Couldn't you have come to me and discussed . . . all of this? Did you have to sneak off in the middle of the night?"

Frank, who had been trying to listen to both the conversation in the captain's office and to what Maggie was saying, stepped up behind Sandy, putting his hands on her shoulders and said, "I think you'd best do your talking in there."

"I'm talking to my niece, and I suggest that you keep out of this. You are already in serious trouble."

Sandy, who had been straining her neck to look from one to the other, was alarmed by the menace in Maggie's voice and grabbed ahold of her aunt's hand.

"Wait! He didn't know anything. He had nothing to do with it. It was all my idea. He didn't even believe who I was at first."

Maggie seemed to be addressing Sandy, but she kept her eyes fastened on Frank's. "And when he did realize who you were, did he recognize any moral obligation to contact your family? Or the authorities at least? Did it occur to him that a fourteen-year-old girl should not be wandering around the countryside like some vagabond?"

"I wasn't wander—" Sandy began, before Frank interrupted.

"Did it occur to you that she might have felt safer taking her chances on the road than stayin' there with you, havin' to take your abuse?"

"Sandy! What is this lunatic talking about?"

Before Sandy could respond, the policeman and the captain were next to them, herding them across the hall to a room with a long conference table in the middle of it.

The captain sat at the head of the table, with the policeman who had brought them in taking the chair next to Frank, and Maggie and Sandy sitting opposite. The captain opened a writing tablet and held a pen poised over it. "All right, now, for starters let's get the correct names and addresses of the concerned parties."

One after the other, their voices cut through the air at varying pitches—uneven and just a little strident, like instruments being tuned before a concert—as the captain judiciously attended to the exact letters and numbers. Next he asked what the relationships were. Sandy stared at the pen as it crossed the page again and again, and realized this was becoming a much graver situation than she would have thought possible.

Maggie and Frank weren't looking at each other, but whenever one of them responded to the captain, the other one grimaced in a rude way that would have gotten someone Sandy's age into a lot of trouble. They were just up to the circumstances and date of Sandy's "disappearance" when a commotion in the hall caused them all to turn their attention toward the door where Buddy appeared.

He was insisting to the young officer that he should be allowed to join the others.

The captain looked inquiringly at Frank. "He with you?"

"A friend."

Looking up at Buddy, the captain said, "You can lend comfort and aid later. Right now this is a private hearing." He tipped his head to indicate the officer should take Buddy back to the lobby.

Maggie shook her head, looked at Frank, and said under her breath. "You're a real piece of work."

Frank gave her a guarded look.

"I mean it. You, Mr. Haggard, are capable of far more harm than even my father—in his somewhat provincial wisdom—gave you credit for."

Frank rubbed his thumb along the top edge of his belt buckle, and his voice took on a lazy, gravelly tone. "Well, I guess I ought to thank you. Considerin' the kind of things you and yours have no doubt been sayin' about me all these years, that adds up to almost a compliment."

"Don't flatter yourself. Once you were no longer an immediate threat to my sister's well-being, we tended to repress any thoughts of you that might have lingered."

Frank smiled, but he didn't look friendly. "You always were good with the words, Maggie. Never too mad, or too sad, or too interested in the truth to resist taking your best shot."

The captain had been sitting with one hand raised. He brought it down on the table with a resounding smack that made all of them jump, and then folded his hands in front of him. "This is not getting us anywhere." A young officer leaned in the doorway and said to the captain, "The judge just showed up. Wants to see everyone over in the court room."

They were led back down the hall and taken into a larger room that had a judge's bench along the front and a raised platform on the right, with wooden pews on it. They went to the front of the room and were told to sit down around one of the two conference tables. The captain had stayed behind making a phone call, and the young policeman who had brought the group together stood by the table, poised to write relevant details into the small note pad he had pulled from his shirt pocket.

A man entered the room from the door next to the raised bench, walking with long, deliberate strides and frowning. He didn't look much older than Frank, and he was wearing a pale-yellow knit shirt with blue pants and white shoes with fringe flaps on the tops. He had a piece of paper with notes scrawled on it that he was reading, and looked up only after he was settled into the chair at the other end of the table.

"I'm Judge Stearns. Let me see if I've got this right." He went through their names and addresses, pausing to study Frank a moment. "You race cars over at 81 Speedway in Wichita."

Frank smiled and said that he did, then asked the judge if he got to the races often.

"Don't go. Too much noise and commotion." He looked from Frank to Maggie to Sandy. "You, young lady, seem to be the instigator of the immediate problem, which as I understand from what your aunt told Officer Nash, here, is that you have been missing from your home in Kiowa since Friday, July fifth, and have been traveling with this man, here, who is reported to be your natural father, and whom you never saw before last Friday. Is that about right?"

"Except in pictures," said Sandy, as she put her hands in her lap and wiped her palms on her shorts. She stared at the moist prints they had left on the brown tabletop. The judge had said "instigated," which sounded legal and a little weighty. She wondered if she was going to have a police record complete with fingerprints.

"Can you tell us why you found it necessary to run away from your aunt's home? I mean to ask why you didn't tell her of your desire to see your father."

Sandy sat up straighter, resting her hands on the table, then remembered the moist prints and jerked them back down to her lap. "It's kind of hard to explain."

"Do your best."

She kept her eyes on the judge. "Well, I always knew that there was something funny, about my other father, I mean. He died when I was three, so I don't remember him very well, but mostly I remember that my mother never talked about him after he was dead. And I used to hear Mom and my aunts talking about things that happened when I was real young or not even born yet. I knew that whenever they started in on the thing that made Grandma Parson spittin' angry that it had something to do with me. But I didn't know what, exactly. And then after she died, I found a box of letters—"

"Hold on, "the judge told her. "When who died? Your grandma?"

"No sir. My mother. Ruth Parson."

"Haggard," Frank added.

"Turner," Maggie corrected.

"Ah," said the judge, raising his eyebrows and looking around the table as if for clarification. When no explanations were forth coming, he shrugged and said, "Continue."

"Well I found these letters from her best friend, Alice, who lives near Kansas City—"

Maggie's voice surprised even her as she blurted out, "Sandy! You didn't!"

Sandy looked at her aunt. "I didn't mean to pry. Honestly, I just wanted to know more about my mother, and the letters talked about things Mom must have written to her friend about. Anyway, they're mine, now, aren't they? They're part of her things."

Maggie pinched her lips together to keep them from trembling, and answered softly, "I guess if they're anybody's, they'd be Alice's now."

Sandy dropped her head. "I didn't think about that. But the scrapbooks are mine." She looked from Frank to Maggie to the judge. "She kept them every year, from 1946 until she died. I knew from the books and Alice's letters that there was one driver Mom was really interested in." She glanced over at Frank, who was leaning over the table, staring at the back of his hands.

The judge, who had been listening intently, asked when she had decided that man must be her father.

She thought for a moment. "I don't really remember. But I showed Grandma Parson an article in the paper about races he was in, and I thought she was gonna have a fit, saying racing was crazy and dangerous and a waste of money and that only crazy people would risk their lives and their family's welfare like that."

"And that made you suspicious?"

"I guess so. 'Cause my uncle Lloyd goes to the races sometimes, and she never says anything like that to him. He even takes us kids sometimes."

"How many kids we talking about here," the judge asked, looking at Frank.

"Just my two cousins and me. Sometimes our neighbor Ralph goes with us."

The judge leaned back in his chair. "I see. And when you found these books and letters you were curious. Natural enough." He tapped his fingers on the page of notes in front of him and looked at Maggie. "Tell me, Miss Parson, when your sister died, did you attempt to get in touch with the natural father?"

"I . . . we'd lost track of him. It was war time. And I was the next of kin."

"No, you were not." Frank's voice was so low it raised goose bumps on Sandy's arms.

"I helped raise her. I was always there. You didn't even know about her. Surely, you don't think that after six years had passed without a word—"

"What about my letters?"

Maggie seemed surprised. "What letters?"

"The letters I wrote Ruth every day."

"There were no letters."

"Hell if there weren't!"

"Watch your language," the judge cautioned.

"If there had been any, don't you think I'd have known? Every day, my sister went to the mailbox, hoping to get some news, some address where you could be reached."

"I wrote. Every day for eight weeks, until I was shipped out. And for months after that."

"When Ruth was taken with morning sickness, I would go and wait by the box for her." Her voice was steady, and she spaced her words carefully. "I swear, there were no letters."

The judge broke in, saying "You two may have some old business to straighten out, but the immediate issue here is where this girl belongs."

"Your Honor," said Maggie, "I have had total responsibility for my niece for nine years. She's surrounded by loving family members and a stable environment. Frank Haggard's life is hardly suitable for raising a child. A girl, especially, needs a woman's care."

"I don't have to defend my way of earning a living. I'm Sandy's father, plain and simple. Isn't that right, Judge?"

Maggie kept her eyes on the judge, saying "Surely some things are more important than natural parenthood, such as the child's welfare."

"I have rights, Maggie," said Frank, turning his full attention to her. "I was cheated out of what was mine fifteen years ago. And you played no small part in that. You know, I never could figure you out. What did it matter to you if Ruth and I got out of that one-horse-town and lived our own lives? Why were you so all fired determined to help them break us up?"

"I wasn't! It was—"

"Were you so scared of being left behind that you had to keep a strangle hold on Ruth?"

Maggie's voice stayed level as she turned to him, but her eyes got squinty. "I don't have to take this from you. I don't care what you think of me. I just want you out of our lives, once and for all."

Frank leaned across the table and pointed his index finger at her like an imaginary pistol. "Not this time, Sister. Not this time." He leaned back, unsmiling, matter-of-factly asking, "You never married, did you, Maggie? Why is that? You're not a homely woman. What kept you tied to that town and those two hard-nosed, narrow-minded, self-righteous hypocrites?"

"You see, Judge, he never tried to understand then, and he won't now," said Maggie. "All he can see is that he couldn't have things his way, and now he's bound to hurt us anyway he can." She turned back to Frank. "That's what this is all about, isn't it. Some sick kind of revenge."

The judge said that was enough, but not before Frank got out that Maggie was so eaten up with jealousy and bitterness that she was plumb crazy. Sandy, who had wanted to break in, to tell them to stop fighting, felt as if she were made of rubber, and her throat was bone dry from trying not to cry.

"Young lady, I want you to go with this officer back out to the front desk and wait there while we settle some things here. You stay right there, you understand me? And while you're sitting there, you might consider giving some serious thought to your actions and their consequences."

"But—"

"Go on, now," the judge said. He tipped his head to the policeman standing in the doorway, who walked over and put his hand on her shoulder, causing her to cringe.

She glanced over at Frank, then Maggie, mouthed *I'm sorry*, and walked woodenly through the door and down the hallway.

Buddy was sitting near the front door, reading a newspaper. As soon as Sandy came into the room, he jumped up and joined her.

"Are you all right? Where's Frank?"

"They're still with the judge."

He noticed that her face was pale and the hair at her temples was beginning to curl with perspiration. "Come on. I'll take you outside."

"Just a minute there!" The policeman asked where they were going, and after looking closely at Sandy, told them it would be all right, but to stay in front of the door where he could see them.

They sat down on the shady side of the steps, and Buddy had Sandy lean forward and put her head between her knees. After a while, she sat back up and leaned against the railing.

"What all do you think is going on in there?" Buddy asked, not really expecting her to have an answer.

"I don't know, exactly. It was complicated. But Frank and Aunt Maggie are really mad at each other."

"Your aunt wants to take you home with her?"

"Yes."

"She's a good-looking woman. I see some of her in you, the eyes. That little pout you get when you don't want to do something. What did Frank say?"

"That he's got rights." She thought for a moment, then said, "But it's lots more complicated than that. It's like it wasn't just about me." She shook her head. "I've never seen Aunt Maggie so angry."

Buddy fanned them both with the paper he'd been reading. "You're right about one thing. This is getting complicated."

Sandy's eyes closed, and Buddy's voice sounded far off. She started to tell him about Frank's letters—months of letters just disappearing—but mostly she just wanted to sit there not moving, not even thinking about all the words that were flying around inside her head, or even worse, still flying around back in that room where she'd left the three grown-ups trying to untangle the mess she'd gotten them all into.

CHAPTER 32

Although the judge decided Sandy was to remain in the custody of her father until there could be a full court hearing, he said she could go with her aunt to say goodbye for the time being. They walked to a café down the street and slipped in a wooden booth with high backs while their police escort sat on a stool at the far end of the counter.

The waitress placed a Coke and a glass of iced tea on the table and took away the silverware they said they wouldn't be needing. Maggie squeezed the lemon slice into her tea and added a spoonful of sugar, looking at Sandy in quick, fretful glances while she stirred. "Drink your Coke, Honey. You need to stay hydrated."

Sandy obliged in silence, the clinking of Maggie's spoon against the glass making her skin prickle.

"Tell me the absolute truth. Were you so unhappy? Is that why you did this?"

Looking up. Sandy saw that her aunt was close to tears and said, "No. I'm so sorry. I didn't mean to hurt to you."

"I know. But you have. Terribly. And your grandmother and Irma and Lloyd, too. You do realize that when people love someone . . . that you can't just—" her voice broke, and she reached for her tea.

Sandy's own voice was barely audible as she apologized again. "Do you want me to just come home?"

"Yes. That's exactly what I want you to do." Maggie leaned over the table and cradled her forehead with her hand. "You don't understand what you've done."

Sandy asked, "What?"

"You," Maggie put her palm down on the table and pressed it there, to emphasize her point, "have created a monster. Sandy, I don't know how all this got started. You were curious, I guess. I can understand that. Maybe it was wrong to keep things from you. But that man is not to be trusted. However innocent his involvement when all this started, he is now interested in one thing and one thing only—getting revenge."

Sandy shook her head.

"It's true, whether you want to believe it or not. He doesn't see that your grandparents were . . . protecting your mother. She was so young, just seventeen."

Her voice rose with exasperation. "He is so self-centered, so unbelievably narrow-minded. He is convinced that our whole family was out to get him, personally." She reached over and took Sandy's hands in her own. "Honey, don't you see, he never came back, not for your mother, not—"

"What about the letters?"

"There were no letters. I swear to you, on my sister's grave. I never saw even one letter!"

Sandy's head drooped, and tears slipped out, skimming her cheek and dropping into her lap.

Maggie pulled a napkin from the silver dispenser and dabbed at Sandy's cheeks, her own eyes moist. "Why didn't you just come to me in the first place? We could have talked about it."

"I don't know."

"Did you think I wouldn't understand?"

Sandy took the napkin and wiped under her eyes. "I didn't know how to tell you."

"Tell me what?" When Sandy didn't answer, Maggie prompted with "You mean finding out about Frank?"

"Not exactly." Sandy used her index finger to deflect a rivulet of condensation dropping down the glass. "It's just that I always felt something wasn't right, but I didn't know what it could be. And then when I found the albums and Alice's letters . . . well, nobody had ever talked to me about him. I thought maybe I wasn't supposed to know."

Maggie fingered the car keys that lay on the table, aligning each key evenly along the top of the ring so it resembled the sun when it's cut in half by the horizon. "I see."

Sandy knew that she didn't. "I think my mother intended for me to know. I think she wanted me to."

Maggie studied her niece's face, looked into her eyes. "Why do you say that? I mean she never talked to you about . . . did she?"

Sandy squirmed on the bench. "No. But sometimes when I'd look at her she seemed so sad, and when I'd ask her why, she'd say maybe when I was older."

Maggie thought that over.

"I have to go to the bathroom," Sandy said, and scooted to the end of the bench. She walked quickly toward a restrooms sign with an arrow pointing down a hall right next to the kitchen.

Maggie felt nauseated, the way she had when Theresa Potter's arm had gotten dislocated in a fall on the stairs and hung strangely in her sweater as they'd eased her in to Maggie's car to go to the hospital. She sensed the underpinnings of her life crumbling, as if she were racing toward the shore down a long dock that was collapsing at her heels. She was even more frightened now than when she'd realized Sandy was missing. Back then, there was still the hope that she would show up, unaware of the commotion she'd caused, and that life would return to normal again. But they were far beyond any swift, happy resolutions now.

Sandy slipped back into the booth across from her aunt, neither of them saying anything for a minute. Finally Maggie held her hands up as if to pray, but didn't get them closed all the way. She had to force the words past the knot in her throat. "Sandy, I'm so sorry. If only I'd known what you were thinking."

"I'm sorry, too. We can go get my things and go home now."

"Oh, Baby," Maggie said, her voice catching. "We can't. The judge said that since I never got legal custody and Frank's your biological father, all I can do is petition in Topeka."

Sandy sat up straighter and leaned over the table as if getting closer would make the words clearer. "What does that mean?"

"That means suing Frank to get you back."

Sandy's eyes opened wider as the enormity of what Maggie was telling her sank in. "You can't! I mean, that's crazy. Anyway, what if I just leave? Just like I came?"

"Then the police would come looking for us, with a warrant for my arrest, most likely. And an order to either return you to him or make you a ward of the court."

"Frank wouldn't do that!"

"He's already said that that's exactly what he will do." Maggie moved over to Sandy's side of the booth, wrapping her arms around her niece and resting her chin on her head. "I'm going to call your Uncle Lloyd before I leave for home and have him line up the best attorney he can find. I hope we can get a restraining order or something, so you can stay in your own home, until all this is settled. In the meantime . . . ."

She released Sandy so that they could wipe their eyes on napkins and blow their noses. "I wish this were just a bad dream I was having," Maggie said, "and that I could tell you about it while we were driving out to check on your grandmother, and we'd laugh and promise not to share it with her." She leaned back, combing Sandy's hair with her fingers. "I don't know how I'm going to tell her what's happened."

Sandy rolled her head back against Maggie's arm.

"Will you be all right?" Maggie asked her.

Sandy nodded. "He's really not like this. Really. He can be really very nice, and funny, sometimes."

"The judge said that he'd better get you settled at his home in Hutchinson for now. He also—the judge—made him promise not to cut you off from the only family you've known all these years—" her voice broke. "Sorry." She blotted her eyes again. "If you need anything, just to talk even, you call me. Do you understand?"

Sandy said she did and glanced out the window. She saw Frank standing in front of the Mercury, his arms folded across his chest and a cigarette in his right hand, the smoke streaming straight up in the hot, still air. The policeman had gone out to join him and was standing with his thumbs hooked in his belt loops while they talked.

'Listen, there's going to be some kind of special race in Wichita. Maybe you could come and . . ."

Maggie squeezed Sandy hands. "I don't know. For right now. I just don't . . . I have to figure this out. But you know you can call me. Any time of the day or night," Maggie told her. "Collect. You know how to do that, don't you?"

"I know."

Maggie stood up and got out her wallet. She put two dollars down on the table and handed Sandy a twenty-dollar bill. They walked out of the restaurant and crossed the street with their arms around each other's waists, Maggie carefully explaining about person-to-person and station-to-station long-distance calls. When they got to where Frank was waiting, Sandy turned to her aunt and wrapped her arms around her waist. Maggie looked over at Frank. "I'll expect to hear from her daily." When he didn't say anything, Sandy looked around at him, frowning. He nodded, then said, "Get in the car, Sandy." He slid in behind the wheel and watched as the aunt and niece who looked more like sisters kissed and hugged goodbye.

The officer opened the door for Sandy, who twisted in her seat to look back at Maggie as they pulled away from the curb, keeping her in sight as long as she could.

Frank looked over and asked, "You all right?"

"I guess. Are we going back to the garage now?"

When he didn't say anything, she said, "I never meant for anyone to get in trouble. I should have told Tina about how I really got that scar on my back. Aunt Maggie never hurt me. You can't think that about her."

Frank gripped the steering wheel tighter. "I don't plan to think about her at all."

From the grim look on his face, Sandy couldn't decide if that would be a good thing or a bad thing. She held her hand out the window pushed back against the pressure of the air against her palm. She wondered how something you can't see and usually can't even feel can suddenly be so heavy.

"How did you get those scars on your back?"

"Going through a fence like that." She pointed to the barbed wire fence running parallel to the road.

"That the truth?"

"Yes, Sir. Ralph and I were running away from old man Hensley."

"Who's Ralph?"

"Our neighbor back in Kiowa. He's about my best friend."

Frank nodded. "Why were you running away?"

"We sort of took a carburetor from this old broken-down truck on the Hensley place. We wanted to use it to make a go-kart. We were almost through the fence when Mr. Hensley yelled at us and my shirt got stuck. Ralph grabbed my arm and pulled me through and a couple of the barbs caught."

"Ouch. That must have hurt like the devil."

She nodded. "It sure did."

"Carburetor, huh?" Frank stifled a smile, then ran his hands through his hair. "What did you do with it?"

"Ralph had to take it back and put up bales for Mr. Hensley. Once they got my back fixed up, I just had to write a letter of apology. Then after it was all over, what do you think?"

"You tell me."

"Mr. Hensley gave us back the carburetor. But by then, I sort of lost interest in making a kart. It's still in the shed at Ralph's. If you ever need an extra one . . . ."

Frank grinned, then turned to look at her. "Okay. Now listen very carefully. There can't be any more lying or secrets. No way, not for any reason at all. You understand?"

Sandy answered as if taking a solemn vow, "I promise."

She turned to face him and leaned her head back against the seat. "So . . . what do you want me to call you?" she asked, trying to sound casual, as if she hadn't been thinking about it since they first met back at that motel in Enid.

He cleared his throat. "I haven't really given it any thought. I guess that's up to you."

"Father sounds pretty formal. Ricky Nelson calls his father 'Pop' on their television show, but I think that sounds kind of hick."

"Not to mention old," Frank added.

They rode in silence until he pulled into an alley and parked by the back door to his house and turned off the engine. "This is home," he said, opening his door. "I guess you can try Dad for a while. See if you can get used to it."

"Okay," she said, opening the door and climbing out. "Dad," she added, trying it out, but he was already walking inside and maybe didn't hear.

CHAPTER 33

The drone of the television in the day room always got on Olivia Parson's nerves and Maggie's were still stretched like piano wire from the events in Hutchinson. She wheeled her mother down to the end of the hall where there was a window that she could look out of while they talked. The summer storm that had chased Maggie all the way to Hardtner was unloading the brunt of its energy right above them.

"Sandy didn't come?"

"I need to talk to you about that."

"Been almost a week hasn't it? She sick?" The left side of Olivia's face still sagged, making her appear dull, but one look into her eyes revealed that her mind was sharp as ever.

"She's healthy."

"Better get it said, then. What's happened?"

"Sandy has gone to stay with someone for a while. She's fine."

Maggie watched her mother closely for any indication of distress, a blanching or shortness of breath, but the old woman just sighed and nodded her head.

"I suspected as much. The way you been tiptoeing around up here like you were on egg shells."

"I'm sorry. If I'd known you were worried, I would have told you sooner."

"No you wouldn't of. Scared you might do something that will pop another blood vessel. When are you going to learn, Maggie, that you can't take responsibility for everything that happens? No one has that kind of control. Now tell me about my granddaughter. She with that Haggard boy?"

Maggie sat back in her chair, her hands dropping onto the wooden arms with a slap, and shook her head back and forth slowly. "I don't believe it. How did you find out?"

"Been expecting it. She's always been quick. And high-spirited like her mother." Olivia stared out at the storm, her pale, angular face etched like a cameo against the gray pane. "That was a bad business." She took a deep breath and gave her head a little shake. "How'd she find out?"

"Scrapbooks. There's a stack of them in the Lane cedar chest filled with newspaper clippings about the races. I guess she just figured it out for herself."

"You know about those books?" Olivia asked. When Maggie hesitated, Olivia said, "Of course you did. Should of thrown them out when I first found them. Barn door after the horse, now. When's she comin' home?"

"Soon. She called this morning from his house in Hutchinson. To say she's fine and misses us. She asked about you especially."

"What's he want with her, you think? He married?"

"No. Well, Actually, I don't know. Lloyd has talked to a lawyer who says we have to take legal action. Something we should have done after Ruth died. Just a formality, really. Then everything will be all right. There's nothing for you to worry about." Her voice was ineffectually bright—like headlights in fog. The old woman's head sagged, and she hugged herself with her good right arm, as if the dampness of the storm had permeated the windowpane and chilled her.

"Sandy says they'll be at the racetrack in Wichita. I'm going to drive up and meet her there."

Olivia nodded her head. "Even when your sister died, Maggie, I never felt weak. I never once felt I wouldn't be able to manage no matter . . . ." Her mother's voice trailed off, and Maggie just stood there and watched reflections of the rain on the window playing across her mother's face. "Do what you have to do," Olivia said finally. "I've money put away for emergencies. Lloyd and Irma will help where they can."

Wheeling her mother back to her room, Maggie couldn't think of any small talk to ease the strain they were under. As she looked back from the doorway with a parting smile, she searched for something that would erase the awful expression from her mother's face. But there wasn't anything more she could say, and she was feeling that for the first time she had truly let the people she loved down.

CHAPTER 34

RED LIGHT FOR "GO"
HAGGARD PUT TO THE TEST

His racing charger turned into a cherry-top special, senior race car pilot Frank Haggard is out to prove the years haven't slowed him down.

Car owner G.D. Parker has ordered a red light installed atop his car so he can tell if Haggard is getting the best possible race out of his machine.

The red light referred to is designed to light up only when Haggard has the throttle floor- boarded.

Haggard is expected to be among the top contenders in a 20-lap feature scheduled for 81 Speedway's Wally Wilson Family Benefit Race Tuesday night at 81 Speedway, one of the last nights for drivers to fine-tune their cars for the first-ever Grand National Championship Race for Jalopies, to be held this Sunday at Taft Stadium, Oklahoma City, Oklahoma.

Several miles before Maggie got to the winding entrance to 81 Speedway, she heard the drone of car engines. It was early evening, and the fields were tinged with the slanting sunlight that always made her think of the natural light Matisse chased along the southern coast of France, a light she had once hoped to bask in, before becoming a surrogate mother circumscribed her to the simpler geography of Midwest America.

In spite of telling herself she was there to check on her niece, as she pulled into the field that served as a parking lot, she felt a mixture of apprehension and anticipation roiling through her that bordered on anxiety.

The woman at the ticket booth surprised her by asking if she was Maggie Parson and, upon having that confirmed, handing her a complimentary ticket.

"What's this for?"

"We were told if you showed up to give you a pass."

"I see," she said, surprised. "Thanks." Maggie snapped her wallet closed and reached for the ticket. "How did you know who to look for?"

"Frank's kid showed me a picture. You resemble her quite a bit."

Frank's kid. Just like that. How easily his world had absorbed her niece. Maggie walked through the gate feeling like an interloper, or worse—a tourist in a hostile country. To the woman in the booth, Sandy's presence at the racetrack probably seemed as natural as the noise of the engines and the stacks of pumpkin-colored seat cushions. Maybe it seemed natural to Sandy, too, to be there with her real father. But surely the newness and excitement would pass, and Sandy would want to come home, to her family and friends and the security Maggie had provided when the child's world had first turned upside down.

Maggie stopped near the photo stand and looked around. The ticket taker was right. In the years she'd been caring for her niece, she had been complacently aware of the evidence that bound them genetically--reddish-blonde highlights in their light brown hair, the well-turned calves. Even the tendency toward a slight underbite that made the Parson women appear, at solemn gatherings, to be indulging in a collective pout. These manifestations of the bond of blood served to confirm the rightness of Maggie and Sandy ending up together, given the crushing wrongness of Ruth's dying so young.

Maggie listened to the rumblings of a race in progress and debated whether to walk up in front of the stands to look for Sandy in the crowd or to wait at the photo booth as they'd arranged. She let her eyes wander across the rows of black and white glossies tacked to the three sides of the booth in no discernible pattern.

Close-ups of smiling men standing by race cars, some with their hands on the hoods in a proprietary gesture were interspersed with long shots of cars frozen in mid flip or roll or locked into tight races, the swells of dust and dirt as much a part of the action shots as the bright paint jobs and bumper-to-bumper advertising names and slogans. There were a number of group shots with trophies being displayed. In those there were usually, but not always, young girls wearing party dresses and high heels and smiling deep into the camera with their hands cupped on their hips and their arms jutting out like wings. They looked as out of place as fruit flies in an ant farm.

Maggie tried to not let her eyes linger over the pictures of Frank, but they were numerous, and she found herself studying them in spite of herself. He'd been one of the best-looking boys in the county and was just as handsome as a man. It wasn't hard to see how Ruth could defy their parents and run off with him. Maggie focused on a headshot of him and tried to imagine how her sister would look if she were alive right then, in her early thirties, tried to picture her face next to Frank's, turned slightly toward him so that their gazes met at some point mid-booth, but she could only call up Ruth's yearbook picture, which had her looking too young. She was young.

"Aunt Maggie!" Sandy wove through the crowd as she ran toward her.

"Wow!" Sandy leaned around to peer at Maggie's nearly backless sundress.

"You look . . . great. A new dress even. How come you're so late? Did you see this?" Sandy pointed to a photograph tacked to the wall nearest them.

"That's me back there."

"What's wrong with your hand?" Maggie asked.

Sandy looked down at the strip of gauze protecting her palm. "Nothing now. I got a little burn working in the garage. It's nothing. Really. Buddy says I'm a natural mechanic." Sandy pointed to the photo again. "See me?"

"Is Buddy the man with the truck camper?" Maggie asked, studying the photograph for a moment before recognizing her niece's face, about the size of a shirt button, peering from behind a race car that looked as if it had been come at from all sides with a piece of heavy equipment.

"Frank's mechanic and partner. His best friend, really," Sandy said, but Maggie was frowning at the twisted metal of what barely resembled a car. It was the sort of picture she had avoided lingering over only moments earlier. That sort of devastation was what she suspected race fans really came to witness, to be in on the excitement of life made more interesting when something so loud and fast and bold goes wrong right before their eyes. Her brother-in-law Lloyd had explained it by saying that no one hopes for tragedy to strike, but if it's going to anyway, everyone wants to be there to see it. It was exactly that air of ambulance chasing that had discouraged her from attending the races with Lloyd and Irma.

"When was that taken?"

"Back at Winfield. The driver is a friend of Frank's. He may be paralyzed. We're going to go visit him."

"That will be nice." Maggie realized that her response was not only inappropriate but inane, and doubted she would improve things by saying more on the subject. "Do you have a seat picked out yet? Or is there someplace back here we can sit and talk?"

"No place to sit," Sandy told her. "Anyway, Frank's in the trophy dash, and it's coming up next. Don't you want to see the races?"

Maggie doubted anyone could carry on a real conversation in the grandstand, but smiled and said, "Shall we get a couple of seats to take up?"

"I already got some for us. Frank gave me the money." Sandy looked to see if Maggie was favorably impressed by Frank's thoughtfulness. Although she'd suggested the seats herself, he had paid for them. Her aunt's face was inscrutable as they walked toward the grandstand. "Oh, I almost forgot, did you get the ticket he left for you?" Maggie nodded but gave nothing away as to what she thought of all the special treatment.

Sandy led Maggie up the center aisle to a row just five down from the press box.

"This is the best place to see everything. Even when people jump up before you do, you can usually see when something happens in the far turns."

"Great," Maggie said, looking for a secure place to put her purse, but there were only benches and foot boards, so she kept it on her lap.

Sandy was beaming. She was obviously caught up in the glamour and excitement of the spectacle, and any coolness on Maggie's part would only alienate her niece.

Sandy pointed excitedly to the track when the announcer gave the names of the six drivers lined up in pairs for the trophy dash and invited the fans to cheer loudly for their favorites.

His encouragement was hardly necessary since the fans were yelling so much he could barely be heard anyway. Maggie assumed from the way that Sandy jumped and clapped that Frank was in the red 65 in the first row, closest to the grandstand.

"He should have pole position, but that screwball Hays ran up over Frank's rear tire and nearly caused him to spin-out. Otherwise Hays wouldn't of won the third heat."

"Wouldn't have," Maggie corrected.

"Yeah. He's really a spook. Keep your fingers crossed."

Glancing down, Maggie saw that Sandy's fingers were indeed crossed, on both hands. Maggie practically had to yell to be heard. "Screwball? Spook? You've been working on your vocabulary, I see." Sandy grinned at her aunt and gave her "what-can-I-say" shrug.

The din from the accelerating cars caught Maggie by surprise, as if the air around them suddenly started quivering, and she looked out over the track where the cars were moving in a clump around the left end of the track and building up speed. The car next to Frank suddenly lurched forward so that it was well ahead of the others. She wondered how she and Sandy would be able to talk. Everything was noise and motion.

"See what I mean?" Sandy shouted. "They'll have to go around again 'cause Hays tried to get a jump on them."

Maggie winced as a man behind them bellowed, "Come on, Shorty, pull it up." A woman's voice chimed in "Don't let that son-of-a-gun get the jump on ya, Frankie!"

"Watch the light now," Sandy yelled to Maggie, who looked over at the flagman who was holding the green flag to his chest, the fabric gathered up like a closed umbrella.

"What light?" Maggie yelled back, "All I see is a flag," but her question was whisked away in a great rush of air as excited fans cheered and whistled their favorites across the starting line. The engines seemed to scream back and the green flag swept around in quick figure-eights.

"There! See there!" Sandy grabbed Maggie's arm and pointed to Frank's car as he came around the far end of the track and passed by in front of the stands. The black-and-yellow car driven by Hays was right next to Frank, but on the inside of the track. "See the red light? It's been on since they went into turn one. Holy sh—" The curse died quickly, like a tire gone flat. "Can you believe that? That ought'a show old Parker!"

Looking from her niece back to the track, Maggie watched the racing cars for a moment before seeing what had Sandy so excited. It was a steady red beacon on the roof of 65.

Maggie leaned over and yelled, "Why does he have a stop light up there?"

"S'not a stop light. It's a go light. It shows when he's goin' all-out, and it hasn't shut off for two whole laps!" Sandy was so excited she was bouncing in her seat, and Maggie realized that she too was growing tense. *Calm down,* she told herself under her breath, which wasn't necessary since she would have to yell to be heard by anyone else. The flagman was holding out the white flag for Frank and the other five drivers to see. As soon as they were all past, he threw it behind him with great flair and bent to pick up the checkered one. As the cars started around the turns for the last lap, the car the man Sandy called Hays was driving took a sharp turn in the first corner, its back-end slamming into Frank's car, which shimmied wide and fishtailed, losing ground.

"No!" Sandy was on her feet, screaming. The rest of the crowd seemed just as caught up in the race for the checkered flag as Sandy was, for all around them people were on their feet chanting "Go! Go!" and "Come on, Frankie!" The red light was still on as Frank's car straightened out and pulled up to Hays again, the two cars diving into the final turns side by side. It wasn't until they pulled around for their last pass by the stands Maggie realized she was whispering "Come on," her fists tight against her thighs as she leaned forward to see between the people standing in front of her. Then, as if propelled by the collective hysteria of the spectators, Frank's car surged ahead. On her feet, straining to see through the people jumping up and down in front, Maggie stared at 65 and had the sensation that she was moving up the track with it as Frank edged ahead and charged across the finish line, engine screaming and the red light still burning.

Maggie's hands were raised as if to applaud, except that they were still squeezed into fists. Frank had circled the track again and pulled up to the flagman, climbing up through the cut-out roof to accept his trophy, before Maggie felt herself start to relax. She felt as if she had been pinched into one of her mother's old girdles and someone was slowly unzipping it for her.

"He did it! He did it!" Sandy was jumping up and down on the bench in front of them until Maggie caught hold of her arm.

"Better climb down, Sweetie. Those folks would probably like to have their seats back."

"Did you see that? Do you realize he had the throttle down for the whole race? Incredible! Bet Parker will listen to Frank now."

Maggie wasn't certain what all that meant, but she figured it must have been some sort of special victory for Frank. She was just thinking that it was going to be fairly difficult to calm Sandy down enough to talk about future plans when penny candy and cricket clickers landed in their laps, tossed by a sad-faced clown in an over-sized tuxedo of bright patches. Maggie noticed that he raised one foot in an exaggerated slapping step that made his trek up the steps seem precarious.

"Hey, Rags," Sandy called out to him, waving.

"Does he always walk like that?" Maggie asked. "He looks like he might topple over."

"It's his real walk," Sandy assured her. "He got his foot mangled by a fly wheel back when he used to race. Now his foot won't hold up right.

Frank calls it dropsy, but that's not it. I don't know what it's really called."

Maggie was torn by a desire to look at the clown as if he were just another performer and the need to look away because staring at someone with an affliction was rude. Seconds into her moral dilemma, the decision was made for her, as Rags approached them and handed a piece of candy to Sandy, then patted her on the head. The announcer, who had been carrying on a conversation with Rags, mostly jokes and questions to the audience to get them involved, announced, "The lovely young woman getting a fond pat on the head from Rags is none other than the daughter of racing veteran and last year's high-point driver, that grand old man of the dirt ovals—Frank Haggard!" Rags raised Sandy's hand over her head as the crowd applauded. She waved back modestly with her free hand, but the pink in her cheeks was evidence of her deep pleasure in the moment. Then without warning the clown made a deep bow to Maggie. "And I believe that lovely lady sitting next to her is her Aunt Maggie all the way up from Kiowa. Let's give her a big warm Wichita welcome!"

The clown removed the daisy from his lapel and with a grand sweeping motion he held it out to Maggie. She reached for it instinctively and said thank you. He winked at Sandy, then turned to work his way Charlie Chaplin style back down the wooden steps.

Maggie smiled at Sandy, aware of the eyes that had turned, however briefly, toward them, and then looked out at the track, rolling the daisy stem between her thumb and index finger. She had driven nearly 80 miles expecting to find herself in hostile territory. Finding herself singled out for recognition, caught up in the halo effect of Frank's reputation, was a surprising turn of events. Even as she told herself to be wary, her hand traveled up to smooth her hair in an unconscious salute to her quasi-celebrity.

With Sandy subdued by the public attention, they watched together in silence as a pretty young brunette was helped out of a brand-new white Ford convertible and taken over to where Frank was waiting by the flag stand. He was talking to two other men when someone called his attention to the girl, who had stationed herself next to the car and been handed a silver trophy.

Maggie had to admit, the grin Frank flashed as he waved to the cheering, whistling fans was dazzling. She watched him take the trophy from the girl and kiss it, then start to walk away before mugging as if he suddenly remembered the order of events. Running back, he handed the trophy to the man Maggie had seen at the police station in Liberal and dipped the girl back in a dramatic embrace that may or may not have included a kiss of the same duration. The cheers as he righted the girl and helped her make her way across the track to the waiting convertible were deafening. Sandy, who was clapping hard and cheering loudly, glanced at the aunt, and taking her lack of enthusiasm to be disapproval, said, "He's just kidding around. For the crowd, you know."

Maggie raised her eyebrows and shrugged as if to say his antics were of little concern, but she was actually remembering how wild and free-spirited he'd been coming by to pick up Ruth, leaping up over the hood of his dark blue Chevrolet instead of walking around the car, whisking her sister off to the movies and drag races and the picnics Ruth would tell her sisters about in minute detail. It seemed to Maggie that there was still a good deal of the rowdy boy in the man, and she was wondering how much longer he'd be able to cope with having a teenage daughter added to his race-circuit life-style. If Maggie could get him to trust her, if only out of respect for Ruth's memory, surely she could make him see that this was no way for a young girl to live, and he would allow Sandy to return to Kiowa where she already had a life. A good life—though clearly not as exciting as the one she was being introduced to now. Maggie could see she had her work cut out for her.

CHAPTER 35

After the rest of the night's races were over, Maggie tried to keep up with Sandy as they winnowed into the stream of eager fans that contracted and expanded its way through the gate and onto the track, heading for the pit area. Sandy ran ahead, eager to share in the celebration of Frank winning the A-Feature. But Maggie wobbled on the oily, pitted track in her sandals even with their wedge soles and felt a grudging respect for the little trophy girl who had minced her way to and from center stage so fetchingly, hips swaying instead of knees knocking.

By the time Maggie was across the track, she'd lost sight of Sandy, even though the pit area was brightly lit by the floodlights that circled the infield. Everywhere she looked, men were working on cars or loading trailers, and clusters of fans gathered around the drivers, who stood out in the uniform white pants and shirts. Every other person she saw was drinking a cold beer, which sounded really good to her right then, given all the dust she'd inhaled. The whole place seemed far more jumbled together without the elevated perspective from the grandstand. She climbed up onto the base of an overhead track light to see if she could locate Frank's car, but there were too many people milling around. She didn't welcome the notion of having to wander around looking lost or befuddled, but that seemed to be the next step—right after the literal step back down to the ground, which looked farther than she'd realized on the way up.

"How's the view up there?"

Maggie looked around and saw the clown sad-smiling up at her.

"Not so good. Would you believe I've lost my niece?"

"Maybe I can help." He grabbed her arm to steady her as she hopped down. "I imagine she's already over with her Dad. I'll show you."

"Thanks." She leaned down to adjust the heel strap of her shoe.

"It's Rags, isn't it?"

"That's right." His bad foot slapped an odd heel-toe cadence as they walked into the pits.

"What do you do? When you're not performing as Rags, I mean."

"Different things. Right now I'm selling cars over in Newton." He reached up to sweep the rag-mop wig, and the top hat that was attached to it, back and off his head.

They stopped to let a man rolling tires in each hand as easily as if they were hula hoops cross in front of them, and she looked over at Rags. He caught her studying him and ran his hand through his damp, matted hair to coax it back to life.

"I used to drive a race car," Rags said, "but I had some bad luck and had to quit." He smiled a little Charlie Chaplin smile, the corners of his real mouth pulling down, and slapped his leg to indicate the bad foot.

As they made their way across the pits, the smells of oil and hot metal were everywhere. Metallic clanging rang out as cars were driven or pushed onto trailers that dipped and rose to accommodate their loads and tools tossed into boxes. She swayed slightly as she walked, struggling with the ruts, and Rags was polite enough to not seem to notice the appreciative glances that flashed Maggie's way, or the low wolf whistle that came from behind them. She didn't let on she'd heard, but she was smiling inside. She wondered how long it had been since anyone had looked at her and seen anything but a high school teacher or surrogate mother to a blossoming teenage girl. And while as a professional woman she generally disapproved of such blatantly crude male behavior, in that place and at that moment, the woman herself was not minding it.

Rags pointed to where Sandy was straddling the side of a trailer, holding a chain that was wrapped through a stack of tires while the man she called Buddy worked a large padlock through some links and snapped it shut.

Rags called out, "Sandy! I've got a present for you!"

Sandy looked over and then waved enthusiastically before swinging her leg over the side and jumping down.

"Hi, Rags," she called out running over, "thanks for the candy." She grabbed Maggie's arm and said, "Come on, you've gotta meet Buddy. He's the best mechanic in these parts."

Maggie thanked Rags for his help and tagged after her niece, wondering what "these parts" encompassed.

"This is Buddy," Sandy said, as they walked up to the trailer.

Buddy wiped his hands on a red grease rag and reached out to shake Maggie's hand. "Nice to meet you," he said, smiling as if he meant it, which she thought was unlikely given his close relationship with Frank. "So, how'd you enjoy the race?" he asked.

"Which one?"

He looked puzzled for a moment, which made her think he was slow. Then he laughed. "All of 'em, I guess."

She smiled back at him, thinking he looked like everyone's favorite uncle, only younger and a little sexy in a down-home sort of way. "I enjoyed them, thank you. Sandy filled me in on some of the inside stuff. Anyway, you had a big night. Or doesn't winning two races qualify as big?"

"Anytime you win the A feature is a big night, far as I'm concerned. But tonight," he turned to look at the red light on the top of the red race car, "we did all right." He turned to Sandy and winked, and she winked back. Maggie was a little surprised by what appeared to be their mutual affection and how quickly Sandy had acclimated into this new lifestyle that was a far cry from anything she'd known in Kiowa.

"So, what do you think?" Sandy asked Buddy. "We ready for the big one this Sunday? That's the national championship," she explained to Maggie. "The first ever. Will you come? It's in Oklahoma City. That's not too far. You've got to come!"

"Slow down," Maggie said. "We'll talk about it later." She realized that Sandy and Buddy were looking past her, and she turned to see Frank approaching, his eyes on her and his expression hard to read.

"Good evening," he said to Maggie, sounding oddly formal for the occasion.

"Hello. I guess congratulations are in order."

"Thanks."

They stood half a car's length apart, and the silence that followed their minimal exchange seemed as loud to Maggie as the car engines had at first.

"Were your seats all right?" Frank asked.

"Fine. Thanks. For the cushions."

"Good."

Buddy and Sandy exchanged a look and she rolled her eyes, which Maggie caught.

"Sandy seemed very excited about that red light up there," Maggie said, "but I noticed that none of the other cars has one."

She couldn't read the look that passed between Buddy and Frank, but something told her she'd picked the wrong topic to try to move the conversation along less awkwardly.

"That light's a one-time deal only. It's coming off first thing in the morning," said Frank.

"Not so fast there." At the sound of Parker's voice, both Frank and Buddy turned so that they faced him without actually opening a place within the circle. That left Maggie and Sandy peering around and between the men to get a look at the man who was telling Frank in a loud voice what an outstanding job he'd done.

"Super performance. And I'll tell you what, I just don't doubt that that red light up there did the trick. It's a real crowd pleaser. Balzer Cadillac has agreed to a $250 sponsorship with it on for the big one. How about that?" He smiled broadly at the others, ignoring their lack of enthusiasm. "Whaddya say, Buddy? Don't you think that was just the shot in the arm our boy here needed?"

Parker's attempt to rest his arm on Buddy's shoulder in a fraternal gesture left him looking more like a chubby little kid trying to attach himself to a much larger one who has something he wants.

"I don't know about that, G.D.," Buddy said, concentrating on wiping his hands with the grease rag, working it under his fingernails that surely hadn't been entirely grease free for years. "We've been telling you all along that Frank's been getting the best ride out of her."

"The best ride yes, now, now that the proof of the pudding is up there for the world to see. Why it's like a beacon, a challenge to all the other drivers out there. Yeah, that's what I'm gonna tell the reporters for the buildup." He raised his hands and shaped an imaginary banner in the air in front of him. "Frank Haggard races with his heart on his sleeve and his determination reflected in a red dome light that shines like a beacon to other wanna-be racing greats." His eyebrows rose up in his glistening forehead, causing sweat beads to flow outward and then down around the outsides of his round cheeks. He smiled and nodded from Frank to Buddy and back again. "That's sheer poetry!"

"That's sheer wrong," Frank said. "I told you, one time. That thing's coming off."

The smile disappeared from Parker's face like a mask being yanked off, revealing the scowl waiting underneath. "Not until I say it does!"

Turning around, Frank grabbed the toolbox and heaved it at Buddy. "Let's get her packed up." Maggie caught the edge of the expression Frank had shown to Parker and put her arm around Sandy's shoulders drawing her closer.

"Now you listen—" Parker started.

"You listen!" Frank said over his shoulder as he put his helmet into the camper. "I agreed to one race. This was it. When I pull onto the track this Sunday, I'm going to have just one thing to think about—the one thing I'm always thinking about—what I have to do to make those laps in less time than anyone else can turn them in."

"You arrogant S.O.B.! Without me and this car, you'd be up in the stands thinkin' about a whole lot of things, but winning the race of the century wouldn't be one of 'em. I say the light stays, it stays. I'm not pissing away a $250 sponsorship for anybody!" Sweat was pouring from Parker so profusely that Sandy thought he looked like he was melting.

"Look, G.D.," Buddy started, but they all saw the furious-faced little man was beyond reasoning with. He shrugged Buddy's hand off his arm and strode up to Frank.

"So what'll it be? You racing for me, or buying your ticket at the gate with the rest of the girls?"

Without even glancing at G.D., Frank picked up a tire iron and swung it across the top of the car, the red glass spattering over the hood of the car like rain on a tin roof.

Parker sputtered so hard that the exact nature of his curses were muddled, but Maggie did make out "you hotheaded" something and watched with disbelief as he swung his right arm in an arc toward the middle of Frank's back.

Buddy leaned forward and caught Parker's fist as smoothly as if they were doing an allemande left in a square dance, and told both men to cool off, they were talking crazy, and that everything could be worked out.

Without waiting to see if good sense would prevail, Maggie pulled Sandy away, where they watched from a safer distance. "Is it always like this?" she asked.

"Huh-uh. Usually Frank just picks up his winnings, and we all go out for steak dinner."

"If this goes any farther," Maggie said, "That G.D.'s going to need his steak raw."

Sandy grinned up at Maggie, grateful that her aunt wasn't blaming Frank for the trouble with Parker. She said, "Hey, it's too late for you to drive back home tonight. Why don't you come back to Hutch with us?"

"I can't do that. Where would I stay? It'd be too late to get a room."

Sandy thought a minute, keeping an eye on the men who were farther apart but still yelling.

"You could stay with me at Frank's house."

"No. No, that I can't do, Darling."

Maybe you and I could stay in Buddy's camper," Sandy said. "It's so fun. Like camping out."

"I don't see how I can. I didn't bring anything with me."

"You can wear my clothes. Please. I've really missed you. And you could see where I'm staying. You'd see I'm all right."

Sandy stepped aside as Parker strode past them, his face an unhealthy shade of red. "He wouldn't really keep Frank from racing in the Grand National, would he?" Sandy asked. "It's the biggest race of its kind ever. There's never been one like it before."

"I'm sure the men will work out their differences," Maggie said, not having any idea if that was true or not. She could hear in Sandy's voice how concerned she was. "Tell you what, I'll get a motel room for us here in Wichita and we can stay here tonight."

After the car had been pushed up onto the trailer and secured, Sandy told the men, "Aunt Maggie is going to spend the night with me. She said we could get a motel room, but I thought maybe we could just go on to Hutch and sleep in Buddy's camper."

"Happy to oblige," Buddy said, grinning, but not at anyone in particular.

"Thank you, but I don't want to be any trouble," Maggie said.

"Suit yourself," Buddy said, "but the offer stands. If you wanted, we could park it by a nearby pond where there's usually a good breeze."

Frank's expression and body language showed that he was still stewing about the confrontation with Parker, but he agreed with Buddy that they should get started back to Hutch and stop off at Skaets' Steak Shop to end the evening right.

"You know your way to Hutch?" Buddy asked Maggie.

"Just follow 95 across, right?"

All at once it seemed settled that she would stay in Hutchinson with Sandy. "I guess Sandy and I can go on ahead and wash off some of this dirt. Where is this steak place?"

Buddy told her which side of the road it was on and how far into town to start looking for the sign.

•   •   •   •   •

On the way to Hutch, Sandy tuned in the car radio, singing and keeping time with her head and shoulders to "Johnny Be Good" while Maggie mused aloud about how much track dust is carried off after every race just by the fans alone, not to mention the mud that gets caked on the cars right after the track is watered. Sandy found Maggie's notion of a slowly diminishing track funny, or maybe just a welcome relief from the ugly scene with Parker, and she milked it for all it was worth. "I bet there's enough dirt in people's shoes to add a turn five," Maggie said, laughing with Sandy at the absurdity of the joke.

By the time they reached the steak house, they were enjoying themselves so much that the other customers took notice, first when they selected a table and again when they emerged from the restroom with fresh makeup where layers of dust had been. With their heads bent together as they chatted away, they could easily have been mistaken for sisters.

That was exactly what Frank was thinking when he and Buddy, along with some other drivers and their families, showed up a few minutes later and pushed tables together for the post-race feeding and wind-down. Frank took the seat on the other side of Sandy, and Buddy sat next to Maggie.

"Here's the plan, Maggie" Buddy told her, explaining they'd swing by his garage to drop off her car and the trailer and park the camper by a small pond where it would be cooler. She liked it that he had said her name, and Sandy kept looking over at her and smiling, clearly enjoying having her there. Even Frank was being accommodating in his fashion. He told her what a help her niece was and said she did her family proud, making friends easily. Maggie smiled and nodded, but was irritated that he would try to tell her what the attributes were of a girl she'd been raising for ten years.

By the time the steaks and fries had been consumed, along with cold beers, Maggie had not only learned the names of several others dining around them, she knew which cars the men drove, where they were from, and a whole lot more about how truly big the upcoming National Championship race was for all of them.

She could see how Sandy had gotten caught up in the excitement and wondered if Frank might regret having laid claim to his daughter at what seemed a crazy busy time. That had to be complicating his life—which was okay with Maggie. Kids are supposed to complicate lives. That was part of the cost, and the reward, of having them. She saw that it would be a hard sell to her niece, but Maggie thought she might be able to convince Frank that it would be better for Sandy to be back in Kiowa while he got ready for the big race. The trick would be to pick the right moment to suggest it, which was even more reason for her to stay in the area a little longer.

That was what she told herself, although she kept studying Frank while he was busy talking with others about the race just past or the big one coming up. His chiseled features had softened only a little with age, and the blue eyes were as intense as ever, the outer corners crinkling slightly as he laughed. But when he focused on his food, or looked off pensively, his face seemed to darken with thoughts not being talked about over dinner—probably, she thought, the scene with Parker and the unresolved argument over the red light—and it was then he showed some of the wear the years had put on him.

She had driven to Wichita expecting to spend a couple of hours visiting with Sandy while the races were going on and head back to Kiowa, perhaps with her niece in tow. Now here she was smack in the thick of things, dining and drinking with the man who'd taken her niece away from them, and she didn't have a plan, except to not return home yet. That wasn't like her, but then desperate times call for desperate measures. And it would be good to see for herself how he was coping with his duties as a new father, away from the glitz and glamour of the race track.

"So Buddy," she said, after draining the last of her second beer. "How far is it to this cool breeze you were talking about?"

CHAPTER 36

After dropping off the trailer with the race car, along with Maggie's car, in his oversized garage-workshop, Buddy drove Maggie and Sandy in the camper to a pond behind his farmhouse and Frank followed. Buddy had run an electrical line out for the camper and put up an overhead light with a switch on the pole. Maggie had wanted to take her own car, but Buddy said since they would be going off road in the dark, it made more sense for him and Frank to drive. She wondered if Frank was worried that she might take off with Sandy in the middle of the night. It had occurred to her, but thinking about the legal ramifications, not to mention how upset Sandy would be, made her think better of it.

Sandy had quickly drifted into the sleep of the innocent, but Maggie, who had hoped for a heart-to-heart talk about the future, couldn't shut her mind off. She took a lawn chair out to sit beside the trailer and try to sort things out. There were too many contradictions to deal with, including her feelings about Frank, who seemed genuinely fond of Sandy, even though it was clear that father and daughter were still in the early stages of getting to know one another. And yet, the anger he'd expressed towards her family at the courthouse in Liberal clearly meant he hadn't gotten over that dismal part of their shared history. She'd wondered more than once at his insistence he'd written to Ruth, intending to come back for her. Surely, she would have known if her little sister had heard from her lost love.

Each new thought carried Maggie back across territory just covered, like a tightrope walker on one of those bicycles that zips forward and backward along the wire, never quite reaching the platform on either end.

When Ruth died, Maggie had been the one to bear up—for her parents and Sandy and the rest of the family—but it had been a false front that she'd put up. Part of each day for the first month, she'd huddled on the hope chest in the closet, crying into a pillow. And she'd dreaded the responsibility of taking on a five-year-old girl when her own grief over losing a sister had created a brittleness between her heart and hipbones that threatened to snap and cause her to collapse in on herself. Only Sandy's own shock and panic at being orphaned and her need for comforting had pulled Maggie from the closet time and again to act the surrogate mother and conjure up reassurances for her niece that they would survive their shared misery, although more often than not she'd doubted it herself.

But they had survived. And somehow aunt and niece had patched together a life as a family. And the love that had always been there shape-shifted into something more substantive, more tangible. In the 10 years they had been destined to make do with each other, Maggie wouldn't have claimed they had become mother and daughter. Not until Sandy wasn't there anymore and Maggie feared that she might not find her, might not get her back, did she realize that she couldn't bear the thought that they might be separated indefinitely.

Yet Frank, in fact, was her father, openly, publicly, after all the years of silence—which had amounted to the same thing as secrecy, she now realized. And in some way Maggie was not yet sure of, Frank cared about his daughter. Given time, he might actually find a way to keep her.

The noises coming from around the pond were familiar to Maggie, but to listen to them all alone there in the night made sounds more intense. She looked down at the T-shirt she'd borrowed from Sandy to sleep in and then out to the water, which looked black and silky in the moonlight.

She could see it was shallow near the bank because of the hoof prints of the cows that watered there. She got a towel from the bathroom, and draped it over the back of a lawn chair, then walked over to the water's edge. She hesitated a moment, but the only lights were far off in the distance, so she pulled the shirt off, tossing it back up past the muddy bank, and waded in.

The water was cooler than she'd expected, a sweet shock of cold against her warm skin, and then blissfully refreshing. She walked toward the center of the pond, sinking to mid-calf, then her knees, and finally to her waist, before realizing that she was in the direct middle and that the water wasn't going to get any deeper. Bending her knees, she lowered herself until her shoulders were submerged, then leaned back and floated. The sky was so brilliant and close that she imagined she could feel the combination of moon and starlight on her face, that glow just as tangible as the lapping of the water over her as she whirled her hands just beneath her to stay afloat.

She was sorry there wasn't a rubber raft so that she could fall asleep there, the pond undulating gently beneath her. Closing her eyes, she imagined what it would be like to wake up there in the early morning, birds chirping in the surrounding trees. She imagined cows standing at the edge of the pond watching her with mild interest between long pulls of water, sunlight striking her body and face. Gradually, a noise that hadn't been there when she had slipped into the pond reached her submerged ears. It sounded like a propeller or car engine. She raised her head and looked into oncoming headlights.

The sudden move sank her to the muddy bottom of the pond and she struggled to get her footing without having to stand up and expose herself any more than she already had.

She muttered to herself, cursing Buddy for parking them where someone else was obviously interested in being that particular night. By the time she was crouched halfway to the bank, the car was parked next to the camper, lights still on. She didn't stand a chance of getting to the shirt she'd thrown down just a few yards away without being totally exposed.

"Who's there?"

"Maggie?"

"Frank?"

"I thought you'd be asleep."

"Then what are you doing here?"

"Checking up." He was quiet for a moment. "Looks like you're fine." She thought she heard a chuckle, but couldn't be sure.

"Of course we're okay. Would you mind turning off those lights?"

With the headlights off, she could see Frank leaning against the car.

"How's the water?"

"Fine."

"I'm surprised to see that much in there this time of the year."

Losing her footing momentarily, she slithered forward on her hands and knees before catching herself and backing up crablike to a more discreet depth.

"You nice and cool now?" His face wasn't clear to her, but she could hear the smile in his voice.

"I'm cool, and as you can see still awake, and perfectly fine."

"Yep."

"Frank."

"Maggie."

She sighed audibly. "If it's all right with you, I'd like to get out."

"Sure thing. Can I give you a hand?"

"You could hand me that shirt over there."

He walked to where Sandy's shirt lay in a heap and held it up. "Here you go."

"All right, you've had your fun," she said. "May I have it?"

He held it out so she could grab it from where she squatted half submerged, mud oozing between her toes.

"Now turn around, and move away," she said, waiting and watching as he walked from the bank toward the camper before pulling the shirt over her head and tugging it down over her wet skin.

CHAPTER 37

Frank listened to the splashes as Maggie stepped out of the water. "Good idea you had," he said. "Wish I'd thought of it myself. I'm surprised Sandy wasn't out there with you."

The bank was slick where the cows had trampled the grass under, and Maggie slipped twice making her way up the bank. "She dropped right off to sleep. The late-night dip was sort of a spur of the moment thing." She walked around him to grab the towel from the chair and started to step into the camper when she realized she had mud up over her toes and splatters on her legs.

Frank, who had followed her, stood close by, looking down to see what she was looking at. "Stay here." He swung the camper door open and stepped in. Maggie looked down and pulled the shirt out from her wet skin.

Frank came back out with a plastic dishpan of soapy water and a towel thrown over his shoulder. "Here you go," he said, placing the pan on the ground. He reached for her hand to steady her as she put one foot into the water and sloshed it around.

"Thanks."

"You missed some." He squatted down and used his free hand to pull the water up over her calf, rubbing lightly until all the mud was off. "Now the other one."

"I can get it."

"Switch," he said, still holding her hand, the earlier teasing tone gone from both his voice and face. He tipped his face up to her, moonlight tracing the edges of his cheekbones and jaw. Maggie felt she was seeing him exactly as Ruth would have all those years ago, and she had the sensation that any movement would bring her down like a collapsed parachute.

"Maggie?"

She looked away and placed her clean foot on the grass, then put the other one into the pan. He didn't seem to be lingering, but Maggie was aware of each stroke of his hand over her leg. When he stopped, she lifted her foot out and let go of his hand, holding perfectly still as he took the extra towel and dried her legs and tops of her feet.

He stood up and slung the water out over the grass, saying, "You should sleep like a baby out here." He looked out over the pond, then up at the sky, and finally back at her. "You're like her in some ways."

Maggie blotted the ends of her hair with the towel, knowing from the tone of his voice he meant Ruth and not Sandy. "I guess so." That wasn't the answer she wanted to give. In what ways, she wanted to ask, what did he see when he looked at her?

He seemed to be making a study of her face, and said, "She smiled more."

Nodding, Maggie realized that was true.

"Walking down the street or riding in the car she was always smiling, like she knew something was up." He rubbed at his arm absentmindedly, as if locating a mosquito bite. "That's why when she cried it was like the world turned inside out."

Maggie was so struck to hear him talk about Ruth with such tender familiarity she didn't know how to respond. To her family, he had been a rash moment in her sister's short life. But to the young lovers, who had been committed enough to run off and get married just before he left for the war, they'd no doubt already envisioned a future together. Maggie recognized then how limited her own understanding had been during those turbulent days of the elopement and annulment.

"Sandy is like that, too," he said. "She's got a real playful streak. But she's always on the lookout, like a small animal in the woods."

"She's had a lot to deal with for a young girl." Maggie's voice wavered slightly, "I'm afraid I haven't always been there when she's needed me. I mean, I'm there, of course, but sometimes . . . I don't always—"

"She's crazy about you," he said. "She thinks you're funny, too. Especially when you mimic some of the local pain-in-the-asses. My word, not hers. You put on a regular show, she says."

If the moon had been any brighter, the flush that swept across Maggie's neck and face would have been clearly visible. "I shouldn't do that, of course," she said. "They're private jokes between Sandy and me. Or at least they were until now. It seems you two have shared a lot."

"Not really." He gave the pan a little shake to get the last drops of water out and set it on the lawn chair. "There hasn't been much time. But we agreed to talk things over honestly. No more games or lying. She's a pretty amazing kid. Buddy's even got her working on the car some."

Maggie clutched the towel to her chest and said, "I want to say something, but I'm not sure it will come out right."

"Won't know till you try."

"I want to say I'm sorry about . . . what happened all those years ago. I don't know who was right or wrong, or what should or shouldn't have been done. But I'm not sorry about the baby—Sandy, I mean." Maggie wasn't certain she could make clear to him what was only the germ of an idea to her, something she hadn't really thought through or tried to express before now. "I guess what I mean is that in spite of the way things turned out—for all of us—we never regretted Sandy for a minute. I . . . I love her. I always have. After Ruth died, I somehow— well, she became . . . she's the most important thing in my life."

Frank had been listening with his face turned slightly to one side, as if to hear what she was saying but not lose sight of some private vision.

When she stopped talking, he looked down at her. She was asking him to give up his daughter. Not telling him yet. That would come later, no doubt, probably in a letter from some law firm. But for now she was asking. And in his own way, he was asking the same of her.

He tossed the towel onto the pan and stood there looking at her.

She was trying to sort out the tangle of feelings that had been stirring in her the past few hours, the way a sentence is diagrammed so that all its parts and their relationships are clear. But some things defy labels and categories, including the conflicting feelings he had aroused in her. She turned away and buried her face in the towel.

"Maggie . . . ." He didn't know what else to say, so he just said her name again, softer this time, but she kept her face buried, only the shaking of her shoulders giving away the fact that she was crying.

He stepped up and put his arms loosely around her back, staring out across the field to a faraway floodlight, maybe half-a-mile off. "Come on now." Her body was rigid and a muffled sob escaped from the wadded-up towel.

"Here," he said, taking one of her hands and pulling her arm around his waist, as if she were a reluctant partner about to be taught to dance against her will.

"Better. But it would help if you could just relax a little." He reached under her chin and turned her face to one side. "And come up for air."

He rubbed her shoulders and back with slow, soft strokes, sighing himself when she began to loosen up, almost imperceptibly at first, her chin dropping lower on his chest. He let his own head drop, resting his cheek lightly against her damp hair.

The comfort he'd meant to give was changing into something more. He curved over her, wrapping his arms tight around her back.

"Wait," Maggie said, but didn't say for what, nor did she attempt to pull away. Instead she asked, "Why are you doing this?"

"Why do you think?"

"I can't think. That's the problem."

"But you suspect my motives."

"Shouldn't I? Wouldn't you do whatever it takes to keep me from taking Sandy back home?"

"You mean like try to compromise you?"

"Why not?"

"I don't know. How far would you go to get what you want?"

She moved slightly, but he couldn't tell whether it was intentional or involuntary. "If I could, I'd have put Sandy in my car and driven us away from here."

"Why didn't you?"

"You know why. It's a legal issue now."

"And you weren't sure Sandy would have gone with you."

She recognized the truth in what he'd said.

"You know, maybe I put my arms around you to comfort you because you were crying. Or maybe because you're a desirable woman, wearing a wet T-shirt, I might add, out here in the middle of nowhere." He let his head drop until his lips were on her neck. "Someone I feel drawn to in a way I haven't felt for a long time."

Maggie turned her face up, and by the time his lips were on hers she was already breathless from all the doubts tangled up with the desire she felt herself giving in to. For the moment, nothing mattered outside of the tight circle of their bodies. It wasn't until she let her head fall back and could see the whorl of the Milky Way that the world crept back in on her and she whispered, "This doesn't make any sense."

Frank pressed his lips against her neck and said, "Tell me about it."

She studied his face for a long moment, and then let her arms relax and slide back down his chest. He held her in check for a moment, finally letting her step back from him.

"I guess we're going to be sensible," he said, looking as if he wanted her to deny it.

Instead, she said, "We're on opposite sides, here."

He let out a long breath. "Are you sure about that?"

"I'm not sure about anything right now, except that this is getting really complicated."

"That it is," he said, reaching over and moving damp strands of hair back over her ear. "You sleep well. I'll see you in the morning."

She watched as he walked to the car and started it up and circled it back toward the road. The tail lights were pinpricks before she turned to go into the camper, bending down to retrieve the towel and dishpan, the memory of his hand sliding along her calf flashing briefly as she pulled dry clothes from Sandy's suitcase.

Everything would be clearer, she thought, in the cold light of day. But there in the shadowy cocoon of the trailer, with moonlight filtering through the screens along with the breeze and the sounds of insects, she allowed herself to replay the night visit as if she were watching a movie over and over, trying to imagine a different ending for the three of them from the one she feared would be inevitable.

CHAPTER 38

Maggie's watch showed 6:13 a.m. when she finally gave up on getting back to sleep and rolled over to look out of the window next to the sleeping platform that stretched above the front seats. Dawn was creeping through the tree line to the east and birds were warbling the morning into shape. She was already too warm to be comfortable. Rolling onto her back, she stretched as well as she could in the confined space and thought about Frank, mostly how his arms felt around her, how hungry his mouth had been the moment she'd let her guard down, giving as good as she got, as it turned out. Her skin was still alive with the memory.

She checked the side window to make sure there were no cars around. Stepping into the tiny bathroom, she sponged off, aware of the limited water supply. She wondered what Frank was thinking, whether he was feeling any regret at letting his guard down. She should be, but somehow it wasn't happening for her. At least not yet.

During fitful bouts of wakefulness throughout the night and early morning, she'd tried to determine whether Frank had been trying to influence her, or perhaps compromise her—the words he'd used—to gain leverage in their struggle for Sandy. But then, he could be wondering the same thing about her. It was a lot to conjure up from a long kiss and an embrace that felt as if it had been a long time coming and might not end. But it had ended, of course. And after much mulling over and little sleep, she was uncertain what the day ahead of them might bring to this complicated relationship.

As soon as she was out of the bathroom, she began the process of waking Sandy. She knew her niece would sleep till noon if left to her own devices, so Maggie continued to harass her with brief back rubs and toe tweaks as she went about organizing things and straightening up the camper. The sky had brightened to a cloudless deep blue, and there was enough of a breeze to prevent the morning from heating too quickly.

Giving Sandy another final warning and a piece of bread with honey that she set on her rib cage, with a warning not to roll back over, Maggie went outside, turned the chair around to where she could see the road, and sat down. The field they were in was obviously used only for pasture. In front and to the left were the oblong haystacks that always reminded her of giant loaves of bread, giving a neat symmetry to sowing and reaping. Hearing the toilet flush, she called out to remind Sandy that they weren't connected to a water supply and couldn't know how much was left in the tank, so not to shower yet. Just as she got up to go in and suggest her niece take a sponge bath, the dust of an approaching car rose up in the distance.

She leaned in the door and called out, "They're coming! Just get dressed. You can finish getting cleaned up later."

Sandy, who was brushing her teeth, leaned out to look at her aunt and asked what the big deal was.

Maggie's jaw went slack a split second before she said, "I don't know what you're talking about. Just get some clothes on. Big day ahead." She backed down off the step to retrieve the chair, then ran her fingers through her hair and shook it out.

Sandy rinsed and spit and pushed open the door. "Then why were you yelling?"

"Who's yelling?

"Geez! Touchy. A person would think you hadn't gotten enough sleep or something."

Glancing at Sandy's expression as the screen swung shut, Maggie decided that it was an innocent remark, and that she hadn't been aware of Frank's late-night visit.

Maggie was standing beside the camper, where Frank had been parked only a few hours earlier, when the Mercury crunched to a stop.

Buddy got out of the driver's side. "Mornin'," he said, swinging around to the front of the car. "You look like the country air agrees with you."

"Good morning." She looked through the windshield, saw that there was no one else in the car. "Sandy's just now getting around," she told him, wondering what it meant that Frank hadn't come out for them. Whatever the reason, she felt as if she'd been stood up, then felt a surge of anger for allowing herself to be so vulnerable.

"No rush," Buddy told her, leaning back against the hood of the car. "I figured you could drive Frank's car easily enough in the daylight, and I'll lead you to his place in the camper."

"I see. You're sure he trusts me with it?" She smiled, but it didn't cover the sarcasm in her voice.

Buddy looked out over the pond and frowned as if studying something interesting there. "It's an automatic. Shouldn't be any problem. He didn't want you to get yours all dusty drivin' through the field."

"Very thoughtful," she said. "I hope we're not putting him out too much." She went to the camper to get her purse and to say that they were leaving. Sandy had made certain that everything loose had been secured and was tying a satiny blue racing jacket around her waist, the sleeves dangling clear to her knees.

"What's that for? It's going to get hot."

She shrugged. "For the heck of it."

Buddy and Sandy greeted each other with the casualness of good friends, reminding Maggie of how much had taken place in her niece's life in the few days she'd been gone.

Maggie gunned the Mercury and then braked to spin it through a tight U-turn, dust spewing up around and settling over the car as they bumped along the cow path after the camper.

"Whoa!" Sandy called out. "What was that for?"

"For the heck of it," Maggie answered.

As they passed the pond, she saw that the water was shallow and brown, not all that inviting after all.

•   •   •   •   •

The alley behind Frank's house was wide enough to accommodate the camper, which Buddy parked far enough ahead so that Maggie could pull in behind him. By the time she had turned the engine off and gotten out of the car, Sandy had run on ahead and disappeared through the back door, the screen closing after her with a resounding slap. Maggie stood there, looking across the top of the car until Buddy walked over.

She was regretting her earlier curtness, especially in light of his loaning them the camper and finding a cool and private place to park it.

"Thanks again. For the use of the camper. It's real cozy."

"Glad to oblige. Shall we see what the old boy's up to?"

She paced her stride to his, and tried not to appear anxious, but her skin tingled.

"Is the race this Sunday really as big as Sandy says it is?"

He held the door for her. "It'll put dirt track racing on the map in a whole new way. It'll mean better crowds, more money, hotter cars than ever before. Eventually. Right now, it's just the biggest purse goin'."

At first, Maggie was so intent upon staging a casual greeting with Frank that nothing else registered. It wasn't until they were seated at the table and Frank had poured coffee all around, Sandy's mug half filled with milk, that she looked around. She hadn't given any thought to the kind of home he would have, or of how he would fit into a domestic scene. She checked out the kitchen and living room beyond while the others talked about how hot it was going to get and Frank and Buddy made plans for the day. She could see telltale signs of hurried cleaning—the paper sack of trash nearly filled to bursting, a bulging dish drainer, the dustpan and broom leaning in the corner nearest the table, surely not their usual spot. The notion of his staying home that morning to tidy the place up for her visit was the last thing she would have thought to suspect him of.

Frank kept glancing at her over the rim of his cup, but his expression was too noncommittal to give anything away. "So, you say you slept all right?" he asked.

He had to be testing her, but he sounded as sincere as a boy scout.

"I don't believe I did say, but yes, we did."

His eyebrows went up at the "we."

"Sandy fell right to sleep, and I didn't have any trouble either."

"Good. It's fairly cool out by the water, I would imagine."

He was definitely toying with her, and the other two were looking from Frank and back to Maggie like spectators at a ping pong match.

Turning to Sandy, Maggie asked if she had plans for the next couple of days, saying that her grandmother was anxious to see for herself that she was all right. She looked over at Frank. "Any objections to our driving down to see Mother? I don't know if Sandy told you, but she's had a stroke."

Frank set his coffee cup on the table and leaned back. "We can talk about it."

It wasn't until Sandy and Buddy were getting up and heading out the door to run some last-minute errands that Maggie recognized a plot was underfoot. The men were so obviously clearing Sandy out for a while so that Frank and Maggie could be alone that Maggie nearly laughed. And she might have after the door had closed if Frank hadn't looked so sober.

"Alone at last," she offered. "So. What's the idea of getting rid of Sandy?" She was trying to keep her tone light, but was glad to be sitting down for the clearing of the air she sensed was coming.

"I just thought we should talk before you head back."

"I agree," she said, frowning down at her coffee.

"So, speaking of plans, what are yours," he asked.

"Well, as soon as we get home, I plan to take a shower."

"Why wait? There's plenty of water here."

She looked at him and raised an eyebrow. "I take it that's an invitation to use your shower?"

"Make the drive more pleasant."

When she didn't answer, he said, "Anyway, it's all in the family. Sandy's got gobs of girl stuff in there you can use."

She was halfway entertaining his offer to wash the residue of pond water out of her hair when he got up and refilled his coffee mug, then held out the pot. She nodded for him to refill her cup too. He sat back down so that they were squared off across a corner of the surprisingly well-polished oak table.

"Did you really get any sleep?" he asked.

"Some. How about you?"

"Same."

She turned the cup around in her hands and smiled at him tentatively. "Well, we seem to have covered the topic of how much or little we slept last night pretty thoroughly."

Pursing his lips as if to avoid smiling, he nodded.

She reached up and ran her fingers along her collarbone—a nervous habit she was almost never aware of anymore. "Frank, I think we both want the same thing."

"I'm happy to hear it." She heard the smile in his voice before she looked up and saw it on his face.

"I'm talking about Sandy's wellbeing."

"That too," he said. He reached across the table and replaced her hand with his, stroking her collarbone. She barely breathed as he ran his fingers up her neck and along her jaw, her lips parting as he ran his index finger around them. Reaching up, she took his hand and pulled it down to the table, holding it there.

"So," she asked again, "a visit to Mom today? An overnight, maybe."

Frank pulled his hand back and ran his thumb across the top of his belt buckle. "She can see the old lady. But I'll be down tonight to bring her back home. Understood?"

Maggie started to protest, then realized that it might be good for him to see Sandy in her familiar surroundings, to see how much more stable her life was there with the family she'd always known. It might be the push he needed to see where Sandy truly belonged.

CHAPTER 39

After the girls left for Kiowa, Frank sat on his back steps with the newspaper still folded across his thighs and closed his eyes. What had Sandy said that first morning at breakfast? She could feel the rumble of the engines in her chest, follow the changes of pitch when they accelerated or idled. His kid, all right. If she'd been a boy, he might have taken her to the track early, put her into the driver's seat and crawled in beside her to guide her through the gears and turns. He could show her how to spot the left front wheel and hang onto the groove, arms firm but flexible, so that all the force of the upper body is joined through the steering column with the horsepower straining underneath.

The thought of Sandy's slender arms braced against the wheel made him smile in spite of his dark mood. She was such a delicate blend of child and woman, he had trouble knowing how to deal with her. Watching the two girls getting into Maggie's car that morning gave him his first real stab of anxiety. The possibility of having to fight Sandy's family for her once they were back in Kiowa set up shop in the back of his head and was doing a bang-up business. Equally worrying was the thought of them alone on the highway. He realized that realistically they were in no danger. For one thing, they were both smart and headstrong. But they had a vulnerability that seemed intensified to him when he saw them together.

His real problem, he finally admitted to himself after Sandy had stalled around and then run back to give him a self-conscious hug, was that these two people had somehow gotten a hold on him and were now driving out of his life together. And he wasn't sure how serious either of them was about wanting their association with him to go on. By the time they were to the end of the alley and turning out of sight, he felt a stab of melancholy that quickly changed into something more familiar, and therefore less galling—irritation.

He lit a cigarette and opened the newspaper, automatically turning to the sports page. There was an article with his name in the lead-in: "Frank Haggard to Pilot Red-light Special." He felt a rush of anger as he quickly read through the piece, then read it again more slowly before going inside and dialing the private line to Parker's Dry Cleaners.

On the phone, G.D. now told him again "That's the deal, hot shot. The new sponsors want the red-light special. You can take it or leave it."

Frank could hear the hissing and clumping of the steam pressers in the background before Parker must have swung his office door shut.

"I kid you not, Haggard. Nobody treats me the way you did in Wichita and gets away with it. I may be just a fat wad of greenbacks to you, but I'm still the one calls the shots. You got that?"

Frank opened the back screen-door and flipped his cigarette butt into the dirt between the porch and spreading cedar. "Yeah, I got it. Now you get this," he said, "you want a side show, go hire yourself a freak. I'm not running another race with that clown's nose on the car. It's too risky for the others drivers. They told me as much."

"Then you're not running period, buddy. I've had my eye on a younger driver anyway, someone who's still got fresh balls."

The sound of Parker's receiver hitting the cradle was so loud that for a moment Frank had the impression he'd knocked himself in the head with his own phone. He dropped it into the cradle and set it back on the counter. Then he opened a bottle of beer and went into the living room, where he turned up the air conditioner full blast and stretched out on the sofa, a sick feeling roiling through him. He rolled the cold bottle across his forehead. He knew G.D. meant what he said. The question was would he be able to find anyone with real skills to replace Frank before time trials on Saturday. And if he did, would Frank be able to find another ride? He thought of that red light and got angry all over again. It was one thing to keep his foot down for three laps when he was in the lead and there was only the handling of his own car to consider. Trying it in deep traffic was a recipe for disaster. Seemed everyone but G.D. knew that.

Frank's head hurt. He twisted it around against the throw pillow, trying to loosen up his neck. Finishing the beer, he lit a cigarette and went back into the kitchen where he dialed the garage. He didn't have to ask if G.D. had gotten in touch with Buddy. As soon as he said, "It's me," Buddy was yelling, asking what they thought they were doing, how could they be so stupid and stubborn, and other questions he wasn't expecting answers to. Finally, Frank gave up, and in response to Buddy declaring he was going over to Parker's Cleaners to try to talk some sense into at least one of them, said fine, he could find Frank at Jack's Nest, where he intended to make some sense out of a bottle of rye.

CHAPTER 40

The quick stop-off at Aunt Irma and Uncle Lloyd's as they got to Kiowa had been a bit of a strain at first, everybody seeming a little stiff as they welcomed Sandy back. She could tell that Maggie had filled them in over the phone before they got there because there was a distinct lack of curiosity about exactly where Sandy had been—and no one asked if she was back to stay.

But when the adults stepped out for a quick pow wow on the porch, her cousins made it clear they were in awe of what she had done. She answered their questions about hitchhiking and actually confronting Frank with a nonchalance that she knew she would probably pay for later—get your nose up in the air, you're bound to stumble, their Grandma Parson liked to say. But for the moment, Irma's kids—both younger than Sandy—were receiving her as a true adventurer, which was how she'd seen herself before she'd accidentally fallen asleep in the Enid bus depot and everything had accelerated out of her control. Now she was back, but still not in control. She wasn't sure who was.

Back home, finally, Sandy flopped onto her bed, scattering the pile of stuffed animals. "Hey, guys!" she greeted them. "Miss me?" Rolling onto her back, she sat Bobby Bear on her chest and looked around the room. The familiarity felt like an embrace.

"Be sure to put your dirty clothes in the washing machine," Maggie called from the next room. I'm going to call rehab to let your grandmother know we're coming by."

Without lifting her head from the pillow, Sandy said, "Hello, Ralph. Still training to be a peeping Tom?"

"It's my life's ambition," he whispered. "Can you come out?"

"Why are you whispering?"

"I thought you might be grounded or something. For the rest of puberty. "

"Don't be repulsive."

"Meet ya on the front porch."

"Not there. I have to start the laundry. Wait for me in your dad's wood shop."

· · · · ·

The air in the small garage that Ralph's father used as a woodworking shed was pungent with the scent of shavings and turpentine. At first, she didn't see Ralph, since it took her eyes a few seconds to switch from the bright sunlight to the shadows.

"Over here." He was sitting on a stool in the corner, sanding one of the cedar horses his father used for the weathervanes he sold at craft fairs.

"Hi." She scooted onto a stool next to him. "So how are you?"

"How am I? How are you?"

"Fine."

He grinned at her. "You look different."

"How so?"

"You look good."

"Thanks. So do you."

"You really did it. Shoot. I couldn't believe it when your Uncle Lloyd came banging on the front door, asking if I knew where you were. Man, was he steamed."

"What did you say?"

"That I didn't know. That I hadn't seen you for two days."

"That was a lie." Her tone indicated that it was a lie she admired.

"No, it wasn't, technically. You were slumber-partying with the girls most of Friday, or getting ready to, and they didn't ask me anything until late Saturday. What was it like, hitchhiking there alone? And what's he like?"

"It was hot in the back of the truck, and then things got kind of crazy when the police woke me up at the bus depot."

"Come on, this is Ralph you're talking to."

"Okay," she propped her feet on the bottom brace of his stool and put her hands on his knees. "It was like . . . kind of scary at first, but then it was exciting. Except not like an adventure, you know, where anything can happen, and it doesn't matter what. More like I was finally going to do something I wasn't sure I'd ever have the nerve to do. Like parachuting, or something."

She gazed into space for a moment.

"And?"

"And he's incredibly good-looking and popular. He didn't believe me at first. And I think he likes me now. It's hard to tell sometimes because he doesn't show his feelings a lot. Except when he's angry. Did you read about the big fight in Liberal?"

"Yeah. Were you there?"

Still smiling, she bit her bottom lip.

"Well, were you?"

"You won't tell anyone?"

"Do I ever? Jeez, Sandy, I could fill this room with the stuff you've told me that I'm not supposed to tell."

"We started it!" The look on his face was exactly what she expected to find there. "Really!" she said. "I even got socked in the jaw. Had to have an ice pack. "

Ralph put down the horse and sandpaper and gazed at her admiringly.

"Which side?"

"Here," she turned and fingered the right side of her face, although the coveted tenderness and discoloration had mostly disappeared.

Ralph reached over and ran his fingers along her jaw.

Suddenly feeling self-conscious, she pushed his hand away. "There's nothing to see now, of course. But it hurt like heck."

He nodded, a curious look on his face.

"What's wrong?"

"Nothing. Only I was just thinking, you really do seem different."

She pulled her feet back under her own stool.

"I'm exactly the same person. Only life is a lot more complicated than it was before. Aunt Maggie and Frank really hated each other at first, but they're trying to be civil to one another on my account. They don't say much when they're in the same room, but there's this incredible tension." Ralph was still looking at her in that curious way, and she hopped down off the stool and ambled around the room.

"Are you going back to him?"

"He's coming here for me tonight. I want you to meet him, okay?"

Slipping down from the stool with the litheness of a cat, Ralph leaned against the workbench studying her.

"Cut it out, Ralph!"

"What?"

"Looking at me like that, like I'm some sort of freak or something."

"You're imagining things. Anyway, how long are you going to stay with him?"

"That's the thing. I don't know what's going to happen. Right now the law says I have to stay with him. But Aunt Maggie has a lawyer trying to get it so I live here legally."

"Which do you want to do?"

That was the question she'd avoided asking herself ever since she'd seen Maggie in Hutch, how hurt and lost she'd seemed. "I don't know. I really don't, Ralph. I mean, now that I'm back—" Ralph was right, things were different. "I wish everyone could just be happy."

Ralph said, "You dope" softly, maybe meaning something else.

"I'd better get back. We have to go pick up Grandma. She's been so upset, the doctor thinks that the only thing that will calm her down will be to have her come home for a day or two, to reassure her sort of. Uncle Lloyd's going along to help get her in and out of the car."

As she crossed to the door he said, "If you decide to stay with him, promise you'll tell me right away?"

She walked over and put her hand on his shoulder, which felt rounder and harder than she remembered. "Don't I always tell you everything?"

Grasping her by the arms, he pulled her into an awkward hug.

"I gotta get back," she said, as he released her. "But I'll call."

She headed back to her aunt's house feeling every waft of the hot summer breezes against her skin as if it were more alive than ever, and her mind, too, expanding to take in all the new and puzzling possibilities that leaving home and even her returning had somehow led to.

CHAPTER 41

By 10:30, Maggie had given up on hearing from Frank about coming for Sandy, and gone to bed. She assumed he'd gotten involved with Buddy and the race car and would call in the morning. She was reading *The Deadly Darling*, the latest Shell Scott mystery, when the hum of a car idling just a few yards from her bedroom window caught her attention. She set her book on the night stand and sat there listening for a car door to slam or for the noise to stop, but all she heard was the irritating drone of the engine. She went to the front door and saw Frank's car parked in the drive, but she couldn't see anyone in it.

She stopped on the porch to look around and whispered his name. When he didn't answer, she tiptoed out to look in the car. "Oh my word," slipped out before she clasped her hand over her mouth and looked around to see if anyone was watching. She eased his car door open, flinching at the prolonged squeak, and tested to make sure it wouldn't fall back on her before she let go and leaned over to turn off the engine. She saw an empty bottle lying on the floorboard, and the smell of whiskey didn't lessen any when she got Frank pulled upright on the seat, his slack mouth next to her chin as she tried to shake him into consciousness.

"How could you do this!" she whispered under her breath, "at this time, in this driveway, with my mother back in her bedroom!" Grunting as she worked his legs out of the car one at a time, she clasped her hands behind his back to pull him to his feet but couldn't budge him. "Mister, what a punishing I'm going to give you if we both survive this." She took a deep breath and grabbed him again. "Okay, third time's a charm." She pulled again, felt him rise up against her. She was about to topple over backwards when she felt his arms tightening around her and he caught his balance.

"Hi ya, Baby. Y'gonna be good ta ol' Frankie?"

"Oh, you'll get yours, Old Frankie. Help me get you inside."

Twisting around so that they were both facing the house, she pushed the car door shut with her foot, struggling to keep him upright. Teetering beside her, he alternately nuzzled her hair and rested his cheek on her head, as if to nod off again.

By the time she maneuvered him up the front steps and through the door, it occurred to her that she would never get him up the stairs to the extra bed in the dormer without waking up both her mother and Sandy. Pivoting, she ushered him into her room at the front of the house where, like a homing pigeon, he zeroed in on the center of her bed and plunged for it, landing spread eagle on his stomach.

Taking a deep breath to reinforce her resolution, she grabbed an arm and a leg and pulled, but it was like trying to lift a sack of wet cement—the weight kept shifting, forming a new, equally heavy center of gravity. Working her hands under his trunk and grabbing his shirt front and belt, she tested her grip, preparing to give one great heave to turn him onto the far side of the bed. "On the count of three," she whispered to herself, "one, two, three, heave!"

"What's going on?" Sandy might just as well have yelled "Boo!" Whether it was the adrenalin released from the scare or superior leverage, Maggie gave a yank that pulled Frank over the edge and onto her feet with a resounding thump she was sure shook the house.

Sandy threw herself crosswise over the bed and peered down at him. "Holy cow!" she muttered, "What's he doing here so late? I thought he'd decided to come in the morning."

Maggie clamped her hand over Sandy's mouth and whispered, "Listen!"

From the small bedroom behind the kitchen they could hear Olivia's thin, sleepy voice calling for Maggie. They looked from one another to Frank and back again. Maggie worked her legs free and leaned out the door.

"What is it, Mother?"

"I heard a noise. Is anything wrong?"

"I just stubbed my toe. Go back to sleep."

"Sounded bigger."

"It was my big toe." Maggie looked at Sandy and shrugged. Sandy clasped her hand over her mouth to contain a giggle, then tiptoed past Maggie to the door of her own room across the hall, from where she called out in a voice meant to sound gravelly with sleep, "It's just me. Grandma. I fell out of bed. I guess I'm not used to being back yet. Sorry. Go back to sleep."

"Good grief, you two, up all hours. Get to sleep!"

"Yes, Mother," said Maggie, at the same time Sandy said, "Yes, Grandma." As soon as the house was quiet again, Sandy slipped back into the front bedroom to join Maggie who was sitting cross-legged on the bed studying Frank.

"Is he, you know, drunk?"

"He would be if he were awake. Fortunately for us, he's graduated to passed-out."

"Wow!" Sandy whispered, "Why would he do that? Something terrible must have happened."

"It did, and it's lying on my bedroom floor." Maggie took one of her pillows and leaned down, working it under his head.

"Are you going to leave him there all scrunched up against the wall?"

"Only until I can get him on his feet."

"Shall I take his boots off?"

"Why bother? It's all the same to him."

"It'll make him quieter when he finally does get up."

"Good point," Maggie agreed, and got down to help Sandy. When they'd made him as comfortable as Maggie decided he had a right to be, she sent Sandy off to bed, saying that there was no point supposing what had happened since it looked like he would live to tell about it in the morning.

The sky turned from black to gray to pink in restless flashes as Maggie dozed fitfully, raising her head to see the clock's progress and then leaning over the edge of the bed to see if Frank was still there. She had to catch the alarm before her mother could hear it. Then she could get Frank out of there early enough for him to return and make a respectable entrance.

He changed position only once, rolling from his side to his back and throwing his arms up over his head, one of which wedged against the bed at a peculiar angle. At one point she reached down to turn his head to stop his snoring, and then ran her hand inside his shirt. Feeling his warmth and steady breathing sent ripples through her, and in a drowsy moment of recollection and forbearance, she thought what a waste to have him supine and virtually useless there below.

CHAPTER 42

When her room began to take on early morning light, Maggie went around the bed to where Frank's stocking feet jutted out. It took several shakes and admonitions for him to keep still before they were communicating, although at a fairly primitive level—mostly jerks and gestures.

Frank looked around from his low station with a mixture of disbelief and alarm, but in seconds his psychological predicament took a backseat to physical matters.

"Give me a minute, will ya. I'm think I might need to die."

"Oh no you don't," she said, gripping his hands so that she could pull him upright. "That's too good for you."

"What are you doing?" He pulled his hands away. "I'm not ready to move."

"Maybe not, but you've got to get out of here and come back like a normal, considerate, respectable person."

"Who you tryin' to kid?"

"Mother."

"Mother?" He opened his eyes wider.

"She's back."

"By back, you mean . . . ."

She nodded. "Back here in the back bedroom at the back of the house. Just a few yards down that hall."

"What hall? Isn't this the hall? You have another one?" He pressed the heels of his hands into his eyes and groaned softly. "When did I get here?"

"Late. Close to midnight. For Sandy's sake, try to pull yourself together."

"Sandy doesn't know I'm . . . here, does she?"

Maggie gave him a look that confirmed his fears.

"Damn."

"My sentiments, exactly."

He reached for the bed and pulled himself up slowly, until he was sitting on the edge, his eyes slightly glazed.

Recognizing that retribution far stronger than any she could dispense had taken hold, Maggie stood back and let Frank work unhampered at attempting to regain enough equilibrium to get him into his boots and back to his car. He sank back on his elbows, took a deep breath, and blew it out.

"Please!" Will you get out of here? Mother is a very light sleeper, and while she doesn't get around well, there's nothing wrong with her ears. Or her mind."

"That's an improvement."

"Don't even," she warned, pulling him to his feet and guiding him toward the front door.

Maggie motioned for Sandy, who was waiting on the porch, to put Frank onto the swing. Then she ran to the car, opened the door, and slammed it shut. Taking the steps two at a time, she motioned Sandy to get back inside and get dressed and ordered Frank to count to 50 and ring the doorbell. Then she slipped through the half-open door like all the sleuths she'd ever seen in the movies and tiptoed into her bedroom.

Frank sat on the swing trying to keep it from moving. He considered just staying there, letting Maggie stew while waiting for the doorbell to ring. He was still weighing his options when a young spitfire on a bike cut across the lawn and slung the morning paper in a shallow arc that stopped at Frank's feet. He jumped and the swing swayed and squeaked, causing the contents of his stomach to stir uncomfortably. He lunged to the side of the porch in time to throw up behind the hydrangeas.

Maggie had pulled on a half-slip, her blue sailcloth skirt, and a white boatneck blouse that showed off her collarbones before the doorbell rang. She stepped into her shoes and rushed from her room to find herself in a bottleneck behind Sandy, who was following as Lloyd pushed Olivia in the wheelchair. Sandy squeezed past and ran to get the door just as the bell rang again.

"Good morning, Mother. Lloyd." Maggie smiled a greeting at the front room in general, which included Frank, who was standing just inside the door. "You remember Frank Haggard. We didn't expect you this early."

"I . . . I thought I'd get an early start. I have some business to take care of. So I thought I'd get an early start."

"You already said that," Olivia said.

Maggie and Sandy nodded and smiled.

"Well, good." Maggie said.

"I hope I'm not inconveniencing anyone, coming this early," he said.

"You wanted to get an early start," Olivia said, looking at him sharply, as if considering whether a pound of ground round she'd been sold was really a full 16 ounces.

"No, of course not," Maggie said. "We get up early around here."

"Yeah," Sandy confirmed, realizing that no one there would believe that of her for a minute since she was notorious for sleeping in.

"Well, Lloyd," Maggie probed, "you're here early. I didn't hear you come in."

"I parked in back. Irma said to check if y'all needed help with Mother Parson, getting her up and around this morning. So I just threw on some clothes and came on over."

Maggie eyed her mother suspiciously and realized that she was wearing a muumuu over her nightgown, meaning she'd been in a hurry to get out of her room.

Olivia wagged her finger to let Lloyd know she wished to be wheeled farther into the room, where she looked first from Sandy to Frank to Maggie and back at Frank.

"So. You're back." Olivia's statement of the obvious failed to invite further comment until Lloyd made the usual inquiries regarding Frank's trip down—route taken, time required to make the trip. The last thing Frank remembered clearly was G.D.'s phone slamming in his ear. Then vaguely, dancing at Jack's Nest with either Faye Jarrod or the Nichols girl. After that, it was all headlights and horns.

"Sixty-one's the best road out," Frank said. "You ever make that drive?"

"You bet," Lloyd said, "taking seed orders all over the Midwest."

"So," Frank said, "what do you figure your best time to Hutch was?"

"As I recall, I've made that trip in around an hour and 15 minutes. That'd be startin' from the office in Medicine Lodge, y'nderstand."

"Hmm, Frank said. "That's pretty good."

"Ya think?" Lloyd said, chuckling, a racing fan pleased with the compliment.

Impatient with the idle chatter, Olivia barked "Who's hungry?" At first, no one answered; then they all chimed in at once speaking to cross purposes, all of which Olivia dismissed anyway.

"Sandy," she ordered, "go help your aunt fix eggs and bacon all around. You staying, Lloyd?"

Not wanting to leave her mother and Frank alone, Maggie suggested she put on some coffee and Lloyd could go get some breakfast rolls, but Olivia insisted on everyone having a real breakfast. Stopping beside her mother's chair on her way to the kitchen, Maggie asked if she would be all right.

"Why wouldn't I be? Am I in any danger?"

Embarrassed, Maggie added more quietly, "I meant your health."

"So did I."

Frank walked around the wing chair he'd been leaning on and started to sit down, pausing mid-way. "All right if I sit here?"

"Suit yourself, Mr. Haggard. So you're living in Hutchinson, Kansas. What do you do there?"

"Off-season, I sell insurance, mostly."

"Off-season?"

"When I'm not racing."

"Oh yes. I've heard about that. Tell me, are you any good at it?"

Frank leaned to one side of the chair and stretched his back. "What have you heard?"

She grunted and looked off to the side, then back at him. "Not much, Mr. Haggard. Not much at all."

Lloyd, on the other hand, had followed Haggard's career closely. He was eager to ask about other drivers he was interested in and how preparations for the Grand National were going. Frank let him talk, giving short answers where they were called for, and keeping an eye on Olivia to see if her expression changed. It didn't.

CHAPTER 43

Popping grease forced Maggie to back off from the large iron skillet of bacon she was frying, and she joined Sandy briefly at the doorway to eavesdrop. The conversation in the living room seemed to be focused on racing. She directed Sandy to butter the toast and finish setting the table, since the eggs were going into the hot bacon grease in two minutes. Maggie was darting and spinning around in a frenzy of last-minute moves to get everything to the dining room table and the whole group gathered around it. Finally, she called to Lloyd, asking him to wheel Olivia in and stationed herself at the head, opposite her mother. It took everyone else a few seconds to realize that Lloyd was leading the short version of their mealtime grace, and they barely got their heads bowed before he beseeched "For what we are about to receive, let us be truly grateful. Amen."

Frank looked proportionally worse in relation to the amount of light there was in the room and the amount of food that passed by him, of which he helped himself to only a piece of toast, a slice of bacon, and one egg.

Maggie, who was trying not to pay him undue attention, was uncomfortably aware of his discomfort along with her own.

"You know, Frank, we didn't even ask if you wanted to freshen up a little after the drive—"

He was on his feet immediately. "Thanks, I would like to do that. If you all will excuse me."

Olivia told Sandy to show him the way, but he said not to bother, he'd be all right, then turned the wrong way down the hall. Righting himself to a chorus of directions, he hurried toward the welcome privacy of the bathroom.

"You call Irma, Lloyd?" Olivia wanted to know. "She know you're taking breakfast here?"

He nodded in the midst of achieving the perfect balance of egg and bacon on a corner of toast. "Just now. I reckon she and the kids will be hightailing it over here any minute."

Maggie had thought to pick at her food, but found instead that her appetite was in good form and her plate nearly empty. Startled, she looked around at the others and put her fork down to sip coffee.

"Said you weren't hungry," Olivia reminded her.

"Cooking must have given me an appetite. You want anything else, Mother?"

"I want to know what he intends to do about her."

Sandy looked from her grandmother to her aunt.

"All that has to be worked out. The lawyers are handling it. I told you about that."

"I know what I was told. And how little I was told. I'm paralyzed, not senile."

Maggie felt as if she'd just bumped into a hot skillet with her stomach. "You're not paralyzed. The doctor says—"

"Don't hold with what the doctor says. I can't walk alone, I can't use my left hand the way I used to before I fell sick. That's paralyzed. You never were one to face things head on. But I'm not too sick to fight for what's mine."

Lloyd wiped his mouth and leaned his arm across the back of the wheel chair. "Don't get yourself upset, Mother Parson. We're all with you in this. But this isn't the time or place to be discussing such matters. Especially in front of the child."

"Why not in front of me," Sandy piped up. "It's my life you're talking about. I'm the one who started all this anyway, and I'm not a child. I'm almost fifteen. If I lived on a farm, I'd already have a driver's license."

Maggie told them both to please calm down. "Nothing can be settled right here and now, and there's no point in getting ourselves upset. Sandy's home safe and sound. That's what matters. The rest can all be worked out." She took the napkin she had twisted up and smoothed it out over her lap again.

When Frank walked back into the room, his hair newly combed and still wet around his face, they were all silently intent upon whatever little business they had left with their plates and cups. He looked at Maggie, who excused herself to get more coffee for everyone, and then to Sandy, who was chewing on a strip of bacon as if she had a grudge against it. Making conversation, he said, "Sandy doesn't seem to have developed much of a taste for eggs."

Olivia glanced at her granddaughter's plate and back to Frank's, where half a perfectly basted egg sat in congealing grease, and said "Seems you haven't either."

"I'm a little off my feed this morning."

Olivia just grunted, then said, "Must be the excitement about the big race," and held out her cup to Maggie, who refilled it and then the other cups around the table.

"So, Frank," Maggie asked, "what are your plans for the day?"

"Sandy and I need to get right back. Some business to attend to."

Not sure how to respond, Maggie stood up and started clearing the dishes. "Why don't you men finish your coffee out on the porch where there's a breeze? Sandy, how about helping me get Grandma back to her room for a rest." Maggie shot Sandy a look, and she jumped up and wheeled her grandmother into the back bedroom without waiting for her consent.

·　　·　　·　　·　　·

Olivia insisted she wanted to remain in the chair for a bit, said she could rest well enough there. She *was* tired, but what she needed was some time to reflect. So Frank Haggard was back. They'd said more to one another with their mutual omission of Ruth's name than with all the other words they'd exchanged. As he'd sat there, shifting in the wing chair and answering Lloyd's questions about where he'd been and what he'd been doing, she had only half listened.

In the far back of her brain had been flashes from the turbulent days when she'd been caught between Ruth's desperate love for that boy and her husband's fierce, unyielding need to protect his second daughter from her rash, romantic nature.

226

The more Ruth's soft face had dissolved into tears, the stonier her father's expression had become, until Olivia had begun to fear his rigidity far more than her daughter's dramatic threats to do herself harm.

And then came Ruth's eerily sober revelation about the baby, her face set hard like her father's with the sense that this was what they all deserved—her tyrant father, her mother, who had refused to intervene, and her annulled husband, who had allowed himself to be cut from her life so completely that she questioned he was ever really part of it. But of course it was soon obvious to the world he had been.

Even after Ruth had given over to her father's solution and married his kind and decent employee Fred Turner, Olivia would catch Ruth running her finger down the page of H's in the new phone books to see if perhaps Frank had slipped back into the area without her knowing he was there. She wanted more than ever for him to slide back into the past and stay there. But from the look of things, he wasn't about to do that. She wheeled herself over to her vanity and pulled out a bottom drawer.

CHAPTER 44

A slight breeze and the shade on the front porch made it tolerable. Maggie came out and asked if Frank wanted a refill.

"No thanks. I think I'm about as sober as I can stand for the time being."

"Did Lloyd go home?" she asked Sandy, who was sitting crossways on the top step with her legs stretched out.

"Yep. Said he'd be back later."

"Sorry about last night," Frank said, looking at both girls and then leaning his head back.

"You were an unholy mess. Sandy thought something awful must have happened." When he didn't rise to the bait, she persisted. "I said that indeed it had, and that it was lying on my bedroom floor." Still no response, except for his glance that passed over her along with the summer air, as he took in the rest of the porch and yard and studied the houses up and down the street.

"Looks the same," he said. "Trees are bigger."

"Dad cut down some of the fruit bearers. Got tired of the birds and the mess. Filled in the goldfish pond out in back, too. Right after Sandy was born. He was afraid of her stumbling into it."

"Yeah, one thing old Parson was good at was protecting what was his."

Maggie didn't like the way the conversation was going and asked Sandy what Ralph was up to.

"Excuse me," Frank said. "Call of nature." He headed into the house, wishing he hadn't staggered in under the influence last night, hadn't made such a weak showing at breakfast, hadn't cared what Maggie thought, or Sandy. Even the old lady. But he did. And there it was. He was back and more off balance than he'd been in a long time. And he didn't know if he'd have a ride for Sunday. He needed to get back to Hutch and see what Buddy had found out.

•   •   •   •   •

If Frank hadn't had a second cup of coffee, he most likely wouldn't have been passing Olivia's bedroom door while she and Irma were debating the relative moral and practical points of turning something over to him what might or might not be his. As it was, the moment the women became aware of his presence in the hallway, they froze in a parody of the guilty being caught in the act.

Irma said, "Hi," looking from him to her mother, who was sitting with her back to him, her head hanging down.

"Thought I heard my name," he said. "Anything I can do for you?"

Olivia's head lifted as she shared a long look with Irma. Frank had a brief vision of the two of them with plates and bowls spinning at the tops of poles like a circus act. If Maggie had been there, he might have wanted to share that bit of nonsense with her, but the time for that, he sensed, had passed.

Olivia slowly turned her chair around to face him. He saw the shoebox on her lap, a thick, red rubber band around it. She pulled the band off and slipped it around her wrist. She looked up at him with an expression he couldn't read, then opened the box, and lifted out a thick bundle of envelopes so familiar that he knew exactly how they would feel and smell if he'd reached in for them himself.

She held them out. "I'm sorry. I didn't know. Until it was too late."

He stared at the stack of envelopes for what seemed like a long time before reaching over and taking them from her. He flipped through them to see if they had been read. They hadn't even been opened.

"He told me about them shortly before he died," Olivia said. "He'd had them held for pick up at the post office. By then, our Ruth was gone. I thought about destroying them, but . . . ."

Frank's head dropped so low they couldn't see his face. He could hear the sounds of breathing. He thought it might be his.

"If we'd known . . . ." Irma said.

Frank looked over at Olivia, waited for words to come. He believed her, that she hadn't known. Any words left to say were meant for Ruth's father—as lost to Frank's building rage as the words in the letters had been to Ruth.

He turned and walked to the bathroom, not sure if what he felt was numbness or a kind of sickness. When he came out, Maggie met him at the end of the hall, looking from his face to the bundle in his hand. "Oh, Frank, I'm so sorry."

He started past her.

"Wait," she said, grasping his arm. "Where are you going?" She was struggling to think of what could be said to carry them past this betrayal and the inevitable anger—back to where they had been earlier that morning, his hand stroking her arm when he was sure the others couldn't see.

He stopped and looked at her. They just stood there in the silence. All the words that mattered now were sealed up in a handful of unread letters. He walked through the dining room where Lloyd, Irma, and the kids were clustered under the archway connecting that room with the parlor, as if they'd heard a tornado warning and were debating where best to seek shelter.

CHAPTER 45

In the living room, Frank called out, "Sandy! Go get your things. We're leaving."

"Why?"

"Do what I say." He gave her shoulder a push to start her toward her room. "Now. Get all of it. Everything you want. We're not coming back."

Maggie had never felt real panic before, but thought she might be heading for it now. She couldn't get enough air no matter how she strained her chest muscles, and everything important to the moment was jumbled just behind her eyes, like a file drawer that had been ransacked. "Wait!" Too loud. She lowered her voice. "Frank. You don't want to leave like this. Sandy won't understand."

He looked at her coldly. "You'd better hope she doesn't."

Her voice shrank to almost a whisper. "Please, be reasonable."

"Reasonable? I wish to heaven I'd been this reasonable fifteen years ago when that meddling old man was screwing up our lives." He swung around on Olivia who had rolled her chair to the end of the hallway and made a noise in her throat. "Don't start with me old woman. Even when your own daughter was dying, you let her go on thinking that I hadn't cared enough to . . ." He rubbed his hand over his jaw. "What she must have thought of me! Didn't that bastard know he must have broken her heart? My heart?"

Irma walked over and placed her hands on her mother's shoulders to lend support, but when Olivia spoke, her voice was surprisingly strong. "Her father may have been wrong, but he did what—"

"Her father was bull-headed, couldn't be reasoned with!"

"And what were you?" she said. "A hot-headed young know-it-all. And for that matter, where were you? One whippin' and you turn tail and run off."

"Because you lied to her. I figured you'd poisoned her mind against me."

"Not true, not true," Olivia was wagging her head vehemently. "All we wanted was for you to wait until she was older. Until you were both older."

"Well," Frank spread his arms wide in a gesture of mock acceptance. "Here I am, old woman. And I am definitely older. And Ruth, she got older, and then she got dead. So what's the plan now? What did you have lined up for Sandy for her next fifteen years?"

The menacing tone of his voice made Maggie sick. She caught hold of his arm to get him away from the others and talk to him alone to try to calm him, comfort him if that was possible. At her touch, he jerked away, envelopes flying into the room and scattering at their feet.

"Just stay the hell away," he said, without looking at her.

"Let's just everyone calm down," Lloyd said, "and remember there are children here." The cousins, who had been sent to Sandy's room by Irma, were trying to keep up with what the adults were saying while interrogating Sandy. Clueless herself, she piled her neatly pressed shorts and capris and blouses into her gym bag, and tossed in Bobby Bear and some favorite books. She saw that the clothes would be wilted and crumpled by the time she opened it again.

Everything was happening so fast she couldn't understand it all, but she was sure that she would have cried if her cousins hadn't been there. Her hands shook as she pulled open drawers, wondering what to do about the things there wasn't room for and trying to listen to the adults over the excited voices of her cousins, who had offered to either hide her if she wanted them to or to keep her Monopoly set if she wasn't able to take it with her. They had a game of their own, but they figured it couldn't hurt to have the extra money.

When Frank swept into the bedroom and grabbed the bag with one hand and Sandy with the other, she felt as if her legs were going to buckle.

Maggie was right on his heels, trying to stop him in the doorway, but he shoved her aside and made it to the front door in the fewest strides possible. Raised voices jumbled around them as they made for Frank's car. He waited impatiently as Sandy hugged Maggie as tight as she could and then got in. Maggie followed him around to the driver's side, leaned down to the window and tried once more to reason with him. "Please, don't do this. You have a right to be angry, but stop and think of what you're doing. To all of us."

He turned to look at her and the expression on his face was so slag-stone hard that she felt as if she must have been deceiving herself. He really was an unreasonable, self-centered hothead, not the decent human being she'd allowed herself to be fooled into caring about.

Maggie's own face and voice hardened. "You can't keep her from us. We're her family." She stepped back as he backed down the driveway, watched her niece until they turned a corner and there was nothing to do but go back inside. She was grateful to see that the others had already gone in. She stood on the porch listening to their voices. She would have to be the one to appease them, now, protect her mother as much as she could by insisting everything would be okay. There was no percentage in fueling the fires of their anger toward Frank, none of which could touch hers.

CHAPTER 46

Frank swung his feet down from the corner of the desk in Buddy's office at the back of the garage, the springs in the chair slinging him upright. He held the receiver high over the cradle and let it drop into place with a resounding clang.

"Hey," Buddy called out, ducking his head out from under a Buick he had up on the rack, "don't take it out on the phone." When there was no response, he shook his head to himself and went back to the leaky oil pan, glad to be working on something he could fix—with his eyes closed, even.

Frank reached over and pulled the office door closed, then sat there brooding and trying to think who else to call. The only cars available were either rebuilts that still needed some expensive work done on them, or else dogs that would require so much building up that there was no point in putting them onto a track with the best field of cars in the country, each one tuned and honed like a thoroughbred race horse. He wouldn't get on the track with a car he wasn't certain he could qualify in, wouldn't set himself up for the disappointment, never mind the humiliation.

Still hungover—more from lack of sleep and the bile of suppressed rage from the encounter at the Parsons' that morning—he folded his arms on the desk and cradled his head there. He should phone home to make sure Sandy was okay, but things were still strained between them. She'd been so hot that she'd slammed every door she could find an excuse to pass through and spoke only in response to direct questions. High-spirited and stubborn. She'd certainly gotten *that* from her mother's family.

Watching Sandy with her aunts and grandmother had been like almost having Ruth there, not so much because of the similarities, but in the way that a missing piece of a puzzle is defined by pieces that surround the space it was meant to occupy.

He pushed back from the desk with a groan. There was no percentage in that kind of thinking. He'd spent the drive back to Hutch playing "what if"—what if one of his letters had gotten through, what if her mother had shown them to her when she'd first gotten sick, what if something in the letters would have made a difference and she'd gotten better instead of worse. Each new scenario made him angrier and sicker in proportion to the likelihood that things would have worked out differently.

Buddy rapped on the glass with his knuckles and walked in, crossing to the file cabinet between Frank and the wall.

"You don't mind if I do some business today, do you?" Reaching into the drawer from the side, he pulled out the paperwork for the Buick and took it around to the front of the desk, where he leaned over to finish filling it out. "You need to get out and get some air, you know?"

"No, I don't know." Frank's response sounded more like a growl than conversation.

"Well, I do. Your breath is makin' the office smell like Jack's Nest at one o'clock on Sunday morning. Worse. There's no hotdogs grillin' to cover the smell of puke. Has Carpenter called back?"

Frank shook his head without looking over.

"Well, he's been talkin' about buying that V-8 from those guys in Alva and fixin' up old 55. It's a chance."

"Slim to none. If he'd had the price he'd be on it already," Frank said.

"Quit growlin' at me. It's a long shot, but it could happen. Go down for the engine this afternoon, still have two days to put it all together, test it out."

Frank looked as if he thought Buddy was talking crazy, but his head and chest were pulsing with the need for what Buddy was saying to be true.

"Course, you could still get in touch with Parker," Buddy said. "Or I could do it for you." He waited for the response he was pretty sure wouldn't be coming. "Just a call. You know he wants you to drive

Sunday as bad as you want to be on that track. Tell you what. I'll tell him you'll go along with that red-light stunt if he's still stuck on that burr, and just before the race I'll see to it that the wire gets pulled loose when I'm making last minute adjustments. By then, the whole thing will be water over the dam anyway. What do you say?"

For a moment, Frank considered it, but that was all the time it took for him to be unable to see anything but red.

He was sick of manipulations, of assholes trying to shape his life according to other people's ideas. The way he felt at that moment, he was physically incapable of picking up the phone and talking to Parker. He pushed himself up from the desk. Carpenter was his only hope, and that was a possibility only if Frank could raise some money toward the engine himself.

He mumbled, "Later," and headed for his car. He needed to check on Sandy, but foremost in his mind was the need to get his hands on some quick cash.

CHAPTER 47

Sandy unpacked by tossing her things onto the bed. She gathered up the toiletries she'd grabbed from her room in Kiowa and took them into the bathroom. Taped to the mirror on the medicine cabinet was a note—"Gone to Buddy's. Get some lunch at the drugstore and come over." There was a pencil mark at the bottom, as if he'd started to sign it and stopped, and a five-dollar bill next to the sink.

She wasn't hungry, but she didn't feel like going to Buddy's, where she knew the atmosphere would be tense and Frank distracted. She didn't feel like sitting in the house, so she walked four blocks to the drugstore. It was cool, and at least there was stuff to look at. She took the latest issue of *Life* magazine from the rack, but it was the covers of *True Romance* and *Love Stories* she was actually reading. Glancing up when the bell on the drugstore door rang out, she finally gave up on the idea of buying one of the spicier magazines and turned her attention instead to a *Reader's Digest* for the jokes and quips at the bottoms of the pages. When the bell rang out again, she glanced up and watched Tina walk over to the cosmetic counter where she sprayed a sample of Evening in Paris onto her wrist and sniffed it. She picked up an atomizer filled with Este Lauder and spritzed some into the air in front of her face and walked through it. Next she looked through the lipsticks, opening a tube and lightly touching it to the heel of the thumb, rubbing it in and holding her hand up to her face in the cosmetics mirror. Sandy stood there transfixed. At first, when their eyes met, Tina seemed not to recognize Sandy, but by the time she'd turned around for a better look, there was a huge grin on her face. "Hey, Sandy!"

"Hi," Sandy said, feeling awkward because of the scene she'd caused about the cat in the Big Well in Greensburg, Kansas, when they'd last laid eyes on each other.

"What are you up to?" Tina walked around the counter to where Sandy was resettling the sample tube into the tray.

"Not much. What about you?"

"Thought I'd buy some more war paint." In response to Sandy's puzzled expression, Tina picked up a tube of lipstick with a plastic tip indicating the color and held it up to her face. "What do you think? Does it scream *most desirable lips in the county?*"

Laughing, Sandy curled her finger and thumb into the okay sign. "What war?"

"The battle of the sexes, of course."

Sandy wondered whether Tina could be referring to Frank, but was hesitant to ask, so instead she said, "I was worried about you. You know, after the Big Well thing. How did you get home?"

Tina brought her thumb up in the classic pose of a hitchhiker.

"Weren't you scared?"

"Naw. I'm used to it. I may not have gone far, but I've sure ridden in a lot of different vehicles to get to where I've been." She pulled a dollar bill from her back pocket.

"Listen, I heard about Frank losing his ride for Sunday. I'm truly sorry, you know? I mean, I'm not still angry with him or anything like that and—well, it's just not right, him being the best around for so long and not getting a shot at the national title." She shrugged and looked out the front window. "I asked L. Ray if he could maybe find somebody looking for a driver, but he doesn't know of anyone."

The mention of L. Ray's name, so casual that Tina might have been saying "Nice day, isn't it," struck Sandy right between the eyes. She realized that Tina was talking about Frank and the race, but all Sandy heard was that Tina had been talking to L. Ray, asking for a favor, as if they were close and he would want to do something like that to please her.

The smile never left Sandy's face, but the air had left her lungs and she forgot for a moment to inhale.

"It's real nice of you to be concerned," Sandy managed to say, "especially after everything that happened."

"Frank's a good guy. We just see things different. And I have to admit that L. Ray's more my age."

There it was again, like a dagger twisting in Sandy's chest. She listened politely while Tina visited a little longer and then said goodbye. "We'll be seein' ya in Oklahoma City, I guess. I sure hope Frank finds a car."

Sandy tried to recall whether Tina had said "Well, be seeing you" or We'll be seeing you." She moved slowly up the aisle, as if trying to find just the thing that she'd gone there for, while she took in the fact that L. Ray was seeing Tina. All because Sandy wanted to go get that stupid dead cat out of the well. She stood there trying to process how all that had happened. Her eyes snagged on a box with a picture of a smiling woman with a cascade of platinum-blond hair rippling down the package. She picked it up and read of the promise of shimmering golden highlights and bounce. She didn't care much about the bounce part, her hair was pretty lively as it was, but her life could really use some shimmering highlights. Maybe it was just the change she needed to make L. Ray and the others sit up and take notice, to see she wasn't some green kid.

When she got back to the house, Frank was there, on the phone. She went straight into the bathroom, leaving the door slightly ajar so that she could hear what he was saying. When she heard the words "prepared for the worst" and "mysterious ways" she stepped out into the hall, fearful that something had happened to her grandmother. But it soon became clear that he was pitching insurance, and she could recognize elements of what he had told her was his hard close, with references to life's cruel surprises and the need to keep the babies' futures secure with a modest investment for the present.

He thanked the person on the other end of the line with great sincerity and said when they made up their minds he'd sure appreciate them getting in touch with him, and if they came to the races to be sure to come out to the pits after to say hello. Then she heard the refrigerator door open and close, a bottle top pop off, and more dialing.

After a few seconds he hung up again. She called out, "I'm back," to let him know she was there.

"Where have you been," he called back. "I was expecting you to come over to the garage. "

"Busy," she said.

"What do you mean busy?" He sounded closer, so she closed the bathroom door behind her.

"I mean I had to get some things at the drugstore."

He didn't respond right away, as if he was giving some consideration to what a fourteen-and-a-half-year-old girl might get from the drugstore.

"Oh," he said. "Uhm, okay. I've gotta go out on some calls. See if I can stir up some business. You be all right?"

Really, she thought, treat me like a baby. "I'll be fine."

That seemed to satisfy him, and as soon as she heard the door slam, she went back to investigating the promise of shimmering blondness that was soon to be hers. She worked feverishly, anxious to get the solution mixed and applied before he returned and could give her any grief about it.

Anyway, it was her hair. There had to be something that she was in total control of. She decided to bypass the step that called for testing a hidden strand of hair to make certain that nothing awful would result. And she found the disposable gloves too large and slippery, so she took them off and began daubing the cotton into the solution and onto the various sections of her hair—parted more or less into four sections as shown in the diagram. She daubed again and again until her whole head was drenched with the runny, sour smelling peroxide solution.

As she sat on the toilet lid, timing the bleach and watching her finger-tips shriveling into white felt pads, she wondered whether she'd burnt off her finger-prints, which—when coupled with the change of hair color—might render her totally unidentifiable. If she chose to be. Clearly, it wouldn't matter to some people. Probably not Frank, who was so wrapped up in trying to find a car to race on Sunday. And it was clear that L. Ray wouldn't lose any sleep if she were never heard from again. Thinking that made her eyes tear, unless it was the chemicals filling the small room, which seemed to smell stronger the longer she had the solution on.

Jumping up every few minutes to peer into the mirror to see what was transpiring on her head, she imagined several brief but poignant dramas involving future encounters with L. Ray. The gist of them was, of course, his realizing she was not a kid. She was one of the tallest girls in her class, and old for her age—according to her aunts. She imagined him handing her a trophy and telling her he would wait for her. There was also a version where she was run over rather severely by Hays, who had run amok in the pits right after Frank and L. Ray tied for grand national champion. L. Ray would cradle her bloody head . . . . The kitchen timer went off. It was time to remove the plastic cap and rinse.

The transition from imagined tragic figure to the strawberry blond in the mirror was a shock. The emphasis was on straw. Her hair felt like dry grass. She rinsed in luke-warm water twice as long as the instructions said. She wondered if L. Ray thought she only had a school girl crush. But what she felt for him had been much more. She couldn't go to sleep without thinking of him, wondering what he thought of her, whether he thought about the gum and the carnival. Back when Tina had been with Frank, before the possibly dead cat in the world's largest hand-dug well had ruined everything.

Now L. Ray was with Tina and Frank was only interested in the big race and selling insurance. She decided she'd been pretty much right about men all along, about her not being important to anyone who might have counted. The old suspicion that she was somehow at fault, flawed or lacking in some way, wrapped its clammy tentacles around her, like the lank strands of hair that clung to her face and neck. Whatever it took for her to be the most important thing in any man's life she didn't have enough of.

She combed her new hair back from her face and then pushed it up into waves, studying the contrast between her brown eyebrows and lashes and the reddish blond hair that was getting lighter as it dried. It wasn't the platinum mane she'd envisioned, but it was different, and a little exciting, in her opinion. She would show them that she wasn't the sweet little nobody that they all thought they could ignore except when it suited them.

Once she got her hair wound onto her pink brush rollers, she went out to sit on the back steps where the hot breeze would speed the drying time. The alley was deserted, and in a rush of daring and defiance, she pulled one of Frank's cigarettes and a kitchen match from the cuff of her jeans and lit up, careful to keep the hand with the cigarette down near the bushes beside the porch where she'd seen Frank flip his butts. It could have been the combination of bleached hair and cigarette smoke that made her feel genuinely older. Or it could have been the dread that she might never be loved the way she longed to be. That harsh truth was enough to make someone grow up fast, and feel low down, regardless of how she might get her hair to shimmer.

CHAPTER 48

By the time Maggie got back with Olivia from her therapy, the scheme she and Lloyd had been working on had crystallized and was weighing heavily on her. He was to set things up with Frank. Keeping it from Irma and their mother for the time being would be tricky, but something had to be done, and fast. This turn of Frank's sickened her in more ways than one, but her primary concern was to get Sandy back where she belonged regardless of the cost. Then after everyone cooled down, they could see how things stood.

Kicking her sandals into her closet, Maggie fished through the shoebox on the shelf for her bankbook. She opened the book to the last entry—July third, when half of her June salary had been deposited in her special savings account against a future when life might be less predictable. And the very next morning, Sandra Joleen Turner had walked out to the highway and caught a ride straight into the deepest, darkest corner of all their collective pasts.

Maggie's balance was one-thousand-seven hundred-and-thirteen-dollars and twenty-nine cents. Lloyd had made some calls and told her it was enough for what she had to do to get Sandy back home where she belonged. She was determined to see to it her niece got all the chances that Ruth had been robbed of and had slipped steadily through Maggie's fingers year after year.

She sat down on the end of her bed and looked into the large mirror over the dressing table. Her hair was curling around her face from the humidity and hot against her neck. She pulled it up on top of her head, not in a teacher's neat bun but in a careless tangle. Studying her reflection, she tried out a pout, then sighed with the realization that she would never pout that way or wear her hair like that for anyone. But there had been moments in Frank's presence when she had felt so drawn to him that just breathing in and out had taken some effort. And then those sad letters had resurfaced. She had gathered them up and put the box on her dresser, and now she was back as well, in the same room she'd inhabited since the second grade, and about to risk everything, to destroy any chance she and Frank might have had to overcome the ugly chasm of the past gaping between them because Sandy was the one thing she could not lose.

She pulled her hair up into a ponytail and went over to the box of letters and took them to the bed. She reached in timidly, as if they might be booby-trapped. At first she studied the postmarks. Since they were out of chronological order, no clear progression was apparent, but it looked as if he'd written a surprising number from right there in Kiowa.

Dumping them out onto the bed, she began organizing them by date, noting when the postmarks indicated the jump from daily to weekly to monthly letters. There were twenty-six in all, the final three coming at three-month intervals. In straightening them out, which is what she would have said she was doing if anyone should have been there to ask, she noted that some of the flaps had come unglued, the result of being exposed to alternately humid and dry air over the years, she guessed.

Placing them in the box like index cards, she got up to look for some string or ribbon to tie them up with, digging through her scarf drawer in vain. She hadn't had ribbons around for years, probably not since the time the letters had been written. Returning to the bed, she placed two pillows behind her shoulders and leaned back against the carved oak headboard.

Just thinking what she was thinking made her so apprehensive that she checked the door and windows to see if anyone might be looking in.

Taking out a handful, she turned the envelopes over and fanned them like a deck of cards on the bed in front of her. Slowly, she slid out one with a loose flap and pulled out the letter. She read quickly at first, then more slowly. The prose was far more graceful than she would have expected, and touching in the way things real and heartfelt are.

So I'll be sent overseas soon, my darling. I feel like a truly broken man since you left. But I'm not running away. This is just until you're old enough to get free of your folks and we can start our real lives together. I don't know why you don't answer. I have to think it's because your old man is on the lookout. But please try. I need to hear from you. If I can read your words I'll hear your voice. In my dreams I hold you every night. Yours forever, Frank

.   .   .   .   .

Maggie felt herself flush as she carefully folded the paper and replaced it in the envelope. She opened another, reading the mix of details about army life and longing to hear from his would-be wife. *We're shipping out, we can't say where, but please write before I go, if only to reassure me that it wasn't all just a dream. One thing I know for sure, that love with the right woman is worth fighting for. You'll be in my dreams every night and in my heart forever.* His signature was in large, neat loops, beneath "Love Forever," and his P.S. reminded her to write to Private 1st Class Frank Haggard.

Maggie replaced the letter and put them all back in the box. There was so much to be sad about—Ruth, the young soldier, herself, and even the Frank she had come to know and care for, but then hate, and yet still miss. She got up and slipped her shoes on, then walked over to Irma's to see if Lloyd had called Frank yet with the proposition.

.   .   .   .   .

A new band was playing at Kirby's, a country and western trio who were trying to segue into rock and roll. For the most part, Frank found their flip-flopping between the two styles irritating. Buddy was still making calls and looking at cars, but the outlook was grim. The likelihood that Frank would not be in the lineup for the first national championship was slowly sinking in.

It had taken a sincere dedication to the pursuit of oblivion for Frank to concentrate on only the beer in front of him and the mildly amusing dialog of the Heller cousins at the next table, who had bought a used fiberglass outboard motor boat that had split wide open on its maiden voyage.

He was doing a fairly good job of keeping the cousins' debate of culpability and stupidity going by asking random questions whenever one of them showed signs of giving up the discussion. It had proved such a good diversion, in fact, that when Frank's name was called for him to come take a phone call, he was halfway to the bar before irritation about who might be calling took over, causing him to bark "Yeah?" into the receiver.

"Still in a foul mood, I see."

"Buddy?"

"Yeah. What kinda shape you in?"

"You takin' a poll?"

"Just testing the waters. You had an interesting phone call a little while ago, and Sandy's here. At least I think it's her."

"What's she doin' there?"

"I'm not exactly sure, and I'd rather not guess over the phone. I told her we'd walk over to Kings-X for a burger. You up to meetin' us there?"

"What do you need me for?"

"Don't, exactly. Just thought you might want to take care of your own business."

"Yeah, well, I'm not such good company right now. You two go on over, and I'll see you afterwards. What about the call? Wasn't Carpenter was it?"

"Huh-uh. It was Sandy's Uncle Lloyd, says he goes to the races. Met you in Kiowa this morning when you drove down to get Sandy."

"What's his beef?"

"Don't know, exactly. He just said that there was a lot at stake and that he had to talk to you right away. I've got his number written down here by the phone. You want it?"

"No. Yeah. Hold on." He took a ballpoint pen from his shirt pocket, clamped the receiver between his jaw and shoulder, and held the pen over his left palm. "Shoot."

Buddy read him the number. "You gonna call?"

"Maybe."

"You want us to bring you back some grub?"

"No thanks, I'll drink dinner here. See you in a while." He hung up and ordered another beer, then dialed the number, his palm sweaty around the receiver. The voice on the other end of the line was pleasant, but Frank sensed the tension. Possibly it was the beer, or maybe the unexpectedness of the message, but he was having trouble processing what he was hearing. "You messin' with me?"

"I assure you that that is not a trick of some kind. Maggie is making a genuine offer in good faith." Lloyd's tone changed slightly, becoming more confidential. "Look, friend, let's be honest. We both know that a young girl, one becoming a young woman, really, needs to be with her mother. Or," he quickly added, "a loving, reliable substitute."

"So let Maggie lovingly and reliably move up here if she's pining to be of some use."

"Let's be reasonable, shall we? She's making you a perfectly respectable offer. Generous, even."

Frank's pulse was racing. Lloyd knew of a Ford flathead engine that a car enthusiast had been gradually working on and where to get hold of the necessary parts to make it race-worthy. Maggie would buy the engine and the parts. They could drop it into Dwayne Carpenter's cut-down roadster that blew an engine two weeks ago in Newton and have two days to try it out. If it worked, if he could run it at Taft, it was his. All he had to do was give Sandy back to Maggie without a fight.

"So I get a ride and you get the girl, that it?"

"A big ride, friend, the biggest ever. No strings attached."

The battle Frank was waging within himself spilled into the phone with a ferocity that caused the other patrons in the bar to look over to see what was up.

"You can tell your sister-in-law that if she wants to deal with me, she has to deal with me. You got that? Is she there? Is she listening?"

Clearly, Lloyd hadn't been prepared for that particular response, as there was a pause and some murmuring in the background.

Maggie's voice was as taut as the wire that carried it to him. "Frank? I'm trying to do what's right for Sandy. For everyone."

"You're trying to bribe me."

"You get what you want, what you need. You know that eventually she's going to come home. Your life isn't set up for taking care of a growing girl."

"And what makes you the expert, huh? Never been married, never had kids of your own. Livin' your whole life in one small town."

"Yes, my life is small and circumscribed and steady and reliable. I've made a life for us. What can you really offer her?"

"Has it occurred to you that I might love her?"

"Yes," she answered. "I absolutely believe you do. And I'm not asking you to stay out of her life. But we're not talking about you. We're talking about a young, impressionable—"

"She's all I have left of Ruth!"

They were both silent for a moment.

"I love her too." Her voice cracked slightly. "I have since the day she was born."

"Yeah, well, you had your turn. Now she belongs to me."

"People don't belong to other people like that."

"You can tell that to the judge."

"Wait," she said. "What about the deal?"

Frank looked at the number written in blue ink across his palm, then squeezed it into a fist, and said, "I'll let you know," before hanging up.

CHAPTER 49

Buddy returned to the garage alone to find Frank sitting in the swivel chair with his feet on Buddy's desk and his head thrown back. "What's happenin', Speedo," Buddy asked, keeping his tone light, but worry lines were etched between his eyebrows.

Frank jolted upright and gave Buddy a long look. "Where you been?"

"With Sandy, gettin' dinner. I told you."

"Yeah." Frank leaned his elbows on the desk and nodded at the chair across from him. After Buddy was settled, Frank said, "We've got a proposition."

"I figured."

By the time Frank had finished outlining the nature of the offer Maggie had made, Buddy had gotten to his feet and was pacing around the small office in a clear state of excitement. "What are you gonna do?"

"What do you think?"

Buddy hesitated a minute, his face pulled into a deep frown, then brightened. "I think you should go look at this engine, and if it's any good, we'll buy it ourselves."

"With what?"

"Maybe on credit? For a percentage of the purse?"

"I thought of that, too. But they didn't happen to mention who has it, and I really don't think they intend to."

Frank unfurled his left fist and read the number written on his palm again. He'd known when he hung up that it was just a matter of time before he would call back.

Lloyd picked up on the second ring and barely said hello when Maggie pulled the phone away from him and said "Yes?" into the mouthpiece. Frank waited a beat, then said, "The terms aren't good enough. You're still trying to play it safe."

When Maggie's voice finally came back at him over the wire she sounded different, calmer perhaps, or tougher.

"What terms would you find acceptable?"

"Well now," Frank sounded calmer also, "what kind of gambler are you? What risks do you find worth taking?"

"Frank," Maggie started in a softer tone, "if you could just have calmed down long enough to talk about—"

"What risks, Maggie? You called to cut a deal, so what's your best offer?"

"You . . . ." She couldn't say what she was thinking without sinking to his level.

"Now we're getting somewhere. I may make an honest woman of you yet." He could hear a muffled conversation in the background, as if Maggie were arguing with Lloyd, who got back on the phone.

"You're a gambling man, right?"

"Go on."

"You gamble every time you go out on the track."

"Make your point."

"Well, what if we make the odds more favorable? Like say," he hesitated, as if unsure of what to say next or uncertain about saying it, "Maggie still puts up the money for the engine. You win, we get Sandy back. All done up legal and proper. You would have visiting privileges, of course."

"And if I lose?"

"Then you pay her back the money, and we go back to square one."

"Which is to court?" It wasn't really a question. Frank thought a minute. "This Maggie's idea?"

"She's agreed."

"I want to hear it from her."

Maggie sounded less certain than resolved. "Is it a deal?"

"Not much risk on your part," Frank said.

"Well, just what guarantee do I have that I'd get my money back?"

He hesitated a minute and asked, "You that sure I'll win?"

"I'm that sure you'll do whatever it takes just to get the chance."

At that moment, Frank both hated and admired her.

After he made arrangements for Lloyd to bring Buddy the engine, he leaned back in the chair and ran his fingers through his hair, noticed they were shaking, and saw the inky numbers had grown blurry from his perspiration. He clasped his hands together and looked at Buddy standing in the doorway. "Well, Bear. Looks like we might still put together a ride."

Buddy let out a small whoop that carried clear outside to where Sandy was pacing on the sidewalk. When she heard Buddy's outburst, she hurried into the garage to see what was going on.

The men had their heads leaned together while Frank read an address to Buddy from a scrap of paper. Sandy had to ask what was up twice before getting their attention, but as soon as she had it she realized she'd misjudged the moment.

"What in the hell have you done to yourself!" Frank yelled, and then just stared at her, which was even worse.

Buddy tried to diffuse the tension by telling her they had good news, that Frank was getting a car for Sunday, "And not just any car," he went on—accentuating the positive, as the song had it. But to no avail. When Frank finally collected himself, it was to tell Buddy that Lloyd was bringing up the engine from Kiowa and to set up the deal with Carpenter. He was going to take Sandy home.

She could smell the bad time coming, tinny and sharp like the afterglow of the peroxide. He didn't even wait until they were in the car to let loose the harangue of typical parental questions, the gist of which was what did she think she was doing? She responded that she knew what she was doing, that it was done, and it was her hair—he didn't have to look at it if he found her so repulsive.

Frank pulled into the alley and put the car into park, leaving the engine running. "You don't get it, do you? You want to look like a ... like someone who's not a nice girl? What would your aunt say?"

"She wouldn't yell."

"Think not?" He rubbed his eyes hard. "She probably would have seen it coming and stopped you." He studied her head for a moment and asked, "How do you fix something like that, anyway?"

His angry scrutiny of her hair was like getting doused with a bucket of cold water. Her face pinched closed against him and anything else he might have to say. Still he persisted, more from frustration and embarrassment over having let her get out of control than from pure anger. Maybe her relatives were right, he threatened her, maybe she deserved to be shut up in a little podunk town like Kiowa where they could all keep close tabs on her, keep her from running wild and looking like a . . . he caught himself before saying the word that couldn't be spoken between father and daughter, and waited only a moment after she got out of the car before pulling out fast, the back tires throwing gravel, as he headed to the garage where he could get back to the kind of business he knew best. Racing could be a tough life, but at least when it came down to it there was only one person in charge—the guy behind the wheel. Raising a kid was a whole other can of worms.

·   ·   ·   ·   ·

Once inside the house, Sandy was startled by the altered appearance staring back at her from the bedroom mirror. With her face flushed and swollen, her whole head seemed shrouded in a pink aura. Frank had told her to stay at the house until they got back from checking out a car, but after the way he'd talked to her, she was in no mood to sit around waiting for him to return and start in on her again. She pulled open the junk drawer and dug out some cigarettes and matches, then flew back out the door. She smoked as she walked, slightly dizzy and not really caring who saw her, her lips moving in a silent but fierce harangue at her father. She was two blocks away before she shortened her stride, remembering what Frank had said about the car. They were back in the race. And she might not be there to see it because she didn't have light brown hair anymore. Her anguish escaped in small smoky spurts. Life really stunk.

She stopped and ground out her cigarette with the toe of her sandal, feeling queasy. The buildings and trees looked like charcoal etchings against the pink glow that still radiated in the western sky. Her favorite time of night. And there she was, more alone than ever while the one she loved was with Tina. And her father thought she looked like a ... whore.

She looked up at the orange and pink sky and blinked to clear the tears from her eyes. The world was so beautiful and so messed up. She couldn't understand how it happened that in following the loose threads her mother left behind everything else had come unraveled. Her past had always seemed fragmented, like the patchwork quilt her grandmother had been making from scraps of all the girls' homemade dresses, and never actually finished. But this was even worse. Her whole life felt as if it was like the shredded bits of newspaper caught up in the spreading evergreens along the fence, twisting this way and that in the relentless summer wind.

CHAPTER 50

It could have been dumb, blind luck, but more likely it involved Sandy's passing by the drugstore three times hoping to run into Tina again. Sandy had been left pretty much on her own Friday morning after Frank had dropped her off at Mimi's Beauty Shop to get her hair dyed back. He and Buddy were working nonstop to get the engine installed and the car ready in time to test it out before Saturday's time trials. On the third pass, she saw Tina sitting at the counter eating a sandwich and flipping through a movie magazine.

"Hi."

Looking up, Tina smiled broadly and said hi back. "Wow. Nice color. You do it yourself?"

"No. Well, yes, at first. Blonde. Then my father made me get it dyed back, but it turned out sort of auburn." She patted the curls hanging by her neck. "I still like it better than natural."

"Looks good. So, what else are you up to?"

Sandy sat down on the next stool and ordered a cherry Coke. "Just keeping out of the way while Frank and Buddy get a car ready for the race. Did you hear about it?"

"Yeah. Good news travels fast. That's great. I'm really happy for him."

They sucked on their straws, and then Tina added, "I guess I was a little too enthusiastic when I heard the news."

Sandy frowned at her.

"I mean L. Ray didn't especially like that I was so happy for Frank to be back in the race. We had, shall we say, words."

Sandy perked up at this unexpected stroke of luck. Maybe this meant Tina and Frank would get back together and free up L. Ray for herself. She smiled sympathetically, shook her head, and said, "Men," the way she'd heard her aunts and their friends say it, as if that one word held a world of meaning about the failings of the opposite sex. Tina rolled her eyes.

"You know," Sandy continued, "Frank feels terrible about what happened. He talks about you all the time. I can tell how much he misses you."

"Really?" Tina asked, looking over at Sandy. "Couldn't tell it by all the phone calls he hasn't made."

"That's 'cause he doesn't know how to tell you. 'Cause he knows it was his fault. He's been trying to think of what to say. And then the car disaster happened, and we heard you were seeing, you know, someone else."

Chewing thoughtfully on a mouthful of egg salad, Tina looked at Sandy for a minute, and then they smiled at each other.

"It'd probably ease his mind some to know that you're not still angry with him," Sandy said. "To hear it from you, I mean."

Tina draped an arm over Sandy's shoulders and finished chewing, then said, "I suppose they've got the car over at Buddy's garage."

"Yep."

"I have to be getting back to work over at the hardware store, but I suppose they'll be getting thirsty later on this afternoon."

"Hot day," Sandy said.

"Well," Tina said, turning around on the stool so that her knees were bumping up against Sandy's, "I reckon it would be a mercy if we were to take some ice-cold drinks over there. Maybe when I get off?"

Sandy grinned. "Very neighborly."

"Meet me at the hardware store at 6:00," Tina said, pointing her index finger at Sandy like a gun while she winked and made a clicking sound with her tongue. Sandy did the same, blowing on the tip of her finger as if to cool it down, then grinning like the Cheshire cat at her reflection in the mirror behind the counter.

•　　•　　•　　•　　•

Maggie had refused Lloyd's offer to drive her to Hutchinson to see Sandy. Frankly, she was sick of men and wanted a chance to check on her niece by herself. She told herself that it didn't matter whether she saw Frank or not, didn't know what she might do if she came face to face with him at this point, but the closer she got to Hutch the more agitated she became. By the time she had asked the attendant at the Mobil gas station where Buddy's garage was and found it, it was almost dinner time. She'd been too nervous to eat lunch. She intended to grab Sandy, get a room at a hotel with a pool so that Sandy could swim, and find a nice air-conditioned restaurant where they could relax and talk. She knew that once she got Sandy started, the news would pour out of her freely, with all her usual embellishments and commentary that could make her seem simultaneously silly and wise. Maggie needed that contact, the reassurance that, regardless of the changes taking place around them, her relationship with Sandy hadn't been drastically altered.

The air in the garage was stifling and smelled of oil and sweat, even with the two bay doors open. Maggie stood just inside, relieved to be out of the sun and go unnoticed while she studied the cluster of people around the blue-and-white car of which she was now bizarrely part owner. She watched as Buddy, who was bending over the engine, reached his hand back and Sandy handed him a wrench. Finally Sandy spotted her and cried out, "There you are!" and rushed over to hug her. "Check it out! We've got a car. They're dropping a flathead Ford engine into it. It's the best. Buddy says it's gonna be bigger and badder than old 65. And isn't this blue paint job beautiful?"

Buddy tapped his forehead with his index finger in a salute and went back to work. Maggie locked eyes with Frank, who was leaning back against the workbench next to a young woman perched on a stool who looked familiar.

"This is Tina," Sandy made the introduction, walking her aunt toward the others. "From Enid, I mean from Hutch, but we, she and I, we met in Enid." Maggie said hello and was wondering what the girl in tight yellow crop top and too much make up for her age had to do with her niece when Tina leaned closer to Frank and linked her finger through his belt loop.

"Hi," Tina said. Maggie noted the girl wasn't much older than Sandy, but had mature curves and an air about her that made Maggie think that she had been old for her age for some time.

In spite of herself—the falling out with Frank, the convoluted business deal she'd struck with him, the voice of reason in her head that seldom if ever let her down—she realized that she was sizing up Tina as competition. Suddenly she was angry with herself, and with Frank, and Sandy, whose hair was the wrong color, and Lloyd, and even, posthumously, her father for getting them all into this high-stakes showdown.

"I drove in for a visit with my niece. If that's all right with you."

"As long as she stays in Hutch," Frank said.

The frostiness of their exchange was not lost on Tina, who sat there swinging her shapely legs and eyeing them both as she sipped her Coke through a straw, her free hand now resting on Frank's shoulder.

"All right, then," Maggie was saying to Frank. "We'll probably be at the Thunderbird out on the highway."

"What do you mean probably?"

Maggie took a small step toward him, her chin up and her eyes locked on his.

"I mean that if they have a vacancy, that's where we'll be. Sandy prefers a place with a pool. And you'll have your hands full tonight getting the car ready."

Frank shot her a stony smirk so brief it was lost on the others, and said, "Nothin' like a cool dip on a hot night."

Maggie's neck and cheeks flushed as she took Sandy's arm to lead her away. "I'll have her back in the morning."

"You do that," Frank said, watching them walk away.

Sandy called over her shoulder, "We'll check on how the car's coming later, and maybe we can all have dinner together."

Maggie kept walking, no one else saying anything as the two got into the car and drove off. Buddy broke the silence with a long, low whistle while Frank fought the urge to run after the car. He had no idea what he'd say if he caught up with them. He could hardly threaten Maggie in front of Sandy, or insist Sandy stay at his place if she wanted to be with her aunt. But the anxiety surrounding the rush to get the car ready in time as well as the crazy arrangement with Maggie had him more nervous than any race ever had. He turned back to the bench and calibrating the spark plugs, but he would be passing by the Thunderbird Motel later to make sure Maggie's car was there.

CHAPTER 51

Irma had balked at leaving for Oklahoma City so early Saturday morning, but Lloyd didn't want to miss any of the time trials. Especially since Frank was leaving a pit pass for him so he could be part of the crew. His prediction had proved right—Taft Stadium was as crowded for the time trials as for a regular race day, just like the Indy 500. Maggie and Sandy met Irma and the kids at the gate and led the way, so that the business of buying tickets and chair backs and drinks was dispatched in record time. They picked up programs as well, and then claimed a row of seats far enough up that the overhanging roof of the press box would eventually give them some shade.

Sandy's cousins clamored in first, followed by Irma, then Maggie, Sandy, and Tina on the aisle. Because the cars were running one at a time, it was possible to talk without shouting, but Sandy's enthusiasm had her nearly yelling as she pointed out cars and drivers to her aunt. Maggie tried to keep track by referring to the program, which listed all the drivers and had stories on the top point earners over the past decade. Frank was right there, smiling out from the top of the article, but if she'd hoped to learn anything substantive about the man who was trying to take her niece away she was looking in the wrong place. While laudatory in the extreme, the write up focused almost entirely on his long string of successes as a race car driver, with no mention of his time in the service during the war or his work for an insurance company. As she read the program cover to cover, she also listened to Sandy and Tina talk like old friends, debating which cars were sure to be hot, which drivers were the best looking, after Frank, they'd agreed. Not wholly inaccurate, Maggie had to agree, in spite of his being a dozen or more years older than many of the drivers.

Sandy was a good sport about accompanying her young cousins to the concessions and bathrooms, which kept her busy and left Tina and Maggie in close proximity without a buffer. Her curiosity getting the better of her, Maggie asked how Sandy and Tina had met.

Tina glanced over, as if to determine whether she was being set up. "I was with Frankie when the police brought her over in Enid." She took a bite of her hotdog, swallowed, and added, "I've been traveling the circuit for a couple weeks. I'm from Hutch, and the hardware store where I work was closed two weeks for summer vacation, so I just took off." She looked over again. "Crazy, huh?"

Maggie shook her head no. "Not if you enjoy the races that much."

"Don't you?" Tina asked.

Maggie hesitated, then said, "I haven't been to many."

Tina pulled a face and shrugged dismissively. "You're a schoolteacher, right? You're watching history being made this weekend."

Ignoring the fact that race results weren't taught in the schools, Maggie said, "You sound like a real fan."

"So's Sandy," Tina said, "though I guess we both really got into it because of Frank."

Maggie seized the opening. "Have you known him long, then?"

"By reputation, most of my life. We've only been dating for a month or so. Less actually, when you consider we had a fight and broke up for a while. But then Sandy talked to me, said he was really missing me, and sort of got us back together."

Maggie nodded and looked away, frowning. Perhaps her niece was seeing Tina as a substitute for Maggie—a sort of step-mother and playmate rolled into one.

Maggie said. "Excuse me. I think I'll walk around a bit." She started to tell Irma that she'd be back in a while, but Tina leaned over and said, "Sandy's a sweetheart. And Frank really cares about her. When we saw those scars on her back and thought that ... well thought that someone had hurt her, he got sick just thinking about it. He told me what really happened."

"I see," Maggie said, looking at her directly for the first time.

Tina nodded, then said, "I'm glad I was wrong, but I'd do it all again if I thought someone was abusing a young girl. There's a lot of that around." She looked away, then added, "Frank's a good dad in his way. He would do anything for her."

Maggie wondered if that were true, if he would deliberately lose the race to keep her and make Maggie take him to court. She missed what Tina was saying and asked her to repeat it.

"I said, it seems like you and Frank don't get along all that good."

Maggie thought about that. "It's complicated. We have some history." She stood up and announced that she was going to stretch her legs and check on the kids, then strode down the steps so quickly that Irma didn't have time to catch her and go along.

Maggie stopped at the bottom of the stands and watched a car gliding around the track all alone, racing the clock for a decent spot in tomorrow's lineup. She was about to go behind the stands where she could pretty much fall apart in private if need be when she heard the announcer saying, "Frank Haggard is up next, folks, starting his warm up lap. As he comes by, please give a round of applause to the long-time racing champ."

Maggie's hands were clasped in front of her chest as she watched Frank in blue-and-white number 55 pull onto the track and head into the first turn. She couldn't take her eyes off the car as it sailed around the track once, twice, gaining speed and flying across the finish line for the first timed lap. It seemed to circle even faster on the second lap. The announcer said that he'd turned the lap in the second fastest time of the day so far and would be a driver to keep an eye on. She, for one, certainly planned to.

CHAPTER 52

When the final time trial of the day was finished, Sandy forged ahead of the others through the throngs of people pouring onto the track for autographs and to get their picture taken with their favorite drivers. She wormed through the crowd gathered near L. Ray's car and found herself just a toolbox and two tires from where he was signing his autograph for a woman whose grin was almost as wide as his. When he finished writing and looked up at the crowd, his eyes locked on Sandy's, and he winked. She stepped over the toolbox and into the center of a tire when she felt a hand grab her arm.

"Careful there," said Tina. "No fraternizing with the enemy." She pulled Sandy away, both girls looking over their shoulders at L. Ray, Tina with a smug smile, Sandy with disappointment and longing.

"Did ya ever see so many good-lookin' studs in one place before," Tina asked, loud enough for L. Ray to hear.

Buddy was keeping an eye on blue 55 as fans milled around, running their fingers along the hood as if it were a talisman. He waved when he saw the girls walking toward him. "How about that time," he said, sounding more like a proud parent than a mechanic. "We may just be in the running."

"Is it good enough to win?" Sandy asked him.

"It'll keep us at the front of the pack, all right. Winning takes something more. My money's on your dad any day of the week and twice on Sundays."

"Where's Frank?" Tina asked, scanning the clusters of people in that section of the pits.

"Um," Buddy started, "he's a little busy right now."

Tina looked over at Buddy and raised her eyebrows as an invitation to go on. When Buddy didn't add to his answer, she said, "Like he's in the men's room?"

"Not exactly."

"Well what, then, exactly?"

"He and Maggie went off toward the camper. They were having a discussion."

"About what?"

"Well now, I'm not exactly sure." He looked over at Sandy, who was listening to them, her face still flushed with the heat and excitement of the day. To prevent her wading into the middle of the heated argument Frank and Maggie were having when they charged off for the camper, he said, "They'll be right back."

"That's okay, I'll go get 'em," Sandy said, loping off.

"Wait a minute!" Buddy said. "Come on back and you can help me load up," but she called out, "I want to find out where we're going for dinner." She hadn't appreciated Tina's reference to L. Ray as the enemy, and was hoping they'd all meet up for dinner the way they usually did.

When she got to the camper and reached for the screen door, she hesitated at the sound of raised voices. She stepped over to the open window above the eating nook.

"Lady, you've got balls, I'll say that for you," she heard Frank say. "First you steal my wife, then my kid, and then you try to buy her back. And you want us all to be civilized about it?"

Sandy instinctively ducked down and kept her ear turned to the window. Frank had used the word "balls" in front of her aunt.

Maggie said, "You took the deal. You agreed that if I paid for the new engine you would let Sandy come home where she belongs. You know you're not about to give up racing, and running around with women far too young for you to become father of the year."

"If I win! That was the deal. If I win, which is the one thing you have no control over. And that's the burr under your saddle, lady. You're not running this show, not this time."

Sandy sucked in a gasp that was audible to Tina, who had stopped a few yards away.

"Are you telling me that you would actually lose deliberately," Maggie said, "knowing I'd take you to court? Not in a million years. You'll do whatever it takes to come out on top. Frank Haggard, the great champion."

"You think you know it all, don't you?" he said.

"And just who will you be if you don't win?" Maggie said. "A has been? That's what drives you."

"At least I know who in the hell I am," Frank said." What are you, anyway? You're not even a real mother. You have no legal claim to her."

The camper was quiet for a moment, and then Maggie spoke in a low tone Sandy recognized as Maggie's teacher's voice. "All right, let's just … let's take this down a notch. Yelling insults at one another isn't going to get us anywhere."

"Now who's afraid of losing," he shot back.

"We'll all lose if you and I can't manage to at least be civil for her sake."

Frank sat down at the eating nook making the trailer rock slightly, so close to Sandy that if there'd been no screen in the window she could have reached in and put her arm around his shoulders. Not that she wanted to. The shock of what they were saying was giving over to a mounting sense of betrayal. She wasn't clear on their agreement, but it was certain that they were each risking losing her to the other. Forever, apparently. A bubble started to build in her chest, and she straightened up a little, as if to relieve the pressure.

Inside the trailer, Frank looked over at Maggie, staring at her legs and letting his gaze slide up her torso, finally meeting her gaze so directly that she shivered.

"We've already come way past wherever civility would have taken us," he said. "Or maybe you've forgotten the night at the lake? Maybe that's what's really got you so riled."

Maggie watched her palm smack across Frank's cheek as if it had happened of its own accord. Her hand quivered between them, her wrist clamped in his angry grip as she tried to pull it free.

Sandy jumped at the sound.

"Hey, Sandy! What'cha doin' over there by the camper?" Buddy called out, trying to warn them that Sandy was nearby. "I could sure use some help over here."

Frank and Maggie looked at each other, and then looked out the window and saw Sandy running toward Buddy.

CHAPTER 53

"Let me in," Sandy said to Buddy, shaking her hands at her sides impatiently. "Come on. You said I could take the car for a ride. You said I drove old number 65 just fine. Like a pro, you said."

Buddy looked at her closely. "Are you crying?"

"I'm just excited. Come on. Or doesn't anyone's word mean anything around here? You promised! You said I could!"

"After the races. I promise."

Sandy scrambled in through the window and dropped down into the seat, her hand trembling on the gearshift. Frank said it was okay," she said, pressing the starter. She revved the engine briefly, then put the car into gear.

"Hey! Hey! Hold up there," Buddy yelled, walking alongside. "You can't take it out now! The track's not cleared."

She was pulling away from him faster than he could keep up. "Circle back around here before you get hurt or wreck the dang thing."

A few yards farther up, Sandy pumped the brakes to a stop as some people crossed in front of her, looking back over their shoulders as the car lurched away again.

By the time Frank and Maggie had scrambled out of the camper and caught up with Buddy and Tina, the car had melded with the steady stream of traffic pulling out of the pits and heading for the back gate.

"What in the hell does she think she's doing?" Frank asked.

"Takin' a spin around the track," Buddy told them. "I told her she could after the race was over. I sorta let her take 65 around with me a couple of times."

"Well of all the hare-brained ...." Maggie said.

"She's upset," Tina told them, staring hard at Frank first, then Maggie as they watched to see if Sandy was coming back in. "She was

266

listening to you two hammering each other in the camper. Hell, I could hear some of it clear over here. What a couple of idiots." She slammed her half-full beer bottle into a trash can and turned back to Frank. "I said it before, and I'll say it again—you're too old to be this stupid!"

Maggie grabbed Frank's arm and pointed at a stream of cars and trucks heading for the exit. Buddy stretched up as tall as he could make himself to see over the cars and crowd. "At least she knows how to drive all right," he told them, "but the brakes are gettin' soft again. I tried to stop her, honest, but ...." He stood there watching her navigate into the line of cars, his forehead rigid with furrows.

Frank hopped up onto the hood of a truck and squinted at the line of traffic.

There was blue 55 moving steadily through the gate. He jumped down and ran back to the Mercury, fishing through his pockets for the keys before remembering that they were hanging on the knob of the cigarette lighter. By the time he'd started the engine, Maggie had gotten in on the passenger's side.

"What do you think you're doing," he said as he started the car.

"Get going," Maggie ordered him, just as the door pulled open and Tina slid in, forcing Maggie over to the middle.

"What the hell!" Frank accelerated, then slammed on the brakes. "You two will just get in the way."

"Yeah, well she's not furious with me," Tina pointed out, "so maybe I can talk to her."

"Stop arguing and go!" Maggie said. "The only damn thing you're good at is driving, so drive!"

Buddy grabbed hold of the door and leaned down. "I'm comin' too."

"All right," Frank told him, "but you take the camper and cover the roads just north of here. I'll check to the south."

Once they had squeezed into the line of traffic leaving the track, Frank honked impatiently as cars ahead kept slowing down for others from the big parking lot to slip in. Swearing, he shot out of line and sped along the narrow strip of grass between the road and the fence around the track, pulling up at the entrance, where he nosed up into a slight gap between two cars. His persistence roused some honking and angry shouts until he leaned out through the window and waved. The other drivers who recognized him squeezed up, making a large enough wedge to let him through the opening and make a hard left to the south.

The thump on the trunk startled all three of them, and Tina twisted around to see if they'd been hit. She saw Adam running along beside them, waving and yelling. Frank hit the brakes and slid to a stop.

"I tried to catch up with her. I saw her cut down a side street. Come on, I'll show you!" Adam dove headfirst through the back window, his legs nearly catching a car passing on the right, all of its occupants staring into the Mercury while the driver mouthed a few words it was just as well they couldn't hear.

CHAPTER 54

Sandy's heart was pounding so hard she thought she could hear it above the grind of the engine as it chocked and backfired. Afraid the car would stall, she swerved between two cars and made a last-minute turn down a side street where the traffic was lighter. She knew they'd come looking for her, if only to get their precious car back. Everything was a lie. She felt ashamed that she'd believed they'd both really loved her. Her chest felt as if it were clamped in a giant vise, a pressure she transferred to the accelerator. She figured they would think she'd head north, back toward home, but she wasn't ever going there again. She took the next corner on the outer edges of the wheels and headed south.

She was oblivious to the houses that had thinned out and the barns and outbuildings that replaced them. All she could think of was the wager that had been made, as if she were a piece of property, their property.

"Who do they think they are?" she said out loud. Hearing her own voice calmed her a little, and she let up on the accelerator slightly. She yelled into the wind, "It's my life, not theirs! And they," her voice broke, "agreed to give me away. Both of them."

She sailed past the mileage sign for Norman, Oklahoma, and swung wide to avoid colliding with cows that were being moved across the road, the car fishtailing as she fought to keep it on the road and get back on the right side. Two men standing by a truck parked on the shoulder with its hood propped up turned to watch her with open mouths, too surprised at seeing blue and white number 55 with a girl at the wheel zoom by to yell out their usual advice to city drivers in a hurry.

．　．　．　．　．

Frank pulled into a truck stop on the south edge of town and told Adam to go ask around if anyone had seen Sandy. He sent Tina to the houses across the highway. At first, Maggie stayed where she was, staring out of the windshield. "It'll be dark soon. Does she have lights on the car?"

"Yeah, right, and a radio for weather reports."

She bit her lower lip. "I just thought," her voice broke. "Well, it's getting harder to see."

Frank put his arm up onto the back of the seat and turned toward her.

"We'll find her. She'll be all right." He did his best to sound reassuring, but he was struggling with his own rising panic. If she slammed into something or the car rolled and she tumbled out just ahead of it . . . He squinted at the road ahead as if to bring her into focus. "She's got to be right around here somewhere. There's not enough gas left for her to get very far. We'll find her soon."

Frank gave Maggie's shoulder a reassuring squeeze.

"I just need her to be safe and happy," she said. "That's all I've ever wanted."

"It's not always that easy."

"It used to be."

"Really? You think she was safe and happy before?"

Maggie looked over at him and hesitated.

"Then what are we all doing here?" he asked.

She shrugged free of his hand and stared at the empty road ahead. "Just find her."

Adam slammed through the café door and ran back to the car, this time opening the back door and ducking in. "Several people have seen her, but she didn't go by here, it was farther back in town, a couple of blocks back, but she was definitely heading south, goin' like a bat out of hell, one guy said."

Frank hooked a U-turn in the parking lot and put the car in neutral.

"Said he'd gone out to let his dog take a—'scuse me," he scooted over for Tina, who was getting into the back with him. Anyway, he saw her go by, so he came on over here to the truck stop to see if anyone knew what was going on. Said he thought it might be someone on a road race who got lost or something." Adam laughed at that, but stopped when he saw their grim expressions. All three in the front seat were staring hard at the road ahead, as if they could will the back end of a small blue car into view.

CHAPTER 55

"What the heck!" Sandy let up on the accelerator and let the car coast along on its own momentum. She knew without checking that the gas line was nearly empty, had heard that sound before as racers shut down and limped into the pits, all hope of victory dashed by a leak in the gas line or an inadequate tank for the extra laps required during the hard-luck races where the yellow flag was out almost as long as the green one.

Looking up the road, she spotted a farmhouse on the right and tested the accelerator. She was rewarded with a sputter and a lurch before the car began to cough and backfire as she turned into the driveway and aimed for the barn. "Please, please, please" she said, under her breath. Jumping out before the car had stopped rolling completely, she pitted herself against the back-end to keep it moving, grunting and straining for several seconds before realizing that the car was completely stopped and wasn't going one inch farther on her account.

She waited a minute to see if anyone had heard and was coming out, but the only sound came from dogs barking behind the house. Staying low, the way she'd seen the chased and chasers do it in the movies, she scrambled along the row of crab apples until she had no choice but to dash across the open area to the barn.

Blinded briefly by the sudden shade, she searched frantically for what she wanted.

"What'cha think you're doin'?"

She turned to see a scrawny boy in too-long overall's with a bowl haircut sizing her up.

She gave him a tight smile and nodded to show she was friendly. "I just ran out of gas, right there by your drive. I was hopin' you might have some stored around here. I can pay you for it." She reached into her pocket and pulled out some dollar bills as proof.

The boy squinted at her as if considering the proposition. He looked only nine or ten, but he might have just been small for his age. He motioned for Sandy to follow him to the far side of the barn to the gas storage tank they used for cars and equipment.

Scrounging around through rusty spare parts and small pieces of lumber, he located a well-dented red gas can and held it up triumphantly. "Holds five gallons. Cost ya three bucks."

"It's twenty-six cents a gallon! That's highway robbery."

He shifted his feet and lowered the can, bracing his elbow against his hip so that the empty can dangled between them. "That's in town. Two bucks. We gotta hurry, before my pa gets back."

She shook her head as she put the dollar bills into his grimy palm. "It's still robbery."

The deal struck, the boy's attitude shifted and his eyes and voice radiated admiration as they approached the race car. "Holy cow! This really yours?"

Sandy quietly and knowingly went about inserting the funnel and pouring the gas as if it were any old car after all.

"Course. Wha'd you think? I stole it?"

"That would be pretty stupid. It kinda stands out. Hey, could you give me a ride?"

"Sorry. I've got a date with destiny."

"With who?"

"I'm in a hurry." Already, dusk was settling over the countryside, muting the colors that would soon be reduced to shades of gray and then nothing. "Here," she handed him the can and climbed in.

Turning the starter, she smiled over her shoulder at him. "Maybe next time, junior." The starter ground, but the engine would not turn over. She tried again, and again, her fingers forcing the starter as far as it would go as if by mere pressure she could get the car started.

"Better not keep that up or you'll flood it and wear the battery down."

"Leave me alone." She tried again, the grinding getting slower and slower.

"Okay. But I know how to get it going," he said.

Turning to look at him, she rested her arm along the side and leaned over it.

"How?"

"Cost you a ride."

"Look, I told you I can't. I don't have time."

"You got time to just sit here?" He took a step back and set the can down beside him.

"Listen, you little weasel!" she said in a tone that meant business, and she started to climb up out of the car.

"Just up to the next road and back!" he called out, backing away.

Sandy gave him a hard look, then dropped back down into the seat. "All right then."

He held the can up next to his ear and shook it. "That'll do 'er."

He told Sandy to get out and hold the hood up while he unscrewed the air filter and set it aside. He had to stretch to get the can directly over the carburetor, where he sloshed what little gas remained in the can down over it. Tossing the can to the side of the drive, he put the air filter back on and climbed up onto the car, looking for a place to lean back and brace his feet.

"Crouch down right here and hold on tight to the door and the roll bar," she said.

She crossed her fingers on both hands and turned the ignition. After some preliminary sputtering, the engine started up with a bang, sparks shooting out from under the hood and the noise clamoring through the still country air like marbles in a mixer.

"Whoo hoo! Let's go!" he yelled. She pulled into the open area in front of the barn and made a U-turn, heading back down the driveway, pausing only long enough to see that there was nothing coming from the left as she turned right and took off down the road. She ground the gears a little getting her speed up, but was intent upon carting the larcenous kid down to the crossroad as quickly as she could so she could hang a U-turn and dump him back home. Glancing over at him she laughed out loud. His grin took up the whole lower half of his face and looked frozen, like a snapshot.

As they approached the intersection, she geared down and pushed on the brakes, pumping them several times before sliding to a stop.

He had to brace himself to keep from banging into the dash and yelled, "Hey, watch what you're doin'!"

"Sorry, but you asked for it." She hooked a tight U and sped back to his drive, pulling in and turning around one last time at the barn.

"Geez, what a machine! Whose is it really? D'ya steal it? I won't tell, honest!"

"No! Now get out." If she hadn't looked up to yell at him, she would have missed the white and buckskin Mercury passing by. "Get out!" she screamed at him. "They're here!"

Climbing hurriedly out through the window, he reminded her that he had nothing to do with anything and wasn't going to get into trouble on her account.

"Wait," Sandy called after him as he high-tailed it back up to the house. "Is there any other way out of here?"

He stopped and looked back at her. "What's it worth to ya?"

"A buck, but we have to hurry!"

"Come on!" He ran between the buildings with her right behind, stopping at the field directly in front of them.

She pulled out the dollar as he pointed to a cow path that led along a windbreak of crab apple trees. "If you follow it back and around to the left, it goes into an old road that nobody uses anymore," he was shouting and running alongside as she rocked and rolled along the rutted dirt path, "but there's a bridge across the creek and then you can follow along east of the pond to where the old road goes back out to the intersection we just drove up to."

"Thanks," she said, as he grabbed the money and she crept along the path slowly so that the engine wouldn't get any louder. She kept her eyes straight ahead without thinking or wishing or even praying. Flight had become pure reflex, like a hand snapping back from the faucet when the water comes out a lot hotter than you're expecting. Which would be what she'd be in if they caught up with her, but she was too hurt and angry to think about that now. Seeing a narrow dirt road ahead, she sped up, the washboard road bouncing her clear off the seat so she had to use the steering wheel to brace herself.

CHAPTER 56

Frank swerved into the long drive and skidded to a stop a few yards from the house, a cloud of dust catching up with them as they jumped out to look around. Tina ran up to knock on the front door and then around to the back, which stirred up a swell of dog barks. She was heading to the car when a reedy voice called out, "Ain't nobody home!"

Everyone looked over at the young boy who'd come around the barn and was eyeing them suspiciously.

"Hello there," Frank called to him.

"Nobody here." Then he added hurriedly, "But my pa's due back any minute."

"Son," Frank said as he started toward him, the boy taking a step back, "we're looking for someone, and we thought that we saw something up here by the house that could have been it."

"What'cha mean 'it'?"

As Maggie and Tina approached, the boy backed up another step.

"A young girl," Maggie said, "in a blue race car. Has the number 55 on it in white." She looked over at Frank to see what his assessment of the situation was, but his eyes were locked on the boy, who retreated farther.

"We just want to look around," Frank told him. "All right?"

"Told ya, nobody here."

Tina walked over and took hold of Frank's arm. "Maybe Maggie was mistaken. Maybe we're wasting our time here."

"I thought I saw a flash of blue," Maggie told them.

Adam stepped up to them, his back turned to the boy so that they formed a circle. "I thought I saw something, too. Something shiny through the trees. I think we should take a quick look around."

Frank turned to Maggie, her face unguarded and vulnerable in her near panic. She was counting on him to find Sandy and somehow make things right again, and he knew that the longer it took to locate her the greater the risk of her losing control of the car.

He knelt down, studying the several sets of tire tracks crisscrossing through the hard-packed dirt and saw the tossed red gas can lying on its side. Frank scratched his head and looked out toward the highway, casually, to cover the growing fear that the increased fuel in the car substantially increased the odds of her getting seriously hurt. "I don't know." Turning back to the boy, he asked, "You ever go to the races in town?"

"Nope."

"But I suppose you'd know a race car if you saw one, wouldn't you?"

"Sure."

"Well, maybe not, what with you being stuck out here in the country and all."

"Would, too," the boy answered, his chin lifting defiantly.

Frank had slowly straightened back up, shifting his weight from one leg to the other, looking around casually with his hands stuck in his back pockets, so that when he made his move, the others were just as surprised as the boy, who twisted and yelped from where Frank held him at arm's length.

"It's all right! No one's gonna hurt you. We just want to know where she went. You understand?"

"Let me go, I don't know nothin'!" He kept up the struggle until Frank, to avoid the flailing feet, grabbed the back of the boy's overalls and held him out horizontally. The yelling stopped abruptly when the boy saw dollar bills spill from his pocket to the ground below.

"That's better. Now just stay calm." Frank set him back down, but didn't let go. "Here, you dropped your money." With his free hand, Frank picked it up and stuffed it back into the pocket in the bib of the boy's overalls. "There now, see? We can be friends. You like money, do you?"

The boy nodded, eyeing Frank suspiciously.

"Like to do chores—odd jobs maybe—to earn a little extra? Sure you do," Frank crooned, as the boy nodded again, this time with more enthusiasm. "How would you like to earn a little right now?" Frank pulled his wallet from his back pocket, flipped it open with his thumb, and worked out the corner of a five-dollar bill. Squatting down, he looked the boy in the eyes. "Listen, Son. This girl we're looking for and that car she's driving are heading for trouble. It's dangerous for her to be driving it out here, and—" He let go of the boy's overalls and rubbed his hand over his own eyes. "Look, she's just upset and running scared, you understand? We want to get to her before something happens and she gets hurt."

The boy was looking from the billfold to Frank's face and back again.

"So if you know anything … she can't get far, anyway, because she's almost out of gas."

"Huh-uh."

Frank looked at the boy's face and fought to keep his voice casual. "Huh-uh what?"

The boy kept his head lowered until Frank reached out and tipped the boy's face up, his eyes nearly closing as he struggled to keep the five-dollar bill in sight that Frank was slipping into the small pocket that was beginning to bulge with the day's opportunities.

"She's not out of gas. I sold her some."

Maggie, who had been edging closer, knelt down beside them. "Please tell us where she went. It'll be dark soon, and the car doesn't have any lights."

A frown crossed the boy's face, and he pointed toward the fields. "There's a dirt path road that runs along the pasture and then crosses the ravine and circles back to that there intersection," he turned and pointed to where Sandy had taken him on his joy ride. "Ain't nobody usin' it anymore."

The four of them ran for the car debating whether they should follow the path Sandy took or go on over to the crossroads she would come out at.

They were headed for the road when Adam, who was staying behind in case she turned back, yelled and pointed back down the road. Frank slowed to a stop and honked to signal Buddy, who pulled in next to them. "You folks have any luck yet?" Buddy said.

"A kid back there says she came through here, bought gas, and took a back route to that road that comes out down there."

Frank turned to Maggie. "It looks like we've got her. It'll be all right."

She looked at Frank and Buddy, then up the road. The chase had the trappings of the hunting excursions her father had taken her on as a child, the hushed excitement when the dog finally went on point and the men settled in for the kill. She tried to imagine what Sandy must feel, the anger and hurt, and probably fear, and now all alone in a foolish, desperate flight on what was to have been a red-letter day. Maggie listened guiltily as they mapped out their strategy, Buddy and Adam going on ahead to where the old road came out, Frank, Maggie, and Tina starting in along the path that led to the back of the property.

CHAPTER 57

Sandy lifted her foot off the accelerator as she approached a rickety one-lane bridge with weathered cables running along either side. She considered the race car was smaller and lighter than regular cars, and she didn't weigh all that much herself. Letting the car roll ahead, she felt a jolt as the front tires wobbled over the wooden planks. She cringed at the sound of boards creaking under the weight of the car. She was a full car length out when the bridge seemed to list to the right, but by the time she realized that it was not safe enough to drive across and had pumped the softening brakes enough times to roll to a stop, she was halfway across. The vibration of the engine was punctuated by the snapping of dry timber as she tried to remember whether the car had a reverse on the gear box and where that might be. Suddenly, the car lurched forward and down as a rotting board split open under the right front tire.

She put the car into first gear and tried to ease forward, but the wheel had dropped too far through the wood to climb back out, and the strain of the car pulling forward caused more boards to crack and give way. Sandy had to brace herself to keep from sliding off the seat and shifting the car even closer to the edge. She clung to the side of the car with her left arm and held onto the steering wheel with her right hand as she stretched up to peer down into the bottom of the dried-out gully. Even that slight movement triggered more settling, each pop of wood like a firecracker under her feet. Clearly she wasn't going to be able to drive the car off the bridge, and the vibrations from the engine weren't helping the situation. She carefully reached down and switched it off.

The sudden quiet slipped up around her, and she saw that the dusk had deepened, long shadows reaching across the scrub at least eight-to ten-feet below the car. She tried to control her shaking, fearing the consequences of any more movement on the bridge, but her body hummed like a vibrator.

"Help," she said almost inaudibly, more like a prayer. "Please help," louder this time, if only to comfort herself with the sound of her own voice. Don't cry, she told herself. Just don't cry, think of how to get out of this.

She could feel her heart thumping in her ears, wanted desperately to put the car into reverse and undo everything, to have 55 safely stowed on its trailer behind Buddy's camper and be tucked safely into the camper herself. The pinging of the cooling engine melded into the raspy utterings of insects and rustling of the dry grasses along the gully below her that seemed to come alive in the hot summer breeze.

She started to cry, softly, afraid to move at all but unable to get a grip on her emotions, which seemed to be cascading into an abyss much like the one she was suspended over. She tried to pretend that it was all a bad dream, closing her eyes and willing herself to wake up in her own bed, but that raised the issue of which bed, the one in Kiowa or the one in Hutchinson, and she cried even harder, her tears blurring what little was still visible of the landscape before her. The weathered wood beneath the car gave out a loud creak and slight shudder as the car sank farther to the right. She grabbed on to the left side with both hands and held her breath until the rocking stopped.

At first, she thought the moon had suddenly materialized just over her shoulder and was casting a pale glow on the dashboard and hood. Then she heard the sound of a car engine grinding its way toward her.

She twisted slowly in the seat until she could look back to where headlights approached, bouncing up and down like glowing white balls. By the time she could see the outline of the car, the white top shimmering in the real moonlight, she knew it had to be Frank. Her heart pounding with both hope and apprehension, she watched as three figures emerged. The slam of car doors made her flinch as she braced for the onset of more vibrations along the splintered boards where she was suspended like a fly in a web.

CHAPTER 58

"Sandy!" Maggie called out. "Are you all right?"

Sandy raised her right arm through the cut-out roof and gave a little wave. She couldn't be sure how they were feeling at that moment, but she knew that, any way you looked at it, she was in some big trouble. It occurred to her that she could just stay there until the car finally crashed through, ride it to the bottom, like a captain with his ship. Maybe that would guarantee their sorrow and regret.

Frank stepped onto the bridge, stopping when his weight caused it to complain. Grabbing the railing with his left hand, he felt it vibrate like a plucked guitar string.

"Are you hurt? Can you move?" Maggie's voice—brimming with familiarity and concern—helped to push aside enough of Sandy's fear to let in a good dose of guilt.

"Stay back," Frank warned Maggie and Tina as they approached the end of the bridge.

"I'm okay," Sandy answered, her voice not convincing, "but when I move, the wood pops."

Frank took another step and waited, stepped and waited, then stepped again, the heel of his boot sinking through a gap in the boards. He worked it out, but the motion caused the bridge to screech.

"Watch out," Maggie called out. He could hear Sandy whimpering in the racer and the blood ringing in his ears. He was sweating, and wiped his palms on his pants. He considered whether it would be better to take long strides to the back of the car or to inch along and sneak up on it. In the dusk, it was hard to see exactly how much damage had been done to the bridge, or how much support was left.

He looked back at Maggie and Tina, gathering his thoughts mostly, not that when they were all collected they were much good to him. He had to do something, and the sooner the better.

"Sandy," Maggie called out, her teacher's voice calm and controlled, "You just take it easy, and we'll have you out of there in a jiffy." She looked at Frank as if to ask what next. "Maybe I should try to reach her," she suggested, "I weigh less than you."

"I weigh less than either of you," Tina chimed in. "What if we form a chain, with ropes or something?"

Frank shook his head. "There's not time. Let me think." He was touched by the women's bravery, wondered what the two of them would do without him right then, if they'd be better off. He slid his foot farther out on the bridge and eased his weight directly over a plank, stopping stone still until the bridge was quiet again. "It's okay, we'll get you out of there. It'll just take a couple more minutes. Don't move." If he didn't do something soon, they might as well be there without him. The fact was, he realized, that without him, they wouldn't all be there in the first place.

"I'm sorry," Sandy called out, and then she began to cry out loud, quietly at first, then more loudly.

"It's okay," he reassured her. "Just stay calm. Can you do that? Try not to move."

She continued to sob raggedly, feeling the panic starting to flood over her as the seriousness of her predicament settled in.

"Listen. Are you listening?"

She managed to choke out a yes, but her chin was quivering, and she was trembling all over.

"We have to get you out of there. So you just sit tight."

"But the car!" She cried even harder.

"Forget the car! It doesn't matter. Just listen to me, and do everything I tell you."

"Look!" Tina pointed across to where lights were flickering through a hedge row, coming their direction. "That'll be Buddy. We can use the light."

Frank leaned some of his weight against the left cable. It was loose but felt secure enough for him to formulate a plan. By the time Buddy and Adam were parked directly across the way, the camper headlights illuminating the scene on the bridge from the other end, Frank had explained to Sandy what they were going to do. All she had to do was ease up to lean through the window and get ahold of the cable on the left side of the car. "No matter what," he cautioned her, "don't let go. I'm going to wait until you've got a good grip, and then I'll work my way toward you. Got that?"

He could see her head bob in affirmation, her wind-whipped hair eerily aglow in the flood of headlight beams.

"That's right, ease up slowly. Don't rush it. We don't want to disturb this cranky old bridge any more than we have to. Everything'll be fine," he told her, hoping it wasn't a lie.

With both hands clamped tight over the top of the door, Sandy pulled herself up by inches, pausing with every creak of wood that split the night air and made her heart pound harder.

From across the way they heard Buddy call out. Frank explained that Sandy and the car were stuck and that the bridge wasn't safe. They heard Buddy say "Holy shit!" and then the snapping of brush as he descended the ravine toward where the car was suspended. "Holy shit," he said again, seeing the right front tire through a split in the wood and the listing support timbers.

"Steady," Frank assured Sandy. "You're doing great. Don't worry, I've tested the cable along this side, and it'll hold up. Reach out for it now with your left hand. There." Frank was easing forward, keeping his feet as close to the left edge as possible.

Sandy could hear Buddy talking to someone as he moved along the ravine below, but she was too afraid to look over. She concentrated on Frank's words, gaining confidence as he talked. Twisting to the left, she raised herself up enough to reach out and clamp her right hand over the cable. She clung there waiting for more instructions, literally up to her arm pits with the race car that was jiggling under her, the bridge groaning with Frank's advance. She turned her head to see where he was, but in the glaring lights he was a shadowy figure suspended somewhere between her and the safety at the end of the bridge. Then all at once a hand reached out and took shape, warm and solid around her left arm.

284

The bridge quivered like a fun house walkway, as if sections of it were trying to go in different directions. She felt the car shimmy against her chest and stomach as it slipped farther to the right, the wooden planks splitting wide enough for the right front wheel to drop completely through.

"Hold on," Frank said, as much to the bridge as to Sandy, while he tried to grab hold of her without having to lean any of his weight over the car. "Here," he said, as he pulled her up by her left arm so that she was partially out of the car with her arm over his shoulder and then around his neck. He was having trouble keeping his footing on the sloping timber. Leaning back against the cable, he braced one foot against the rear wheel so that he could get his right arm clear around Sandy. "Grab hold of my neck and don't let go. I'm going to lift you out."

She reached up and locked her arms around his neck, squeezing her eyes shut as he eased her up, her feet braced on the seat for a moment before she pulled her knees up and to the side, just clearing the top of the door.

"Now grab onto the cable again with both hands," Frank said, as he turned and lowered her to her feet between him and the side of the bridge, "and go ahead of me." Keep your feet as close the edge as you can, one in front of the other. Go on. You've got this."

The wood beneath their feet was slipping and shaking as the shifting weight of the car caused more timbers to give way, the screeching complaints of the old bridge filling the air, along with gasps from the women.

"Come on, we have to make a run for it," Frank said as he grabbed Sandy's arm and they sprinted toward the end of the bridge.

CHAPTER 59

Maggie and Tina reached for Sandy and Frank as they scrambled onto solid ground. Then they all turned to watch as the bridge continued to shudder and the screeching grew louder before it gave up the ghost, blue number 55 riding it down through crisscrossed beams of headlights—a slow, stuttering descent that dropped the bridge and car ten feet, coming to a cacophonous halt in the dried-up bed of the Canadian River.

The silence when it was over was as striking as the dust cloud that rose up, obscuring their view. From below they heard, "Holy shit," then heard it a second and third time, Buddy's lament rising with the dust motes from the bottom of the dry river bed.

Sandy buried her face against her aunt's shoulder, and whimpered, "The car. The car."

Frank looked over to where Maggie was rocking her niece slightly and telling her everything was going to be all right, and then looked over at him as if to ask if that was true. He put his hands on their shoulders. "All that matters now is that you're safe, you hear me? It's just a car. It can be fixed, or we can get another. You, you're one of a kind. A little too hot-headed, for my taste, and the darnedest truth bender I've ever met." He and Maggie locked eyes, and he saw she was crying silently. "But we're gonna work all this out. Why don't you two go sit in the car while I talk with Buddy?"

• • • • •

News of the chase and bridge collapsing accelerated through the racing community like an oil leak being burned off the track. It took Buddy less than an hour to get a tow truck to come out along the road he'd taken to the bridge and backed as far down into the gully as was safe. Several others from the track, when they learned what had happened, had followed in their cars and trucks to see if they could be of some help, and several vehicles of spectators who had gotten wind of the excitement brought up the rear.

The scene had a surreal air, with headlights from both sides lighting the ravine and casting shadowy outlines of the men around in an effort to raise the car without doing it any more damage. Adam climbed back up to the Mercury to get a pair of gloves from the trunk and told Sandy it might not be all that bad, but the expression on his face told her that there was next to no chance that the car could survive that drop.

Maggie and Sandy chose to stand at the end of the bridge with their arms around each other's waist watching the rescue operation. The men's voices and feet rustling the dry brush punctuated the otherwise quiet of the country evening. Tina had moved a little down the slope, shifting from time to time to stay out of the way of the men, including L. Ray, who'd been one of the first on the scene, who lined up some of the fallen planks so the car could be pushed up to where the tow truck could latch on.

Finally, the motor of the winch started up, and the men called out amid grunts as they helped balance and position the car onto the trailer. Cheers broke out as blue-and-white 55 crested the top of the ravine. Local police lined a path to the road for the tow truck to keep the spectators out of harm's way, and a photographer from the *Oklahoman* finished up one last roll of film, which included a telescopic shot of Sandy standing on the opposite side of the ravine with her arms over her chest, fingers crossed on both hands, and dried tear tracks on her dust-covered cheeks.

·   ·   ·   ·   ·

The only conversation in the Mercury as they headed back into town was a brief discussion about dropping the girls at their respective motels and Adam at the track, but Sandy quietly asked to stay with Frank and the car for the time being. Maggie and Frank decided it

287

would be best to just follow the tow truck and Buddy to Petty and Son's Garage where they could get the car up on a rack and begin the process of assessing the damage. The girls could drive themselves to their motels after things had settled down.

Sandy sat hunched over on a stool by the workbench, a study of misery, and it seemed enough for the time being for Maggie to have her arm tight around her niece's shoulders while they waited for the verdict on the car. Tina had made reassuring noises for Sandy's sake, but she kept a discrete distance from the others, finally saying she could walk the few blocks to her motel and check in with them later. Only Maggie noticed when Tina actually left.

It took Buddy half an hour to finalize a list of what needed immediate attention, including fixing the drive shaft and track bar, straightening a slightly torqued differential, replacing the fuel pump, and recalibrating every moving part—not to mention replacing one wheel. It was going to be a long night.

By nine o'clock, Buddy finally shooed the others out of the garage so he could concentrate without distractions, telling Frank to check back in a couple of hours. Everyone was too restless to go to the motel, so Frank suggested they go to a nearby truck stop and get something to eat. Adam went with them and tried to get Sandy to talk, but she didn't have much to say except that she wasn't hungry. Maggie ordered a hamburger and fries for her anyway, and the others ordered the usual steak with fries and a salad, but Frank seemed not to have much of an appetite either.

Suddenly, Frank put down his knife and fork. "Nothing like this is ever going to happen again, is that understood? From now on, we'll talk things out. And that means that you, young lady," his hand warm against the nape of Sandy's neck, "have to learn to face things square. No more running away, no more hiding things." He continued as if he were still talking to her, but his voice softened a little and he was looking into the space between Maggie and Sandy as he said, "You keep that up, and after a while you don't even know what you're running from, or where you're headed." He squeezed her neck gently and turned back to his steak. "By the way," he said, "where the Sam Hill were you going, anyway?"

Sandy studied her hamburger and then looked up at him. "I don't know, really. Home, maybe?"

Frank shook his head and a slow grin formed. "Well the way you were headed, you'd of had to circle the globe to get there."

For a minute no one said anything, and then laughter broke out, and with it came ripples of relief that saturated the table. Sandy grinned sheepishly and then came the brittle sound of a dish dropped in the kitchen, the waitress stopped by to ask if they needed anything else and refilled their water glasses, and the moment passed.

Iced teas and beer bottles were lifted, knives moved through steaks, and the talk returned, as it always did, to the track and cars and the men who drove them. What no one talked about as Frank and Maggie pushed their food around on their plates was blue 55 and what the odds were that Buddy would be able to pull her together quickly enough to make her race-worthy. And even if it could run, Sandy wondered, how could it possibly carry Frank to victory against all the other drivers whose daughters hadn't gone nuts and wrecked their cars and lives?

CHAPTER 60

By 9:00 a.m. Sunday morning, the north end of Taft Stadium was already crowded with race cars and trucks, and there were trailers parked all around loaded with tires and tool chests and coolers of beer that would be iced down for after the races.

From where Sandy stood watching, up high in the center of the stands, the infield buzzed and bobbled like a circus parade lumbering into town as the drivers set up in their assigned pit areas.

Frank had bought her a pair of binoculars—small enough to fit into a pocket—and she had spent much of the morning scoping out the long procession of cars and trucks pulling in to unload and set up early for the two o'clock race and later the milling crowds of spectators who were making their first trips of the day to the souvenir and concession stands. She kept her eye out for Adam, who found her first with a complimentary Coke and Baby Ruth, said he'd look for her afterwards in the pits.

•   •   •   •   •

Frank pulled in from his turn at practice laps and parked with the nose three inches from Buddy, who said, "That's right, come to Papa."

"Holy shit she's handlin'," Frank said. "You are one righteous miracle worker."

"You keep her on the track and this engine will get you to the front."

Frank followed Buddy's gaze and saw that he was watching Parker walking past with some of his pit crew and a young driver up from Fort Worth, Texas, who was brought in to pilot red 65. "We'll be fine," Frank said following Buddy's gaze. "You sure about the gear ratio?"

Buddy spit, then walked over to the tool box to check the contents once again, like a surgeon examining a tray of instruments every few minutes while the patient is being put under, not wanting to start racing the clock until everything is primed. Lifting and replacing wrenches and gauges as casually as he would finger change in his pocket, Buddy told Frank to make himself useful by getting them some iced tea. The day was promising to be a scorcher.

·　　·　　·　　·　　·

The stands were already starting to fill by noon, fans from as far away as the gulf of Texas, the corn fields of Iowa, and wheat fields of Nebraska eager to secure good seats and not miss any of the hoopla. It would include the crowning of Miss Grand National Jalopy Champion of 1957, who would serve as trophy girl.

Sandy was looking up at the small plane trailing a banner that read *Shop Lawrence Autorama* and didn't notice Frank sprinting across the track toward the grandstand. By the time he had climbed to where she sat, enough fans had shouted out their good wishes that she would have had to have been deaf and blind to have missed him climbing the steps. The pride that she felt when he sat down beside her puffed her up like an inner tube a couple of pounds over.

"The rest of the Kiowa crowd aren't here yet, I take it," he said to Maggie.

"Not yet. We expect them any minute."

He nodded.

Sandy saw a look pass between them, as if they might want to say more, but there was a pause.

Maggie looked down and asked, "Is everything okay? With the car, and everything?"

He smiled at her and nodded slowly. "We'll see what we see."

Maggie looked over at him but just nodded and smiled. He looked at Sandy. "This where you want to be?"

"I guess. You think we should move somewhere better?"

"Well, now," Frank said, I never get to see things from this side," he said, "so you're a better judge of the best seats than I would be." He scanned the track. "Looks good from here. Real good."

As much as Sandy was enjoying the attention she was getting, she couldn't help wondering what had brought him up there. He'd never said anything before one way or another about where she sat. She thought it might have to do with Maggie being there, about the seeming truce that had settled in between them after the scare and trauma of the night before.

"Listen, Junior," he said to Sandy, "it's a big day. Lots goin' on, thousands of people millin' around, so you look out for yourself and Aunt Maggie, okay?" He put his arm around her and gave her shoulders a squeeze.

She looked up at him and said, "You too."

"Nothing to worry about. I'll be fine. And no matter how things turn out today, everything's gonna be all right. We clear on that?"

She nodded, not at all clear as to how things were going to be at all, but finding that she needed to believe him, that he would not just disappear the way he had all those years before.

He looked over at Maggie and then pulled a small packet of tissue from his shirt pocket and handed it to Sandy. "I've been saving this. I wasn't really sure what for. I guess now I know."

She unfolded the square of crinkly white paper and saw that it held a gold chain with a small gold cross on it."

She heard her aunt inhale sharply and turned to look at her, and then back at Frank.

"It was your mother's," he said. "She'd want you to have it."

Sandy fumbled with the fastener, then handed it to Maggie and sat very still as the clasp was fastened. She slid the cross along the chain so it hung straight down, then leaned over and kissed his cheek. "Sometimes I feel like she's watching out for me."

He put his arm around her shoulders and pulled her to him, kissing her forehead. "I'm sure she is. You might ask her to keep an eye on number 55 today if you think that's all right."

She buried her face against his chest and said, "She loved you. I do too."

He rested his chin on the top of her head, looking at Maggie, who was smiling but looked ready to cry. "Me too, you," he said, and then he was on his feet, forcing down the lump in his throat, as he loped down the stands and to the gate, his right hand raised in a friendly salute to the refrains of cheers that washed down over him all the way to the end of the bleachers and chased him back across the track.

CHAPTER 61

The jostling was intense where Sandy held her ground at the chair stand nearest the ticket gate. Even with the stands practically filled there must have been another thousand spectators milling around behind the bleachers. Irma discovered Sandy first and waved futilely as the troop from Kiowa edged closer. When Sandy finally noticed them, they were stopped in the main thoroughfare with foot traffic spilling around them like a stream around boulders. The cousins were too taken by the array of carnival-type food to remember that they'd just eaten lunch and could in no way actually be hungry. Sandy broke the standoff by promising to bring her cousins back down for a pass along the concessions after everyone got shown to their seats and Aunt Irma could get her bearings.

Sandy led the way. Maggie admired her niece's ingenuity. The girl had changed that summer, seemed more sure of herself. Perhaps because she had gone off on her own, or because she had found her father, after all those years of uncertainty and wondering. And probably fantasizing too, if Maggie remembered her own youth correctly.

Sandy let the others go in first, even Maggie, and sat next to her on the aisle. They smiled at one another, from very different wells of pleasure, Maggie suspected. Sandy's excitement about the race was so obvious that Maggie hugged her, in silent anticipation of any disappointment that would strip that glow of pure joy from her niece's face. And the hug was for herself as well, to push away the doubts she had been plagued with ever since her call to Frank, her attempt to force him into giving Sandy back to her without a fight.

She leaned toward Irma to hear what she was saying.

"I said, I wonder how it feels to be a driver right now, getting ready for the biggest race of its kind ever—or even to be a car owner." She winked at Maggie.

Maggie got her meaning, but didn't respond. In truth, she wasn't sure what her status was. Part owner, previous adversary, now a fan, or something more. She had been genuinely stunned by the size of the turnout and considered that perhaps she had a fairly provincial outlook about racing. It was clear to her, as she took in the panorama that had been advertised as the racing spectacle of the decade, she had backed into something very big indeed. "I'll be honest with you," Maggie said to Irma, "it feels as if a house is about to cave in and I'm holding an umbrella."

"We still talking about the race?" Irma asked, knowing full well that this day meant much more to Maggie than she had at first let on.

Sandy, oblivious to the barely audible chatter of her aunts leaned down between her cousins' heads from time to time to tell them some bit of news about the cars and drivers and owners pictured in the program they pored over. She was surprised at how much information she'd picked up in a relatively short period of time. It was as if she had been around racing all her life instead of just nine-and-a-half days. Adam had been teasing her, but maybe there was some truth to what he'd said, maybe that sort of thing could be in the blood.

"Frank's heat race won't be for a little while," she told them, saying that if they still wanted to visit the concessions they would need to do it soon or wait until much later. She didn't want to miss anything, especially any races that L. Ray might turn up in.

She took the cousins at their word when they indicated that they were more interested in watching the action from the stands for a while than in running around below, so they all got snow cones from one of the passing vendors. The breeze blowing over the stands earlier in the day had either died down considerably or was hampered by the additional bodies all around her.

Sucking red syrup through the crushed ice, she watched intently as a string of young girls in shorts and bathing suits filed up and across the stage that had been erected in front of the stands. At one end of it rose a partially enclosed press box on stilts. The announcer, who was

295

introducing the girls, was cautioning one of the judges to stop hanging out over the railing for a closer look or he might end up watching the race from the back of an ambulance. The crowd laughed and applauded enthusiastically. Sandy watched to see if the girls with the biggest chests got the most applause, but it was hard to tell because some of the candidates who looked more like her were hometown favorites and so got resounding cheers also.

Eventually, Miss Enid, Oklahoma, was named runner-up and Miss Blackwell, Oklahoma, was crowned Miss Grand National Jalopies Champion Queen 1957."

While the girls were driven through the back gate, more announcements were made and the drivers pulled onto the front straightaway one by one to start the slow quarter mile circles that would warm their cars and calm their nerves as they got the watered-down track ready for the first heat race.

· · · · ·

Because the field of entries was so large, they had to stage four heats instead of the usual three, and the wait through those extra eight laps made Frank, who was scheduled for the fourth and fastest, uncharacteristically anxious. The car had handled better with each trial run they'd made, but he was still getting acquainted with it, and there was no better way to feel out a machine than in an actual race, with everything on the line. But in this case, there was very little recovery time if something were to go wrong first time out.

He waited until the third group of cars had taken the checkered flag before fastening the strap on his helmet and climbing into blue-and-white number 55.

Buddy, who still had the hood up, pulled it closed gently, as if he were tucking a blanket around a baby, then stepped back and gave Frank the thumbs-up to pull out and head for his spot in the lineup.

As Frank sat there waiting for the flagman to work his way down the rows holding crossed flags above each car as the drivers were announced, he glanced to his left at Shorty Mullins, who had drawn the pole position, and they grinned at each other, Shorty tapping the bill of his helmet in salute to a time-tested comrade. Frank felt the familiar purr of excitement rise in his chest, every inch of his body on alert.

He looked up into the grandstands, a sea of humanity so vivid and immediate that it seemed to threaten to break over them all in waves. Then the flagman signaled for them to start the pace lap and the crowd and the day were gone, everything but the track ahead telescoped into the distance. Engines growled in different octaves as the field of cars opened and closed like a Technicolor accordion, squaring up for an even start. Then the green flag dropped. It flapped in Frank's peripheral vision for a full second, the time it took for Shorty and Frank to lead the pack past the starting line and twist into turn one.

Frank locked hard onto Shorty's rear, tried to slip under him in turns three and four, but couldn't be sure the race was an actual go until they were on the front straightaway and he could see the green flag still aloft, signaling that all cars had cleared the first turn and the track was wide open. Without turning his head, Frank knew that there was a close race for third because the car behind him was lurching up on the outside and diving back down to hold off the car in fourth place. For a tense moment, the driver challenging from behind nearly jammed his front left tire up under Frank's rear end, but lost ground when Frank nosed so tight along the infield his own left front wheel was hobbling over the loose dirt clods. The whole car vibrated, but by the time they pulled out of turn four he'd put daylight between him and the guy right behind fighting to stay in the money, and Shorty had drifted just high enough that Frank was able to squeeze up on the inside.

Not giving up without a fight, Shorty lay into it coming into the front straightaway, straining to keep the lead as the two cars seesawed back and forth at the start of lap four. Gearing through turn one, Frank felt a slight lurch, like when a car hydroplanes on a wet road. Then the engine took hold again and he began to pull up on Shorty, first by only the span of the back wheel, which he fought to keep through the rest of the fourth lap and into the fifth. Then he managed to inch up to Shorty's doorpost and finally pulled even as they headed into turns three and four where Frank held the advantage.

Unable to regain the lead on the outside, Shorty slipped up into the groove on turn four and shot back down to the inside to sneak around Frank there, but his momentum was gone, and so was 55 as Frank put half-a-car length between them.

By lap six, the field had stretched out, and even the tight race for third seemed far behind as Frank circled the track and glanced over at the slower cars on the opposite straightaway. He managed to hold the lead and keep the car wide open, to feel out what it could do when asked, but what he was thinking of as he crossed the finish line was not that he'd won the race but that they might have trouble with the gear ratio as the track dried out and got slicker. And he wanted Buddy to check the brakes, which seemed soft. He took a fast lap, playing through the gears as he made his way back to Buddy and another tense session of fine-tuning.

CHAPTER 62

Waiting in line to get cold drinks during intermission, Irma turned to Maggie and asked, "Have you seen the kids?"

Maggie shook her head and scanned the crowds around the various concessions, not really concerned. "Sandy knows her way around. They'll be fine."

"Sister?"

Irma only called her that when she wanted to talk about sensitive matters. Glancing over Irma's right shoulder as if studying the menu on the back wall, Maggie prepared herself for a conversation she was pretty sure she didn't want to have.

"Lloyd and I are worried."

"Regarding?"

"With this whole crazy thing. Risking your savings on this, and, well, what about the deal you made? What were you thinking? Even Lloyd thought that you and Frank, well, that this deal is pretty crazy. Oh he's all in, of course. Gets to be a big shot in the pits, all involved with the car and the big race. When he put on those white uniform pants, he did a little jig as if he was five and it was Christmas morning."

Maggie sighed and looked at her. "First, the arrangement I had with Frank went south when Sandy found out about it, obviously. My attempt to circumvent a risky legal challenge has failed. What happens after tonight is anyone's guess."

"I don't know what in the world ever made you think that betting on the outcome of a race was the answer."

"I wasn't. I was betting on a driver." Maggie turned away and looked for the children, but it was Frank she was thinking about. Hoping that win or lose, he'd realize Sandy belonged in Kiowa. But Maggie had also witnessed the bond that had sprung up between father and daughter, and she knew that regardless of how this day ended, none of their lives would ever be the same again.

Irma paid for two Cokes and handed one to Maggie as they turned back toward the grandstand, saying, "You've always been so level-headed, but this is all pretty far—

"You've already said that."

"Yes, I can't help but wonder if you know what you're doing."

"Well, Sister, no, I can't say as I do know what I'm doing exactly."

Irma hesitated, unsure what to say, now that the reassurance she'd expected to get wasn't forthcoming. "So what do you think will happen?" she asked.

Maggie laughed out loud, astonishing them both, and then Irma joined in, although she had a quizzical expression on her face. "Damned if I know, Sister."

"Hey! Over here!"

They looked up and saw the kids clustered at the entrance to the stands, the two youngest with helium balloons tied to their wrists. They had attained an impressive collection of photos and plastic propellers on sticks and cardboard containers of drinks and snacks.

"You kids," Irma chided, "have you spent every last cent already and the races only half over?"

Lloyd Jr. assured her that they all had money left, but that he'd had to argue his clunk-headed youngest brother out of getting a tee-shirt with a two-headed, fire-breathing dragon and the words Derby Dare Devils emblazoned across it.

By the time they made their way back up to their seats, Irma was sufficiently distracted to have let go of her $64,000 question, but it had gained purchase in Maggie's brain. Whatever it was she wanted, not just for herself but for all of them, her mother included, seemed to be on hold temporarily, making way for her immediate concern for Frank's safety. She didn't know what Sandy might do if he were to be injured, or worse.

Just sitting through Frank's heat race had exhausted Maggie—even though he led it most of the way and won. The trophy dash had been mercifully brief, even though Sandy had insisted that with another lap

300

or two Frank would have taken first. It was as if Maggie had felt every jolt of blue 55—every twist of metal and rubber through the turns— with her own body. It was even worse when she tried to look away, putting her at the mercy of shrieks and moans of those around her. Finally, she determined to keep her eyes on number 55 no matter what else was going on, telling herself that as long as she did so nothing terrible would take place. It wasn't exactly offering a virgin for the volcano, but a tentative bargain she struck with her own God, aware that it was spur-of-the-moment and probably not terribly binding.

·   ·   ·   ·   ·

The atmosphere in the pits just before the championship race got underway was electric. Even those who had nothing more left to do than sit and rub a cloth back and forth over a visor or read a gauge for the tenth time did so with more concentration than usual.

Buddy's instincts had been to gear the car high so that by the second half of the race, when the track would be even drier and slicker, the car would be getting maximum horse power and still be handling its best. Probably. Frank found Buddy's continual tinkering with the car nerve-wracking. He was ready, the car had darn-well better be ready. He wanted to get this show on the road.

There was a strip of shade to the side of the camper, and Frank settled into a lawn chair there to sip one last glass of water laced with lemon juice. One hundred laps in Oklahoma City in July would dehydrate a camel. He could feel the blood pulsing in his neck and moved his shoulders around to loosen up, air cooling the strip of sweat between his shoulder blades. Nestled where he was, he couldn't see much, but the voices and noises from nearly a hundred surrounding pit areas gave him an encompassing awareness of all the others gathered there. The scared and brash newcomers—those who'd won the one A-Feature on their home tracks that had gained them entry to the Grand National, and who'd won little else worth a line of print. And the more seasoned veterans—friends, and even some loose cannons, alike—though few as seasoned as himself. The grand old veteran. He laughed harshly out loud, causing Buddy and Lloyd, who was happily serving as Buddy's wingman, to turn their heads, but no one said anything.

Frank tipped his chair back against the camper and closed his eyes. For many of them, this would mark a grand beginning. National recognition. A whole new era for dirt-track racing. But for him—it could very well be his one and only chance to be the best at the only thing he'd excelled at in his whole hit-and-miss life. Mostly misses. Even Ruth had been a miss. A near-miss, closer than he'd realized at the time, himself full of hurt pride and self-doubts. He tried to picture Ruth there, dead-center in the stands, her hand with the dime-store gold band shading her eyes as she looked for him. Tossing her head slightly to coax her hair back over her shoulder. No, it was Sandy who did that, her hair sometimes catching at the corner of her mouth as she bent over the car with Buddy, discussing everything from how to set a cam to boys she'd known and almost liked a lot. Sandy was a hit.

Leaning forward to right the chair, he opened his eyes and ran his thumb over his belt buckle. And he had let Maggie egg him into waging his claim to his daughter, like next month's paycheck or a steak dinner. Only this time ... maybe he'd needed a talisman to appease the race gods. Here. Here's what this is worth to me. Just let me win this one last race, it's only another race after all. I've won hundreds. But just this one more, that says I'm still on top. And my life isn't gonna fizzle down to ... he put his face in his hands and gave his head a shake, a growling sound escaping involuntarily.

"Yo?" Buddy called out to him. "You sayin' somethin'?"

Raising his head slowly, Frank looked over at Buddy, who was leaning into the car through the opening on the driver's side.

Frank shook his head, said, "You ever gonna make peace with that pile of bolts, or what?"

"We're ready as we're ever gonna be. You peed yet, Sonny?"

Getting up slowly, as if there was nothing more pressing than taking a casual glance at the car, Frank put on his helmet and climbed into the seat. He fastened the chin strap, then the seatbelt, and pulled on his gloves. He ran his hands over the wheel and gear shift in a quick caress, and reached for the ignition. "We copasetic?"

"You better believe it. Hold up." Buddy pulled a sheer aqua-blue head scarf out of his back pocket and tied it around Frank's upper arm.

"What in the hell—"

"From Sandy." He swatted Frank's hand away. "She made me promise. It's what they did back in the days of the knights and stuff. Anyway, little extra luck can't hurt."

Frank lifted up his arm and looked at the wispy blue-green fabric, it's two ends fluttering with the vibration of the car. "Right, unless it cuts off my circulation. Or gets caught in the machinery."

"You're gettin' to be an old lady."

"So you keep sayin'."

"Here," Buddy took out a pocket knife and sawed off the ends of the scarf.

"Satisfied? You're gonna make a little girl very happy."

Frank looked at the scarf once more, thinking don't be too sure, and eased ahead. Buddy walked alongside, his right hand against the sun-warmed metal like a trainer steadying his horse into the gate.

"Remember she's set a little high right now. May take some extra handlin', maybe not. Hard to figure how much the extra semi-final affected the track. Just keep her—"

"Hold up! What the hell!" Frank pumped on the brakes repeatedly before the car finally rolled to a stop.

In a flash, Frank was out of the car and Buddy had lunged in head first, pushing on the brakes himself with his hand. He yelled for Lloyd and another guy nearby watching them to come over and roll the car back into the pit stall with Buddy still draped over the side. He dropped down to the ground and scooted under before it had completely stopped. The others rushed to drag the tools and flashlights closer and formed a taut half-circle around Buddy's legs. They were an eerily silent gathering in the midst of the commotion of engines revving and men shouting as the featured event began to get under way.

"Come on. Come on," almost a chant from Frank. "How bad is it?"

Buddy twisted around to stick his head out. "Can't find it. If there's a leak, it's too small to see this way."

"Didn't you check the brakes after the heat race? I told you then they felt soft."

"Of course I checked them. Think I'm gonna ignore something like that?" He told one of the men to get some brake fluid, sending them all scrambling through the chests and trunks, but with no results.

There was only a small amount left in the can he'd used to top it off after the first race. Frank climbed up on the back of the camper and called out to those nearby, asking if anyone had any brake fluid. The question was repeated by others like a diminishing echo with no positive reply coming back from the few within hearing. The one remarkable response was from Hays' crew, four cars down, who discussed it among themselves and then all raised their middle fingers his direction in an un-neighborly yet predictable salute. Pulling off his helmet, Frank hopped down and walked back over to the car. He felt as if he'd swallowed brake fluid himself and was about to give it back up. "Nothing?" he asked the others, who shook their heads and looked at one another in alarm. Frank stared at the car, unable to move or speak. After all they'd been through.

Buddy scrambled out from beneath the framework. "Get me some plumbers tape from the box, some water, and a funnel. Move it!"

No one moved until it sank in. Then the men standing around all talked at once, sure that it wouldn't work, but then again, there was no reason why it shouldn't, just a hydraulic system after all. What's wanted is pressure. Just a certain amount of pressure. They only had a few minutes to get the car into the lineup. It would have to work.

•   •   •   •   •

Up in the stands, Sandy couldn't sit still. All the other cars had already lined up on the track and the drivers had been announced for the second time that day. But Frank wasn't among them. The position he'd drawn, second back on the outside, gaped like a missing front tooth, even as the cars started on the parade lap, slow and wobbly behind the red corvette convertible with the Grand National Queen waving from the top of the seat. "There!" Sandy screamed.

Maggie thought at first that something terrible had happened, with Sandy the first to witness it, followed by others around them who had also taken up the cry that sounded raw and desperate, "There! There!"

She looked to where they were pointing and saw blue number 55 poised at the edge of the track, gleaming in the sunlight. Then it gunned across the track fishtailing at the back of the line before straightening up, racing along the outside. Fans all along the grandstand were cheering as it passed the bright cavalcade of cars.

Frank shot around the first two turns in an attempt to catch up as the leaders were finishing the parade lap, bunched up like a mechanical beast, roaring toward the starting line. The entire stadium seemed to be yelling "Go! Go! Go!" as blue 55 barreled down the front straightaway and slipped into the empty slot seconds before the flagman burst into action, swooping the flag to waist high and holding it there. Taft Stadium exploded with the roar of accelerating engines and fans screaming and whistling through the first full lap.

Maggie held her hands over her ears, but still the noise was deafening. The crowd didn't settle down until it was clear that all the cars were still on the track to start lap two and that the first grand national championship for jalopies was officially underway—99 laps to go.

CHAPTER 63

Maybe it was the rush of adrenaline from making a grandstand entrance, but on the second lap, with only Al Surrey, Pee Wee, Shorty, and Mac ahead of him, Frank was still shaking as he pulled up hard on Surrey coming out of turn four. By mid-straightaway he eased past him on the inside, and cranked hard into turn one. He slipped to the outside and went nose to nose with Pee Wee as they moved into turn two, and Frank stood on it to pull ahead. Halfway down the backstretch, he felt a slight bump on his left rear as Pee Wee bobbled into him. Frank caught sight of the yellow blur as Pee Wee careened toward the infield before hooking sharply to the right and pulling back onto the track.

Only Shorty and Mac out in front, battling for first. Frank stayed hot on their tails, drafting behind Shorty for the next two laps as Mac got a car length out ahead. Feeling Shorty out, Frank teased him low on the pole and then slid right to ride just a shade high, to keep Shorty guessing which way he'd be coming for him.

Rounding the turns, Frank could see that Pee Wee had gotten back in and was trailing the Texan in Parker's red 65. Hays in the Hornet— black and yellow 98—had worked his way up to sixth. Fine with Frank, who knew that the more fighting for positions that went on behind him the more distance he could put between himself and the rest of the field. Frank had already lost count of the laps and would have to rely on Buddy and his chalk board in turn four to keep track. By lap six or seven—the car was handling so well Frank didn't know how much more he could get out of it without pushing too hard and risking a blown gasket or tire. He decided he had to make his move soon, in case the engine didn't hold up and wouldn't have the juice he'd need later to fight his way into first position.

．　　．　　．　　．　　．

Sandy's fingers were starting to ache. She tried to relax without uncrossing them. It wasn't until the tenth lap, when Shorty challenged Mac on the outside that a hole opened up along the pole and Frank's blue-and-white 55 finally slipped under—forcing them both wide—and shot into the lead. Sandy smiled over at her Aunt Maggie, who grinned back and hugged her.

With Frank out ahead, Sandy could give more attention to the struggle that L. Ray was having breaking out of the middle of the pack. The slowest cars had fallen back so that Frank was about to start lapping them, but the racers in the middle of the field were still locked into fierce battles as they jockeyed for position. During the early laps, L. Ray had passed a car with red and orange flames painted across the hood that Sandy hadn't recognized, and he was now having to go after it again. She narrowed her eyes for a tighter focus and tried to will him ahead, which seemed to be working. Seven back, she counted. Not bad, but with a gazillion laps to go, anything could happen.

．　　．　　．　　．　　．

Buddy held up the chalk board with 20 written on it as agreed to let Frank know he was already well past the total laps he'd run in the previous race when the brakes had gotten soft. So far, there had been little need for them. For the most part, just backing off the throttle had taken care of his maneuvering. But Frank would need to test for grab soon. In the back of his head loomed the unwelcome thought that, if he wasn't going to be able to bring the car to a stop under its own control, he needed to know so he could pick his spot when the time came to let off the gas and try to avoid crashing into anything or anyone.

Shooting up the backstretch, he swung right to lap the trio bringing up the rear of the field. He almost hung back until the two cars just ahead of him finished their fight, but then thought better of it and started around them on the outside. With the traffic slowing him down some, Mac would be knocking on his back door any second, fighting to regain the lead.

Frank was preparing to ride a tire's width wide in turn three to use the momentum of the embankment on turn four to maximize his speed when he saw a tire sail across the track up ahead of him. Instinctively, he slid down to brace for a possible collision. Two cars had locked up and were skidding high toward the wall along the front straightaway. Frank pumped the brakes, felt them grab, giving him time to find a hole in the dust-cloud and bore through it, hoping it was clear on the other side. By the time he'd made it back around the track, the red flag was out.

He banged his steering wheel with the heels of his hands and shut down, cruising slowly through traffic around to the finish line to save the brakes. He pulled up to wait for the restart of the race, shaking his head at MacElroy and Shorty, who had rolled to a stop right behind him.

•   •   •   •   •

Her hands clenched together, Maggie asked Sandy, who along with half the people around them had climbed up onto the benches to get a better look, "Can you see anything? Is it bad?"

"There are too many people. Wait . . . nope, can't see if they're out yet."

Just then, a surge of cheers and applause traveled along the stands from where one of the drivers gave an okay sign as the ambulance, which had been parked just off the track, rolled to a stop. Maggie felt her insides twist, and every time she looked over to where Frank was, either crouching down to look under his car or talking with Buddy who looked like he was pouring something into it, her insides got another stir. More than winning, she just wanted this to be over with, for Frank to come out of it all in one piece. But she knew that the only thing he wanted was to get back in the car and chase the gold.

"There he is. They've got the other driver out," Sandy yelled over at her.

"Is he moving?" Maggie asked.

"Doesn't look like it. His head rolled to the side."

Maggie winced and crossed her arms over her ribs.

Even before the ambulance got off the track, the mangled race cars had been turned right-side up and hooked to tow trucks.

The announcer, busy trying to give the exact lineup of cars one lap back from when the race was stopped, interrupted himself to give an update on the injured driver. "We've gotten word that he's recovered consciousness and is going on in to the hospital to be looked over. I know I speak for every man, woman, and child at Taft Stadium today in sending good wishes his way. Let's have a round of applause for the fine medical crew standing by for just such emergencies, and for Ace Wrecking, for their fast, efficient services in clearing the track."

Sandy jumped down off the bench clapping hard. By the time the race was started again, Maggie's watch showed twelve minutes had passed since the shut-down.

"This isn't so good." Sandy leaned against her aunt's shoulder and pointed to the cars as they started around the track again for a second green flag. "That creep Hays is in fifth. L. Ray will have to be careful getting around him. And that's the new driver in red 65, Dad's old car, behind L. Ray." She sat up straighter and checked her crossed fingers. She had it all worked out, had thought about it for two nights. L. Ray had to take second or even third place. She would go up to him after the race and make some gracious gesture as the winner's daughter. She had to do it right away, as soon as she saw him, so it would seem spontaneous, a congratulatory kiss. Just like some of the trophy girls did, no matter who was around.

. . . . .

It took two pace laps before the flagman was sure the cars were in the right order and gave them the green again. Fighting to keep his nose down, Frank pushed the throttle all the way in through the first turn and kept it flat out on the backstretch, the newly acquired cluster of contenders hot behind him. The car felt a little sluggish, maybe because it had cooled down some, and he struggled to find the right combination as he geared through the turns and then blasted across in front of the stands. He could feel Mac's breath on his neck and thought he caught the flash of Shorty's car slowing down and rolling into the infield. Frank gunned it down the back-stretch and held tight through the turn, gaining inches as Hays plowed into Mac, knocking him wobbly for a few yards, just long enough for Hays and L. Ray both to slip under him to move into second and third. Frank thought he got a glimpse of Parker's 65 behind Mac.

The track was all oil and hot rubber, and the ruts made when the track had still been damp were now as unforgiving as concrete. Frank ran a finger across his goggles to clear off the dirt and grabbed for the wheel again as he felt a buck from behind. It came again, and he stomped the throttle into the floorboard, sensing without actually looking back that he'd cost Hays a few critical inches.

Just ahead were the slow cars, ready to be lapped again. Frank sucked in more dust than air as he came up behind them and started under as they moved to the right at the flagman's signal, two, three, four cars out of the way.

He was back to turn one, and again the jolt from behind told him that Hays had slipped through too, had not lost the same seconds Frank had to give up while the move-over signal had been given and obeyed. Fighting to hold the lead coming down the backstretch, he nearly missed Buddy's signal that it was lap 40. Nearly halfway.

CHAPTER 64

Maggie looked over at Irma to check the laps again when a woman nearby screeched, "No!" causing Maggie to jump and look back at the track. Every face in the grandstand turned to the south end where two cars were spinning in the same direction, sparks flying up where metal ground against metal, and then the car highest up clipped the cement retaining wall and bounced back into the other car. It seemed to Maggie that they skidded in slow motion, locked together, before coming to a stop against the retaining wall. She looked to the flagman, who held the yellow flag straight down by his side. "Why isn't he warning everyone?" Maggie asked.

"No need," Sandy yelled, to be heard over the noise without turning her head. "No one's hurt, and the cars are out of the way up there." She pointed to where the drivers had climbed out of their cars and stood up on the top of the concrete wall, leaning against the wire fence there.

"Hey, that's red 65!" Sandy yelled. "Our old car. Old Parker's gonna shit bricks!"

Both aunts and her cousins turned to look at her.

"That's race-track talk," she said, smiling sheepishly.

Maggie rolled her eyes, and Irma reached over and thumped Sandy on the head, telling the other kids to close their mouths and turn back around. They all watched as the drivers that had spun out together pushed their cars farther along the wall and over the embankment, as far out of harm's way as they could get them. According to Irma's markings, there were 54 laps to go. Maggie 's heart was pounding so hard she didn't know whether she would make it to the end.

• • • • •

Back at turn four , Frank saw Buddy hold up the chalk board to signal lap 55, and then he threw it down, holding his hands up to indicate that there was very little distance between him and the car behind. Frank wiped at his goggles and fought off the black-and-yellow hood crowding up on the inside in turn one. He heard Hays inch up as far as his rear wheel, gaining the inside. Frank fought to keep the steering wheel tight, its vibrations jolting all the way up into his chest and neck as he held the lead through the turn. Just before straightening out into the backstretch, a slam into his left rear sent him fishtailing. In the seconds it took Frank to straighten back out, Hays and then L. Ray shot under him. The anger that flooded through him used up half a lap before he got his concentration back. Third place. Not worth shit on a shingle.

• • • • •

Frank was able to stay on L. Ray's tail, leaving just enough air between them to keep out of trouble. The kid was gunning for Hays like a man possessed, roaring up on his tail, then gliding down to get under his left rear, then back up on the right, looking for the chance to blast past. Hays was sliding right and left to keep L. Ray from slipping around. They were both working their tires hard and Frank knew that with this being the longest race any of them had ever been in there was no telling how the rubber would hold up. The whole idea of taking cars pretty much all out for 100 consecutive laps was a crapshoot anyway. Frank and Buddy figured this race would quickly separate the men from the boys, and from Buddy's last chalkboard message, the field was already down by half. Not that that made much difference to Frank, who was only concerned with the cars running at the front, the ones most likely to make it to the finish.

．　　．　　．　　．　　．

Frank kept his eyes glued to L. Ray's rear-end, and went into auto pilot, holding on and playing the long game. He didn't think the kid had what he needed—either from the car or from himself—to get around Hays in the yellow and black hornet, who was running hot and knew all the tricks in the book. But that was okay. Frank had been studying their battle for about two dozen turns around the track, and was waiting for what he knew would be his best shot.

．　　．　　．　　．　　．

As agreed, Buddy signaled when there were twenty laps to go. Exhausted, parched, and fighting off a cramp in his right thigh, Frank tapped into what Buddy jokingly referred to as his spare tank, the reserve it took to battle from behind to the last hundredth of a second it took to reach the checkered flag.

It was four laps later that L. Ray made the move Frank had been waiting for. The kid had a habit of pulling wide a little early on turn four to try to use the sling from the embankment for an outside pass. So far he'd been quick enough to settle back in behind Hays to keep his second-place position locked up. On the next lap, Frank hugged the pole in turn four like white on rice, his left front tire vibrating over dirt clods along the infield. *Pedal, meet metal*, Frank muttered, as he ground the throttle into the floorboard and pulled his car up under L. Ray's, even with the back tire, then the door, and pulling past him into second position. *That takes care of the rookie*, he thought, as he drafted behind Hays around turns one and two. Now it was just him and the loose cannon in the hornet. Anything could happen.

•　•　•　•　•

Lap 95, Frank made up his mind to attempt an outside pass. He'd been riding Hays hard on the inside to keep him low, and was pretty sure 55 had the juice to power around if he could get the right start. Hays had to know it as well, and wasn't giving an inch. With Hays biting hard and low through turn one, Frank took 55 all out, inching up outside until his hood was almost even with Hay's front wheel and holding along the backstretch. In turn three, Hays swung his rear-end wide, sparks flying where it careened into number 55, forcing Frank to settle in behind him again. Lap 96, Frank made the same move, but this time he kept so close that Hays had no room to repeat his earlier maneuver. Frank could feel the heat radiating from Hays' engine as he pulled even on the backstretch, and they rode through turns three and four like Siamese twins. As they flew past the grandstand, the roar from the fans swept over them like a tailwind. Two laps to go. They were still running even when the white flag swung above them in figure eights as they took their 99th trip over the oily, chewed-up, beat-down dirt oval. This was it.

Frank kept the throttle wide open along the backstretch and into turn three. He came out of turn four so fast the centrifugal force tugged him a few inches wider than he wanted to be, but once on the straightaway, Frank was able to push 55's nose past Hays by the time they reached the flag stand. That was all he needed to know.

Frank held his slight lead through turns one and two, but on the backstretch, Hays gunned it, and the cars seesawed back and forth trading mere inches. Entering turns three and four for the 100th time that hot July afternoon, the black-and-yellow Hornet and blue-and-white 55 were running neck and neck. And then like a thoroughbred that has been held in check and was finally given its head, 55 pulled away.

•　•　•　•　•

In the stands, Sandy held her breath, every muscle taut as she leaned forward to see around and through the standing crowd. Four-thousand pairs of eyes followed the front two cars on the straightaway as blue 55 pushed past the hornet's nose by six inches, eight inches, and then a foot as Frank Haggard shot across the finish line of the first-ever Grand National Jalopies Championship. To Sandy's relief, L. Ray hung on to finish just half-a-car-length behind Hays in third place. She felt the footboards of the bleachers tremble as 4,000 fans jumped and danced, their cheers nearly drowning out the riotous cascade of engines gearing down—the checkered flag looping figure eights as the rest of the field gunned across the finish line.

CHAPTER 65

Frank tapped the brakes repeatedly as he rounded the track, gearing down even as adrenalin was still raging through him. When he got back to the finish line, he reached out to shake the flagman's outstretched hand before taking the checkered flag and heading back out for his victory lap as national champion.

Holding the black and white checkered flag overhead, he took in every inch of Taft Stadium as if it were his first time to see it all, the sea of faces that swiveled in unison as he headed into turn one, the fence with its panorama of ads, the infield where the hard-working pit crews were waving and cheering, raising two fingers in a victory salute.

By the time he got back around and pulled into victory lane, the single lap seemed to have taken almost as long as the race itself. He sat there for a moment vibrating, then realized the car was still running. He shut off the engine and let the reality ease up over him as he climbed up through the cut out in the roof and handed back the flag, and then balanced there while he removed his gloves, helmet, and then goggles, dropping them onto the seat. He raised both hands, waving at the crowd, and then looked around for his pit crew. He spotted Buddy and Lloyd standing near the edge of the track and motioned them over for the photos and trophy presentations.

As soon as Frank swung his legs over the top of the car and jumped down, Buddy grabbed him, lifting him off his feet. He bounced him a few times for good measure before setting him back down.

Buddy said, "You might be an old dog, but you're still top dog!"

"We did it," Frank said, slapping Buddy on the back. "Someday you're gonna tell your grandkids about the car you pulled out of a ravine, and the next day it won the biggest damned race of its kind!"

Trophy presentations passed by in a blur of flashbulbs and congratulatory handshakes, Miss Grand National's pink prom dress was a like a blush in the midst of gritty white uniforms moving around her as they joined up and repositioned for photos.

All at once, Frank was up in the air, carried along on the shoulders of other drivers and their crews as Lloyd did the honors of pulling 55 back into the pits where more pictures would be taken. The first fans that poured onto the track rushed into the pits with programs and cameras hoping to get autographs and pictures of themselves shaking hands with their favorite drivers and touching the hoods of their favorite cars.

By the time Sandy and the rest of the family fought their way to where blue 55 was parked, Frank was surrounded by a huge ring of smiling fans calling out congratulations, some asking questions about the car and peering in at the engine as if some magic formula for success would be revealed.

Pushing her way through the wall of admirers, Sandy threw her arms around Frank's neck as he lifted her in a bear hug. "We did it," he said, giving her another squeeze before setting her back down. He looked out over the crowd to where Maggie and her family were standing and waved them in, the others parting to let them through.

He nodded at Maggie, and then handed her the trophy and raised her other hand overhead. The crowd cheered wildly, flashbulbs popping all around. "Well partner," he said, "how's it feel to win the big one?"

"I'm a nervous wreck" she said, and laughed.

He saw her hand was actually shaking and took the trophy back, handing it to Sandy, saying, "Take care of this, Junior."

Sandy eased to the edge of the crowd and climbed up onto the trailer to get a better view of the infield. The trophy stretched from her waist to her head, so she balanced it on the side of the trailer to get a closer look. It was lined up exactly against the late afternoon sun so that a bright halo radiated around the gold race car perched on top. Her arms shaky from its weight, she lowered it to balance on her hip, and then looked back over to where Maggie and Frank stood in the circle of friends and fans, right next to the car that had taken her father farther than he'd ever gone before.

"Hey!"

Sandy looked down and saw Ad walking over. "Nice hunk of metal." He hopped up onto the trailer. "You must be bustin'-your-buttons proud."

"I am," she said, realizing that even though it was a new sensation there was something familiar about it, as if the months of pouring over the scrapbooks and daydreaming of what it would be like to be with Frank had all been in preparation for this moment.

"Wow, that's a beauty," he said, "indicating the trophy. But it doesn't hold a candle to the beauty holdin' it."

She looked at him for a split second before starting to smile, then glanced over to where L. Ray was still talking with fans, and saw Tina wave at her. Sandy lifted her hand to wave back, nearly dropping the trophy against the edge of the trailer.

"Whoa," Adam said. "I'll make a deal with you. I'll hold it while you climb down so it doesn't get banged up."

"Okay," she said, turning her hip toward him so he could take it.

"Hold up there, Missy. I said I'd make you a deal."

She looked at his eyes, which were a light blue, like her father's, and shining with anticipation. "I'm not so hot with deal-making these days," she said, remembering the near disaster of the previous day.

"This is a good one," he said. "I'll help you with this monumental one-of-a-kind trophy if you'll let me give you a congratulatory kiss. Just one tiny one," he said quickly. "A beautiful, experienced woman like you won't miss one little kiss." He grinned at her and raised his eyebrows. "Who knows, maybe some of the luck you brought your dad will rub off on me. I'm planning on getting a ride in a couple years myself. I'll be old enough to start trainin'. No more concessions for me."

She studied him for a moment. She was also thinking about L. Ray. She decided it wouldn't hurt to practice a little, so she leaned in, closing her eyes part way as she did, and kissed him on his lips, which were softer and warmer than she expected.

When she pulled back, she saw his eyes were still closed and his lips were stretching into a slow smile. "Wow," he said, opening his eyes. He

318

hopped down and reached out for the trophy and offered her his other hand. "Madam?"

She grinned, and said, "Thank you, Adam," as she jumped down beside him.

By now, the adults all had cold beers and the crowd was thinning out. When Sandy walked up, Maggie leaned her mouth close to her ear and said, "What was all that about?" She motioned toward the trailer with her chin, and was smiling in a way that didn't seem like a tease.

Sandy blushed, but pulled Ad over by the arm and said, "This is Adam. He works the races. But in two years, he'll be a driver."

Frank looked over and shook his head. "Hot damn!" he said. They just keep gettin' younger and younger."

The people standing around laughed and asked questions as more hands were shaken. A clearly star-struck young boy held out a strip of leather to be autographed.

"This is a first," Frank said. "Where's the rest of the cow? Anyone got a Magic Marker? What's your name?"

"Hold on," Buddy told him, as he fished one out of his tool box.

"Name's Jesse. Jesse Reed, Sir."

Frank wrote on the leather piece and handed it back, saying, "Here you go, Jess."

"Wow," Jesse said, grinning ear-to-ear. "Thanks. Thanks, Frankie. I figure this oughta last forever."

Frank reached over and shook his hand, saying, "Let's hope so, Son."

He glanced over at Maggie. "Let's hope so."

Adam pulled Sandy aside and handed the trophy back to her. "I gotta go, or I'll miss my ride. But I'll see you around, okay?"

"Hope so," she said, wondering whether she would or not, wondering where she'd be this time next year.

A reporter for the Oklahoma City paper asked if his camera man could get a couple more pictures with Frank, Buddy, and the trophy beside the car, and the crowd shifted slightly to let them line up for the shot, the trophy balanced on the hood between them.

"So, Frankie," the reporter asked, the light bulbs making the gold plating of the trophy seem to throw off sparks in the late afternoon sunlight, "I hear a rumor you might be thinking about retiring. Going out on top. Any truth to that? Gonna let the others have another shot at you?"

Frank said, "I can guess who started that rumor." He looked over to where G.D. Parker was scowling at the twisted frame of red 65. "It's a little soon to start thinking about the second national. Just let me enjoy this one, all right?" The fans nearby cheered and whistled.

Maggie and Sandy stayed close by taking it all in while Frank and Buddy answered a string of questions about the race and car and what it felt like to win the big one. Maggie felt as if she'd been caught up in a whirlwind and set back down but still didn't have her bearings. She was just a short drive from Kiowa, but the scene and the sensations she was feeling were so new she might well have traveled halfway around the world.

Every few minutes, unable to contain her excitement, Sandy bounced up and down. She wondered how many newspapers would run the stories of the first race of its kind. They would have to stop to buy newspapers all the way back to either Hutch or Kiowa, wherever she was going to end up. She might even find pictures that were taken while she was standing beside her father and holding the trophy. And there would be photos of the others, including L. Ray with his trophy for third place. She turned to ask her aunt if they could start a new scrapbook, said she wanted to put the remains of her lucky blue-green scarf in it, and saw that Maggie had moved closer to Frank, his arm slung over her shoulders.

Sandy looked over to where L. Ray was still talking with fans and didn't see Tina nearby, so she meandered over, taking a pack of juicy fruit from her pocket and opening it. Even in the hot, steamy air in the crowded infield, Sandy felt goosebumps rising along her arms when L. Ray spotted her.

"This here's the current champ's daughter. You're lookin' at track royalty right here, fellas. Ain't she a beauty?" He put an arm around her waist and pointed at the gum. This my prize?" She nodded and said, "Congratulations. Your trophy is really nice, too."

"Thanks, Sandy. Tell you what. Clearly you brought old Frankie some serious luck this year. I'm thinking next year is my shot. How about throwing a little this way for good measure?" He bent down, offering her his cheek. She glanced around the circle and then kissed him so quickly her lips barely made contact with grit and bristles on his jaw as people around them whooped and yelled their approval.

"Bye," she said, blushing from head to toe, but with a smile that would cause Maggie to study her niece for a moment when Sandy got back and swung in through the window of blue 55. Dropping into the seat, she put on the helmet and ran her hands over the steering wheel. A bulb flashed and popped as people laughed and the photographer called out to her, "Nice ride. What's your best time?" Sandy pulled herself up through the cut-out roof and straightened up the over-sized helmet. Grinning over at Frank, who had his arm tight around her aunt's waist—which was definitely significant—she called back, "Not sure. You'll have to ask my dad."

FRANK HAGGARD CROWNED 1STGRAND
NATIONAL JALOPY CHAMPION

Oklahoma City, Oklahoma—Frank Haggard engaged in a savage duel until he took the lead for good on the 99th lap, successfully defending his high-points standing Sunday in the first-of-its-kind 100-lap Grand National Jalopy Championship on the quarter-mile track at Taft Stadium. A record crowd of 4,000 witnessed Haggard in a new entry—blue and white number 55, a '34 Ford Coupe with a flathead Ford engine--and Floyd

Hays in his number 98 black-and-yellow hornet battle it out through the last several laps.

When asked how it felt to win the first-ever national race of its kind, Haggard said, "It's been quite a ride. It's an honor to compete against these outstanding drivers, and to see so many fans turn out for the show. My crew is just the best anyone could ask for. Couldn't have happened without them." When asked whether he expected to be in the line-up next year to defend his title, Haggard said, "I guess we'll have to wait and see. It's sort of become a family affair."

Winner of the first Grand National Jalopy Championship, Frank (Frankie) Lies (left) of Wichita, Kansas, and car builder Kenny Riffel of Herington, Kansas, Taft Stadium, Fairgrounds, Oklahoma City, Oklahoma, 1957.

And Now for the Rest of the Story . . .

By Bob Lawrence

The primary race promoter for that first National Championship was Raymond Daniel "Ray" Lavely, who was originally from Houston. In 1957, Ray was the regular race promoter at Taft Stadium. He decided to invite Jim Davis, the promoter from Hutchinson, KS, O. L. Douglas, from 81 Speedway in Wichita, Jack Merrick from Dodge City, and the promoter from Enid, OK, to join in a joint promotion of these races. Note that Lavely excluded his main rival—Bud Carson, who was soon to become Oklahoma City's premier race promoter.

Each of the five (including Lavely) was given 20 qualifying spots at the first National, and each promoter could fill those spots in any way he saw fit. For the heat races at Taft, there were five 20 car heats made up of the 20 cars that had qualified from each participating racetrack. For instance, there was a Wichita heat race made up of the 20 drivers who had qualified from Wichita. From each of those heat races, 10 finishers went to the A feature and 10 to the B feature. This assured that the cars in those two feature races would be dispersed equally from each of the 5 qualifying racetracks.

At some point during the races on championship race day, Ray Lavely skipped town with the ticket office receipts for the weekend. Lavely was found in Colorado several months later, assisting another race promoter, but once he was discovered, he skipped town again.

Several years later, Lavely was discovered in Gardena, California watching the races at Ascot Speedway. Ironically, the man who recognized him was Shane Carson--son of Bud Carson whom Lavely had excluded from the National Championship race at Taft. Lavely disappeared again, and in 1980 he passed away in Harbor City, California.

None of the participants in that first National Championship (including the new champ Frank Lies) ever saw a dime of their prize money. The whole situation sort of soured the other promoters, so when Jack Merrick asked them if he could use the name and move the 1958 national championship races to Hutchinson, KS, none of them objected.

The rest is history.

You can read more on Frankie Lies' colorful racing history as well as other drivers and cars of that period at
https://kansasracinghistory.com/Cejay/Lies/Lies_Web_Page.htm.

ACKNOWLEDGEMENTS

I am enormously grateful to the following family members, friends, and fellow authors for their input and generous ongoing support—

For the technical observations of my subject-matter experts: Joe Hoffman, who knew my step-father, winner of the first National Championship for Jalopies in July 1957, and who saved me from the faux pas of installing a Jiffy Lube in Oklahoma several years before the company existed; collector-of-the-archives Bob Lawrence; and finally, Jim Petty, who tirelessly tracked down leads and fact-checked the history for me, dug up a photo of Dad (Frank Lies) at the first national championship—confirming the car was a five-window 34 Ford Coupe—and for whom, I think, the hardest job was to get me to understand the breadth and impact of a three-second lead between speeding cars. (Any errors/inconsistencies are entirely mine.)

For my stalwart Leawood Library critiquers (the "Read and Rip" gang) who have no qualms about letting me know when my writing shines and when it can use a good polishing: Joyce Brown, Richard Brown, Tim Brown, Frank Cook, Gregg Coonrod, Charlotte Henderson, Heather McCartin, Kent Moore, Shawn Parkison, and Adam Sales.

And ironically, in this age of Covid 19 and quarantines, I'm grateful for electronic connections to a marvelous band of fellow writers and critiquers from around the world—thanks to Kathy Ver Eecke, whose contagious enthusiasm for authors and their efforts through her Pitch to Published program has been the weekly shaking that keeps us all steady.

And of course for my closer-to-home readers, Heather Chapman, Mike Reed, and fellow wine/book club peeps: Bettie Jean Auch, Teresa Dunn, Carol Galloway, Linda Kircher, and Alice Martin.

A very special thanks to Reagan Rothe and the dedicated staff at Black Rose Writing for their belief in and support of this book.

And finally, my constant champions—editor-extraordinaire husband Glenn J Broadhead and our children—Linda Klein, Nancy Culp, Stephen Klein, and Emily Reed.

This pretty much makes up my writing village. What a privilege to dwell here.

ABOUT THE AUTHOR

A former creative writing instructor, Marlis Manley has award-winning short stories and poems in literary magazines—including *Kansas Quarterly*, *Crosscurrents*, and *Kansas Women Writers*, and founded the annual Mendocino Coast Writer's Conference. The winner of the 1957 National Championship for Jalopies was her step-father, Frank (Frankie) Lies, and for this story she has drawn from family scrapbooks and website racing archives, as well as memories of her early life around race tracks. She lives with her husband and a small menagerie on a modest horse ranch just south of Kansas City, Kansas.

NOTE FROM THE AUTHOR

Word-of-mouth is crucial for any author to succeed. If you enjoyed *Trophy Girl*, please leave a review online—anywhere you are able. Even if it's just a sentence or two. It would make all the difference and would be very much appreciated.

Thanks!
Marlis Manley

Thank you so much for reading one of our **Sports Romance** novels. If you enjoyed the experience, please check out our recommended title for your next great read!

The Fat Lady's Low, Sad Song by Brian Kaufman

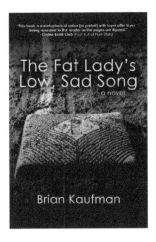

"This book is a metaphorical onion (or parfait) with layer after layer being revealed to the reader as the pages are flipped."
-Online Book Club (Four out of Four Stars)

CPSIA information can be obtained
at www.ICGtesting.com
Printed in the USA
JSHW030931080721
16614JS00005B/3